COMET WEATHER

COMET WEATHER

Liz Williams

NewCon Press
England

First published in March 2020 by NewCon Press,
41 Wheatsheaf Road, Alconbury Weston, Cambs, PE28 4LF

NCP220 (limited edition hardback)
NCP221 (softback)

10 9 8 7 6 5 4 3 2 1

ISBN:

978-1-912950-45-4 (hardback)
978-1-912950-46-1 (softback)

Cover by Ian Whates

Text edited by Ian Whates
Book interior layout by Storm Constantine

PART ONE
WHEN THE COMET COMES

BEE

Beatrice Fallow was in the orchard, waiting for Dark, when she heard the voice in the tree. It was an evening in early October, with the windfalls scattered among the blown leaves. The orchard smelled of cider and of rot. Above Bee's head, there were stars in the branches of the apple trees; Orion climbing high to the east with the blue dog at his heels, the bright handle of the Plough. Bee watched the clouds scudding over the thin rind of the moon, and that was when the voice came from the elder tree.

She'll soon be home. It was a cold voice, as small and hard as the moon itself.

Bee was more surprised at the content of the message than by the nature of its delivery.

"What? Who?"

Why, your far sister.

"Are you talking about Nell?" Bee frowned. The trees were prone to speak in metaphor. "She's my cousin, not my sister. From America. I spoke to her this evening, on the phone." *A more reliable method of communication,* she almost said.

Not the one from over-water. The starry one.

"Stella?" Her heart leaped, beat, subsided. "But Stella –"

Stella had said she was never coming home again. Not after what had happened last time. Bee thought that her heart had adjusted to the rhythm of loss: first her mother, then Stella. But now it leaped painfully in her chest.

She'll soon be here.

Bee did not know exactly what this meant. To the trees, time was a fluid thing, stretchy as elastic. They did their best and she did her best, too, to help them.

"What phase of the moon? Can you tell me that?"

The new moon. Before the comet comes.

Bee had read about this in the paper: Lerninsky's Comet, coming round to the world again after a handful of thousand years. She tried to keep up with astronomical news, to keep her grandfather's professorial legacy alive. None of the girls had followed in his footsteps, but Bee felt someone ought to take an interest. Just in case Abraham did not already know about these things, but might want to be informed. And this would be a winter star, visible until the end of the year, so the papers said. Like the one that had heralded the birth of the winter child, at Christmas, at Solstice. It did not surprise Bee that the elder tree seemed to know all about this, but it did make her sorry to know that neither her grandfather nor his daughter would be here to see it. Abraham would have had a professional fascination; Alys would have seen the romance.

"About Stella. Do you know *why* she's coming?"

But the elder tree was silent. Bee could see it in the light of the moon, a collection of spindly twigs, stripped down beneath the remaining leaves. In spring, the tree was a frothy mass of sea-foam blossom; in early autumn it had been laden with sticky black berries that looked as though they should have been poisonous, but which had already been picked for jelly. Soon the elder would be withied and bare, prone to spurts of sudden temper.

"All right," Bee said, in resignation. "Then I suppose we'll just have to wait."

The elder lapsed into silence. Bee kicked aside windfalls, sending them rolling into the long grass and trailing the smell of ferment. She listened, for the sound of Dark's footstep among the trees, and soon enough, she heard it.

SERENA

Serena had a mouthful of pins when her mobile rang. She spat them into the palm of her hand and scattered them across the table. Under the needle of the sewing machine, the dress was as pink and folded as a woman's flesh.

"Sorry," Serena said, indistinctly. "Didn't catch that, Bee. Everything okay?"

"I *said* – have you heard from Stella lately?"

"Yes." Serena wasn't surprised by the question; it was like Bee, the mother hen, to check up on them all. But since Alys wasn't here any more... Bee had taken on the role, as the eldest daughter. On the family frontline at thirty four, if you didn't count a small bevy of ancient great-aunts, which Serena did not. Cards at Christmas and, if you were lucky, a handknitted object, all the way from Inverness. How old was Cousin Nell, though? Bee said something unintelligible, interrupting Serena's familial calculations. In the background, Charlie's machine hummed and whirred; Charlie was bent over it, her face frowning with concentration. "Hang on a minute, love. It's a bit noisy in here."

Picking up the phone, she wandered down the stairs to the first floor. A chilly light fell in through the long windows, casting shadows across the floorboards. Serena shivered, though the room itself was not cold: decorated in shades of eggshell pink, its walls were scarcely visible between the mass of pictures. Gilded wooded letters spelled out her initials and Bella's on the mantelpiece, between incense holders and carved spheres and goddesses and photos and flowers. Above the fire, her own face, a long beaky-nosed oval like an Italian portrait, gazed down, serene indeed.

But sometimes Serena thought that her mother must have had a very poor sense of humour, to give her the name that she bore. 'Serene,' indeed! 'Panic' might have served her better. Chaos?

"Serena, are you there?" Her sister's voice was tinny over the phone.

Distracta? Dishevel? "Sorry, Bee, what did you say?" She decided to lie. "Honestly, this is a *dreadful* line. Builders next door – the whole

9

place is like a warzone."

She'd apologise to the house later, she thought.

"I *said,* when you saw Stella, did she say anything about coming down to Somerset?"

This time, Serena was genuinely startled. She perched on the arm of the sofa and fumbled one-handed for a cigarette. "No. God! Frankly that's the last thing I'd have expected her to do. She said something about a gig in Ibiza, but that's all. Mind you, you never know with Stella. She's not staying with me, anyway."

"Because someone said she might be coming down here. Implied she might be abroad, which would account for Ibiza, I suppose."

Serena frowned. "Who told you that?"

"One of her friends." There was the tiniest pause before 'friends.'

"I wouldn't put much store in anything one of Stella's mates said. You know what they're like. Half of them are my friends, too and honestly, Bee, if some of them wished me good afternoon I'd look out of the window to see if it was dark. Loads of fun, but... Anyway, what was one of that crowd doing down your way out of festival time? Did they get lost?" Another, more pertinent, thought struck her. "Why don't you just ask her?"

"Actually, I tried. I texted her. Despite – well, in spite of that. But she's not answering her phone. Maybe she *is* out of the country?"

"I wouldn't worry about it. If she's changed her mind she'll let you know soon enough. And I wouldn't worry about the row, either. It wasn't your fault. Stella knows when she's being unreasonable. You just have to give her a bit of time to get over herself and then she'll apologise. If she was wrong, anyway. And on this occasion, she was. You did all you could, Bee. And Stella didn't have any more luck with the police than anyone else did."

"I suppose so." Bee sounded dubious and changed the subject. "So how are you?"

Even though her sister could not see her, Serena grimaced. *What, you mean apart from Mum?* But they'd stopped talking about Alys, by unspoken consent, and Bee had just dodged that very subject. "Oh, you know. Getting on with it. Business is okay. I've got a big show booked up for London Fashion Week – I'm really pleased about that."

"That's great! When is that?"

"Not till February."

"And how about *you?* Are you still with Ben?"

"Yeah, as far as I know." Bee had always been one for the direct question, but to Serena's irritation, her answer had sounded more snappy than she'd intended. It caught her by surprise and made her snag her breath, like pricking yourself with a pin. "He's off doing a gig in Liverpool at the moment, though. Coming back in a day or so's time. We'll have to see how the land lies then."

She was grateful that Beatrice, sometimes, had learned not to push. Instead, her sister said, "Well, I hope it goes well."

"Thanks. How are things with you? Are you still coming up to London next week?" That had been almost as surprising as the idea of Stella going back home. When Bee had told her, by text a few days before, she'd said, before she could stop herself, "But you never go anywhere!" *Nul points* when it came to sisterly tact.

Now, Bee said, "We're planning to. Nell gets in tomorrow – I'm picking her up at Bristol. She wants to spend a few days here going through stuff and recovering from jetlag."

"But she doesn't want to spend the whole trip holed up in Abraham's study."

"Well, she won't. She's planning to go down to Cornwall for a day or two to see a friend, and then we'll come up to town on the Wednesday, if that's still all right with you. Maybe I could see Stella then…" Her voice faded doubtfully away.

"Maybe." Serena hadn't meant to sound so dubious, either. "Why don't you text Stel again? She doesn't seem to be answering her Facebook messages at the moment, either. But it would be great to see you." She meant that, anyway. "Let me know what time you and Nell arrive and we can meet up for lunch. Or you can come here straight away and dump your bags."

When Bee had put the phone down, Serena remained on the arm of the chair and lit the cigarette. She couldn't smoke upstairs: Charlie didn't like it and there was too much fabric around for safety. With the cigarette in hand, feeling the familiar guilty pang – she really should think about giving up – she went back to the window and looked out. It was now dusk, with the streetlights showing in dim misty globes through the murk. More like November than October… Serena shivered. She tried to turn her thoughts back to the dress, to the new collection, but somehow her mind had become stuck in a spiral, circling

11

around Bee and Stella and Nell, whom Serena had met once in New York, for lunch, and once at a wedding in Connecticut. She wished the family could be closer, but they were all so different – Bee the home body, looking after the house down in Somerset; Serena with her fashion; Stella with – well, whatever Stella happened to be doing to eke out a living – and finally Luna, going off to live in that bloody van and now who knew where? Four sisters, like the four winds, the four corners of the Earth: all scattered now.

And Alys, mother to them all. Gone gone gone.

Outside, it was now completely dark. Serena took her mobile out of her pocket and checked it; there was nothing. More to the point, nothing from Ben. Sighing, she made her way back upstairs to the light and the clatter of the sewing machine.

Ben did not call. Serena stayed up until midnight, working on a new frock. Charlie had long since gone, heading out for a night in the Bellnote, then the Soundhouse. She'd suggested that Serena go with her, but the thought of all those hyped-up people, hellbent on enjoying themselves, made Serena feel old.

"Oh come *on*," Charlie said, when Serena told her this. "You're only thirty-one, for God's sake. It's not like you're totally ancient."

"I feel ancient." She spoke sepulchrally, to make Charlie laugh, and succeeded. "I just want a quiet night in for a change. With my zimmer frame."

Charlie giggled again. "With your cocoa and your slippers."

"That's the one."

Years ago, her mother's voice: *I hope you're not staying in because some boy might call, Serena.* That had been in the days of the single landline, just on the cusp of every teenager having their own mobile, but reception at Mooncote hadn't been good then and still wasn't. Now, with all these choices, there was no excuse. No excuse at all, only the ache of your heart. *Well, what did you expect, going out with a musician?* This time the voice in memory was Beatrice's, exasperated. Serena had bit back a sharp reply, because of family lore, the part of it that said that all they'd ever wanted for Bee was for her to find someone of her own and not moulder away down in the country, still living with her mother and granddad, before that all changed, seemingly content and yet…

Yeah, I know, she told herself, looking at her reflection in the mirror.

What did *you expect?* For answer, she held up the frock: a black froth, its hem dangling with hundreds of tiny rosebuds. Goth was back, again, but it had to be pretty. Against the black lace, Serena's flicks of blonde hair looked even paler. The black would wash her out, too severe. Lucky it wasn't for her, then. And the dress would dominate her too much if she put it on; she didn't have the height of the models.

You, she told herself, *want to start making dresses for real women again.* The whole point of the new collection was the exposure: drama and flash, but alongside that had to come the clothes for people who weren't professional clothes horses, her regular customers.

At nine, the phone did ring and she bolted for it, to find that it was Bella.

"Mum? Sorry. Didn't know if you'd still be up."

"It's only nine."

"Yes. But –" Old people go to bed early, Serena mentally supplied.

"You okay, Bells?"

"Yeah. Tired. School."

"Is your dad there? Do you still want to come back here tomorrow?"

"I suppose. Yeah. Is that still all right?"

"Of course," Serena said, and her daughter hung up. She looked out of the window again, into the north-east dark to Highgate, where Bella had just put down a phone.

STELLA

The Mediterranean light fell hard on the coast, slamming down onto blue sea and black rock. Around the tables and chairs of the café, the shadows pooled like ink. Stella shuffled bare feet against hot stone and tapped yet another text message into her mobile. Why did things have to get so complicated?

Do the gig. Come back home, flying into Luton on Easyjet. Take the train to Somerset, from Paddington. It wasn't rocket science. It would be a quick trip and when she returned from Somerset she would stay with Serena and figure out her next move. Goa or Amsterdam, perhaps: wherever Liam wasn't. But this trip was straightforward.

Except nobody else seemed to agree with her. Especially the railway booking service.

I know I said I'd never go home again. But that was then and this is now. It wasn't so raw any more and she never thought she'd say that. With a sigh, Stella put the phone back into her backpack and rose.

The route from the café took her through bright white streets, narrowing into pools of shadow. It was late afternoon, with the sun deepening down from midday. The air smelled of thyme from the hillsides and a nose-wrinkling tang of exhaust and fried food from the town below. Stella walked past closed shop fronts, admiring printed dresses and ornate jewellery: expensive, rich-boho gear of the kind her sister made. Maybe Serena's stuff was even sold here; Stella did not know. She didn't shop in places like that. Her reflection – white vest, azure sarong – flitted alongside in the mirrors of windows and her flip-flops slapped against the stone. Her reflection wasn't entirely disappointing, she thought: she still had a swimmer's strong calves, the broad shoulders. Not too bad, even if she was just about to hit thirty. Perhaps thirty would hit back? She'd never got into the habit of siesta but she liked the fact that the town was so quiet, settling into somnolence before the evening, when the bars and the shops and the clubs re-opened into mayhem.

When she came to Nightside, she slipped around the back of the building rather than through the front doors and stepped into the small makeshift kitchen that lay behind the bulk of the club. Someone had not washed up, again. Stella ignored the mess and went through into the huge echoing space in front of the stage that, later, would be filled with thrashing bodies and strobe lights. Her deck stood on the far side of the stage. Stella did a quick equipment check, but she knew what she was planning for the evening. Something a little bit different tonight, before she had to head back to London. Something for them to remember her by.

Her nerves were on edge in case Liam showed up and wanted a re-hash of the discussion – she was determined to keep thinking of it as a discussion – of the night before. Stella gave an exasperated sigh. She didn't think she could cope with more tears. In theory it was great to be in favour of men showing their more sensitive side, just not right now, and especially not when she thought she had made it clear all along that it was just a seasonal thing. Anyway, best to be brisk now and not keep the poor bloke dangling. But she didn't like having to be cruel to be kind. She did not feel good about the whole thing.

When she had finished, minus an appearance by her now ex, she went back out into the sunlight. After the hazy dimness of the club, the heat hit her like a blow. Smiling, blinking, Stella took the winding road that led past Nightside up to the little cafe at the top of the hill. It was taking her out of town, above the bay. When she reached the small patch of scrub halfway up the hill, she spun on her heel and looked back, squinting out over the gilded line of the sea. A white sail flickered across the water. The town was a distant hum. From the waste ground, a voice said, *You'll soon be home.*

It was hard to tell whether it spoke in English or Spanish, or something else. Stella turned. An olive tree stood in the middle of the patch of earth: an old tree, contorted.

"How'd you know that?" Stella asked.

The moon told me.

"Moon should mind its own effing business, then."

The olive tree was silent.

"Why tell me," Stella said, "what I already know?"

When you go home, the tree said, *you should mind the man who is cold.*

Stella frowned. "Do I know him already? Or is he someone new?"

Both. All.

"You got a name for him?" Stella asked, but the tree was subsiding, drawing its shadow up into itself, shutting itself up into silence.

"Typical," Stella said aloud, and walked on towards the cafe.

That night, she stood behind the mixing deck, ready to roll. She'd put a new line-up together, some tried and tested favourites, some new stuff, brought over from Manchester. A couple of new bands, Bristol-based, that she did not think the clubbers would have come across, even though the majority were Brits.

"Are you ready, Nightside?" Stella cried. "Are you *ready*?"

They were. Stella set the deck on stun, and the club roared into life.

Two hours later, wiping sweat from her face, she ran down to the toilet. A ten minute break and Stella was in need of air. Swigging water from a plastic bottle, she inched through the door that led into the yard, into the warm darkness. The grid of lights below ended in the shadow of the sea. Stella stood for a moment in the doorway. There was a flicker of movement across the yard. Stella strained to see. A dog? But no, it was a person, getting up from their hands and knees. Christ, please don't be bloody Liam. Stella switched on the arc light and the person, a girl, gave a little gasp.

"Sorry," Stella called. "Didn't mean to make you jump. You okay?"

"Yeah." The girl stood, black hair fanning over her shoulders. Stella saw a thin frame, black jeans, a retro punk t-shirt with a diamante design sparkling across it. She had an indeterminate English accent; impossible, unusually, to tell origin or even class. Her face was angular and striking, cast into prominent planes by the harsh light. "I was looking for the loo and I think I dropped my lighter."

"Oh, bad luck. I'll leave the light on."

"Thanks."

"The toilet's through there. Everyone always gets the wrong door."

The girl nodded. "Thanks," she said again. Stella turned, leaving her in the floodlit yard, and went back in to the melee of the club.

LUNA

Waking into frost, Luna sighed and turned over. Sam was warm against her back, cocooned in a pod of blankets. Luna didn't want to get up, but her bladder was insistent. She grabbed her coat, bundled it on over the clothes she was already wearing: sweater, shirt, an old vest, combats, thick woollen socks. Moth raised his long grey head as she passed, but Luna whispered reassurance and the lurcher sank back down with the sigh of the much put-upon dog.

It shouldn't be this cold, so early in the autumn, but Luna stepped out of the van into a white, misty world. Wisps of morning fog curled up through the spines of hawthorn and over the tips of winter wheat.

They were somewhere in Wiltshire; white horse country, following what had once been old drove roads. His family had followed them for hundreds of years, Sam had told her, but Luna wasn't quite sure if she believed that. Sam liked to wind her up: gorgio that she was.

"You and your big house," he said. "What would you know?"

It should have sounded crueller than it did, but Sam teased, he didn't judge. He'd been smiling when he'd said it. Then, "I'd like to see your house, mind."

"Maybe. One day."

"And your sisters."

She had the impression that, for Sam, her sisters had achieved a kind of mythic significance, like muses, or graces. It annoyed her. He asked a lot of questions about them: flaky Stella, superficial Serena, stick-in-the-mud Bee.

"They're just... you know." She'd shrugged, sullenly.

"They sound okay to me. Stella's following her heart, so you said. Her music. That's a good thing, isn't it? Serena makes clothes, doesn't she, now? And you said she's not all that into being the big fashion designer, just likes making pretty stuff. That's cool. And Bee grows things and makes cider and looks after books. Nothing wrong with getting your hands in the earth if you've got a bit of land." Sam in candlelight, round faced and reflective. "Don't be so hard on them, Lune. They sound okay. And they're your family."

"I suppose." Too hard to say: *but I don't know what to be. I don't know*

17

where I fit in. Did she fit out here, on the road? Not really here, either.

Sam told her, when they first met, that his family were not gypsies. "Romany, you mean?" she'd said, anxious to get the word right, to not offend.

"No, not Romany. Not travellers, either, although we do travel, obviously. Older than both. So I sometimes say *gypsies* because everyone knows what it means but it doesn't tie us into the New Age lot or the Rom."

"How old are your people, then?" Luna had asked, intrigued.

"I dunno really," he'd said, with what she now recognised to be a deliberate vagueness. "Well old, anyway."

Luna had not met many of Sam's family yet. That was to come. For the last year, ever since she'd got together with him at a festival – a small, local thing, a few tents, a roundhouse, on a farm on Dartmoor – they had been travelling. Not in a painted vardo, or a modern streamlined trailer, but a high-sided thing that looked as though it was made of wood, but was not. It was drawn by two hairy piebalds: saved on road tax, Sam said, not to mention the petrol.

Now, the piebalds grazed peacefully on the starry, frosted verge. Luna pissed in the hedge, unravelling from layers of clothing, and stumbled across the clotted field back to the van. Once inside, the windows misting, she put the kettle on the little gas stove and lit it. Sam was still a huddle under blankets; he rarely woke much before ten if he wasn't working. Moth, too, remained still, a curled grey shape in his own blanket. Luna didn't bother to glance at the clock: a year out of normal time and she'd learned to know what stage of the sun it might be. Now, it was around eight. The sun was coming up over a ridge of ash trees in a bright smoky blur. Luna sipped strong tea and waited.

She had not lost hope that she'd meet her mother on the road. It wasn't likely, but it wasn't as unlikely as her sisters pretended. Luna knew that they remembered Alys as she had been: long legs curled up under velvet skirts or in faded jeans, nestled in an old paisley beanbag, book in one hand, tea in the other, or her silver-fair, blue-eyed head bent over embroidery. Alys in the heart of Mooncote, as she had always been.

But Luna knew that this was not true. Because when her mother had been a girl – some time between the months of modelling for Zandra Rhodes, some time between the later seventies glam rock *Vogue* shoots and the girl-about-town London snaps, some time even between the hippy trips to India (Alys with grinning tribesmen on some high Afghan pass) and Marrakesh – Alys had done another kind of journey.

"The Gipsy Switch," she'd told Luna. "That's what it was called."

They had been in the long panelled attic at Mooncote, surrounded by painted roses and the high-beamed ceiling, getting Alys' old clothes out of the trunk. Flared velvet trouser suits and Persian cotton kurtas, still smelling of joss sticks. Long flounced skirts, lacy blouses with high Victorian necks. A crocheted sleeveless tunic which looked like a bedspread, at which both Alys and Luna had grimaced. "So arky," Alys said, her word for out-of-date. Luna never knew whether it meant archaic, or from-the-ark. But a lot of the clothes had become magical again, the seventies back in fashion, and they were looking through the trunks partly for Serena in London, for ideas, and partly for Luna to wear, even though she was so much shorter than her mother, and not as slim either. Good thing some of the clothes were wide, Luna thought.

"The Gipsy Switch?"

"The route of the horse fairs." Alys had smiled. "Land's End to John O'Groats, round the top and down again. It took a whole summer. We slept in hedges."

"Who were you with?"

"Oh," Alys said, far-away-eyed, "A man. There was usually a man."

Luna knew better to ask: *was he my dad?* It would have been too long ago; Luna was only twenty-five now. But she wondered anyway. Alys had never told them who their fathers were, but occasionally a little sidelong hint slid out. Stella's father: a visiting musician. Bee's dad: someone local, apparently, and they'd spent a few months listing possible suspects. It was, of course, easy to make some genetically-educated guesses about eye colour and perhaps hair. Luna had wondered for a while if she and Bee had shared a father: shorter and stockier than the other two girls, brown-haired and amber eyed, but then Alys had said something about dates which seemed to rule that out. But Stella's blue eyes were Alys' own and Serena's fine fair hair was identical to Alys' blonde.

"The Fallows," Alys had said once, "never stay with a man for long."

"What about Grandpa, though? He was born and died here."

"That was a bit different. He married a woman who liked to stay put. Like Bee. And anyway, Grandpa *was* a man. Maybe it's different for male Fallows."

But the Gipsy Switch… Luna thought of it now, in her own van, with her own man asleep under the blankets. Alys' loss was a sharp ache in her heart, sometimes pinprick, sometimes rapier. It would be a good thing to do, retrace the Switch, follow in her mother's footsteps. And maybe, just maybe, she'd find her, where her sisters and the police and the newspapers had failed.

BEE

With Sarah, one of the girls from the village, Bee cleaned Mooncote from top to bottom on the day that Nell was due in from the States. It wasn't as though the house ever got really filthy, but Bee was determined for Nell to see it at its best: her cousin had not visited the place since her teens, and now Nell was forty. But Bee knew what the house had meant to her, for it had appeared in Nell's novels over and again, in different guises. In the latest book, the one that had won that big literary award, it had been the homestead of the three silent brothers and their overbearing mother, a tragedy played out in shades of monochrome, delicately portrayed. Bee had read it with interest, recognising rooms and views from windows, although the house in the book had been situated in the Hudson Valley, where Nell now lived. She barely remembered the brothers' names, but she remembered the house, and now, before Nell was due to visit, Bee sat down with the book on her knee while Sarah did some last minute dusting, and undertook a quick scan of first and last chapters so that she would have something intelligent to say about the novel. In her experience, Nell rarely talked about her work and certainly wouldn't have expected her relatives to have read it, but that wasn't the point. It was polite, and that meant much to Bee.

When Sarah had gone, and her own little bit of homework had been done, she wandered through the house. Plenty of time. She was going over to Amberley for a few hours this afternoon, then on to the airport for six. Hopefully Nell's flight would land on time, wouldn't end up in Cardiff because of fog, or somesuch. *Stop finding things to worry about,* Bee told herself firmly. The staircase swept down in an arc, banisters gleaming, to the acorn-shaped newel post. Bee did not have an inner small boy, but if she had possessed one, she thought, she would have wanted to slide down those banisters. The hall smelled of polish and woodsmoke, and the chrysanthemums that fireworked from the big blue and white Chinese vase. From here, Bee could see the stone flags of the kitchen and the worn Persian rugs that covered the living room floor. But she went upstairs, onto the quiet landing. There was a sudden flurry of disappearing cat, which meant Fly, who was prone to panic at noises.

"Oh, come on, you silly thing," Bee said aloud. "It's only me."

Fly did not reappear. Bee walked on, checking that the Welsh quilt on Nell's bed was straight and untroubled by further cats, and that the chrysanthemums in her room had enough water. Outside, through the leaded windows, she could see into the orchard, and this made her think of Dark, and the previous night. Dark had a secret, which he was not divulging. She could always tell, and wouldn't give him the satisfaction of asking him.

She paused before the door to Alys' room. It dismayed her too much to think of pushing open the door, to find her mother sitting on the bed, brushing her hair into a silver shine, looking up into the mirror. "Oh, Bee. It's you, darling."

She opened the door anyway. The room was empty, just as Alys had left it, although Bee had put away the clothes that had been left on the floor in the haste of Alys' packing. It had been most unlike her mother, Bee thought, frowning, to want to go on a sudden hiking trip and the police, certainly, had seen it as suspicious. They thought, Bee knew, that Alys had staged her own disappearance, but Alys would have never done that to her daughters, although she might have done it to a man.

But there had not been a man, not for some time.

Bee went over to the rocking horse that stood by the window: Alys' old toy, from childhood. She touched the white mane and the horse creaked forward, then back. The patterns on his back were a grey-dappled map of the moon: Grandpa's little astronomical joke. A moonhorse, to ride all the way up to the sky.

A flicker of motion in the mirror made Bee jump. She looked up, heart suddenly in mouth. "Mum?"

There was a figure in the mirror, a reflection of someone who was not in the room. Her long full dress was a dull gold; her hair was red and laced with pearls. She carried a lump of polished jasper in one hand, a sprig of plantain in the other. "Arcturus," Bee whispered. She knew her Behenian stars. The spirit in the mirror regarded her gravely for a moment from yellow cat-eyes, then flicked out of sight. Bee sighed, and went to open the window to let in apple-scented air.

In the afternoon, she drove over to Amberley in a sudden rush of rain. It was a bigger house than Mooncote, and not quite as old. Bee had always liked it, regarding it, like her sisters, as a second home. Whereas Mooncote was late summer coloured, honey-stone, Amberley was wintery: a grey stoned, slate roofed house of elegant proportions, warmed with yellow lichen. Mooncote was more homely; of the two, Amberley was the debutante. A magnolia, beautiful in spring but now dropping its hard leaves, stood before the tall, square windows of the lower floor and Caro's roses, neatly tied, decorated the borders.

By the time Bee had come into the drive, the rain had swept down the valley towards the coast, leaving a wan light in its wake. Caro Amberley came out to meet her, a tall woman, chestnut hair turning to grey, and brown eyed.

"Bee! I thought you were coming tomorrow."

"No. Today. It's in the diary."

"Honestly." Caro rolled her eyes. "Sorry, I'm sure you're right. It's just – I don't know whether I'm coming or going, this week. I keep getting muddled up."

"That's not like you." Normally, Bee knew, Caro was one of those women of whom other women said, *I don't know how she manages, when you think of everything she does, she's a miracle, she really is…* Not like Alys, Caro's best friend, dreaming vague through life.

Caro spread her hands. "I know. I've been running about like a headless chicken for the last month – I'll be glad when all this is over." *All this* was showjumping, gymkhanas, fetes: the usual manic round of summer in a horsy family. Bee gave her a sympathetic smile. "I know. Well, you can calm down for a bit. Before the jumps season starts, anyway."

"God! Richard's dealing with most of that, anyway. Although some of his clients at the moment –" She pulled a face. Training horses was high pressure, Bee knew. She'd rather stick to books. "And then there's Apple Day."

"Well, that's why I'm here."

They had been planning it since the spring. An Apple Day, at Mooncote. It had been Caro's idea and Bee had thought it a good one.

"Part of this Celebrate Somerset campaign they're doing. Jamie's been involved in it – raising the profile of the county."

"A lot of people are running Wassailing events now – look how popular those are, and that's in the middle of January. We went to an Apple Day last year over near Somerton. It was fun. Lots of cider."

"Anyway," Caro said now. "Come on in."

They went straight up to the turret room, a creaking oak spiral leading into the tall pale interior, with its leaded windows looking out across the vale. Bee had always envied the Amberleys this room, a Victorian folly, but now it was, for the time being, her office and she was grateful for that. It was not, however, tidy. Boxes of books littered the floor, stacked on top of one another. Caro repeated her earlier grimace.

"They seem to have bred," Bee said, looking at the boxes.

"They *have* bred. Julian brought more over this morning in the back of his car and he couldn't see out of the back window."

Bee eyed her askance. "I hardly dare ask. Are there more to come?"

Caro nodded. "'Fraid so. He says they've cleared out about three quarters of it."

"So does Ward want any of this?"

"I don't know. He's still in New York and when I emailed him I got a reply that said, basically, *don't bother me now.*"

"He's coming back for the funeral, though, is he?"

"Yes. The play will be over by then – he's flying back as soon as the run ends, he said, and that's very soon, it might even be tonight, I can't remember. It's sort of worked out because they're going to have to do an autopsy on poor old Harold, even though it's pretty clear it was heart. But Julian was just keen to get the books out of the way first, and do a full inventory, and then they can see what's what in the rest of the house. Honestly, Bee, you didn't see it but the man must have lived like a vole – the cottage was a warren of books, with little tunnels between them."

"I knew he was a bit –"

"Bonkers, Julian said. I didn't know him very well, even if he was a cousin. He kept himself to himself. Probably couldn't get out of the front door."

"So did *Ward* know his uncle all that well?"

"I don't really know. That side of Richard's family's always been a bit off with one another, as far as I can see. I lost track of who was not speaking to whom ages ago and, anyway, it kept changing. In the meantime, we've got to cope with the books. I'm starting to feel a bit sorry I've dragged you into this, to be honest. I didn't realise there were so many."

"Well, you are paying me," Bee said mildly. "Or Julian is, to be accurate. And I don't mind. I am a trained librarian, after all. A book whisperer."

"While you're whispering to the books," Caro said, "I'll bring you some tea. And cake. This is a job that needs cake." But then she put her head back around the door. "Oh. By the way, I had a word with this chap Tam Stare about your car – he knows all the scrap people. He says he'll pop over in the next day or so and pick it up. Is that okay?"

"Yes, fine. It's not worth repairing, the garage said, and I've still got the Landrover. And thank you. I'd rather deal with someone recommended by a friend."

"I don't know how reliable he is, to be honest. He seems all right. His sister's a friend of Ben's. She's a model – a stunning girl, actually."

"That's nice," Bee said, thinking little of it.

Left alone with the boxes, she went to the faux-mullioned window of the turret room and looked out. Behind the house, across the beds of lavender and box, the hillside was a sudden startling green in a shaft of sunlight. A white horse stood by a stand of bronzing beech and as Bee watched, she kicked up her heels in a flurry and galloped across the field, a flying heraldic form. Cloud Chaser, Richard's prize winning racehorse, enjoying her moment of freedom before the jumps season began later in the month. Bee was reminded of the moonhorse and smiled, imagining Cloud Chaser racing up into the sky, following her name. She supposed that the mare would be taken up to Cheltenham: cream of the jumps tracks and National Hunt racing, and Cloud Chaser had won a handful of races last year. A lot of money for the yard. Caro's daughter Laura would be up on the hill with her, keeping a close eye on the rising star. Meanwhile, Bee herself had a job to do. She opened a box at random, wondering what she would find. Julian's uncle's library had been, to say the least, eclectic. She did not know whether to expect Victorian fairy stories, birds of the British Isles, a history of the Great Game or the works of Aleister Crowley.

And in fact, the box contained none of these: they were all on the subject of gardening. Bee sat down on the floor, and began to sort through the box as the sky darkened and the rain, once more, began to patter against the leaded windows of the turret.

25

SERENA

Serena walked quickly through mist, having coming up out of the relative warmth of the Underground. Outside, Camden was a roar of noise: taxis hurtling past, a man shouting, incoherent. Serena ignored it all, dodged through traffic, headed north towards the Lock. It was already close to half past ten and people were streaming in the opposite direction, making for the Tube, but Serena's night was just beginning. A school night, too: she would be working tomorrow. She felt a little guilty, but only a little.

Ben's band, Coldwar, were playing in a club that had once been a warehouse, an arch under the Lock. It was typical North London: grimy, reached by an uneven alley of half-cobbled pavement, the stone of the arch black against the dirty orange sky. Serena half looked up for the moon, then decided she didn't want to know. She could feel it, however, very faint in the heavens, a bright and easterly eye.

The bouncers, both young and black, heads shaved with fashionable patterns, recognised her and smiled. She smiled back. Inside, it was stuffy and dark. A band Serena did not recognise was doing a sound check on the narrow stage. She slipped through the crowd – too many people, too much noise already, and she longed for the quietness and peace of the studio. She made her way to the back of the stage, through a heavy black curtain that smelled of age and mould.

Two of Ben's band were there already: the bass player, Mont, and Seelie, who played fiddle and flute and who was thin and blonde like Serena, but ten years younger. They got on well; Serena liked Seelie's vagueness, her unforced ability to be kind. And she liked her clothes: a shredded lacy vest with ragged Victorian sleeves and PVC jeans as black and shiny as a sealion's skin.

"Ben's gone to get some cigs," Seelie said now. "Said he'd be back in a bit."

"Okay," said Serena. She wandered into the empty dressing room, found a bottle of white wine and poured some of it into a plastic cup. Sipping, she went back to the main club to a squeal of sound. She didn't want to get in the way. But halfway down the room she ran into Ben himself.

He smelled of night and rain and tobacco. He had a pint glass in one hand. "Hey!" His long face lit up. He swept Serena into a one-armed embrace against his donkey jacket and kissed her. His brown curls were starred with water.

"You're all wet," Serena said. She shook herself like a cat. "It wasn't raining a minute ago."

"It's *pissing* down outside. I went to get some fags."

"Seelie said."

"This lot are on until eleven. We're next. You all right to hang about out here?"

"I've got wine," Serena said. She liked to see people going about their business. She waved him on and watched until he disappeared through the curtain. Fifteen years and not a lot had moved on, really: she'd first met Ben on a rainy night in a dingy club, him with a guitar in one hand. But then the drinks had been cider and black, snakebite or lager, and the clubs had been in Yeovil or Taunton, not Camden Lock. Ben hadn't changed much; Serena hoped she had. But it hadn't been a case of childhood sweethearts. That had come much later.

It felt okay, tonight. Didn't it? Ben's recent absences, those had been work. And the other absences, Serena asked herself? Those unanswered texts and messages. Those sudden, uneasy silences, and things not said, hovering like the ghosts of moths around the edges of the room. She had told herself she was just being stupid. Ben had apparently agreed. *It's a bit paranoid for you, isn't it, Serena?* – said with a frown. *You're not normally like this.*

"But are we – all right?"

"Yes, of course we are. I'd tell you if something was wrong."

Along with the faintest edge of male exasperation: the woman is making a fuss again. Serena hated that. It wasn't about being too cool for school, it was about trust and love. Yet she hadn't been able to push the feeling, the wrongness, back into the box in her head.

But he was probably right; she was being paranoid. There you are, tonight has proved it. He was fine just now. You need to get over yourself.

She leaned against the bar and sipped her wine, watching people, and making mental notes. The support band came on and fired up into a wall of sound. Serena didn't mind, once her ears had adjusted to the din. But after a while it got too much and she unpeeled herself from the bar and made her way backstage. Here, the noise was muted but still intense. Blinking, Serena went down the corridor and pushed open the door to the dressing room.

Immediately it was like stepping into a soundless bubble, the noise of the stage muted and muffled. Her first thought was that the girl was standing far too close, and that Ben looked far too comfortable with that. He took a quick step back, but the girl remained where she was.

"Hi," Serena said. The word fell into the room like a stone. She hoped that nothing showed on her face.

"Hi." The girl uncoiled herself from her perch on the table, which brought her even closer to Ben. Serena saw a pointed white face and a fan of shining black hair. "Aren't you going to introduce me, Ben?"

Her teeth, Serena thought, were much too small. Her eyes glinted like oil. But her face was as symmetrical as a mask and she was familiar: a model? Serena was sure that she'd seen the girl somewhere before.

"This is Dana Stare," Ben said. "Dana – my friend Serena."

Friend. Serena wasn't going to have the indignity of correcting him. She gave an entirely inauthentic smile, which was mirrored by Dana, and fell back on platitudes.

"Dana. Nice to meet you. How're you doing?"

"Good," Dana said, then turned her back and drew a long-fingernailed hand down Ben's sleeve. "See you later," she whispered, and glided out through the door.

"Wow," Serena said. "You couldn't have a more obvious vamp, could you?"

"Sorry," Ben said. He had the grace to look slightly abashed.

"Well, whatever." Serena wasn't going to start getting into some jealous snit over it after she'd spent a week talking herself down. She told herself she had too much pride. And bands were surrounded by groupies all the time, especially those that were on their way up. She turned away and walked back out into the club, trying to ignore the sudden churn in her stomach.

STELLA

Stella hated airports. She loathed the burnished white, the artificial lighting, the no-smell of cleaning fluids. The rush and the strain of the international sausage factory, even in a relatively small airport like Luton. She charged through arrivals, and out into the swimming day. Then the coach into London, the capital emerging and receding through the torrents, and down to Paddington.

When Stella stepped out onto the concourse here, she finally felt able to take a breath. Railway stations weren't like airports. There was something substantial and dignified about railway stations, especially this one, with its high arched girders and neat rows of platforms. The Exeter train was on time, and she was able to find a seat at the end of the carriage, where she could squash herself in with her book and her iPod and watch the wet countryside roll by. The dreary suburbs of West London first, reminding her of Portobello and Serena, and then Reading, the landscape growing more rural after that. They crossed the placid expanse of the Thames. Stella glimpsed a white chalk horse on a hill. Yellow oak and burnt beech flamed like torches. They came to small towns, then smaller yet, and eventually, an hour and a half after leaving London, the train pulled into Castle Cary, embraced by green fields and a smell of cows. Stella, with some trepidation, crossed the bridge to find her sister Beatrice waiting. They studied each other for a moment, with the row hanging between them like summer thunder, and then it was gone.

"Bee! I didn't think you'd make it. I was going to wait for the bus."

Her sister gave her a big, sudden hug. "I've got Nell in the car," she said.

Nell and a spaniel – Nelson.

Stella said, "Ha! Nelson and Nell."

"It's gonna be hard to tell us apart," her cousin said over her shoulder.

"Nell, you look nothing like a spaniel." Stella shoved her backpack into the boot of the Landrover and clambered into the backseat, shoving over a muddy, feathery dog. Her cousin twisted round so that Stella could see her properly and Stella's heart twisted with her: the blue eyes were so like her mother's, and so was her face. And Nell had fair hair, too, almost white, but very long and plaited into two. The schoolgirl style made her look old and young at the same time.

"Hey, Stella. This is a surprise. It's great to see you."

"I'd forgotten you were coming," Stella admitted. She wasn't sure that she'd even known. She was embarrassed to find that her voice was hoarse, a frog-croak. The shock of Nell's resemblance to Alys was starting to ebb. "It's good to see you, too."

"Bee said you've just come back from Ibiza."

"Yeah. I had some gigs. It went okay. It's such a change to be back, though. I haven't seen rain for a week and now –" The landscape was washed out behind the blur of the weather, but as they pulled onto the Glastonbury road, with the Tor a hummock on the horizon, a thin stripe of blue appeared over the hill with its tower.

"I think it's brightening up," Bee said, invoking the British mantra. They pulled down the lane, the maze of tracks that led to the house, and Stella felt her heart begin to lump about in her chest. Her throat grew dry. The Landrover scudded over fallen leaves, the deep copper of rain-wet beech mast, as they turned into the gates.

Stella stepped out into silence. After the cacophony of the island, and then the plane, the train, the car, everything seemed far too quiet. A rook cawed once, high up in the beeches. Mooncote sat across the lawn, a ramble of wet plastered walls under the russet tiles. Stella could smell apples and damp earth. There was a tangle of dahlias along the beds that bordered the lawn, their colours drenched out. The blueness was growing over the ridge of hills, but raindrops still spattered her face. She shouldered her bag and hauled it inside to the familiar house, thinking resolutely of laundry, and not of Alys, no longer waiting.

Downstairs, Bee was making lunch. Stella scalded herself to cleanliness in the shower and wrapped herself in a bathrobe; she was in her own old room. The teenage band posters had long since come down, leaving the faint spoor of bluetac on the plaster, but the walls were still a buttery cream between the woodwormy beams. The leaded glass of the windows cast the lawn and the distant hills into a comforting distortion. Stella turned, at a non-footstep, and saw a woman passing by the doorway. She was tall, with a thread of garnets in her hair, and her long gown was the colour of rubies, or perhaps raindark brick. She carried a bristling thistle, held before her in both hands, and she did not look at Stella. A moment later, she was gone, and Stella knew that if she looked out of the door and along the passage, no one would be there.

So they still came. Well, why not? They had not been tied to Grandpa and his astronomical work; they were from a time earlier than that, and though Abraham now lay in the Hornmoon graveyard, just down the lane, the stars still came.

"Why," Stella said aloud, "Can't *you* help me find Mum?" They had asked, but the trees, and the Behenian stars, and other things, too, had been silent. Stella thought she might go down to the church later, all the same. Have a word with the old boy. She'd never seen why death needed to put a stop to conversations.

When Stella, dressed, came downstairs, she found a stranger in the kitchen. Bee was slicing bread and the whole room smelled of it. Nell was arranging plates of ham, cheese, olives. It was all very calm and homely and the stranger wasn't like that at all; Stella looked at him with interest. He was medium height, thin-faced, young. His hair was black and spiky; his eyes were a pale, fierce blue. He wore a leather jacket and jeans, the same colour as his hair.

"This is Tam Stare," Bee said, without looking up. "He's popped over to pick up the car."

"The car?" Stella said.

Tam Stare gave her a lopsided smile. "Your sister's old Corsa. Going to the great scrap dealer in the sky."

"Oh dear."

"The back end went," Bee explained. "Whatever that means. It failed its MOT."

"It's not a problem to get it up on the truck," Tam told her. "You should get at least a ton for it."

"I only paid £250," Bee said.

"The tyres alone should fetch a few quid. I'll see you right."

"You'll need the log book," Bee said. "And the keys." She handed over a folder, while Stella put the kettle on. Minutes later, the sound of a winch ground in through the open half of the back door. Stella stepped back and trod on a cat.

"Who's he, then?" she whispered.

"I've not met him before. He's a mate of Jamie Amberley, he was saying, and his sister's a friend of Ben's. Deals in scrap. Possibly deals in other substances, as well, if the rumours down the pub are correct."

At the table, Nell raised her eyebrows.

"Bit worldly for you, Bee," Stella said, although Sherlock Holmes had been right about the countryside: it was just as criminal as the town and drugs were rife throughout the county.

Her sister laughed. "He's not any kind of love interest, believe me."

Stella said, through a mouthful of cheese, "So is anyone, then?"

"Mind your own business." But Bee smiled, all the same.

After lunch, Stella pulled on wellington boots and went out into the back yard, leaving her sister and cousin to look up train fares on the internet. A slick of oil on the flagstones was the only trace of Bee's deceased Corsa. Bee would be accompanying Nell up to London; it was, she said, good that Stella had arrived when she did, as she could feed dogs, cats, chickens, ponies, herself. There'd been a vegetable box delivery. There were eggs, bread, honey – if she was still vegetarian, was she? She was.

Stella liked this idea, and of being alone in her childhood home with just the animals. And the Behenian stars, and the ghosts, and whatever else might care to show up. She hunched into her rainslicker, stepping like a child through the puddles which spotted the lane. Above, the chestnuts still carried a few damp flags of leaves. It was no longer raining, but the air was moist and cold, invigorating after the Ibizan heat. Stella listened, but the chestnut trees had nothing to say to her. She stooped, picked up a conker as shiny as a horse's coat or a polished shoe, and put it in her pocket.

At the end of the lane, the church rose up, squat behind the gathering yews. Unlike a lot of Somerset churches, with their improbably tall fortress turrets, Hornmoon was small and grey. Stella was reminded of Dylan Thomas' poem comparing churches to snails. She pushed open the creaking gate and went inside. In early spring, the churchyard was starry with snowdrops, but now there was only a row of Japanese anemones along the wall, the faded pink of old curtains, and chrysanthemums on a few graves. Stella shut the gate behind her, and brushed underneath the yew branches to her grandfather's tomb.

A pyramid. Pointed, so that the devil would not be able to sit on top, her grandfather had told her: there were similar, older, graves in the churchyard. An astrolabe was etched on one side of the pyramid;

on its base, rested her grandfather's name: Abraham Bendigneid Fallow, and his dates. It made him sound very patriarchal, Biblical, and he hadn't been like that at all.

"Hello, Grandpa," Stella said, and grinned.

BEE

Together, the two women stood looking at the box.

"How old is it?" Nell asked.

"Elizabethan." Bee smiled. "I think. It's not as though I'm an expert on antiques. But look." She turned the box around. In the middle of the back panel, beneath a galleon in full sail, the numbers '1570' were inscribed in curly, flaking paintwork.

"I like the cute little ship," Nell said. "Where does it come from?"

"We don't really know. It's always been in the family." The galleon sailed across the lid of the box, a swallow flew towards one corner: on its side was a bowl of roses, their petals drooping. "Granddad Fallow told me it was a wedding gift for a Fallow bride, but we don't know who she was."

"What's inside it?"

"Take a look." Bee put the box down on the windowsill and lifted the lid. Inside, bands of painted herbs followed the contours of the box: buttercup, juniper, fennel, rosemary, others which Bee could not so readily identify. And there was a bag of ancient black velvet, reposing like a mole at the bottom of the box.

"Better and better! What's in the bag?"

"Another bag. No, actually, it's these." Bee undid the drawstring and tipped the contents of the bag into the box. "These aren't supposed to be taken out of the box for long, so we don't." She picked up one of the stones, rough and tumbled, a clear toffee brown. "Jasper. And this is a topaz." She held up a black oval. "This is onyx."

"It's quite a little collection," Nell said.

"There are fifteen of them." Bee drew the string tight and replaced the bag. As she closed the lid, she could see the faint tracery of stars among the herbs, visible only in certain lights. "But Grandfather once told me that one was missing."

"What a lovely thing," Nell said. "It's a house full of treasures, really."

"It's an old house," Bee said.

Later, when Nell had gone up to her room, Bee sat with the box in her lap. In her mind's eye, her mother sat at the kitchen table, with herself and Stella. It was years before. Bee was eighteen, or thereabouts, Stella five years younger. They had been doing their homework after school, but Alys had been reading a letter. Eventually Stella, whose powers of concentration were not great when it came to the academic and trying to create a distraction, said, "Who's that from?"

Her mother waved the letter. "This, Stella, is from a professor in Oxford. Her name is Frederica Rimington and she is a lecturer in English lit, specialising in Elizabethan poetry. She is a friend of your grandfather's – she's quite elderly now. I sent her something in Latin. It used to be in the box with the gemstones and I think it and the stones really should be kept together, but the parchment on which this was written originally is about four hundred years old and when we last looked at it, Abraham said it was starting to fade. He thought it was too fragile to stay there, so he took it out a few weeks ago. I copied it out and sent it to Freddie to ask if she would translate it. So she did."

"What does it say?" Bee asked.

"I'll read it out." And she did. It had been a sonnet, Bee remembered, and although she could not recall the words she had been left with a lasting impression of stars and herbs and gleaming things, of gardens and running deer.

"Wow! Who wrote it?"

"A very minor Elizabethan poet called William Fallow."

"Oh, Grandpa told me about him," Stella said. "He's a great umpteenth great grandfather, isn't he? He wrote a play and it was terrible and everyone hated it, so he returned home to Somerset and never went anywhere ever again."

"Yes. But he did do something when he came home. He met a girl in an orchard and he married her and she was your umpteenth great grandmother, and mine. I'm going to show you something else," Alys said. "I put this on this morning." She reached into the neck of the kaftan and pulled out a locket. It was dull gold, etched with concentric lines, and in the middle was a star.

"I'm not going to open this, because what's inside it is very fragile. But it's a portrait of William Fallow and one day I'll show it to you."

Now, years later, Bee wondered what had become of that locket.

She packed for London, wondering what to take. All of her clothes

Liz Williams

seemed, over the years, to have narrowed down into a selection of old skirts, jeans, moth-eaten jumpers. Really, she was starting to dress like a fifty year old and not a modern one, either. A fifty something from the fifty somethings. Serena was right to despair. She did have a couple of smart black dresses, and one in deep green: these would have to do, with Spanish riding boots. But you didn't really have to bother in the country and it wasn't as though she was into the dating game. Dark – well, Dark didn't care, did he? But London was a different kettle of fish. She put all the dresses into her case, then took one of the black ones out again. Outside, a blue dusk was beginning to settle.

STELLA

Stella's grandfather had become a star. She might have known, really, although she had been surprised when she first found out. He hovered, a small blue light, above the tip of the pyramid.

"How is that working for you?" Stella asked, perched on a nearby, flatter, tomb. She had apologised to its inhabitants, hoping they would not mind. The yews dripped steadily, revoking rain.

The star danced. Inside her mind, her grandfather's voice said, "You came back."

"You knew I'd gone away?"

"Bee told me."

"Ah."

"We had – a bit of a row. Actually, a lot of a row. Over Mum."

"Ah."

"I think I ought to apologise but we're pretending it didn't happen, so... You don't know where Alys is." It was not a question.

"She didn't tell me where she was going." The blue star danced.

"She said she was going on a hiking trip, which was a load of old cobblers." Stella examined a chewed thumbnail. "I think she's dead."

"Do you? I think I'd know if she was. I think she would have come home, if death had overtaken her."

Stella watched a burnet moth climb laboriously up the side of the pyramid, fairy-tale monochrome and red against the black marble.

"If she's not dead, then where is she? It's completely bloody inconsiderate to just push off without telling any of us where she went." *Oh, you know, darling. Hills and stuff. I'll leave Bee all the details.* But she hadn't. Luna had mentioned something called the Gipsy Switch, some kind of horse-trading route, and Stella herself had an inkling that Alys had gone to Dartmoor, but she couldn't have said why: just a hunch. It was part of the Switch, apparently. She'd even gone down to the moor and asked around, feeling sleuthy and foolish, but to no avail. The police had looked into it, as well, with similar results, and it had been a splash across the papers for a week or so, before other news had pushed a missing woman aside.

"No one would hold a middle-aged mother of four prisoner, would they? It's not as though we're fantastically rich."

"She has not cried for help, or if she has, I haven't heard her," the blue star remarked.

"I suppose that's something."

The yews rustled, murmuring, but Stella could not hear what they said. The blue star sank into the pyramid, which glowed for a second or two, then faded to black. But Stella was somewhat comforted, all the same.

That night, she dreamed of traps.

There was a hollow in the side of the hill, surrounded by the roots of beeches, so exposed and smooth that they seemed closer to stone, a medusa's coils. The trap stood in the middle of the hollow and in it, caught by the leg, was a white vixen.

"Don't move, lovely." Stella skidded down the slope, slipping on damp black earth. She was back in her sabbing days, outwitting the local hunt. "Don't move – I've got you!"

In the dream, the vixen made no sound, only looked up at Stella out of suffering golden eyes. Stella put one hand on the trap, its cold sharp teeth, and one on the nape of the fox. The vixen bared her fangs and fell apart, horribly, in Stella's hands, jointing into rawness and sinew. There was no blood. The vixen's mask dropped floppily onto the earth and Stella found herself putting it on. Seeing through the vixen's blind eyes, she looked down at the trap and saw a shark's row of teeth jutting up through the soil. Stella stumbled back, but the lamprey mouth was coming up after her, arching over her head – she screamed, and woke.

Bee suggested leaving the car, but Stella liked the idea of being stranded for a couple of days. It removed the necessity of making decisions, and Bee could leave the Landrover at the station car park for a few quid. She sat, still with the remnants of her dream about her, at the kitchen table with a stoneware mug of tea. Warming her hands seemed to diminish the chill of the trap; the ticking clock drowned out the echo of the vixen's cry. She could hardly wait for Nell and her sister to leave and when they had done so, she took the tea, closed the top half of the back door so that the house was sealed against the cold and wandered up the stairs. There was a cat on each bed: Fly, Sable, Tut. Both the spaniels were curled in their basket and to Stella's secret pleasure, it had started to rain again. Her mobile would not receive a signal, here in the hollow of the hills. No one was expecting anything of her, and would not get it if they had. She found a paperback book, an ancient edition of *The Dawn Treader,* in a bookcase, where it had always been, and settled onto the bedroom window seat to read it.

She looked up often, but it seemed the Behenian stars were not visiting today.

Towards noon, a sound from the yard roused her and she looked out to see a Landrover, not Bee's and almost indistinguishable from the surrounding mud, pulling into the yard. The dark figure of Tam Stare got out and stood, hesitating, on the flags. For a moment, Stella was tempted to pretend she was out, but she thought it might be better to let him know that there was someone on the premises. She knew a dodgy geezer when she saw one. By the time he had his hand on the kitchen bell, she was downstairs.

"Hello." He looked at her with open admiration. Not a leer, nothing so obvious, but Stella could tell what he was thinking.

"Hi." She smiled politely at Tam, who, after all, was guilty of nothing but being iffy and attractive: the kind of combination which Stella was starting to recognise as a pattern, and problematic.

"I brought your sister's scrap cash." He handed over an envelope, thick with notes. "Two hundred and fifty. I kept twenty, as agreed – you can check it with her. I've written it down."

His pale eyes were owlish, round with the effort to show honesty, but there was a flicker of something behind them. He couldn't quite pull *sincerity* off. "It's cool," Stella said. "She can sort it out with you when she gets back."

"You're a DJ, aren't you?" Tam said.

"Yes. Well, it's one of the things I do." A bit of admin, a bit of care work. Things that made ends meet. It struck her that they might not be all that different. He seemed to acknowledge it, giving her his lopsided smile.

"I do all sorts, meself."

Stella leaned against the dresser. "You're a friend of Jamie's?"

"Sort of. I suppose you all know each other."

She nodded. "My sister goes out with his brother."

"Ben, yeah?"

"Yes. At least, I think she does. It's been going a while, but I think it's a bit up and down, on and off, these days." She felt a pang of disloyalty.

"She's got a daughter, hasn't she, your sister? If it's the one I'm thinking of." The pale gaze was suddenly direct; the irises ringed with a faint fire. His skin, she saw, was very white: Celtic skin, even though he must spend much of his time outside. There was a flicker of silver at one ear.

"Yes. Her name's Bella."

"But Ben's not her dad, is he?"

Stella smiled. "No. She went out with Ward Garner for a bit – Richard Amberley's cousin, the actor?" He nodded; Ward was, after all, famous. "Then she had her little girl with someone else but that didn't last. She started going out with Ben a few years ago." Fallow women do that, she nearly said, *run off,* but caught herself in time. And why was she telling a stranger all this? It felt as though he was spinning the words out of her. Well, Rumpel-bloody-stiltskin, Stella thought, it's time to keep your trap shut.

"My sis knows Ben," Tam said. "Dana."

"I don't think I've met her."

"You'd know if you had."

"Is that in a good way or not?"

"Hard to tell. She's – mercurial," he said, surprising Stella with the choice of adjective. "Quicksilver." His accent, which up until now had been bog-standard sarf-east, suddenly sounded a lot plummier.

"That sounds good, to me. I like quick people."

"Maybe." He did not seem sure. He said, suddenly awkward, "I'd better be on my way."

It was only later that it occurred to Stella that she could have offered him tea. On the whole, she thought it best that she hadn't.

SERENA

Serena stood very still, not wanting to breathe. Eleanor touched a tiny tip of gold to the fin of the dolphin, and sat back in her chair.

"It looks so fragile," Serena said. "How could anyone bear to touch it?"

"It's not nearly as delicate as it looks, you know. That's the beauty of metal. Secretly strong." The table was crowded with objects: the dolphin salt cellar, a small bronze faun, spoons and handles and a huge tarnished platter. Eleanor sat, dishevelled, among them, in a man's shirt with the sleeves rolled up. Her hair, iron grey, was piled onto her head and her dark-eyed hawk's face was focused on Serena. The rent for the Portobello house lay on the table between them; Eleanor had an old-fashioned preference for cash, and it gave the two women an excuse to meet every month.

"I suppose so."

"Whereas those frippery things you make, all flimsy..."

"*They're* not nearly as delicate as they look, either." Serena reached out and picked up a tiny silver spoon. "Look at this. It's like a fairy's spoon."

Across the room, a cabinet took up the whole of the opposite wall: an apothecary's case containing shells, ammonites, roots, geodes. Eleanor, an alchemist, transformed them into silver and gold: the heads of spoons, the handles of cups, the curving body of a bowl. At the centre of the table stood an enormous piece: a silver boy riding a porpoise and bearing up a cornucopia that overspilled with golden grapes.

"It's for one of the vintner's associations," Eleanor said.

"It's amazing."

At the far end of the room a door opened, and a young man glided in; Ethiopian, dressed in white. His head, balanced on his long neck, was as graceful as a cat's. He smiled vaguely at Serena, drifted through the room and disappeared down the palm-fringed fire escape. She did not know if he was adopted son, lodger, lover, and did not feel able to ask. Eleanor behaved as though he was not there. Briefly, Serena wondered if the other woman could even see him.

"Would you like more tea?"

"I'd love some, but I've got to get back. My sister's coming to stay for a day or so, with our cousin. She's American; she's over for a bit."

"I like Americans," Eleanor said, unexpectedly. "So go-ahead."

Eleanor herself was hardly slacking in that regard, Serena thought. The certificate proclaiming her a member of the Goldsmith's Guild stood on the cabinet: someone had been obliged to cross out 'boy' and substitute 'girl', in copperplate.

"Nell's great," Serena told her. "She writes. I'll bring you a copy of her book."

"Books are always very welcome guests."

Serena made her way down the fire escape, difficult to negotiate in heels, into the back yard and out onto the street. The rain had blown out overnight and left London pallid and washed in its wake. She pulled her scarf tighter against a sharp east wind and turned the corner into Red Lion Square.

The square was empty apart from a girl on a bench. Serena, minding her own business, paid her no attention as she walked past but then the girl looked up and Serena saw that it was Dana Stare.

"Oh," Dana said. She gave a twisted little smile that, oddly, looked more genuine than the effusive greeting she had given Serena two nights before, at the club. "There you are," – as though she'd been looking for Serena. Today, she wore a tight black leather jacket with a high collar, and a long black skirt. Her hair sprayed out around the collar in a polished fan.

"Hello," Serena said, warily.

"Cold, isn't it? Where are you off to?"

"The Tube," Serena said.

"I'll walk with you." It wasn't an option.

Dana Stare had a long stride, not a townswoman's step, Serena thought, despite her spiky heels. She said to Serena, "So how long have you and Ben been an item?"

"A few years." On and off, but she wasn't going to tell Dana that. Other people doubtless would, and probably had.

"Childhood sweethearts?" Dana smiled her little cat smile. There was a ragged edge of accent under the London speech, Serena thought, but she couldn't quite place it. Irish? Northumberland? Something of each. "He said he's known you for years."

"Yes, he has." *Childhood sweethearts* wasn't true but she wasn't going to say that to Dana.

"That's really cute." The Americanism sounded off; it was as though Dana Stare was saying something quite different, beneath the conventional words, just as her accent kept lifting up from the surface. And Serena thought she knew what that subtext was. But she wasn't going to get her claws out just yet. She said nothing at all, and this seemed to disconcert Dana. She pursed her lips and looked at her boots as she walked.

"Where are you from?" Serena asked, abruptly. Dana looked surprised by the question.

"What? Oh, all over the place. My family's from different parts. My brother's in Somerset, at the moment."

"Really? My sister still lives in Somerset."

"I know." Perhaps Dana felt that more explanation actually was required, because she said, "My brother's a mate of Jamie's."

"I see. And that's how you know Ben."

"Yeah. Tam – my brother – has known Jamie for a while. I met Ben at Jamie's dad's. And Laura and I are really close. She's such a sweetie."

"Laura's lovely. Amberley's not very far from us."

"I know," Dana said, again. Serena was starting to feel out of her depth – it was like having a stalker, but she could hardly accuse Dana of that just because she knew the same people. She felt an unpleasant tugging at her gut, a sinking feeling, and recognised it as the sensation of boundaries being impinged. They were nearly at the Tube. She said,

"So what do you do?"

"I do things for people."

What did *that* mean? Care work? PR? Prostitution?

"And I do a bit of modelling."

"Catwalk?"

"Some. Mainly magazines."

"I'm surprised I haven't heard of you."

"I'm not one of the big names," Dana said, and smiled as if something had amused her, rather than with the usual anxiety or sour grapes that Serena had become accustomed to with members of the modelling profession. Maybe Dana was in porn.

"Well," Serena said, "Here we are." She wished her voice didn't sound so falsely bright. "Nice talking to you. I'm sure we'll run into one another again."

"I'm sure we will," Dana Stare said.

LUNA

The interior of the van was very dark and it took Luna a moment to adjust. She stood uncertainly in the doorway, with the brightness of the day closed off behind her.

"Gran?" Sam's voice said. His hand was on Moth's collar. The lurcher whined a greeting. Moth's long, rat-thin tail began to whip from side to side.

There was a flicker and a lamp came on. Gradually, Luna saw a divan bed and a small table beside it. The trailer was a modern one, blocky and long, but the windows were covered over with black paper. It stood parked at the end of a field, near a slow-running stream that would, in spring, be thick with watercress. The chalk shoulder of the hill stretched above.

"Sam, come in. Sit down. Bring your friend with you. And the dog." The voice was surprisingly strong. Luna groped her way to the divan and perched on the edge of it. She could see Sam's gran, now, peering out of the shadows. Not all that old, but her face was all bones and hollows, like the hillside, and her skin was white as chalk.

"Hello, doggy."

"His name's Moth," Luna said.

"Yeah, he's the new rescue — remember I told you, Gran? After Bolt went back in the spring."

"I do remember, Sam. What a lovely boy. And what's *your* name, lovey?"

"Luna. Luna Fallow." Normally, she didn't give her surname, but now it seemed right and she wondered why.

"My name is Ver March. I'm Sam's grandmother, his mother's mother."

"It's nice to meet you." Luna, who was reticent rather than shy, felt herself to be shy now and it made her sound gruff and reluctant.

"Sam," his grandmother said. "Go outside and do stuff."

In the halflight, Luna saw Sam grin. "All right, Gran. I'll take the dog, shall I? Before that tail knocks something flying."

He left, letting in a shaft of thin sun, and closing the door behind him.

45

"This must seem a bit strange to you, lovey," Ver March said. "But I've a problem with my eyes at the minute and I can't see too well in strong light. So I'm living like a mole."

"Or an owl," Luna said.

"Or an owl, yes. I'm pleased to meet you. Sam told me a bit about you, more than he usually tells me. Not that there have been all that many girls and not many at all whom he's brought back to meet me."

"I think it's working," Luna said, hesitant.

"He's a good boy. Decent. He's always been like that, tried to do the right thing. He lost his mother when he was young; it's not been easy for him."

Luna knew better than to ask where Sam's dad had got to: her own family history was not stellar in that respect.

"I lost my mother, too," she said.

"I know. Sam told me. But she's not dead."

"How do you know?"

"The cards." Ver March reached for a battered pack that sat on the table.

"Ah." But Luna's expectations about old gypsy ladies and the Tarot were wrong. The cards that Ver drew out were not the Tarot, or any that she recognised. She looked more closely, seeing a curling vine, a moon, a glowing border.

"Three of Joys," the old lady said. "That's for you. Eventually. Wherever she is, your mum, she isn't dead."

"I've never seen those cards before. I do the Tarot myself, a little bit. I'm learning."

"It's a marvellous book. These are older. Not this actual deck: my husband painted these, before he died. But the symbols of these cards are old and they deal with deeper things than even the Tarot does. Wilder things." She handed over a card. A white fox ran down between beech trees, a chalk hillside behind.

"Do you – could you use them to see where my mum is?"

"I did try," Ver said. "But I've not met your mum, you see. So maybe you should draw a card."

She fanned out the deck. There were not so many cards in this deck as in the Tarot. Luna pulled one out and looked down at a snow covered landscape. The chalk horse raced silver on the hillside; below, two winding black shapes coiled through the branches of a blackthorn hedge. She could not see, in the dim light of the van, quite what they were. Maybe snakes? She held the card out to Ver March, who looked at it without expression.

"Rifle through them. Get to know the cards." Luna did so, but the images seemed to drift and swim, leaving an impression of strong beauty behind, rich as good wine.

"They're lovely," she said at length, inadequately.

"My husband was a painter by trade."

Luna smiled. "Yet you don't have a painted wagon."

"No. We prefer to be anonymous, you see. Not to call too much attention to ourselves."

"Sam," Luna paused, afraid of giving offence, "Sam said you weren't Romany."

"We're not Rom, no. We've always been here. The Rom came later, but we made them welcome. Someone had to." She reached out again and took something wrapped in a scrap of velvet, handing it to Luna. "Take hold of that and tell me what you see."

Luna did so. It was a shard of hollow bone. She curled her hand around it and closed her eyes. The wall of the trailer peeled back behind imagination's wall. Luna stood looking out onto the chalk hillside. It was covered in snow, like the card, and the Great Bear curved above it, with Arcturus yellow as a buttercup over the white ridge of the hill. One benefit of growing up in an astronomer's house: you knew your stars. Luna took a step and her boots crunched on ice; she looked back to see a line of beech, and far away, something howled. She dropped the bone in surprise and the landscape vanished. The inside of the wagon felt suddenly stifling and hot. Her head was swimming.

"Deep breath, lovey," Ver March said. Slowly, Luna's vision cleared.

"That was a long time ago."

"Yes, a very long time."

"And your –" 'family' seemed wrong, "*People* have been here ever since then?"

"I knew Sam had been sensible," Sam's gran said.

BEE

Bee stood on the Embankment, looking up at the Sphinx. The Sphinx, inscrutable, smiled back; its enormous bronze face reminded her, for some reason, of the faces of the Behenian stars.

"I wouldn't be surprised if you spoke," said Bee, encouragingly, but the Sphinx remained motionless on its plinth, with the grey oily Thames gliding along behind it.

Nell and Serena had gone to the British Library: Nell to look up something historical, and Serena to search for a particular volume on Victorian embroidery. Left to her own devices, Bee found herself enjoying the capital. The dark green dress was a reasonable success and her sister had lent her a fifties coat with a collar like moss to go over it rather than her usual Barbour. She felt more presentable than she had done in years, and although she missed Dark, it was good to get away for a few days. She knew she'd be tired of London by the end of the following day, and that her feet would hurt, and that she'd be sick of the deadening smoke-smell of the city. But this morning she'd had breakfast in a patisserie, had spent forty five minutes in a bookshop, and was now talking to a Sphinx: for the moment, Bee Fallow was content.

And there was lunch on the agenda shortly, but for that, she'd have to make her way back up to Bloomsbury. She turned, leaving the river behind, and headed towards the Tube. But just before she crossed the road, she looked back. The Sphinx was holding a bronze claw to its smiling mouth: *hush*.

"They're going to send the book to Nell," Serena said. She flopped into a chair opposite her sister. Her fringed shawl sparkled with crystal beads; her brocade coat bloomed with dusk-pink roses. Bee felt a sudden pang at her own sartorial restraint; Serena was, albeit discreetly, turning heads.

"Well, that's good."

"They said she could collect it from Harvard, from the library. They've got some kind of system. Inter-loan thingy. She's really pleased."

"Is she still there?"

"No, she came down with me. She's in a second hand bookshop round the corner. Can't get her out of them. I said I'd meet you, otherwise we'd both have been late."

"That was kind," Bee said.

"And you? Did you have a good morning?"

"Yes. By the way, I rang Stella but she didn't answer the phone. She'll be all right. Probably wasn't up."

Serena shook her head. "I can't believe she's back at the house. You said she just showed up?"

"Well, she called to say she was on the train. We picked her up."

"And how is she? I mean, really?"

"I don't know. She seems all right. We haven't talked about – it."

"Did she mention the row?"

"Not really."

"Oh, Bee. I wish she'd apologise."

"We're avoiding the subject. I'll try and talk to her when I get back. It – well, it did hurt. I did everything I could think of to find Mum."

Serena clasped her wrist. "I know you did."

Bee felt her eyes begin to sting. "I was on the phone for hours, and I went down to the police station every day – I practically haunted it. But I can't blame Stella. It's just been so –"

"It's been shit."

"And part of it is the gossip. People still go quiet when I walk into the village shop and they give you that *look*."

"Probably think we murdered her and buried her under the patio."

"Serena, I'm sure that's what they *do* think. Some of them, anyway. I can hear them thinking 'It's always the relatives, you know'."

"I think that's usually those awful missing kids cases where the father turns out to have done it."

"It's not everyone. Caro Amberley's been a star."

"Ben's mum's always had her feet on the ground. And she was Mum's best friend, after all."

"People think we're weird, anyway. What with Alys and all her kids with different fathers, out of wedlock – I'm surprised we haven't featured in a Daily Mail double spread."

"We're too middle class."

"And the – other stuff."

Serena gave her sister a piercing stare. "Are they – the *you know* –"

"Yes, they are."

"Good," Serena said stoutly. "I like them."

"I like them, too."

"Capella was my favourite, when I was a little girl. That sapphire crown. And she left sprigs of thyme about the place."

"Serena, we shouldn't –"

"What? No one would know what we were talking about. Or care. You should hear what some of my clients believe. One of them thinks she's the reincarnation of a Babylonian priestess. Trust me, no one's going to care about a load of star spirits."

"I liked the Pleiades," Bee said, after a pause.

"Yes, rock crystal and fennel, so pretty. And there was always one you couldn't quite see."

"There still is."

"And the – others."

"Stel went down to the church and spoke to Grandpa."

"I miss Grandpa. I ought to come home," Serena said. She hunched into the brocade coat, while the waitress took their order. The café smelled of ginger and aniseed, chilli and soy: warm scents, against the cold.

"Why not, Serena? You could bring Bella."

Serena nodded. "She likes it there, but she's got stuff this weekend. She's going to her dad's. I want to get the collection out of the way."

"Are you planning to come back at Christmas? You're coming back for Apple Day, anyway."

"I think so, for Christmas. Ben's going home. Not that it necessarily means I'll do the same. Bee, do you know a girl named Dana Stare?"

"No. I know a bloke called Tam Stare, though. He's just sorted my dead car out."

"He's a friend of Jamie's, I gather."

"Yes, one of Jamie's dodgy friends, though."

"What sort of dodgy?"

"Dealing. Not anything hardcore, I don't think, but all the same... He's one of those people that people always know, if you know what I mean. Fixers. They meet them down the pub."

Serena nodded. "I know a lot of people like that. But you don't know Dana? The sister?"

"No, I don't think so. What's she like?"

"Dodgy," Serena said, with gloom.

STELLA

The rain had washed out over the Severn Sea when Stella came back down the lane from her second trip to the churchyard. This time, Abraham had proved skittish and elusive, so Stella had decided not to stop at the black marble pyramid and had gone into the church itself instead, since the vicar was just emerging and held the door for her.

Hornmoon was wreathed with roses. Tudor and stylised, they marched up the white plaster walls in rows, and thence over the roof, occasionally dodging between the beams, where the artist had been obliged to accommodate the uneven surface of the ceiling. All of them were a dull scarlet, with small green leaves. Carol services, Easter and the occasional wedding or funeral had been spent in counting them, but Stella and her sisters had never been able to agree on the exact number.

The church was supposed to have Templar foundations, but Bee, the historian of the family, was uncertain how true this might actually be. It was, however, a most unusual building, and on any given day one might find hushed academics inside it, making notes or undertaking careful illustrations of the roses, the carved wooden cherubs, or the admonitions that ran in a racing cursive script around the walls: *Lovest Thou Thy Lord* and *Praise With A Glad Heart*. Recently, a pleasingly large grant had been given to the church for a restoration project: the previous summer had seen a group of historical artists in residence at the vicarage, notable both for their prodigious imbibement at the Hornmoon Arms and their skill in repainting the decorations and restoring them to their original Elizabethan grandeur. Now the roses leaped from the walls like splashes of blood, even in the rainy autumn light, and Stella sat for a while in contemplation of the thoroughly familiar. Someone had made a competent arrangement of white roses and the churchyard's Japanese anemones in front of the pulpit, and Stella's gaze rested on this composition with satisfaction. She always felt more aligned to Buddhism than Christianity, but there was something pleasing about the routine patterns of the year, as though they tied her back into time. The last eighteen months, with missing Mum, various men, to-ing and fro-ing from Ibiza and London and Dublin and Amsterdam, the whole manic round of it, made her realise how grateful she was to be islanded here. By tomorrow, she might be glad to have Bee and Nell back – but for now, no.

She stayed later in the church than she had intended, and by the time she slipped the key into the slate hollow in the porch wall, dusk was blooming over the horizon. There was a clear green strip of sky in the south west, and the hills were black whalebacks of shadow against it. Stella could see a sliver of moon, right on the new, above the hills. It was not on its back, holding the water in, but upright, like a sickle about to cut. The evening star rode near it, sailing through green.

As Stella walked past the marble pyramid, there was a blue flicker and her grandfather's voice said inside her mind: "The comet's coming. Don't forget, Starry."

"A comet? Really?"

The voice was impatient. "Don't you keep up with these things? Lerninsky's comet. Once every few hundred years, so you won't see it again. Although that depends."

"I'll be a little blue star myself by then," Stella said, and walked home in the badger-light.

She took the orchard path to the house, the long grass fringing wet against her shins. By now the moon was hanging up in the apple branches and more stars were coming out. Stella looked towards the house and thought of supper: the glow of the living room light, which she had left on, was just visible through the window. So the figure stepping out from under the apple tree made her jump.

"Who the hell's that?" She brought a warding hand up; too many years spent in clubland not to be willing to thump someone.

"I'm sorry, mistress," a voice said. "I mean no harm. I thought you were Bee."

Stella saw black clothes, a white collar. Dark wore a pearl in one ear and a neat black beard. Maybe early thirties? Also rather good looking, Stella noted.

And she could see the glow of the window through his chest.

So. One of the no-longer-living, then. Somehow, she shied away from other words: *dead, ghost.*

"No, it's Stella. Who are you?" But she was starting to relax.

"My name is Ned Dark."

"You're a – friend of Bee's?" Stella asked. She sat down on the canted apple tree, the one that the spring gales had brought down in a shower of snowstorm blossom.

"Yes. We meet most evenings." He sat down beside her, a respectable distance away.

"Can you come into the house?"

"Most of it."

"Oh," Stella said, "Did you live here, then?"

"I was born in Hornmoon. But I died in –" he frowned. "I can't recall. I was at sea. Dark and Drake! We used to make light of it."

"You sailed with Drake? Oh, wow!"

"They were exciting times," Ned Dark said, modestly.

"And now you're stuck here in a mouldy old apple orchard," Stella said, sympathetic. "Do you miss the sea?"

"Sometimes I'm there. But usually, here. By choice, I might say."

"That's all right, then."

"You don't look like your sister."

"No. Different fathers."

He smiled. "Ah, Fallow women."

"Oh dear. Did we have the rep in your day?"

"'Rep'? The women of the family are known to be – independent of spirit."

Stella sighed. "We're sluts. It's all right. I'm used to it." She studied his face, the slope of his nose. "Are you a Fallow, then?"

But Dark shook his head. "No. My father was called Dark, as am I, and my mother was a Horne, from down the valley. She was a milkmaid here. This was more home to me than the hovel we lived in."

"I went to school with some kids called Horne," Stella said, and Dark smiled.

"Then they'll be my family, still. But my home was here, and the sea."

It was growing cold, the air dank, and Stella shivered.

"You should go inside," Dark said.

"Are you coming with me?"

He shook his head. "I'll stay out here. The comet's coming, did you know?"

"Grandpa told me."

She bade him goodnight and left him standing under the apple trees in the dying light. When she looked back, he was a shadow, and then gone. She opened the back door to a cacophony of dogs. She had always felt safe here, the heart of things, but knowing that Dark was out there in the orchard made her feel safer yet. She considered, briefly, going to the pub, the Hornmoon Arms, and she thought this was a good sign: ready to face what passed for the outside world again, after her nun-like seclusion of all of twenty-four hours, but then she decided she couldn't be bothered, with that or social media. Facebook could wait. Music, however, never could: it was all about the vibe. She loaded a trance remix onto YouTube and bopped around the kitchen as she fed the dogs and the clamouring cats. Then she diced vegetables for a pasta sauce: tomatoes, onion, flat chestnut mushrooms and garlic. Stella could only cook a couple of things, but she did them properly and she usually didn't burn them. She stood back and surveyed the results, feeling adult and sensible. Looking after yourself and all that. When the sauce was simmering on the stove the phone rang. Stella's hand hesitated above it for a moment, then she picked it up.

"Bee?" A woman's voice, familiar.

"No, it's Stella. Bee's in London. Who's that?"

"Oh, Stella! Good to hear you. This is Caro. Caro Amberley. I'm losing my voice – I think I'm coming down with something. I was hoping to speak to Bee, but if she's not there... How are you?"

It seemed odd to be chatting to Ben and Jamie's mother, as if Alys was still there, and everything was normal. At last Caro said, "It's a bit complicated to leave a message, but I wanted to run an idea past Bee. I mentioned it to her a few days ago. But since you're there, I'll run it past you, instead. You do events, don't you?"

"I've done some events planning, yes. Festivals, mainly. Raves."

"I remember. You did that little music festival up at Oldstone, didn't you? For the leukemia charity."

"That's right. Moonrise." It had gone well; well enough for Stella and Luna to have considered making it a regular thing. But then Alys had disappeared, and Luna had gone on the road, and everything had fallen apart.

"The thing is," Caro said now, "We're having this apple day, like a festival. Just a really little thing. Bee's probably mentioned it. And I know it's way too late and we should have asked you ages ago, but I was wondering..."

An hour or so DJ-ing in their own orchard did not sound too bad. Stella had no firm commitments between now and Christmas; it would give her the excuse to stay.

"Bee mentioned Apple Day, yeah. I'd be up for that."

"If you have any thoughts…"

"Classy," she said at once. "You want to make it classy. Posh food and a good marquee. Make it something to remember."

"That's what we're intending. We had a little play planned, actually, but now the woman who runs the Am Dram society here fell out with some of the people who were going to be in it, because someone's sister had an affair with someone else's husband, and, well…"

"Am Dram ensued," Stella said, in order to take the moral high ground and not interrogate Caro on local gossip, even though she almost certainly knew the protagonists and was secretly dying to find out.

"Yes, quite. Do you think – I know your sister must be really busy…"

Stella knew that she meant Serena. "A little catwalk? I can ask her."

"Jamie and Laura will help, obviously, and Richard. Ben might come down if Serena's involved."

Stella found a pen and a pad, and started making notes. When she had put the phone down again she sat for a moment, staring into the fireplace. She could see someone out of the corner of her eye, but this time chose not to look. It was good to have a project. Despite what her sisters said, she was not like her mother, always drifting. Alys, languid, had never bothered with good works, except insofar as Caro or other women friends dragged her into things. Stella remembered her helping out on village jumble stalls, tall and elegant, smiling vaguely as she handed over hideous china cats, or fir cone Christmas ornaments, or knitted shapelessnesses that other people had made. But she had never taken the organisational initiative, unlike her friends or, indeed, her daughters. Serena had been focused on fashion since she was a tot: first the local college to do textiles and art, then Central St Martin's, then her own business. Stella remembered her cutting up an antique quilt to make dolls' clothes, at the age of seven or so. The ensuring row had been remarkable: Alys could be fiery, when roused, although she had a very long line to anger. Stella herself, never the most ambitious of girls, had done enough events to have Caro request her help now and had once had a chance at being a champion swimmer – never quite good enough, though, but she had given it a go. Even if she had been secretly relieved when it became clear that it wasn't going to happen; bit too much like hard work, thought Stella. Mind you, the number of times she'd heard *oh, a DJ. But when are you going to get a proper job?* Bee kept the house going, had been a trained librarian before the bloody council had closed the library, and still ran her second-hand book business from home. Even Luna had once been planning on a career in environmentalism, before life had whirled her away into the loops of the Gipsy Switch. But Alys, butterfly Alys, fluttering about the ancient house, had never really bothered with ambition once her modelling career was over, except insofar as looking after Abraham was concerned, and her daughters. Stella had always got the impression that Alys had wafted into modelling by accident; probably you could do that, all those years ago.

But basically, they had all been very lucky. The house was theirs, inherited, and if you had a roof over your head, you were privileged, right at the top of the heap, and no point in denying it.

Stella had not thought to criticise her mother, particularly. Everyone to their own path, and all that. But now she wondered whether Alys had actually been all that happy, if Abraham's death had not thrown her into more of a spin than they'd realised. The hiking trip, so out of character. Bee, Stella and Serena had talked about it to Caro, shortly after Alys went missing: if her mother had confided in anyone, Bee had said, it would be Caro Amberley. But she had apparently told her best friend very little, least of all a destination, and Caro was at as much of a loss as everyone else.

"Oh, Alys," Stella said aloud. "Where the hell *did* you go to, my lovely?"

BEE

"He's probably just down the pub," Bee said. Serena, back at the studio, was sitting on the sofa, glaring at the screen of her mobile phone. Bee hated seeing her sister like this, the barely-hidden agitation, and over a man at that. However, she'd made a few mistakes herself, in her twenties; enough to put her off until Dark came along. So now she could, perhaps, afford to be smug: Dark was, after all, long dead, and safe. There were, he'd told her, no ghostly girls who'd prove a rival for his affections, not even the Behenian stars.

"They're like my sisters. All of them. But I don't see a lot of them. And they don't say much. You might have noticed that." For the star spirits tended to keep their own counsel, inscrutable and austere.

Now, Bee said, "How's it – been going? You know, with Ben?"

"I thought it was all right. We've had a few ups and downs... It wouldn't be the first time his eye has been caught by someone else. You know that, anyway. He promised it wouldn't happen again, but... Anyway, I was getting this funny feeling that things weren't quite right. But now there's this girl. Dana, I told you about her. She's been setting her cap at him."

"That sounds so old fashioned," Bee mused. "I suppose we are, though. Comes of growing up with Abraham and no TV. I hear things he used to say coming out of my mouth. I talk about the *wireless,* for god's sake. I shouldn't be living in the twenty first century."

Serena ignored this. "Believe me, there's nothing old fashioned about Ms Stare. She looks like something out of *The Matrix.* Although that probably is old fashioned now, isn't it? Time goes so quickly. Oooh." For her phone had shrilled in her hand.

"Laura? Hello. No, he isn't. I don't know where he is. Sorry? He might be. Bee's here, by the way. Sure." She passed the phone over.

Bee said, "Laura – yes, in London, with our cousin. Stella's at the house. Are you? She'll be pleased."

To Serena, ringing off, she said, "Laura's going over to see Stella, tomorrow. Some idea of Caro's, apparently."

"I haven't seen her for ages," Serena said.

"She's just the same." Laura floated before Bee's mind's eye: tall like her mother Caro, but white-blonde and cocoa-eyed. Nothing like Jamie or Ben, except in height. If Bee didn't know better, she'd have suspected Caro of Fallow-like impropriety, but Caro and Richard were as solid as a pair of apple trees, their marriage as enduring. Impossible to think of Laura without thinking of horses, centaur-esque. She was a show jumper, the reason why the kitchen door at Amberley was starred with multi-coloured rosettes. It occurred to Bee that Laura may well know this Dana Stare, and she thought she would ask her. As if her sister had read her mind, she said,

"Dana said she knows Laura. Said they were really close."

"She can't be that bad if she's a friend of Laura's."

"That's what I would have thought, but – well, she *is* bad, Bee."

At this point, Nell came back into the room, with a stack of books. "I'm going to mail these back home to myself, Bee. They'll bump up the luggage allowance too much, and they're too heavy to carry about."

Bee saw Serena retreat into herself, away from worries of Ben. "I'll open some wine," she said, drifting in the direction of the kitchen. "Bee, can you find me some glasses?"

Bee went over to the white-painted cupboard with its border of roses, and opened it to retrieve the glasses. As she was reaching up, she heard Nell say, "Oh my God!"

Bee turned. Her cousin was staring open mouthed at the door. The star Spica stood within it. Her black hair was weeded with a skein of emeralds; she held a sprig of sage, green against the darker fir of her gown.

"Ah." Bee said, horrified, and the breath broke the spell: Spica was gone.

"One of Serena's models," Nell said. She sat down abruptly onto the couch. "Sorry. She gave me such a shock; I wasn't expecting anyone to be working this late. But what a lovely dress. Serena is so clever, isn't she?"

At this, Serena came back in, holding a bottle of red.

"Serena, I was just saying to Bee, that green dress on your model was so pretty."

"The green –?"

"And matching it with those herbs like that – are you going to do that with all your models? That's a really neat idea. The natural world picking up the colours. Kind of like a sympathetic fallacy."

"Um," Serena said.

Quickly, Bee added, "She caught a glimpse of Spica. With the sage." Understanding, and a trace of alarm, flickered in Serena's face.

"Oh! Yes, the green dress. It is nice, isn't it? She's, er, yes, been working late. Final fitting. For a show."

"Just gorgeous," Nell said, and accepted a glass of Shiraz.

"Can I borrow you for a minute, Bee? You're better at these things than I am. I'm not sure how long this lasagne should go in for."

In the kitchen, Serena hissed, "What was she doing here? They never come here. I've never seen one of them."

"I don't know! And they were all over the house, when Nell came. Stella saw one of them. But Nell didn't say anything."

"Didn't you tell her?"

"Tell her what? The tea's in the left hand cupboard, the hot tap in the bathroom is a bit dodgy and, by the way, you might see these lavishly dressed women carrying plants wandering about the house, but don't worry, because they're not human. They're stars."

Serena gave her sister an owlish look. "Point taken."

"I was hoping that she wouldn't be able to see them, and in fact, I didn't think she could, because she didn't mention it. But she obviously can."

"But why here?"

"Haven't a clue, Serena."

Serena collapsed into a chair. "Damn."

"We've gone over this – they started coming when Grandfather was a boy, at the very least, but Abraham thought they were probably there before that. I mean, we always said that the dresses look sort of Elizabethan."

"They are Elizabethan. I know my fashion history. You think they're connected to the gemstones in that box, don't you? You're probably right. Grandpa thought so, too. And Grandpa said that the Behenian stars were called that in the Renaissance, the ones that move across the sky from season to season, the main stars of the sky."

"The ones that show up tend to be the ones that are actually overhead at the time."

"Could Spica have been some sort of warning?"

"I hope not. Where's your phone?"

Bee waited for a few minutes, the mobile pressed to her ear, until with relief she heard Stella's voice.

"Stel? Everything all right?"

"Yes. Why?"

Bee told her.

"I haven't seen Spica yet," Stella said. "Wonder why she showed up at Serena's? She's never had a particular thing about Serena, has she?"

The star had not, as far as Bee could recall. Luna, now – Polaris (magnet and succory), had often been seen sitting by her cradle, watching over her, dangling the sprig of succory over the baby's brow. And Polaris, Bee remembered, was also linked in astrology to the moon.

"Two other things," Stella said now. "Caro rang. She wants to have some music at Apple Day. I've said I'll help." She hesitated. "If it's okay for me to stick around for a bit."

"Of course it is."

"She wanted to ask Serena if she could do a little fashion show. I said I'd ask her. And –" Stella paused. "And I met Dark."

"Oh." Bee was aware of a complicated array of emotions: relief that she didn't have to explain Dark to her sister, a flicker of homesickness, and the faintest touch of jealousy, not of Dark or Stella themselves, but for the fact that Dark was no longer her secret alone.

"It's fine," Stella said. "He's really interesting. And I'm not ungrateful that he's around."

"Why? Has anything –"

"No. Well, Tam Stare brought your money back. For the car. I'm sure he's cool, but –"

Bee shared the 'but.'

"Dark will help, if you call him. If you need."

"I think he would," Stella said.

LUNA

Luna was up on the Ridgeway, high over the rolling world. At this time of the day, midweek in October, the landscape was deserted apart from a small ploughing tractor, furrowing down a long slope in a flurry of gulls, and the little black box of her own trailer behind the layby hedge. She could not even see Sam or Moth; they would be inside, Sam putting the kettle on. While she was out here, up under the blowing sky. The wind tasted of rain. Luna's heavy boots were clogged with mud, the wet chalky earth making the trackway hard going. To the west, the unlikely pudding basin shape of Silbury Hill was a green cone against the fields, with Avebury and its rings of standing stones beyond.

The entrance to the barrow lay ahead. Luna did not know why she had been so keen to come here: she had woken with it, full-blown obsession. Eyes snapping open in the morning and *I've got to go to West Kennet, Sam. Got to.* He hadn't argued, bless him.

"All right. No worries." Hitched up the piebalds and clopped along, arriving not long after noon. Once there, he'd left her to it: she'd taken food with her, bread and cheese like a ploughboy, and a bottle of water, and headed up the track. Now, boots clagged with slimy chalk mud, she was on the ridge itself, with the barrow looming ahead. An English Heritage placard, rather weathered, bore information about the site, but Luna didn't bother to look at this and marched straight past. She would learn all she needed to from the barrow itself.

At the entrance, she paused. The barrow mouth was a black gash against the green and white of the down, and the rich corduroy texture of the fields. Its rim of stone – two huge slabs, with a third placed on top as a lintel – seemed organic, part of the landscape itself, rather than placed there by man, as though the land had cast the barrow up, out of itself. The dark mouth was inviting. She had not been expecting that.

Luna, being short, did not have to duck low beneath the lintel, or in the narrow tunnel beyond. She followed the passage down into the barrow, pursuing the dim light ahead. She could not tell where it was coming from. Occasionally she had to put out a hand to steady herself against the cool, rough stone, for the earth floor of the passage was bumpy and uneven. At last she stepped out into the egg-shaped final chamber and saw that someone had placed three tea-lights, burning, on a small rock ledge. Their flickering light cast puppet shadows over the walls; Luna raised her hand and made a bunny. When the barrow was dug, perhaps that ledge would have held a tallow candle, or some ritual item significant to the chieftain who had been buried here. His bones were long gone; the barrow fully excavated and its secrets revealed, or at least, those that were visible.

She left the little lights burning away and sat down, cross-legged, in the middle of the chamber. She closed her eyes, thinking back to the stuffy darkness of Ver March's caravan, the underlying cologne and musk odour, the walls peeling back to reveal the ancient land. This did not happen now. Instead, it felt as though the walls of the barrow chamber were closing in, narrowing, but Luna, who liked small dark spaces, was not unsettled. Instead, she felt encased and enclosed, sinking down into the earth's embrace. There was a rhythmic, muffled thump like the beat of a distant drum, or the world's heart. She felt earth settle on her eyelids, on the backs of her hands, between her lips. It was like a blanket; it reminded her of the dry scratch of wool. Luna continued to breathe, steadily in and out, and the earth contained her.

This was all it was. She experienced no sudden vision, no revelations. She saw nothing except red-black dark and felt the increasing weight of the soil. But when at last she forced her eyes open and realised that only one small guttering light remained, she knew that something had changed within her. She did not know what it meant.

As she stood stiffly up, the light went out. Luna made her way to the mouth of the barrow in darkness, groping her way along, and when she reached the entrance she realised that twilight had fallen outside, too. A cold purple haze lay over the land, with a shine only to the west, over the cone shaped hill. She heard an owl cry out and that sound was comforting, too. She felt as though she had become part of the land, no inside or outside. But down by the hedge a square of yellow light showed that Sam had lit the lamp. She went down the chalk track towards it, under the emergent prickle of the stars.

STELLA

Next morning, Stella was in the kitchen when someone knocked on the back door. She opened it, to find Laura Amberley standing on the back step.

"Hello. I'm sorry, I wasn't sure if you were up. Am I very early?"

"It's half eight. That's just about acceptable." Over her shoulder, she said to Laura, "I suppose you've been up for hours."

"Since half five." Laura was apologetic. Her beanpole figure followed Stella into the kitchen; she wore mud-stained jodhpurs and riding boots, a quilted sleeveless jacket with the stuffing coming out. 'Exercising.' She brushed her fair hair back from her forehead; tendrils were coming down, like wild clematis. Her dark eyes were anxious.

"No rest for the wicked." Stella poured tea.

"Mum said you've been in Ibiza."

"Clubbing. Working. I had a series of gigs. It's nice to be home, though."

"Stel – I'm really sorry about your mum. I didn't get a chance to tell you, you know I was in the States last year, and – anyway. I'm sorry."

"Thanks." Stella did not know what else to say. She looked down at her mug and curled her hands around it. There was suddenly a very British silence.

"Anyway," Stella said, to break it. "How are things with you? How's the riding?"

"Okay. The riding's going really well, although I pulled a tendon in my leg a few months ago."

"Ow!"

"It could have been worse." She gave a vague, loose-shouldered shrug. "It held things up a bit. Mum said she'd spoken to you about this apple day. She wants me to organise pony rides."

"Yes, she did. I thought," Stella said, "that we could have deck in the orchard, maybe. I've made a couple of phone calls. And if Ben's coming down –" *Good question*, Stella thought. She'd spoken to Bee the night before, out of Serena's hearing; been debriefed. But she didn't want to quiz Laura about her brother's relationships; it didn't seem fair.

"He is. And Mum's spoken to an orchestra."

"An *orchestra!*"

"George Hazelgrove. She knows him through something or other."

"God, he's famous. Even I've heard of him and I don't know much about classical music. Is she – she can't be paying him, surely? I don't mean you're skint. Just that he must charge a fortune."

"Apparently it was his idea. Proceeds to go to charity, and collecting boxes. He wants to do something based on Holst's planets, because of the comet."

"Outside?" Stella was thinking of autumn, dark nights, damp air, plus musical instruments.

"She'd have to have it in a marquee. You couldn't risk it actually outdoors, because of the weather. I think she's spoken to Tam Stare about hiring one."

"He does that sort of thing, does he?"

"He does a lot of things." Laura's voice was very neutral. *You don't like him,* Stella thought.

"Serena knows his sister, I gather. Dana."

"Does she?" Still that studied neutrality.

"She says she's a friend of yours."

"She said that, did she?" Laura paused. "I think she's really fake, actually."

Stella perked up at this. Coming from Laura, who was legendary for seeing good in everyone, even the biggest local tosspots... Since she had given Stella an opening, Stella said, "Do you? Look, I'll be up front. Bee thinks Serena thinks that Dana's after Ben."

Laura's mouth turned down. "She *is* after Ben. Totally. Without question. Can't think why."

"That's because he's your brother. A bit famous. Very good looking."

"No, I mean – she knows a lot of people. She's got this knack of inserting herself into situations – you never quite know how she's done it but suddenly she's everywhere. Including in your house. I think they're both after money. She and Tam. After what they can get."

"Okay," Stella said. "Thanks. That gives me some ammo for Serena, anyway."

"Ben's an idiot. I know it's sometimes been rocky with Serena and he's been – anyway, they're really good together, when they're good. And your sister has her own stuff – she's got her career. Dana's just a gold digger. She doesn't really *do* anything, except a bit of modelling. But she's sticky."

"She's –?"

"Sticky. Like when you brush against cobwebs or those strings that glue makes, and suddenly it's everywhere? Do you have your legs waxed?"

"Sometimes. In summer."

"It's like that. A little patch off-piste and then it's all over the place and it takes days to wear off. Dana sticks to people."

She had best, Stella thought, think twice about sticking to Ben.

Bee and Nell were coming back on the 7.30 from Paddington, so would be into Hornmoon around ten, unless the train was late. It was the last train of the night from Paddington, infuriatingly early, but the alternative would be Bristol and an hour and a half drive at the end of it, plus the parking.

"I suppose," Serena had said once, returning home for Christmas, "they think we've all got to get up at the crack of dawn and milk the cows."

But now it was after four, and already dark. Stella was feeding the dogs when she heard the sound in the yard.

It was a clattering noise, like metal on stone, and if the half back door had not been open, she would not have heard it. At first she thought it was her relations, returning early, but there was no sign of the car. Nor was it Laura. Stella went out into the yard, tasting rain, but could find nothing. The dogs, accompanying her, snuffled busily about, but in a haphazard manner.

"Anyone there?" Stella called. It was all very quiet, apart from the rooks over in the chestnut trees, but she knew she had not imagined the sound. Wondering, she summoned Nelson and Hardy from their busy investigations and went back into the house.

Above the living room, the floorboards creaked. Stella froze. The Behenian stars never made a sound, and the dogs were downstairs. She could see all three cats occupying armchairs, to the detriment of anyone who might want to sit down. Stella went back into the hall and looked around. The umbrella stand stood by the rarely-used front door, full of umbrellas, few of which worked, and – *result!* – a golf club. No one in the family played golf, so Stella had no idea why this was here, but it was the sort of thing that found its way into umbrella stands and she was not about to look a gift club in the mouth. She pulled it out, in careful silence, like spillikins. It was a number 9 iron.

Iron. She liked the sound of that. She hefted the club in both hands and began to creep upstairs.

There was no one on the landing. Stella peered into the first bedroom, Bee's. Jacobean oak, a moss green carpet, curtains embellished with gold Latin letters. Bee was tidy: everything was in its place.

Nell's room, the spare bedroom, held her cousin's big suitcase: Nell had taken a smaller bag to London. This was Alys' old room, the one with the moonhorse, and it was rocking. Stella flattened herself against the wall and watched it. The moonhorse sometimes moved of its own accord, but this was too extreme: a wild unbalancing which soon enough slowed to a halt, not the moonhorse's own steady unnatural gait. Stella waited until it stopped, then crept through the door.

She went through the whole of the first floor, but there was no one and nothing. Then, as she came out of her own room, she heard the creaking floorboard again and it was definitely a footstep, someone walking across the loose board in the room with the moonhorse.

Stella took a breath, raised the golf club, ran onto the landing and through the door of the spare bedroom. The horse was once more rocking from side to side. She heard a step behind her, turned, saw a figure looming over her. It was black-clad, hooded, huge. Something protruded from the sides of its head – stubby bone coloured horns. There was an overwhelming stink of blood and soil and shit. Stella flailed out with the golf club. It connected, but the figure struck out, a rock hard hand like a metal bar slamming against her arm, and threw her against the wall. The back of Stella's head connected painfully with the plaster; she dropped the golf club. She saw myriad points of light, then something was between herself and the figure. It was a whirling mass of bees: she saw, with sudden pinpoint precision, their striped bodies, and heard them hum. She saw the figure turn and flee out of the door; footsteps pelted down the stairs. The bees, the mass of the swarm collapsing, resolved down into Dark. Across the room, the golf club was bent to form an L.

Stella and the spirit stared at each other.

"What was *that*?" Dark asked, at last.

"You know what? I was hoping *you'd* know."

Stella had never taken a ghost to the pub before, at least, not knowingly. It wasn't so much the thought of alcohol, although she felt that she could certainly do with a drink, as being in a place which was not empty of people. Firelight and company and booze: the perennial allure of the tavern.

With Dark, she had searched the house, feeling a great deal braver with the spirit by her side. They had found nothing, and the cats were still all peacefully asleep, the dogs excited, but not more than usual. Now that she'd seen what Dark could do, as well as his visible concern, Stella felt even more reassured by his company. He treated her with a kind of friendly gallantry: the kind of attitude you might expect from your sister's long dead Elizabethan lover.

Why don't we have the same sort of problems as other people? Stella had wondered this before. But she appreciated his presence. Dark was certainly attractive, but not in that dangerous subtext way that belonged to Tam Stare – to take one example. As they walked in silence down the lane to the Hornmoon Arms, with the new moon sailing above the chestnut trees, Stella undertook a brief mental review of recent partners and was not impressed by what she saw.

Patterns. Musicians, mainly. Young. Unruly hair, dark doe-eyed, skinny. They often seemed to be Celts – Irish, Glaswegian, Welsh. Although one had come from Padstow, which probably counted. Golden tongues, exciting to be with, completely unreliable. Poor Liam had been a bit softer than that, though, and look what had happened there. She'd been the unreliable one. Mentally, Stella rolled her eyes; she had not behaved as well as she'd tried to.

Girlfriends: a rather better track record there. Mel – that had been a pretty good connection, couple of years, but they both wanted to do their own thing and then Mel had gone off to Bali to do reiki. Stella pulled a face at the cliché but she wasn't much better, was she? How about Su? At least that had made the six month mark, which was more than could be said for the fling with Katia. Going out with Katia had been like stepping into a kaleidoscopic centrifuge: dazzling until one was flung unceremoniously into the outer darkness, ears bleeding.

Perhaps, Stella thought to herself, *it is time you grew the fuck up.*

Next year would see her thirtieth birthday and maybe she should just stop gallivanting about all over the place, a gig here, a rave there. Waking up in someone's tent or someone's squat. Someone else's bed, anyway. Regardless of recent events, Stella thought of Mooncote: enduring, of the earth, a place of sanctuary. The thoughts of the last few days, her decision to stay and help out with the apple day, her relief at having an excuse to stay put, were starting to coalesce into a sequence of firmer decisions. But she didn't want to join the civil service or get married or bloody settle down either. She needed to decide what she wanted out of her life. She needed a breathing space, to figure things out.

"Dark," she said. "Did you miss this place, when you sailed?"

"I always knew it was there," Dark said. "Sometimes, yes. Dangerous days. Many times, I thought I was going to die –" he laughed. "Then of course I did. And I came back here."

"Did you – see anything? When you died? Speak to anyone?" She had in mind the Egyptian hall of the dead, the place of going-forth-by-day. A Tibetan bardo. She knew, from Abraham, that the dead were cagey about such information. A guard placed upon the spectral tongue, perhaps. But Dark said simply, "No. I took a bullet in the heart, I think. A privateer; they boarded us."

"Pirates!" Stella said with glee, immediately thinking of Johnny Depp, and then silently berated herself for insensitivity: they'd killed Dark, after all.

"I found the mark, later, a hole in my chest, but it's gone now. The ball might have lodged there – it aches a little in wet weather, still. I remember being on the ship, the salt blue air – then I was waking up here, in the orchard. It was summer. Bees were humming in the lavender; I could smell the box hedges in the knot garden. I went into the house and my mother was there standing over a butter churn. I knew something was wrong because, well, I'd been so far away and anyway I knew she was dead. But she smiled at me. "Ned!" she said. "You've come home." I said that perhaps I had been dreaming and she laughed. "No," she said. I remember the churn going up and down, up and down, and the light was all golden around her. "No," she said, "it's just life, that's all. It goes on." After that, things were different and the same."

"Is your mother still here?"

"Sometimes. But rarely. And there are others. But you know that."

"No mysterious fucker with horns, though."

Dark smiled. "No. I didn't recognise that."

"Did you ever – fall in love with someone else? Another ghost? A human?"

"Not until now."

"Bee," her sister said.

"It's hard to know what I can offer her."

"I think," Stella told him, "that if you are a part of the house, it will be enough."

"And you, Stella? You are a musician, Bee says."

"I'm – well, sort of. I'm a DJ. Do you know what that is?"

"Not really. Bee tried to explain but I do not think I quite understand."

"It's a bit like stand-up comedy," Stella said, and instantly regretted it because he probably didn't know what that was, either. "It's a little bit like the theatre."

"That, I do understand. I have been to a theatre."

They had reached the pub. It stood on what passed for Hornmoon's main street, sloping down the hill towards the little river Horne. It had been built around the same time as Mooncote, and like the house, it seemed to have settled into the ground: low roofed, leaded windowed. It had no rooms that were not bowl-shaped. If you placed a marble by the skirting board, it would be in the middle of the bar within a minute.

Stella had to duck slightly under the lintel. The pub was half full and this would have to do: she had slightly dreaded a packed bar. She did not know the barman, who was new and middle aged. She ordered a medium white wine – there was a grown up drink for you.

"If I sit over in the corner," she said to the barman, "Will I disturb anyone if I talk?" She held up her phone. "I'm recording some notes for something."

The barman grinned. "Half the buggers in here talk to themselves. I don't suppose anyone will mind. If they even notice."

"Cheers," Stella said. With Dark at her side, she went to the furthest booth and took out a notebook. Drinking with the spectral required some preparation, she thought. But it was good to be back. The walls were plastered a dull red, pooled with golden lamplight. Years ago, this place had been a fug of smoke, but now that was banned the only drift was from the fire, burning low in the grate across the room. Horse brasses lined the fireplace and Stella had counted all of them many times as a little girl, brought into the pub for a lemonade with her sisters. A hare, running. The moon, a crescent, above the evening star. The green man, gaping and vine mouthed. The brasses were to protect against evil, guarding the plough horses from elf shot. Stella liked to think of those horses: hairy at the heel, their manes plaited with hagstones and ribbon, the brasses on their harness reflecting the arrow bolts of the fairies.

"This place has not greatly changed," Dark said.

"It was here in your day?" She pretended to speak into the phone but no one was looking anyway. Stella took a sip of wine.

"Yes. Although there was not all this – stuff – in it." He gestured to the bar with its rows of optics. Stella smiled.

"Just barrels?"

"Sack. And ale, of course. Not wine, that was for the gentry."

"It's a girl's drink these days."

It was Dark's turn to smile. "It was then."

"Did you ever see Queen Elizabeth?"

"Once. I went to London. A great journey, then. And what a city. There was a bridge, with houses near to falling off it, and a great maze of people. She was walking across a green lawn starred with daisies and I had never seen anyone so fine – you would not have believed her, a Venus. Her dress was all pearl and cloth of gold and ruby. She was like the sun come to Earth." His eyes shone in the firelight.

"She must have been one hell of a tough cookie," Stella said.

"She was our world. We did all for her, at her bidding."

It sounded a bit like a cult to cynical Stella, but she reminded herself that her ancestors' mind-set would not be her own. Another culture, and surely some of them would have had issues with the Queen otherwise there wouldn't have been all those plots... But she was beginning to suspect Dark of being a romantic. It was certainly interesting to talk to him, though, and he did not seem to mind. She sipped her wine slowly, ordered a veggie burger and chips, and waited for the text on her phone that would tell her that Bee and Nell had arrived back at the station and she would not have to go back to an empty house, should Dark disappear. The ghost rolled up his sleeves, as if he felt the heat of the fire. There were tattoos on his sturdy forearms,

71

blurred and smoky. An anchor, a swallow. Designs that were familiar to Stella now, but mainly in a rockabilly context. Dark followed her gaze.

"The anchor, that means I've sailed the Atlantic. And the heart – well, that's obvious. There's a bee, further up." He showed her, rolling the linen past his elbow. His skin still bore a faint tan.

"They all have meanings, then?"

"Yes. A dragon means you've sailed to China but I never got that far."

"And the swallow?"

Dark smiled. "It's said they never fly more than twelve miles from land. So when you see a swallow, you're close to the coast. That's why we had them inked upon our skin. A talisman."

"That can't be true, though. They migrate so they must cross the Channel. And that's quite wide."

He laughed. "Yes, I'm sure it's just an old sailor's tale. But I'm an old sailor, after all."

Very old, Stella thought, but she did not say this aloud to her sister's lover, the ghost.

SERENA

Bee and Nell had gone, taking a taxi to nearby Paddington, and when they left Serena could no longer put a brave face on things and pretend that everything was all right, because it surely was not. Ben had gone into radio silence and she had made the decision not to phone him: she felt demeaned by it, needy.

"Sod him," she told herself. "*Bollocks* to all this shit." Swearing made her feel a little better. She went into the studio kitchen and made mint tea, because wine wasn't a good idea either. She was damned if she was going to sink into a bottle just because her man had gone AWOL. And there was Bella to think about; tonight was a school night and Bells had already gone to bed, albeit probably to check up on Whatsapp. She needed a clear head, Serena thought.

It wasn't just Ben who was preoccupying her. There was the collection, which had reached that point where you look at the whole thing and aren't happy. Serena knew that this would pass: it always happened and it was always the same. She'd given up lamenting her own lack of talent, the awful clothes – less of the drama queen, these days. Just grit your teeth and forge ahead, telling yourself it would all work out in the end. The only way is through and all that. A bit like relationships, really.

And then there was Spica. The sudden appearance of the Behenian star, not glimpsed since, had completely thrown Serena. It was as though she'd been keeping her life in involuntary compartments: the stars belonged to Mooncote, to Somerset, not here in London. It wasn't as though London didn't have its own stuff, and she'd seen quite a bit of *that*, but the stars were not part of it. A warning, or a benediction? Or something else? Serena did not know and it unnerved her. She felt as though she had begun sailing upon uncharted waters, with solid land receding fast in her choppy wake.

She drank the tea and picked up a magazine that was lying by the chair: not one of the big ones, but a small, alternative fashion and music publication that had recently come onto the stands. This sort of thing usually went straight online but Serena preferred paper editions: she could clip and cut and paste. It was like being a kid again, but it played a real part in her creative process. She had not yet had a chance to glance through this one. Serena flicked through the pages and found Dana Stare's face looking back at her: it hit her like a blow. Mesmerised, she scanned the shoot. Dana in black leather, standing on a moorland outcrop, in ebony lace against a candlelit mirror, in velvet like an Elizabethan mourner. Her hair fanned out; she wore her little secret smile in all the photos. Her face was cat-like above a ruff, feral glimpsed from the depths of a hood.

A sudden overwhelming fatigue struck Serena. Her eyelids drooped, she felt herself reel back in the chair. If she hadn't known better, and been alone, she might have thought that someone had dropped something in the tea. As though Dana had cast a spell on her, from the pages below.

Right, thought Serena. *Enough of this nonsense. You're going to bed.* She stuffed the magazine back in the rack, picked up the teapot and the cup and went upstairs to the large light room on the second floor. Once, this had been Eleanor's studio, before she'd divorced whatever the husband's name had been – some politician, Serena remembered – and moved out to the Judge's house near Red Lion Square. Now, Serena had pulled a Miss Havisham on it, somewhat overdoing the lace even by her own standards, but if you couldn't go for overkill in your own bedroom, where could you? The bed was a four poster, festooned in Victorian petit point, and candles filled the old iron grate. Serena lit a few, for firelight and fragrance, and the room slowly filled with freesia, vanilla, lavender. She collapsed onto the bed and shut her eyes.

And her mother was there. She sat by the side of the bed with an open book in her hands, just as she had done when Serena was a little girl, feverish or tooth-achey and wanting to be read to. Spica stood behind her like a lady in waiting, the sprig of sage pale against the forest of her dress. Her hair was threaded with the green fire of emeralds; her dark, arched eyebrows and firm mouth lent calmness to her face. Alys gave no sign that she knew the spirit was there.

"And *then*," she said, and glanced up. "Ah, you're awake."

"Mum! Where are you?" Serena felt that she was speaking through a fog. The words fell out of her mouth as if she was spitting wool.

"I'm here, dear." Alys seemed amused.

"No, I mean, where did you go? For your hiking trip. The one you never came back from." She felt desperate to make her mother understand. But to her great surprise, Alys gave her a straight answer.

"Dartmoor."

"What?" She felt a cold bolt of shock: Stella had thought that Alys had gone to Dartmoor. She'd even gone down there, Serena remembered.

"I went to Dartmoor, darling. Part of the Gipsy Switch, but I went on the train. I changed at Exeter, I remember – not sure where it was after that. Tavistock, maybe."

"What the hell did you want to go to Dartmoor for? And why didn't you drive?"

"I didn't take the car, darling, because I wasn't sure if I was coming back."

"You didn't even leave a bloody note! Nothing with the solicitors or anything. And you said you'd leave all the info with Bee. She had a terrible time – she thought she might have lost it."

"I didn't kill myself," Alys said. "You know I'd never do that to you girls."

"Why haven't you told us this before?"

"I couldn't reach you. But the comet is coming and things are starting to open up. Thank God. It's been really frustrating for me, too."

"But why did you go in the first place?"

"You don't know this, Serena, but someone stole something from us. Something very important, after Father died. Father and I knew we had to get it back, and I'd heard on the grapevine that the thief had gone to Dartmoor, to trade the thing in."

"What on Earth was it? Jewellery, or an antique – I didn't think we had anything that valuable in the house."

"I didn't say 'valuable', Serena. I said 'important'. It was a bone flute."

"I've never seen such a thing in the house."

"No. You wouldn't have. *I* didn't know it existed until Father died and he left instructions, but by that time it was too late: the flute had already gone."

"Why is it so important? Is it worth anything?"

"It probably is – it's very old – but that's not why it was stolen. It's the key to something to do with the family – it's a magical thing."

"Who stole it?"

75

"I don't know their name. I know what they are."

"What's that?"

"Something old," Alys said. She looked up, and the book fell from her fingers to land on the coverlet. Behind her, Spica's lips were parted; they were both staring at something beyond Serena, beyond the bed. Serena turned to look and saw a fire, flickering against a dark wall.

"Alys?" But when she turned her head again, her mother and the spirit were gone.

BEE

Bee dropped her bags onto the hall floor. Why was train travel so exhausting? All you had to do was sit down for a couple of hours and watch the world go by.

"Stella?" But there was no sign of her sister, or the dogs. That was suspicious. Bee strode into the living room.

"Dogs! Nelson, Hardy!"

They were behind the sofa, like kids watching Dr Who. They crept out anxiously, their feathery tails giving an apologetic mini-wag. The reason for their shame was obvious: a bag of potatoes, only slightly chewed, strewn about the living room floor.

"Oh, *dogs*. You don't even like potatoes," Bee said. But they had been bored, their fawning looks said, and abandoned. She reassured them with fuss.

"Bee, I'm just going to freshen up, and I think I'm going to go to bed," her cousin called from the top of the stairs.

"Okay. I think Stella must have gone out."

Bee poured herself a glass of water from the kitchen tap, just to prove to herself that she was no longer in the city, with its multiply-filtered hydration. Then she opened the back door and went through to the garden.

It was quite dark. A sheaf of stars were scattered overhead, but the grass was damp. The garden smelled of apples, with the tart-spice fragrance of the chrysanthemums weaving its way through the air, and woodsmoke beyond. Bee took a deep breath, forcing London's dirty legacy out of her lungs, and went into the orchard. They would soon need to start thinking about bagging the apples; there were too many windfalls already, cast down by the autumn gales, and although she usually left some for the fieldfares and redstarts, winter visitors who would need something to peck when the frosts came, Bee did not like waste and there were only so many apples that one household could eat, even if it was a jelly-making household. Hence the new small cider press, which she was dying to try out.

She paused by the elder.

"It's coming," the tree said.

"The comet?"

"No. The other."

"I don't understand."

The elder gave a rustling sigh, as if in exasperation, and fell silent. Bee looked around for Dark, but he was nowhere to be seen. She spoke his name.

Then there was a flash of white at the orchard gate, from the lane.

"I can see a light," Stella's voice said. "They must be back."

"Stel! It's me," Bee called. She did not want to make her sister jump.

"Bee!" Stella threaded her way through the windfalls, the dogs at her heels. Bee could see the shadowy figure of Dark behind her. Her sister was muffled up in a cowled sweater and jeans. "Bee, I'm bloody glad to see you."

That was sweet, thought Bee, touched. But then Stella told her why.

"I don't really want to involve Nell," Bee said. Council of war, in the kitchen: Bee and Stella and Dark, voices lowered. "It doesn't really seem fair —"

"She'll think we're *nuts*. 'You see, Nell, I attacked a horned man in your room with a golf club and then Bee's dead boyfriend appeared as a swarm of bees and chased him away.'"

"Operative words, *nuts* and *your room*."

"God, what if something happens in the night?"

"I could watch over her," Dark said.

"To be brutally honest, mate, I'm not sure if that's an improvement. What if she wakes up and sees *you?*" Stella said.

Dark sighed. "She is not like you, your cousin?"

"Well, that's it, isn't it?" Bee said. "We don't know. We've never had that sort of conversation. 'We see ghosts, Nell. And other stuff. Do you?'"

"I suppose we could risk it and ask her," Stella said. "She seems pretty cool. And she's going to be here for a while, isn't she?"

"She saw one of the Behenian stars. Spica."

"What? Where?"

"At Serena's house."

"You're kidding me."

"No, we both saw it. Except that Nell thought she was a model, thank God."

"Oh yeah. That would explain the clothes, of course. But I don't think she's seen one here or she'd have said something, surely."

"Let's just leave it for tonight," Bee said. "And see what happens."

"I think we ought to tell her that I surprised an intruder," Stella mused. "We don't have to mention the whole antler thing."

A half solution found, Stella went upstairs to break the bad news, leaving Bee in the kitchen with Dark. They looked at one another. Bee had not quite got past the oddness of seeing Dark in the company of someone else.

"It is the comet, I am sure," the spirit said. "They are ill omens. They bring forth evil."

Bee started to say that they were just lumps of celestial rock, but then she thought of the Behenian stars and fell silent. Abraham had explained astronomy to them, when they were little. About the orbits of the planets, the motion of the stars. How Aldebaran and Spica and Arcturus, Regulus and Procyon and Algol, the stars with their Arabic names and ancient lineage, proceeded in their fixed paths across the seasonal sky. How the stars themselves were great blazing suns, their physical composition and age determining the light that we see now: cold blue or fiery red, orange or sparkling pale. And those vast distant suns were obviously not the same as the calm-faced women with their jewels and their sprigs of herbs who paraded throughout the house, just as the moon was not the same as the dappled wooden horse who galloped over the spare room floor, and yet, somehow, they were the same: their appearance in the minds of men forming something other, something real. Microcosm and macrocosm: a system of correspondences, star and jewel and flower; number and planet and colour. Bee did not understand quite what the Behenian stars were, but she knew they were spirits in some manner of the same reality as Dark, and as the woman with the skirtful of apples whom she sometimes glimpsed in the orchard at dusk, her brow crowned with roses. Or the girl in the dawn-coloured dress whom Serena used to meet on the stairs, her forehead marked with the smudge of an ashy cross, or the little bright lizards that Bee had seen in the flames as a child. All of these things were part of Mooncote, and sometimes of other places, too, and Bee knew that many other places held their own mysteries. She thought of the smiling Sphinx by the shore of the Thames. It was, Bee thought, time to go to bed. She reached out and took Dark's hand.

LUNA

Luna didn't want to say anything to Sam, just yet. She did not think that she wanted to know herself, even. It would be a secret from everyone, from the world, held within the dark like a flickering flame. Luna found that she did not want to speak to anyone today, even less than usual. Since her decision to run the switch, she had discovered a need for seclusion; she'd never had all that much time for the world, not even for her own family, although whenever she said this to Sam, he smiled as though he knew better. Although she thought that she would not mind speaking to Ver March...

With this in mind, Luna was annoyed to hear a pulse from her phone and to discover a text from Serena. *Can you call me? It's important.* She didn't want to. It had started to rain outside, heavy drops spattering over the roof of the wagon, and churning the earth to mud. Sam had taken one of the horses into Marlborough, to buy supplies at the Spar. Luna was on her own and wanting to stay that way, but she heard from Serena so rarely these days that she was afraid something might be wrong. After twenty minutes' indecision, she picked up the phone and called her sister back, hoping that she'd get the answerphone.

But Serena replied.

"Luna! Thanks. I'm really sorry to bother you." Of them all, Luna reflected, Serena had seemed to most understand how she felt. That made her feel prickly.

"You're not bothering me," Luna lied. "Are you all right?"

"Yes. But I had a dream."

Immediately, Luna's attention sharpened. She knew dreams. She could have this conversation, just not small talk. "What was it?"

She listened as Serena told her. There was no question in her mind that this was a true dream. It struck her that she needed to see Sam's nan, tell her about it, and she did not pause to consider that it was an odd reaction, to want to discuss family business with someone she had met only once.

"Dartmoor. We're in Wiltshire, now. We were heading down to Cornwall, though, before the winter."

"I wasn't sure where you were, Luna."

"We've been up north. Yorkshire, Northumberland."

The landscape was still with her: its vastness, ending in the thundering coast. The moors shadowed with heather and the sudden treasure of gorse, under racing cloud shadow. They'd visited a horse fair, Sam meeting cousins by the river race, although he didn't seem to have much time for the most of the rest of the people there. Luna had found the scene interesting but unsafe, an undernote of aggression running through it, but she'd liked Sam's quiet cousins. She did not explain to Serena about the Gipsy Switch, but she thought she might have to.

"I don't know what to do with this, Luna."

Luna felt a sudden surge of certainty and strength. "It means we have to go. I'll talk to Sam. He'll understand."

"Will he?" Serena's voice was filled with doubt.

"Yes. He gets it, Serena. He knows things about stuff."

"Okay." Serena sounded reassured and that made Luna feel good about the conversation. Maybe Sam had been right. Maybe she could be closer to her sisters than she'd thought.

"Talk soon," Serena said. "I've got to go – Bella wants something. And take care of yourself."

"You too," Luna said and meant it.

Dartmoor. She put the phone down on the table and sat back. On the woodburning stove, the kettle began to shrill and she poured tea. She did not question the information: Serena had dreamed it and Alys had told her.

"You should have told me, Mum," Luna said aloud. But perhaps Serena had been the only one she could reach, who knew why, and perhaps she had been prevented from speaking to anyone before now. Luna felt that this must be the case. Her mother would not simply have abandoned them, and from what Serena had said, Alys had seemed unwilling to expose them to danger. She had taken a big risk and – what? Failed? Succeeded? Luna could not say. But now they had a place: the moor. And where they had a place, they had a plan.

STELLA

Light flooded in through the open curtains and Stella could hear a dove cooing in the eaves. She blinked. Survived the night, then. She knew she had been dreaming and those dreams had been disturbing, but she couldn't remember a thing about them. She chased the memory, but she chased it away. Sighing, Stella climbed out of bed and went to the window to find one of those perfect October days waiting for her, a cloudless blue sky, with the leaves ablaze against it. One of the cats – Sable – was strolling across the lawn, tail held high like a lemur. Stella felt a sudden lift of the heart: her family were back, the day was waiting, there were plans to start putting into place. She thought she might go over to Amberley, speak to Caro and Laura.

Once dressed and downstairs, she found Bee up and about in the kitchen; her sister had always been an early riser and now here was Stella, following suit, for it was not yet eight.

"Toast? Tea?"

"Yes, please. You didn't have any – visitors – last night?"

Bee shook her head. "I slept like the dead, to be honest. London tires me out. So does travelling. Stupid. It's not even all that far."

"I think it's the psychic strain. Someone once told me that your astral self has a maximum speed of 30 mph. So yours has probably only just reached Trowbridge round about now."

"Belting down the track…"

"Wheezing and gasping."

"No wonder I'm tired. Oh, do get out from under my feet!" The last was addressed to a dog.

"What are your plans for the day, Bee?"

"I've got some work to do this morning. Catching up. I said I'd help Mrs Dyer with her accounts, and I've got to answer some emails. I have to pack up some books and wait for the courier. And do some laundry. Then I thought I might make some bread. Not a busy day. Although we ought to get some bags for the apples."

"I was thinking of going to Amberley," Stella said. "If you lend me the car, I can pick some up from Richard and Caro."

"Good idea. When were you thinking of going over? If you wait till the afternoon, I'll come with you. I need to have another look at those books of Julian's."

"Great," Stella said. After the excitement of the previous day, she thought she could do with a quiet morning. She took *Dawn Treader* out to the sunlit garden bench and sat amongst the explosions of the dahlias, surrounded by bees.

The weather remained fine. Bee brought lunch out to the lawn and they ate soup and bread in a contemplative silence. With Nell present, neither Stella nor Bee wanted to discuss anything that might sound too weird, so they talked about impersonal things, instead, and where Nell might visit that afternoon.

"I could take a bus. I thought of Glastonbury, or maybe Cheddar."

"Glastonbury's got bookshops. And the Chalice Well, which would be lovely today. Cheddar – well, caves and cheese."

"There's a gorge at Cheddar, isn't there?"

"Yes. And a lot of tourist tat, but the gorge itself is spectacular. I'm not sure about buses, though – if you want, we'll go tomorrow, in the car. But it's interesting. It's been inhabited for thousands of years."

"They found that bloke, didn't they?" Stella said.

"Which bloke?"

"That maths teacher. They did DNA tests and it turned out he was a descendent of one of the original inhabitants. Thousands and thousands of years ago."

"Wow," Nell said.

"She's right. He was astounded. There were people living in the caves, just after the ice retreated. They've found bones. Some of them were cannibals, but they drove horses and ancient cattle over the cliffs into the gorge and lived off the meat, too."

"You mean to tell me that a descendent of someone who was living near here *forty thousand years ago* is – well, is?"

"Yes. I don't think he's a numpty, either," Stella said. "Not if he teaches maths."

"A –?"

"Think of the Appalachians. There's a lot of inbreeding in Somerset. They put 'NFB' on patient charts in Taunton hospital."

"'NFB'?"

"Normal For Bridgwater."

"Aw, that's unkind," Nell said, but she was smiling.

"True, though. Webbed feet and all sorts."

"Well, our family's been here for a good long while," Bee said. "And we remain unwebbed."

"I wouldn't call us normal, though." Thinking that she had perhaps said enough, Stella shut up and brushed an exploratory wasp from the cheese board.

"Actually, I think I'm just gonna sit out here this afternoon and write," Nell said. "It's so lovely."

"We were going to Amberley," Bee said. "You're welcome to come." But Nell shook her head.

Going to Amberley around the back lanes by car took almost as long as walking across the fields, but neither Stella nor Bee could carry a hundred apple sacks back. So they bumped down the lane, the recent rain having conjured muddy ruts, and through the ford at the bottom of the valley. Stella did not like driving through the ford, and she could tell that her sister was holding her breath. Serena had once, in a different car, got stuck and needed to be rescued by Landrover: it had taken an entire can of EasyStart to get the vehicle going again. Then the road climbed, heading up between steep sided, bramble twined hedges, to the rise on which Amberley stood.

At the back, out of sight of the main drive, stood the stables and the pony ring, which was where they were most likely to find Laura. But they went to the back door, all the same.

Caro, in jeans and Fair Isle, was bending over the Aga.

"Bloody thing," she said, without turning round. "I thought it had gone out."

"Ours does that," Bee said.

Caro straightened up. "Stella! Nice to see you. I thought it was Laura." She smiled at Bee, the more regular visitor. "Would you like tea? Something to eat?"

"We've just had lunch. We'd love some tea."

"I'll call Laura." She went to the back door, and Stella followed: up on the slope she could see Cloud Chaser, running. The mare was like an animated chalk horse across the green swathe of the hill. "Laura!" Caro gave a stentorian bellow in the direction of the stables. "She'll be a minute, I expect."

"I spoke to Serena. She's up for doing the little catwalk thing."

"Brilliant! I've been banging the drum, as well. In addition to what we had already, we have two cake stalls and a man who makes Spanish doughnuts. And a nice burger stand – not the MacD's sort. And someone who does Thai food."

"And the orchestra?" Stella said.

"Yes. 'Classy,' you said. I'm trying to keep it that way."

"In that vein," Bee said, "I spoke to the person who took over the Astronomy Society from Grandpa, and they're going to bring some exhibits about the planets."

"That's a really cool idea," Stella said.

Her sister looked smug. "I thought so."

Laura came through the kitchen door, smelling of horse.

"Oh, Bee. You're back. Great."

"I spoke to Tam Stare," Caro said and Stella pricked up her ears. "He's up for doing a marquee. He's supposed to be over later, with some equipment for Richard."

Bee and Stella gave polite smiles, and Stella felt grateful for her sister's implicit support. She hoped to avoid Stare – he was trouble, she knew it, and that sense of getting away from old worn-out patterns was still at the forefront of her mind. So she was not pleased when there was the sudden roar of a Landrover from the yard and through the window she saw Tam Stare himself jump down.

"Caro," he said, coming in through the back door. "All right?"

"I'm fine, thank you, Tam."

"I've brought Dana with me." He did not explain, or apologise. *Treating the place like your own, aren't you?* Stella thought, bristling. From this angle, she could not see Caro's face. A girl came through the kitchen door, her black hair shining like her leather coat in the sunlight. She looked pale, punk, urban; even her lips were bloodless. She looked Stella up and down and then she gave a little smile. Stella was suddenly aware that she had put no makeup on that morning. Caro said, "Tam, did you bring the stuff? Shall I come and have a look? Laura, could you give me a hand?" The Amberley women went out into the yard, leaving Bee and Stella with Dana.

"Hello." The voice was cool, confident.

No wonder Serena doesn't like you, Stella thought. *I don't, either.* And there was something familiar about the fan of black hair, the pointed pale face. *I've seen you before.*

Dana sat down, uninvited, at the table. She looked with mild, slightly insolent interest at Stella and Bee. "Don't think we know each other, do we?" If she and Stella had met, she gave no sign of it now.

Stella gave her a chilly smile. "I don't think so, no." There was a pause.

Bee, always more prepared to be gracious, said, "I'm Beatrice Fallow. Bee. This is my sister, Stella."

"I'm Dana. I know your sister. Serena. And Ben, of course."

"I don't think she's mentioned you," Stella lied.

Dana just looked at her, a flat black gaze, and Stella knew that the girl had detected the lie. "Really. We're such good friends." She spoke with indifference, as though it did not matter whether Stella believed her or not. Then she looked up, all sparkling friendliness. "Laura, hi, sweetie! How was your ride?"

"Good, thank you." Laura was polite. Then she said, "Stella, Bee, I wondered if you'd like to come out and see the new jumps? Bee, do you remember I was telling you about having problems with that electric fencing and I wanted to ask you…"

With relief, Stella rose and they followed Laura out to the yard. Caro and Tam were bending over some crates, filled with what looked like mowing blades. As Stella walked passed, Tam looked up at her and winked. Stella gave him a stony stare; she was unwilling to entertain any suggestion of complicity. She thought of Dark, and Tam seemed to recede against the sunlight, grow smaller. Stella, with surprise, realised that this had nothing to do with the spirit's attractiveness: it was, suddenly, as though she had a brother. Dark slotted into place in her personal constellation, fitting easily and without conflict. She felt her spirits rise, but even so, it was a relief to get into the stable yard; it felt like sanctuary. A long chestnut face with a white blaze peered over the first half door. He blew at Stella, who went across and murmured to him. There were eleven horses in all, some grazing up on the slope, some here. Something very soothing about horses, thought Stella, though not necessarily when you were on board one of them. She followed Laura's tall, retreating figure through the gate and up onto the hillside.

Looking back, Amberley lay in a slight hollow. She could see the long beds of lavender, a hazy mauve against the green, and the golden trees. From here, too, she could see Mooncote, like a blown leaf in the dip of the valley, and the square tower of the church. The river was a bright thread through the landscape.

"I see what you mean," Stella said to Laura. "About Dana Stare. I didn't take to her." And then it came to her. The sudden blast of light, and a girl rising from hands and knees. Ibiza. The girl who had dropped her lighter in the yard behind Nightside. Stella had thought nothing of it at the time, had forgotten. But now it came back, with new significance.

She said nothing to Bee or Laura. She wanted to mull it over a bit first.

Bee said, "I didn't take to her, either. She felt clammy."

"She did?"

"I don't mean, physically. Although she doesn't look the sort for a firm handshake. Psychically."

"I know what you mean," Stella said, and Laura nodded.

The ring was impressive. One of the yard girls was taking a pony around it as they watched; a roan with a rolling gait. Laura looked at her critically, but forebore from comment.

"Where's Cloud?" Bee asked.

"In her stable. I rode her out this morning."

"You said something about doing pony rides at this apple day?"

"Probably. Yes. Mum's got a lot of ideas. You know what she's like when she's organising something. She wants you do put some music together for the afternoon, Stel. Before the classical bit later on."

"I know. I've sorted it."

When they went back down to the house, the Stares had gone. Caro was making more tea. Stella did not want to mention Dana to Caro; she thought that Laura would do that particular job for her, if need be.

SERENA

She had nearly finished the collection and, finally, Serena was verging on being pleased. She gazed out at butterflies and roses, moths and moons. Mossy tumbles of wool curved along collars; embroidered lichen climbed up from hems. The froth of wave foam spilled from a sea coloured gown, etched with tiny cowries and a shoulder strap of overblown roses decorated a garnet sheath. The collection, seen on the rehearsal catwalk, was a mixture of darkness and light, night and day; Serena's vision finally coming together as though a thread had been pulled, bringing it tight. She was not, yet, able to relax, but she did feel as though she might be starting to calm down. Finally.

"I think it's awesome." Charlotte was impressed. Serena eyed her askance.

"Since when did you start using words like 'awesome'?"

"Sorry. I think it's the evil influence of the internet."

Serena squinted across at Charlie's notes as they sat in the front row.

"That taffeta skirt – that worked better than I thought."

"I like that. And I like the mossy green thing."

Serena smiled. Sage and forest: Spica had inspired that. She'd wondered before how much of a formative influence the Behenian stars had been: her own private collection of muses. More than she'd realised, perhaps.

The last few days had been enervating. She'd closed herself off from Ben, telling him – when he finally texted her – that she had to work. They'd met once, in the local pub, for a constrained drink. She'd found him silent, but he was used to her nerves and fizzy fritteriness before a collection was completed and she hoped he'd put her own silence down to that. They seemed to be careering towards some kind of derailment and Serena, bewildered and hurt, didn't know how to stop it. All she could do was put up the walls and hope for the best, trust in fate, trust in the stars. She had not been to any of his gigs; she had not wanted to meet Dana Stare again. If she had only been convinced that Ben wasn't interested – but she could not be, and it was this that sapped her capacity for action.

Then, the day after the rehearsal, she saw them. It was in Neal's Yard, at the back of Covent Garden, and Serena had been to see a customer. It was a lingerie shop: very burlesque influenced. You stepped from the street into a dark crimson interior, accentuated with mirrors: it was supposed to look like a high class bordello and Serena had to admit that it succeeded. The proprietress was German, with an almost engineered scarlet bob of hair and very thick, black-framed glasses. She wore suits that reminded Serena of Berlin in the thirties. Muttering, clasping Serena's arm, holding up piece after piece, she selected her range.

"One of those, I like this, darling, in the coffee, and the burgundy, notice you haven't bothered doing red, so wise, so *tarty…*"

By the time Serena got out, she felt as though she'd been spat out of a whirlwind. She needed tea, and somewhere nice to drink it, not one of the chains. The café in Neal's Yard fitted the bill and she rarely had the time to visit it.

The Yard was swarming with multi-coloured pigeons, Serena did not know who dyed them, nor even whether it was legal: they always reminded her of Lord Merlin, in Nancy Mitford's novels. They tumbled up into the roofscape, fairy-winged, as Serena came into the Yard.

Ben and Dana were sitting at a table, outside one of the coffee shops. Their heads were close; they seemed to be studying a piece of paper, conferring. Then Dana looked up at Ben, her long black eyes slanted and alight. She gave a wicked grin and murmured something into his ear, nuzzling the lobe. Serena stood, frozen, at the entrance to the Yard. Everything seemed to slow down alongside her, even the flight of the pigeons retreating into slow motion. She did not want to watch and could not look away. Ben was the same as ever: leather coat, faded jeans, hair flopping over his face. Dana was speaking and he was listening to her. Serena recognised that intent look.

Then Dana glanced across the Yard. She was staring directly at Serena, there was no way that she could have failed to have noticed her, but her face did not change. It was almost as though, Serena thought, Dana had known she was there all along. A ghost of a smile appeared on her face; it reminded Serena of a skull, the white skin framed in shadowblack. Then, slowly and with indifference, she turned back to Ben; Serena, the spell snapping, fled.

She did not remember getting home. It felt like one of those dreams, when suddenly you are in one place rather than another. She went straight up the stairs, ignoring the studio where she could hear the murmur of voices – Charlie and one of the other girls – and into the bathroom. She was not sick, somewhat to her own surprise, but it was easier to simply stay put for a while, bending over the basin of the sink with her hands clasped firmly to the cool white china. At last she looked up to see her own face in the mirror: everything stripped down, her beaky nose pink-rimmed, arched brows high with surprise as though she had just received a shock – *but I have* – and everything faded, bleached out. She felt too shaken to cry.

She wandered back downstairs to the kitchen. She did not feel up to speaking to anyone, so she slipped into the living room and quietly closed the door, then, with shuddery hands, lit a cigarette. It made her more light headed, and, paradoxically, clearer. She would speak to Ben, and sort things out, one way or another.

But Ben could not be found. She left two messages, and then stopped herself from calling back. She did, however, send him a text, a classic *I think we need to talk*. After that, she thought that she would not have been surprised to receive no reply: he was like that, head-hiding in the sand. Maybe there was an innocent explanation – but Serena, remembering that cool, monochrome little smile of Dana's, knew that there was not. Maybe it was just a fling… but to Serena, there was no such thing. She'd found that out the hard way, both ways.

Serena herself was not her main concern, once the initial impact of the punch had started to recede a little. Bella must be the priority. She would be home from school soon, and Serena did not want her to find her mother sitting shell-shocked on the couch and reeking of cigarettes. She crushed the stub out in the ashtray, took it into the kitchen and emptied it, then opened the living room window so that the cool autumn air flooded in. She felt empty, but had no interest in eating: she would suggest to Bella that they order a takeaway. She had never not felt like eating Chinese. The prospect of this little trick on herself made her smile, for the first time that afternoon. She thought: *you'll survive, whatever happens. You have Bells and your family and the collection. You have a life*. But she was grateful, all the same, when she heard the bang of the front door and the clatter of her daughter's feet up the boards of the stairs.

LUNA

They had gone down towards Devon on the back roads: to Sam, there were no other kind. Luna, with Moth at her side, watched from the driving seat of the wagon as the chalk hills turned to blue shadow in the distance behind them, and the countryside became increasingly familiar, as they left Wiltshire behind and came down into Somerset. They skirted Bath, creamy in the October sunlight as it lay in its bowl of hill. Sam did not trust Bath; said it was a bit too posh, that people would look askance at himself and Luna in their raggedy sweaters and dreads and boots, a couple of Medieval jesters behind the hairy piebalds, and Luna, her hackles going up at the thought, said he was probably right. There had been enough encounters with the police already.

"Do you mind telling me how long you're planning to be here, sir?"

"You are aware that this is private property?"

"There's been a complaint that this vehicle is causing an obstruction…"

After the first episode of this, Sam had told Luna to stay in the van while he handled it.

"I'm used to this, had it all my life."

"I'm used to it, too," she'd replied.

"You're used to protests and demos. It's a bit different. Even with your hair like that, Luna, they can still tell the difference. No offence, but your accent – it's still middle class." He'd smiled. "A nice girl."

"Is that how you see me?"

"It's not an insult. It's just what is. The law takes one look at me and they see – troublemaker, thief, drugs probably, all round dodgepot. Even though I don't have particularly long hair, actually. They just know. It's like I can always spot undercover coppers at festivals. We know each other – gut instinct. They're mostly okay, anyway. They're just doing their jobs. I know there was the Beanfield but that was a long while back now and the police did have to reckon with what they did. One of the nobs, actually, made them accountable. It's not that I don't trust you to handle them but you can get a bit bolshie and they don't like that."

"But it's not fair," Luna said, as she had been saying for all of her life. "You've never stolen anything. You've never dealt in drugs. You don't even claim benefits!"

He laughed. "Straight as a die, that's me. A model citizen. But it's the way of the world."

So classy Bath — that would be a no. They rolled on, following the old Roman road that took them over the hills and faraway, up above the little Mendip villages where rabbits played over the barrows of the dead and there was often cloud down even in summer. Beech woods covered the lower slopes, framing the prosperous farms. They even stopped at a farm shop and bought home-baked bread and greens for a treat, round golden beets to bake on the stove: very middle class, Sam said. Model citizens!

As they pulled up over the final ridge, Luna saw Glastonbury Tor, an improbable hummock in the blue reaches of the Somerset Levels. They stopped for a minute to look at it.

"Avalon," Sam said, with a smile. "King Arthur's under there, you know."

"Don't Arthursplain to me! I grew up near here. There he lies with all his knights."

"Just waiting till Britain has need."

"You'd think he'd have showed up before now."

"What makes you think he hasn't?" He looked at her. "So. You've got a decision to make, madam."

"I know," she whispered.

"To stop, or not to stop." Sam made a sweeping gesture which encompassed the hazy expanse before them. "Up to you. But we're going to have to decide sooner rather than later."

Luna nodded. "Can I tell you right at the last minute?"

"If you say to me, gee 'em up and let's charge on through, my lady, that's what I'll do. Like a knight on the battlefield."

"My family's not *that* bad," Luna said. But she knew that she had already made her decision; it was hovering around her heart, fluttery and bird-like, giving her the shivers. It would have been so easy to just keep going, down to the next long ridge and the next — the Quantocks, and Exmoor beyond, into that rolling blue. After that was Dartmoor and whatever was to be found there: they were on a mission, she reminded herself.

But Sam had taken her to meet Ver March. You don't take a girl to see your gran unless you're serious. You don't take your bloke to meet your sisters unless – well. It was serious, Luna knew that. She was a serious person. Just because she didn't have a job as such, or any plans to get one, didn't mean that she was a layout, or undisciplined. She helped Sam with his itinerant gardening jobs and she worked hard. Nor would she live off the state, or theft, or anything underhand. They were travellers; this was their work.

The piebalds took them down the steep beech-fringed slope and past Wells, then onto the flat road which took them over the mercurial rhynes towards the Tor and its tower. Luna told Sam stories about the fairy king who is also said to live under the hill, his pack of red eared white hounds, and Sam gave a sidelong smile that suggested to Luna that he was familiar with all this already, had probably dropped in for tea and a natter with Gwyn ap Nudd many a time, but he listened anyway; he was good at that. The lurcher yawned, ghost-grey. One of Gwyn's pack? She wouldn't have been surprised.

When they came to the top of the town, above the green park that held the ruins of King Henry's clerical depredations, a roundabout led in two directions: towards the town of Street and the road south, or the road that led past the Chalice Well, around the foot of the Tor, its orchards heavy with ripening apples. Taking that second road would also, ultimately, lead south, down the old Roman way of the A37, but it would also eventually lead past the road which led to Hornmoon, and Mooncote, and Luna's sisters.

Sam turned to Luna and opened his mouth.

"On!"

"Right you are." He clucked his tongue and shook the reins. They went on past the Tor, a queue of irritated traffic tailgating behind.

As they drew closer, Luna became more and more nervous, answering Sam's observations in monosyllables. Sam, in turn, grew more focused. At length, he kept his comments to himself and concentrated on driving: up, over, down, along. Luna pointed to the signpost as the countryside became increasingly familiar.

"There. It's there."

"All right."

Sam steered the piebalds down the lane. Immediately, they were enclosed: the gilded leaves of beech arching overhead. The road was not wide enough for two cars: Luna kept her fingers crossed that they would not encounter another vehicle. The piebalds could not back up and she didn't really want to piss the neighbours off. But it was quiet, mid-afternoon before the school run, and the beech avenue came out into the wider expanse of the village, the church just visible at its end, and the little stream running through it, unchanged.

"Where to?" Sam asked, for the road had forked.

"Off to the right." Her hands were clammy; she wiped her palms on her trousers. She could see the chimneys now, through the gaps in the chestnut trees. Sam looked like a small boy catching sight of the beach.

"Really excited now," he said and she had to laugh.

"We are, in fact, nearly there yet."

She took over the reins, swapped seats and took the piebalds in through the gate. The wheels of the wagon crunched on the gravel and Luna brought it to a halt.

"Jesus," Sam said. "This is a bit posh, isn't it?" But he sounded admiring, and not defensive.

"I did tell you."

"Old England. Nothing wrong with that. What a great house."

There was the slam of a car door at the back of the house and the sound of voices. Luna got down from the driving seat just as Stella came round the side into the drive. Luna's sister had not altered a great deal since the last time Luna had seen her; her fawn hair was now shoulder length, sun-streaked, not as straggly, and she wore jumper and jeans rather than her rave rags. Silver leaves dangled from her ears.

"I *thought* I heard – oh my God. Luna!" She ran forward and gave Luna a hug. Moth thrust his long sad nose into her hand. "And a dog. Hello, dog."

"His name is Moth," Luna said. "I didn't know you were here. You said you were never coming home again."

"That's because I was a prat."

"Fair enough. This is Sam. My bloke."

"Sam." Stella shook hands. "What an amazing wagon. And I love the horses. We've got a stable. It's in a bit of a state, though. We did have a horse but he died, he was ancient, a year or so ago, and the ponies stay down in the field. I'll clear the crap out of the stable but you can put them in the field if you think that's better."

"That's really kind of you," Sam said. "They'll be fine in the field. I like your house."

"It's all right. Would you like some tea? Bee made a cake."

"I should have said we were coming. But we didn't know. Until the last minute."

"That's okay," Stella said. "I was last minute as well."

She turned, leading the way to the house. Luna detached the piebalds and took them round to the yard, where she tied them temporarily to a ring. The feel of the smooth, cold metal brought back memories of childhood ponies, bareback up on the hill and the swish of bracken against her legs – Luna blinked. For a moment, she'd almost been there.

When she came into the kitchen, Sam was sitting by the Aga with a cup of tea and a slice of cake. He should have looked out of place, New Age traveller in old age kitchen, and yet he did not. He fitted in, and this scared Luna, a little, but also pleased her. Her sister Bee turned and smiled.

"Hey, Luna. Horses okay?" She gave Luna a hug.

"Yes. I tied them to the ring. I'll take them down to the field later."

"…over the Mendips," Sam was saying to Stella. "But we've been up in Yorkshire, the north. Scotland. Way up."

"Back down south for the winter, eh? Did you do any of the festivals?"

"Horse fair. And some of the folk festivals. But there's too much money in it these days for the bigger ones."

"Yes, Pilton – Glastonbury, that is – costs a bomb now and it's so hard to get tickets. You have to be right on it as soon as they go on sale. Sorry, you probably know all this."

"Yeah, pretty much, but that's okay. I'm a bit of a loner, me. I don't do the crowds. I pick up gardening work, here and there. Luna helps me."

"I know what you mean about crowds."

Luna accepted a slice of ginger cake and was re-introduced to Nell, whom she had not seen since she was a little girl. It was a shock, to see how much her cousin looked like Alys. She wanted to mention Dartmoor, find out if Serena had said anything to Bee or Stella, but it did not feel quite the right time, somehow. Not that she didn't appreciate the urgency: she felt itchy, that need-to-get-on-with-it sensation. She told herself to chill out. Alys had been gone for a year and yet – *time's getting on. The winter clock is ticking.* She sat up straight, suddenly alert, wondering where the words had come from. When Stella rose and suggested getting the stable cleared before dark just in case the weather turned and they wanted to put the horses in there, Luna seized her chance. Stella must know that the piebalds were out in all weathers, all the time. It was an excuse for a private conversation and she intended to make the most of it.

Her sister, occupied in moving boxes, heard her out in silence. Then she said, "Dartmoor, eh? Mum didn't say anything about that but then she didn't not say anything either. I wish she hadn't been so bloody cryptic."

"Did you talk to Serena?"

"No, but Bee says she's having problems with Ben so her mind might be on other things. Also she's more likely to have talked about her dreams to you, not me or Bee."

Luna took that as a compliment, because without quite knowing why, she felt that it had been meant as one. Then Stella said, "Why don't I drive you down there?"

"What, by car?"

"No, by my team of tame unicorns. What did you think I meant?"

Luna opened her mouth to say, *We can't,* and then thought, *why not?*

"It'll be a damn sight quicker than going down in your admittedly brilliant vehicle. It's only just over an hour from here. I can borrow Bee's Landrover. Bee can *drive,* if she wants to come with us."

"She might do."

But in the end, it was Stella and Luna and Sam who went, Stella at the wheel.

SERENA

She'd had enough. Ben hadn't called her for days, but worse, he hadn't called Bella either and that was just unfair. Eventually Serena unloaded her worries onto Charlie, which perhaps was a little unprofessional, but they were friends, and Eleanor, who had called round to see about a leaky gutter at the back.

"My dear," Eleanor said, unconsciously imperious. "You've got to tell him his short term future or release him into the wild. Nothing else will do. Otherwise the man will just run roughshod over you."

"I think she's right." Charlotte was more hesitant, but indignant all the same. "What does he think he's playing at?"

"I imagine he thinks he's playing at screwing someone else."

"Perhaps it's an early midlife crisis."

"I don't care."

"You know," Eleanor said, "everyone always gives artists far too much license. If you're creative, you're supposed to be marvellously Bohemian and free, especially men, but usually they just end up making a mess."

"That would be Ben."

"Why don't you go off somewhere for a few days? Bella could stay with her father, I'm sure."

"I don't want to shove her from pillar to post," Serena said, but in fact a weekend was coming up, and Bella had mentioned something about wanting to stay with her dad because there was a thing on. Serena had not got any further with that.

"You could go and stay with Bee. Sisters. That's the ticket for man-trouble."

"I think she's right," Charlotte said. "Maybe they could assassinate him for you."

That, Serena thought vindictively, was by no means a bad idea.

The M3 was congested, even first thing on Friday morning. Sitting in the alleged fast lane, which had slowed to a crawl, Serena was beginning to regret taking the car, but she hadn't wanted to put Bee to the trouble of endless lifts back and forth from the railway station and it did mean more flexibility. Then it started to rain and Serena felt her spirits give a further lurch, but this time for the better. She liked rain. At the moment, it matched her mood, but it also made her feel safe. By the time the little car came to the turn-off for the A303 and the long stretch of westward road, the downpour had slowed to a shower and there were patches of pale blue sky showing above the downs. Wiltshire, and the high country, bleached under the autumn chill. With care, Serena overtook a horse-drawn wagon, curving and colourful and surely illegal on the main road, and thought of Luna who was, as far as she knew, heading south.

When she reached Stonehenge, the rain had almost completely stopped. Serena pulled the car into the visitors' car park, located her English Heritage membership card with ease, greatly to her own surprise, and slipped in through the turnstile and onto the bus. She passed a party of Italian tourists coming back, but everyone else must be at lunch, for Serena found herself the only person on the bus and then on the circular path that led around the monument. It was here that she finally felt able to breathe. She stood, looking at the impenetrable grey forms of the stones, encrusted with lichen and crowned by squabbling jackdaws, and took in a lungful of damp air. The short, sheep-cropped grass beneath her feet was thick with clover. She walked slowly around the perimeter of the henge, as another coach trundled along, until only the distant hum of the road and the low wire fence betrayed the presence of the modern age.

"Well," Serena said aloud. "Well." It had an air of finality.

In the middle of the stones, movement caught her eye. Something brown, low in the grass. A rabbit – but as Serena looked, it sat up. Much bigger than a bunny, with long, narrow ears and folded back legs. A hare. It came quite close as she stood as still as she could, a few yards, until she could look into its wise, golden eye. Then the sound of voices came from further along the path and, unhurried, the hare looped away among the stones. When Serena followed the path around, it was no longer visible. But she felt it had been a sign of some kind, a symbol, and surely of nothing that was bad. Hares and the moon, shapeshifters, Luna had said. Old stories about women who could change their form. She walked slowly back to the bus stop, as a cloud drew over the sun and the first few spots of rain touched cold on her skin.

STELLA

Dartmoor always looked particularly dark, Stella thought, regardless of the time of year, as though it had its own perpetual cloud layer, its own night. They took the turn-off to Moretonhampstead, coming onto the moor itself just after midday.

"You know what we need?" Stella asked.

"What?" her sister said. Luna had drawn her knees up onto the front seat. Wrapped in layers of charity-shop woollen shawls, with her dark red henna'd dreads, she looked like a hitch-hiking Medieval peasant. Sam sat in the back, staring out at the hedges and fields.

"We need a pub."

"Do you think we should stop?"

"I think we should grab some lunch before we start our investigation. An hour or so won't make much difference, I'm sure."

"Outstanding suggestion," Sam said. "And as if by magic –"

The pub stood all alone, high on a spine of road. Below it, the moor fell away in long lines of wet bracken, the shade of Luna's hair, and black stands of pine. Far to the south, the sky had that faint shine that appears above the sea, but the coast itself was invisible. The moor looked far larger than it actually was. Stella parked opposite the pub and they got out into a cold wind.

The pub was called the Warren House and there were old photographs of it buried up to its roof in snow. It was, Stella learned with interest, the second highest pub in the country. There were fireplaces, made of brick, at either end and rabbit stew on the menu. Sam had a pint and ordered the stew; Luna, slightly to Stella's surprise, asked for a tonic water rather than a beer, but asked for egg and chips, which Stella also opted for. Her sister seemed on edge, a little ragged, but that was not unusual for Luna. Stella had always thought that she suffered from her anger; she could not have said why, but Luna often seemed to be fighting to keep some emotion under control. It was probably hormones, or simply being the youngest. But that was a bit patronising. Ever since she had been a teenager, Luna's social conscience had been strong. Stella herself had confined her protest to a bit of sabbing (her teenage years had been before the badger cull, otherwise that might have been an outlet, too) and the occasional anti-war march, but Luna, after her not-very-good GCSE results, had simply bailed into the university of life and the anti-fracking protests. Fair enough.

"Sorry," Luna said, as if catching the tail end of Stella's thought. "This is winding me up."

"I'm not really surprised," Stella said. "We've all had a lot to put up with."

"Must have been fucking awful," Sam said to her now. "Having your mum vanish like that. I know what that's like. My dad went off when I was a little kid; didn't come back for three years. We thought he was dead."

Stella did not say: *but you're travellers*. Instead, she said, "Where'd he go?"

"I don't know. He wouldn't tell us, the old bugger. And we're a bit more used to it than many, like."

Stella nodded. Her egg and chips arrived; she applied herself to it. She found herself liking Sam. Having your little sister run away with a traveller in a van, away with the raggle taggle gypsies-o, was not the sort of thing that middle class people were supposed to approve of, but Stella didn't do *approve*. She thought Sam was all right. He reminded her, very slightly, of Dark: a faint similarity in build and colouring, perhaps, but it was more of a vibe: a determination to look after people. Stella liked that, and liked his voice, too. She couldn't place the accent, but if she'd been forced to pin it down, she'd have said that it was old fashioned, without quite knowing what that meant.

After lunch, they got back in the car and headed, with a growing sense of anticipation, towards Tavistock. Heading down the hill, Stella's phone buzzed with an incoming text.

"Can you look at that for me, Lune?"

"It's from Bee," Luna said, after a moment. "Serena's home."

"Oh, fantastic!"

"And she says: *don't mention Ben*."

"Oh bollocks. I wondered if that had turned to ratshit."

The winding lanes made travel across the moor twice as long as it should have been. Towards two they pulled into Tavistock. In unspoken agreement, everyone got out of the car and went into the ticket office.

"Excuse me," Stella said to the morose man behind the panel. She gave her best social smile. "We're looking for a woman who might have come through here a year or so ago. She's our mother and I'm afraid she's missing." She pushed a photograph of Alys under the grille.

The station master looked disapproving. "You've left it a while to come looking, haven't you?"

"We've only just found out that she was headed this way."

Stella's smile remained fixed in place; she did not want to irritate the man, but he seemed determined to be unhelpful. He had no recollection of her. The station was equipped with CCTV, but this went back only three months. When asked who might have been on the desk at the time, he simply shrugged. Eventually Stella thanked him, with gritted teeth, and led the way back out into the afternoon sunshine.

"That was a waste of time," Luna said.

"No, he couldn't be bothered, could he?" Stella, however, was determined. "There's a shop over there. We could try that." She hoped they wouldn't have to traipse round the whole of Tavistock, which was quite large.

Here, the woman behind the counter was only too happy to be drawn into a drama. "Missing person, is she? I saw it in the papers. But I didn't see her, otherwise I'd have reported it. I did hear, though, that there was a lady staying for a few nights at the pub up the road, the White Horse, and the landlady did say that she looked a little like the one in the paper, but she had red hair and she was a lot younger."

"It couldn't have been her, then," said Luna, but Stella asked, "Where's the pub?"

It lay at the bottom of the road, on a corner. It was whitewashed, plain, with late nasturtiums in pots outside the door. They found the landlady behind the bar, and she studied the photographs carefully.

"I don't think it was your mum, I'm afraid. I did wonder at the time, because it was a week or so before it was in the papers, but the lady who stayed here was younger." She rifled through the photos. "Now that – that looks a lot like her."

She pointed to a photo of Alys in jeans and a Bowie t-shirt, holding a stout infant Bee on her lap. It had been taken in the garden of Mooncote; Alys' long ponytail swung over one shoulder, and there were narcissi growing about her feet. She looked like a rock-group version of Persephone, Stella thought.

"I'd have said that was her. You can't tell the colour of her hair, this being black and white."

"Did it look as though it might have been dyed? Her hair, I mean?"

"Yes, it might have been. Your mum didn't have any sisters, anyone who looked like her?"

"She was an only child, as far as we know. My cousin Nell looks a lot like her, actually."

"But Nell would have been in the States then," Luna said.

Stella was thinking hard but none of the ideas that she was coming up with seemed anything other than paranoid. "She must have given you her name."

"She did, but I can't remember it – let me look. She might still be on the system." She went into the back, and Stella glimpsed her scrolling down a computer screen. "Here we are. Lynette Horne." She spelled both names out.

They looked at each other. "Mum's middle name was Linnet," Luna said. And they all knew about 'Horne'. Stella felt as though the blood was rushing into her face, as though she was suddenly burning up. After all this time, after the police search and publicity, going on a dream, they had found a trace. The landlady was staring.

"So you think this might have been your mum?"

"Very possibly."

"Oh, I do hope so. But what happened to her? You poor girls. It must be such a nightmare."

"It's been pretty awful." Stella was afraid she might cry. She blinked hard, focusing on the postcards from Marbella and other places which were tacked up on the other side of the bar. She took a breath, aware of the familiar odours of polish and beer.

"You all right?" Luna said in an undertone.

Stella nodded. "So how long did this Lynette Horne stay here? Several nights, you said?"

"Three. Right at the end of August. I remember it, because the weather was so horrible – like a monsoon one day, just after the Bank Holiday, and I remember thinking what a shame it was, because it was just before the kids went back to school. But she went up onto the moor all three days, no matter how much it rained, and I do remember thinking that she was very clever because she never came back wet. Always nicely dressed – casual, you know, jeans and a jacket. But good quality. Barbour. And proper hiking boots."

"Do you know where she went?"

"No, she didn't say much about it, although she did say that she didn't know the area but she'd got a map. I know she went to Postbridge, because we talked about the old bridge, and I know she was very keen to go to Wistman's Wood. She said something about doing that before she went home, so it would have been on that day, and she didn't come back, of course, but then we weren't expecting her."

"She didn't have a car," Sam said. "How did she get up onto the moor? On foot, I suppose."

"There are buses. She had a timetable and I know she was asking someone questions about the bus to Newton Abbot – the wood's on the way and there's a bus stop."

"Would there by anyone there who'd remember seeing her, do you think? Is there a pub or anything?"

The landlady looked amused. "No, there's nothing there except a farm. I think they do take guests, though, so you could ask."

"Okay." Stella looked at Luna and Sam. "Anything else you can think of to ask?"

They could not, but Stella took the landlady's phone number in case, and she showed them the location of the wood on the moor: some miles distant, a tiny indication of an ancient monument. "And there are the stone rows, as well."

"Stone rows?"

"Very old. Like little standing stones. No one knows who put them there. They're markers, I suppose, up on the moor."

By the time they were back up on the heights dark clouds were running in from the coast, leaning a line of yellow light over the sea, and splashes of rain spattered the windscreen. They drove in silence, Luna huddled further in her shawls, like a hedgehog trying to hide. They came past the road to the prison, making Stella think of the Hound of the Baskervilles, and then the long rolling road over the moor. Stella found the track that led to the wood with some difficulty, and parked the car.

When she got out, it felt very quiet. She saw Luna looking at the information placard. "It's National Trust." They studied it.

"Dwarf oaks," Stella said. "I didn't know you could get little oaks. Like bonsai."

The illustration on the placard was finely drawn, a twisted knot of trees above a dry stone wall. It reminded Stella of a Japanese drawing. It made her want to go into that Celtic knotwork of branches, see what there was to be found there.

The rain had blown over, for now. Stella led the way, striding over the grass with its outcrops of stone. A bare, bald landscape, honed down to the last layer before the earth itself. They saw no one except sheep, masses of dirty wool trundling over the grass, and once, a raven high against the racing cloud, its harsh honk unmistakeable. Sam looked up at that.

"Old dark lady," he said. Stella said nothing; the raven seemed to go with the day, and she hoped it was not an omen of foreboding. It seemed strange, to be walking over the land which might have been the last place on which her mother had walked, and she was beginning to be afraid of what they might find, in the twisted oak wood.

SERENA

Serena pulled into the drive of Mooncote around lunchtime, having crawled across the landscape from Stonehenge. There had been an accident just outside the Salisbury junction, a lorry overturning and causing a tailback for miles. The enforced time in the car had given her time to think, however, without even the distraction of the radio, which was on the blink, and her attitude had gradually hardened. Enough. It had been good with Ben, when it was good, but she'd seen relationships go this way before, ending gradually and then suddenly, with a very slow deterioration in quality, and then people all of a moment not speaking to one another any more. She was finding it hard to believe that this had happened to her and Ben, but it seemed that it had. And if so, it was over, and Serena was reluctantly free.

She got out of the car and went across the lawn towards the quiet house, but halfway over the lawn she paused, and headed to the orchard instead. She had not expected to see anyone, but the girl was there: the one in the dusk-rose dress. Serena had first seen her when she was a little girl herself, perhaps even before that as a baby, because Alys had told her how she had held out her arms to someone, or something, that no one else could see.

The girl never changed. Now, she looked very young to Serena, who had not seen her for a year or more, but when Serena had been a child, she had thought that the girl was very grown up, and beautiful in her rosy gown. It was Elizabethan, being a sequence of hoops and ruffles, and there were pearls in her ears and around her neck. Her hair was a pale, satiny brown, and her eyes were hazel. Now that Serena was herself grown up, she realised that the girl was still beautiful, but there was a vulnerability in her face, a trepidation, which made Serena fear for her: foolish, because the girl was surely long dead. They had never known whether this sort of spirit, who had presumably been alive and a member of the household, was sentient, conscious and aware, or whether she was merely a kind of action replay, a loop. But she did not seem to have many set patterns, even if Serena had often seen her on the stairs, or in the attics, this had been at different times of day, and the girl's behaviour had been different, too, sometimes faltering, sometimes smiling.

Now, she was doing neither. She stood with the skirts of her gown vanishing into the long grass, contemplating – apparently – the ripening apples. Serena broke a rule and spoke.

"Hello."

She was not expecting a reply. The girl had never answered, never acknowledged her existence, but now, to Serena's great surprise, she turned and smiled. She seemed to see Serena, to look directly at her, and Serena was so startled that she took a step back. Then, in a blink, the girl was gone. Serena turned and went slowly to the yard.

First Spica, manifesting at the studio, and now the smiling girl. Things were changing, Serena thought, and she did not know what they would bring.

Later, she sat at the window of her old room, looking out into the darkness. She had given her mobile phone to Bee ('don't let me look at it.'). Bee, resolute, had not. Best, she said, if Serena just let Ben stew. Assuming he was in a stewing mood. But she had also spoken to Serena about Dana Stare.

"Stella didn't like her, either. None of us did. It was like school, everyone smiling from the teeth out and glaring inwardly."

"But Caro *does* like her."

Bee had hesitated at that. "I'm not sure. Dana's – around. But then I think her brother's made himself useful to Caro and Richard, and maybe they're fond of her... She strikes me as someone who can worm her way into things. That's what Laura said."

"Yeah. Like into my boyfriend. Ex boyfriend. Oh, I don't know." Serena had the feeling that she was starting to crumple, but where better place to do that than in your own old home? Nell and Bee were calm presences: Stella, Luna and the latter's new boyfriend were not there. They had gone to Dartmoor, Bee said, and at this Serena had experienced a sudden curious lightness, as though a window had opened a crack and let sunshine into a shadowy room. Perhaps it was just that someone else was taking care of business.

"Do you know if they've found anything?"

"Last thing we heard, they were in a pub." Despite the seriousness of the situation, Serena smiled at that.

And now Nell, Bee and herself were going to the local before supper. Serena got the impression that Bee thought she might disapprove of the suggestion, accustomed as she was to more sophisticated nightlife, but Serena had had enough of sophistication. The Hornmoon Arms sounded ideal: going out, thus Friday night not a total loss, but safe. A known quantity.

Unless, of course, Dana Stare showed up. But what would she be doing here, when she could have been prancing around Camden with other people's men? Then again, what had she been doing here yesterday? And at this, Serena was struck by a sudden very odd thought: *time*. She had seen Dana in Neal's Yard, unmistakeable, sitting beside Ben at a café table. Yet Bee had said something about Dana being at Amberley yesterday afternoon, and not even someone as devious as Dana was likely to possess the ability of being in two places at once. She did a quick calculation. A quarter of an hour to the station. An hour and a half at least from the station to London. Forty five minutes on the Tube. Public transport was thus ruled out. Twins? Not very likely either. Really fast driving? Possibly.

There was a knock at the door. "Serena? Are you ready?"

"Yes." She took a quick look in the mirror. Surprisingly presentable, and not red eyed, either. Encouraged, Serena followed her sister down the stairs.

"Bee!" Caro turned, smiling, from the bar of the Hornmoon Arms. She was holding two gin and tonics, and she was elegant in a knitted silk sweater and velvet jeans, in shades of gold.

"Oh, Serena! I didn't know you were coming down. How lovely to see you!" The greeting was obviously sincere, but to Serena, who knew her well, there was something a little constrained in her manner. Serena smiled in return.

"Last minute decision."

"The best kind." She hesitated. "Look, I'd ask you to join us, but – I'm with someone."

Serena felt small icy feet creep down the back of her neck. *Oh no. Please tell me he hasn't come home.* She felt a weird, unreasonable sense of betrayal. This was supposed to be her haven – but it was Ben's local too, when he was at his parents'. Who gets the pub in the break up?

"We don't want to intrude."

"It's just that – well, actually, it's Ward."

The icy feet stopped dead, but only because Serena was too relieved that it was not Ben – or Dana – with whom Caro was sharing a table. "*Ward?* I thought he was in New York."

"He was. But it's his uncle's funeral in a couple of days' time – did Bee tell you poor old Harold had died?"

"Yes. I told her about the books," Bee said.

"It was his heart, by the way. I don't know why they bothered with an autopsy but I suppose rules are rules. Anyway, his play ended its run and that's meant that the poor man could actually get back in time for the funeral."

"Look, you don't need to worry," Serena said, taking the plunge. "He's on my Christmas card list. We email each other from time to time. I actually saw him a couple of years ago. We had coffee. We spoke. In a non-recriminatory manner that was not fuelled by adrenaline, bitterness, regret or any of those things."

Caro smiled, evidently relieved. "Well – in that case, will you join us?"

"We'd love to," Serena said, before Bee could open her mouth.

Ward had not changed greatly since their split, some considerable time before. He still had the long, blondish hair, the brown spaniel eyes and the handsome, lugubrious countenance: 'saturnine' was an adjective which had been made for Ward Garner, and he played up to it. Typecasting had, Serena gathered, long been an issue. Villains, Shakespeare, or Jane Austen. Maybe even Jane Austen villains: she had not kept up with all of his screen performances. A great many people assumed he was gay; Serena knew that he was not. At least, not most of the time.

"Hello," she said. They exchanged air kisses. "So how was New York?"

"Much as usual." Ward turned the stem of his wineglass in fastidious fingers and looked pained. "Like Ernest Thesiger's description of the Somme. My dear, the *noise*. And the *people*."

She was not up to theatrical camp right now. "Play go all right?" In fact, Serena knew perfectly well how the play had gone: well received, but no awards. She'd even looked up clips on You Tube. Ward had played a literary critic with an alcohol problem: it was the kind of sarcastic part which suited him.

"They seemed to like it. They laughed."

"I hope you mean the audience and not the critics."

"Oh, *critics*." He made it sound like *Nazis*. "But yes, it went reasonably well. The rest of the cast were all very keen." The rest of the cast had been much younger, Serena recalled.

"Will it transfer to London?"

"I don't know. There was talk. But you know what it's like." Ward looked even more gloomy.

Serena nodded: fashion was similarly fickle, and she knew enough about the theatre to be able to relate. First world problems, though. It was odd, sitting down with Ward like this, after so many years. It was as though nothing had changed, and at that thought, Serena nearly choked on her wine. He was, after all, Richard's cousin and therefore Ben's as well– she seemed fated to date Amberley relations – and it should have been more awkward than it had, when she had started seeing Ben. But she and Ward had broken up by mutual agreement, some time before she and Ben became an item; it had been more situational than otherwise. Hollywood had beckoned to Ward; Paris to Serena. Indeed, she echoed her earlier thought, it had been a very first world reason for splitting up with someone... and Hollywood had apparently only intermittently worked out, as it happened. As had Paris. Ward had grown tired of playing flamboyant British baddies, and sought the sanctuary of the stage, but by that time Serena and Ben were an item. She understood from the tabloids that Ward had recently parted company from Miranda Dean, whom Serena always thought of as a siren. She had never met the woman and probably Miranda was nothing like that at all, but it entertained Serena to cast her in that sort of light ("Ward? He is going out with a Siren of the Screen"). Very childish, probably.

"And you, Serena." Ward didn't do that 'I am staring deeply into your eyes' thespian thing, which would have made her giggle, but he did sound sincere. "What's been happening with *you*?"

"Oh." She could hardly say in front of Ben's mother that she thought they might have split up. Instead, she said, "I've just done another collection."

"Very nice."

"Well, I hope so. I hope people will like it."

"We hope Vogue will like it."

"Yes, of course. But also normal people."

"Do you really design clothes for normal people, Serena?"

"I do try," she said, a little nettled. "The diffusion ranges, certainly. Why shouldn't Mrs Bloggs at the Post Office get a chance to wear nice clothes, as well as some beanstalk model? Or an actress," mischief compelled her to add. "And the diffusion ranges are affordable."

Ward raised a sceptical eyebrow, as if he doubted this. Serena, glancing around for support, realised that they were temporarily alone: Caro had gone to the loo and Bee had taken her turn at the bar.

"What about you?" Serena asked. "I'm sorry to hear about your uncle, by the way." Ward grunted; Harold's loss did not appear to cut deep so she changed the subject. "I keep seeing pics of you in the Daily Mail." Then, digging a little, "With the lovely Miranda."

"Oh. That."

She hoped he was referring to the overall situation, and not to the girl herself. Then he said, "That didn't last, actually."

"You surprise me."

"Unbeknownst to me, she's been having a thing with her latest director. For some time. As in, for some time before we officially parted company. Expect even more photos in the Daily Fail."

"Oh dear."

"He's married. To another actress who tends to compete with Miranda for similar roles. Tabitha Foss. You'll have heard of her. They have two small children."

"Oh *dear*." Mischief also made her add, "I thought she was really good in that film about the American Civil War."

"She was up for an Oscar. Alongside Miranda, for *Roanoke*. Neither of them won. You know, Serena, I may have been a bit of a tit."

"In what way?" Maybe that wasn't the most tactful thing she could have said.

"Going off to LA like that. Leaving you behind."

"You make it sound as though you abandoned me on a railway platform. Waving my red-spotted hanky. I was in Paris, in a lovely Left Bank flat, hanging out with people like Amanda Harlech."

"And then along came Ben."

"I'm not sure Ben's still coming along, actually. It's why I'm down here."

"Oh really?" He looked much more interested than she had expected. And then Caro came back from the loo.

LUNA

It took longer than they had thought to reach the wood. There seemed to be acres of barren moorland, with no sign of anyone but sheep, and no sign of any wood, either. Luna was used to walking, and so was Sam, but Stella eventually insisted on stopping for a cigarette.

"Otherwise my lungs might pack up with the shock."

Looking back, Luna could just see the maroon roof of the Landrover, tiny as a toy against the huge expanse of the moor. They had long since passed the farmhouse and there had been no one visible in its yard. "I suppose we ought to press on," Stella said. In silence they trudged along the track, and at length the end of the wood appeared further along the moor, in a shallow valley. They skirted a dry stone wall and found themselves at the edge of Wistman's Wood.

To Luna, it looked like something out of a fairy story. The trees were like thorns on the coast, blasted into streaming shapes by the wind, but these trees were oaks. Their branches curled and curved, a dragon's sinuosity, and the last of the leaves were yellow rags in the cold air of the moor. They were, for oak trees, tiny: not bonsai, but hawthorn-sized. Stella, Luna and Sam looked at one another.

"Shall we go in?" Stella said.

Among the trees, it was as though all sound had suddenly been cut off. The wind died; it was almost warm. Sam went ahead, with Stella wandering behind. Luna, suddenly, wondered what they expected to find; somehow, this had not been a question which had occurred to her in the car and she berated herself for being stupid. In the back of her mind had been thoughts of her mother's scarf, a fragment of thread, a silverfair hair on a branch. But not a body. At that thought, she turned her foot on a round globe of bone and stifled a yell. The others did not hear. She sat back on a fragment of wall and shoved the bone with her foot. A sheep's one eyed skull came loose from the moss and grinned at her. Luna swallowed fright and fury. She called to Stella, "Have you found anything?"

But the words might as well have been spoken underwater. Stella did not turn her head, and shortly vanished from sight among the trees. Luna imagined the words floating upwards, bubbles of air. And although she had been a vegetarian for some years, Luna plucked the sheep's skull from its bed of moss, and holding it to her face like a Venetian carnevale mask, looked out through the single hole of its eye.

At once, everything changed. The trees blurred and twisted, snake-writhing against the ridges of moss-covered stone. Above her, the glimpses of sky were quite black, while the trees themselves were silvery pale, and the moss green as emerald. Luna watched the spirit of a mouse run up the dry stone wall and into a hole; a minute later, it did it again, caught in a hangman's loop of time. She turned and with a shudder of shock saw her mother.

But it wasn't Alys, not quite. The woman who stood, calmly staring at Luna in return, was younger. She wore the dappled skin of a deer over one shoulder and a whiter skin about her waist. One breast was bare. Her hair, as red as Luna's own, spilled down her back in a complex dreadlocked mesh, marked with fir cones, clay beads, and a single bright blue glass sphere, very small. There was ochre between her brows. But it was Alys' face and a moment later, Luna was not so sure that this was not her mother.

Alys said something, in a language that sounded like water.

"*Mum?*" Luna breathed. Because it was Alys – not quite. The woman put a finger to her lips. She was looking at something beyond Luna and instinctively Luna turned, still holding the sheep's skull to her face.

Something was standing among the silver flickering oaks. She couldn't make it out, but it was big and dark, a bulky shape that was the colour of peat. It looked furred, beneath the tatters of its leather cloak. Stubby horns protruded from its head: not really antlers, for they were too thick, too short. The face was a blank oval, with no eyes visible, although for a moment she thought she saw a tiny brightness, like looking down into very dark water. She froze, icy with wanting it to go away. Behind her, there was a rustle: Alys had stepped forwards. Her hand came into Luna's vision, the wrists banded with old blue tattoos, and holding up a piece of what looked like bronze. Luna did not recognise the shape, but it was not a cross, for it had too many arms. Alys spoke again, that long rippling sound, and the horned thing turned abruptly and sprang up onto one of the dry stone walls. Luna saw it there for a second, outlined against the negative-bright trees, and then it was gone.

Alys bent down to Luna. She smelled of her familiar French perfume, tuberose and musk, but also of the earth itself. Close to, she no longer looked so young. She said, in perfectly intelligible English, "Luna, I'm glad you've come to find me but it's dangerous. Not just for me, but for you, too. All of you. Do you understand?"

"Yes. But –"

"You need to guard the house. I'll come back with the comet, I promise. Speak to Bee. Tell her to look after the house. Tell your lad's gran, too."

"You know about Ver March?"

"And the hare. Yes, I know. But it's Caro who really needs to –" She broke off. Her head went up like a startled deer's and Luna saw that beneath the red dreads, there was a faint line of silver-grey around Alys' old-young face.

"Throw the skull in the water," she said, urgently.

"What –"

"Just *do*."

So Luna took the skull from her face. Immediately, her mother vanished, and the trees returned to their shadowy twilight selves. The sky above the wood was rainy-black. Luna hefted the skull in her hand and threw it into the trickle of a stream that ran between the oak roots, down the slope. She did not think there was much water running through, but the skull disappeared as if she'd dropped a pebble into the ocean. Luna gave a sudden shiver of cold. Stella's voice, coming from behind, made her jump.

"Luna? Are you okay?"

Luna turned to her, trembling, and for the first time since she had been a very little girl, sought her sister's embrace.

BEE

On returning from the pub, Bee thought that she needed to speak to her namesakes, even though it was well past sunset. They were not yet dormant; the waning warmth of the autumn sun still drew them out into the lavender and sometimes they became drunk on the rotting juice of the windfalls, fighting the wasps for the sweetness. Telling the bees. Grandpa had always done it, and so had Alys, when she'd remembered. The hives were situated at the end of the orchard, just before the edge of the nettles and the tangles of bramble which separated the orchard from the field. Bee, wellington-clad, trudged through the long grass to the hives. She gave them an edited version of events, as they hummed inside their tall wooden home. When she had finished, the voice of the elder said, *The man who is cold is here.*

"What do you mean?" Bee asked.

The man who is cold. The ancient.

"Sorry," Bee said. "I have no idea what you're talking about."

He'll reach his power when the comet comes. You need to be careful.

But the elder would say no more. Irritated, Bee went back into the house through the fading light to find a message on the answerphone. Stella's voice: *we're on our way back.*

The expedition reached Mooncote an hour later, as Bee and Serena were in the kitchen. A casserole simmered in the oven; Serena had opened the wine. Bee found that she was dreading the return of her sisters, and Sam; she felt as though she was sitting on a bed of pins.

"Stop twitching," Serena said, without looking up. "This isn't like you."

"I know. Sorry." Then the half door banged and Sam and Luna poured in. A moment later, Stella followed.

"Where's Nell?"

"Having a bath. Did you –"

"We found her. Well. We think we have. She was definitely down there – she was using the name Linnet." Stella flopped into a chair. "Can I have some wine, please? Cheers."

Bee felt her heart hammer and jolt. "You're sure it was her."

"Luna *saw* her."

"What?"

"In a wood. Wistman's Wood. I didn't see her, neither did Sam."

Luna looked sulky and defensive. "I did see her. I didn't make her up."

Stella leaned across the table and put her hand on her sister's wrist. "I didn't say you did, Lune. No one's saying that. We believe you, so chill out."

"She didn't look like she used to," Luna said. "She had red hair, but it was dyed. I could see the edges. She had tattoos but they were old ones."

"She had that butterfly on her arm," Serena said.

"These were round her wrists. Old and blue. And she looked younger, too."

"Are you sure it was Mum?"

"Yeah, I'm totally sure but it was like – another version of her," Luna said. "A parallel version. And she spoke to me. She said we were in danger, and that you ought to look after the house, Bee."

Bee felt the slight sting of implied injustice; it was her turn to become defensive. "What the hell does she think I've been doing?"

"She said she'd come back when the comet comes. And," Luna added, turning to Bee, "There was this *thing*. This shape. We talked about it in the car and it's the same as the one Stella saw."

"It's a horned god-style entity," Stella said. "But not the sort of neo-pagan one that looks like a rock star. More basic than that. Creepy as fuck."

"Someone – a tree – told me to be careful of a man who is cold," Bee said. Stella's mouth fell open.

"I got told that, too. By an olive."

"An olive spoke to you? What, like out of a dish?"

"An olive *tree,* you muppet!"

"This was in Ibiza?" Bee asked.

"Yeah. Up on the hillside near the club. I asked it what it meant but it wouldn't tell me."

"Neither would the elder. They seem to think we should know what they mean."

"At least they talk. Not like the star spirits."

"Grandpa doesn't think Alys is dead," Stella said.

"Now, neither does anyone else," Bee told her.

*

That night, Bee woke with a start. Someone was standing over her, bending low. She flailed out and the person hissed, "It's me!"

"Stella!"

"Shhhh! There's someone outside."

"Where?" Bee got out of bed and, clad in her chaste white nightgown, padded across to the window. A new moon hung above the trees, still too slender to cast any light, but the outside yard light shed a glow over the buildings. "I can't see anything."

And Dark had not alerted her. Why not?

Stella leaned against the wall like a spy and peered round the edge of the curtains. "Don't let them see you!"

Bee kept obediently still and after a moment saw a shadow slink around the edge of the old stable. "See him?" Stella whispered. Bee wanted to say: *maybe it's Luna or Sam,* but somehow she knew that it was not, that it was an enemy. It did not have Luna's sturdy shape, or Sam's ambling grace. "Downstairs!" Stella said. For the first time, Bee realised that her sister was dressed, or at least wearing tracksuit bottoms and a t-shirt emblazoned with a band logo. Stella's jaw was set. Bee snatched up a navy dressing gown. They went quickly down the stairs to the hall, where the clock was ticking with that peculiar echoing resonance characteristic of clocks at night: a secret marking of the minutes and hours. The back door was still closed; the kitchen peaceful and dark. Stella herded the spaniels into the hall and shut the door.

"Ever thought of keeping Dobermans, Bee? Rotties?"

Bee had. The spaniels, feathery and melt-eyed, were perhaps not as effective as guard dogs as they might be and more of a liability. Very gently, Stella eased the half door open and they slipped through. A very faint sound came from the old stable. Stella held a finger to her lips. Then there was a sudden warbling, yodelling yell and a long grey shape shot past Bee in the darkness, nearly knocking her flat. She yelped in turn. Moth, Luna's dog: Bee had not even known he was out. Maybe the shadow was Sam, but then why would his own dog bark, for Moth's cry had been challenge.

"Christ!" Stella said. "What was that?"

"Sam's lurcher." But Stella was running towards the stables.

STELLA

Inside, the stable was like a refrigerator and Stella paused. It had not been this cold outside, even in the autumn chill. She blinked. The pallor from the yard light fell over her shoulder, and she could see the large, placid shapes of the piebalds, munching hastily-gathered straw. They had put them in the stable after all, for a break, Sam had said. But beyond them was shadow, and something moved within it. Stella called out sharply, "Who's there?"

There was no reply. She could not see the dog. She went between the piebalds, breathing in warmth and the odour of horses, her footsteps muffled by the hay. But the warmth was soon gone, leaving Stella in the black. She blinked. No, it was possible to see, after all – the stable went back much further than it should have done. Like a Narnian wardrobe, and then Stella began to be really scared. She turned. The door was gone. An immensity stretched behind her, a wasteland covered in a pale blanket of snow. She looked up. A full moon hung overhead, a white eye. Down the slope, a river raced black with boulders of ice, in full spate, but as Stella watched, horrified, it slowed and froze. It was like watching a film, now speeding up, now slowing down. Her knees actually started to knock, something she thought only happened in metaphors. She was standing on a ridge of land, snow crunching beneath her feet; she was glad she had thought to pull on her trainers, but the cold still burned and bit. She looked behind her and saw a ring of huge grey boulders, standing like teeth in the snow. Something was crouched beside them, a ragged black shape.

"Who's that?" Stella shouted. She wished a golf club was to hand, anything. The figure did not reply, but Stella thought she had startled it, for it lurched to its feet and bolted down the slope, stumbling unevenly through the snow. A long cloak, made of skins, streamed out behind it. Then there was movement from behind one of the stones and Moth, barking, raced down the slope. Stella saw the dog hit the figure from behind. It threw up its arms and went down into the snow. She heard Moth growl, but then the dog turned tail and ran back up.

"Moth!" Stella cried. "Come *here*!" The dog skidded past her; Stella turned and found a star spirit standing in the snow. Sirius: the dog star was blue above her head, bright-chasing the heels of the Hunter. Orion strode across the sky and Sirius held out her hand. A sprig of berried juniper twined about her fingers; she wore a coronet of beryls, a pale blue-green in the white blaze of her hair. Something about her face reminded Stella fleetingly of Caro Amberley, but of all the spirits, Sirius looked the least human, like a drawing by Richard Dadd. Her long mouth curled in a smile; she beckoned to Stella. *Come.* So Stella did, staggering through the soul-stealing cold in the star's wake, and out into the fusty warmth of the stable.

Three o'clock in the morning and all's well. Stella and Bee sat silently over steaming tea. Stella had dropped a shot of whisky into her mug, saying that this was no time to be worried about turning to drink. The lurcher Moth lay at their feet, beneath the table. In the nearby hall, the clock spoke the hour.

"It was Tam Stare out there at first," Stella said. She felt that she might never be warm again. "I'm sure of it."

"Did you get a look at his face?"

"No. I just know."

She was grateful that her sister forbore to ask how she knew; she could not have answered that question. Nor could she have said how she understood that what she had just seen, what she had experienced, had not been real. She had walked into someone's mind, someone else's magic, and it had the sense of Tam Stare: darkness and white, the pale fierce blue of the moon, or an eye. By degrees she anchored herself back into reality: the residual heat of the Aga, the presence of Moth under the table, and the ticking of the clock.

"We've got a week or two," Bee said now.

"For what?"

"Until the comet comes. Until Mother comes back. Until Apple Day."

A week or two, Stella thought. A lot could happen in a fortnight. Until the comet came.

PART TWO
WHITE HORSE COUNTRY

LUNA

He'd rarely spent so long in one place, Sam said, not for quite a while. Luna shot him an anxious glance. They were sitting on the low wall outside the terrace of the house, still in sunlight, but the air was cold and the morning had seen the first frost.

"Do you want to – move on?"

"Did I say that? As long as your family's cool with us being here."

"I think so."

Serena had gone back to London and so, Luna knew, had Ward Garner. She did not know what was happening there, or with Ben, but that was Serena's business. She did not want to interfere. Nell was busy writing; Bee was busy cataloguing books and Stella, too, was spending a lot of the time at Amberley, helping to organise the Apple Day. The only people who were not technically busy were Luna and Sam, but Sam had made himself useful around the house, bagging the windfalls, which now stood in neat sacks beneath each tree in readiness for the cider press, and cutting the grass. In exchange for board and lodging, he said, and he had made a run to the some co-operative farm behind the Tor (rather than evil Tesco) and bought a box of vegetables as a contribution, which had now become a weekly occurrence. The piebalds now grazed in the back field and the wagon stood, moored for the time being, in the old stable.

One evening, Sam had come into the kitchen and said to Bee, "There's a bloke in the orchard."

Bee had blushed. "Oh. I know." She had not pretended to misunderstand him.

"A dead bloke." Sam was not accusatory or even greatly perturbed; he sounded intrigued. "Elizabethan. Must have had an amazing life. Says he sailed with Drake."

"I didn't know until recently that we had an Elizabethan ghost," Luna said. Bee went even pinker.

"I used to see him sometimes when I was a little girl. Then he started appearing more often, a few years ago now. And then – well." She was now full-on beetroot red.

"Bee! You didn't say anything."

"He was my secret," Bee said. Luna nodded. She understood that. She had a secret of her own, now.

But it wouldn't be a secret for much longer and although she hadn't told Sam, she wasn't sure that she was going to have to. She thought he already knew. She wasn't suffering from morning sickness, and there were no visible sign as yet, but Luna felt that she was sinking down into the earth, becoming gravid.

Sitting on the wall, she glanced up to find that Sam was looking at her. "So, what do you want to call it?"

"I don't know." It was as if they'd already had the first part of the conversation, the important part, and were now into the calmer waters beyond those rapids, but she wanted to make sure. "Do you – mind?"

"No, I think it's amazing. You know what? If it's a boy, I think we should call him Ned. After Dark."

Dark had become Sam's hero. It amused Luna; she'd never seen Sam in male-worship mode before, but he was spending a lot of time with the spirit, sitting in the orchard late into the cold evenings, talking about running away to sea, and other things.

"If it's a girl, we should call her after your gran," Luna said. "Vervain."

He nodded. "That's good with me. So when do you think it's due?"

"I think I must have been pregnant for about a month. So probably it's due in June." She wished she hadn't been drinking, but she hadn't drunk a lot. The occasional glass of wine. She hoped it hadn't hurt.

"A summer child," Sam said. "Like its dad." For Sam was Leo. "Have you told your sisters?"

"Not yet. I will do, though. I don't want a lot of fuss."

"Is this why you've seemed to – not want to move on?" For Luna had resisted any suggestion that they go back on the road, and Sam had not pressed the issue. From not wanting to come here, now she did not want to go; perhaps this would change when the baby came, or the spring. It worried Luna: Sam was not the landed kind, but she simply did not want to move. For the moment, however, he seemed to accept this.

Among her remaining sisters, Serena being in London, there was a tacit understanding of two things. One was that they would follow Alys' instructions, no matter how little they liked them, and wait for the comet – which should be appearing in the eastern sky any day now, if the newspapers and Abraham's ghost were to be believed. The second was that someone should be at the house at all times, and this was why Bee had been grateful to Luna and Sam, for staying put and allowing everyone else to get on with their jobs. Luna was not sure how much Bee had told Nell, but Nell too had become part of the household, a quiet semi-permanent presence. Sometimes she went across to Amberley to help Bee with the book collection, and sometimes she went up to London, staying with Serena and haunting the British Library, but mostly she stayed at Mooncote. She had not mentioned noticing anything untoward.

Tam Stare was around a lot, in the village. Sam had run into him in one of the garage yards, when picking up a spare wheel for the Landrover, and they had gone for a pint: to get the measure of the man, Sam had said.

"And what did you think?" Bee had asked, that night at dinner.

"He's got a high regard for himself," Sam said. "Full of himself, you might say. I think they call it 'entitled'. But seemed to think we were the same. I didn't agree. I didn't say so."

"I think he's really shady," Stella said.

"Yeah, I'd say you were right, at that. I've spoken to a couple of people, who might know him. They did."

"And?"

"He and Dana were brought up in Norfolk somewhere. No one seems to know where the family's from. The mother's English, but not the father, but I don't know what he is. Or was. They're both dead, apparently. The old man had a reputation for violence, which is saying a lot. The mother – now that's interesting, because a couple of people said she was originally posh, like landed-gentry posh."

"I can't place his accent," Stella said. "Or his sister's. Sometimes it sounds like he's trying to be working class and sometimes it sounds genuine. There's something underneath it."

"Perhaps they moved a lot. Maybe that explains the way they speak," Bee said.

"I don't think they did. I heard – conflicting reports, as they say in the newspapers. Someone said they'd been to the house when the kids were growing up and it was proper posh, a real old school stately home out in the middle of the fens. But then I spoke to another bloke and he said he'd been there and there was nothing but a caravan or two. Maybe he was thinking of somewhere else, though. He said it was a long time ago. It sounded like they weren't popular. And the people I asked – you know, they're no saints themselves. But there are limits."

Luna was grateful to her sisters, that they hadn't launched into self-conscious, class-guilty justification. *Of course, you're different, Sam. We're not prejudiced against travellers, you understand, it's just that...* All Stella had said was, "I don't like the bastard."

"Neither do I," Sam said.

So now Luna and Sam were waiting. For the comet, and the baby, and anything else that might be on the way.

BEE

Bee had been expecting trouble around Hallowe'en. That seemed to fit in with her ideas about the season. It was Samhain, which some people said was the old festival of the dead and stolen by the Christians, though Bee had heard other versions. A tricky time, when the veil between the worlds of the living and the dead, between those of fairy and of men, were supposed to grow thin. In Bee's imagination it resembled a net curtain full of holes, through which things might slip. She went to Tesco all the same and bought some bags of sweets, in case of local trick or treaters. The house felt on edge, as if waiting, but the comet was not due for a while yet and Alys had said – well, they would just have to repel any boarders, said Stella, who seemed to be picking up a nautical vocabulary from Dark.

When the day itself dawned, it was clear that it was going to be wet. The sky was lowering halfway through the morning and they had left the kitchen lights on.

"Should put the kids off, anyway," said Stella. "Maybe we should dress up."

"As what?"

"I dunno. Ghosts?"

"We could just get Dark to answer the door. And make sure he's see through."

Stella looked seriously tempted by this option and Sam grinned, but said, "I like the way you think but maybe keep it under the radar, yeah?"

"You're probably right."

Bee had to drive into Taunton to pick up a new cartridge for the printer. It should have been sent to the house, had not turned up, had eventually gone to the shop. This was the sort of tedious and unnecessary errand which caused Bee to muster all the patience she could, but she went anyway, picked up the wayward printer cartridge and a sandwich for lunch. Then she drove home through the lowering day, avoiding the dual carriageway and taking the road across the Levels instead. It was a curiously primitive landscape, extensively managed but frequently flooded: some years previously, the government had been obliged to call the army in to rescue people and sheep and cows, stranded in waterlogged pockets of land. The old name for Somerset, Bee reflected now as she eyed the brimming rhynes that ran along the road, was taken from the Summer Country: it only appeared in summer. It other months, it lay submerged. Moved by a whim, she pulled off the road into the car park by the little hummock of Burrow Mump. A ruined church stood on the top of the hill, echoing the slightly higher Tor some miles away. Bee climbed the slope in the blowing damp, causing the resident sheep to amble away from her. At the top, she leaned against the wet stone and looked out across the landscape. Very flat, bisected by the silvery rhynes. A chessboard, Bee thought, and herself and her sisters pieces upon it. But moved by what hand? Along the swimming ditches marched row upon row of pollarded willow, looking stumpy and mutilated, but Bee knew that in the spring the long whips would uncoil themselves from these skull-like stumps and block out the fields in a delicate haze of green. They were still used for basket-making and she liked that old link with the land.

She'd come up here with some vague thought of connecting with the spirits of place on this day of the dead, some faint pagan impulse, but now she was up high above it all, she wished she hadn't. She couldn't shake off the feeling that she was being watched. She even turned, quickly, to see what might be looking back out of the ruins of the church, but only the mild sheep were there, drifting across the close-cropped grass. Below, she had the sudden sense of the willows' hooded eyeless shapes; wasn't there an old story that if you turned your back on one of the trees it would creep after you? Bee went quickly back to the car, stumbling a little on the wet slope, glad of the vehicle's sanctuary.

At five o clock there was a thunderous knock on the front door, making everyone jump. "I'll go," Sam said. With Stella at his heels, they disappeared and Bee heard the sound of voices. She waited, nerves on edge, until they returned to the kitchen.

"It was a very small devil. With a very large father."

"I hope you gave them some sweets."

"I did."

After that there came a trickle of village children until seven, then no more.

"All gone home for their Hallowe'en parties," Stella said. "We could bob for apples."

But in the event, they just opened more wine.

That night, Bee woke with a start. Dark was not by her side. It took her a moment to come to her senses. Hallowe'en and nothing had happened after all. Bee had a hurdler's sense of relief: at least *that* was over. She had lit a nightlight in the window, with some atavistic memory of it being the thing to do on this day, a glow to guide the spirits home. It had now burned out and the room lay in darkness. Bee got up and went to the window to draw the heavy curtain further aside. Rain spattered on the pane, making her start. She looked down.

Something was standing in the yard. She recognised it from Stella's description, and Luna's. It was the horned thing, a column of night in the shadows of the yard. It was half turned away from her, staring up at the window of the room that had been Alys' bedroom and which was now occupied by Nell. Its face was a muzzle, the long head shared by dog and goat and deer, strange when you thought about it, as though they were interchangeable. But the body was that of a very tall man: beneath the hem of its cloak, she could see one bare foot poised on tiptoe, and its arm, visible through a ragged hole in its garment, was also bare, and human. She saw the blur of tattoos or paint spiralling up it.

Bee felt herself begin, uncontrollably, to shake. Once, not that long ago, she had looked out of this window on a summer evening, and around the round bales of hay in the opposite field she had seen a roebuck and a doe, with a fawn. The baby had been playing with its parents, running around the bale and then dodging back, just like a human child. And Bee, charmed, had nonetheless had the feeling that she was seeing something that she was not meant to see: a secret thing, private. Despite the horror of the figure that now stood in the yard, that same sense of transgression overcame her.

Don't look. This is not for you.

She had to do something, she must wake Stella or Sam, it was looking right up at Alys' window and surely this was to do with her mother, message or warning – Bee swallowed, stepped back and when she next dared to peek, the yard was empty.

STELLA

Stella wanted to see the comet with Abraham. It had become a fixed idea, a focal point. She kept a close eye on dates and newspaper reports, logging onto astronomy sites once a day. When the first apparent sighting was due, she pulled on a coat and boots and walked down to the graveyard at twilight, to wait.

Her grandfather was there, a dancing blue flicker above the grave. Beyond, the bulk of the church towered up, with the weathercock shining a sudden occasional gold, as if powered by its own light.

"Hello," Stella said.

"Hello, Starry. Come to see the fire in the sky?"

"Yeah. It's supposed to be due tonight." She was conscious of a fierce, repressed excitement, like being a child again and on the verge of seeing the sea for the first time in a summer, or going to get a Christmas tree.

"It will be," Abraham said. A tawny owl called, up in the church tower, making Stella jump. The sky was a deep blue-green, but no stars were visible yet. She suspected that another frost was due: it had not melted in the lee of the church wall, but still shone faint and silver. Stella remembered a snowy land and standing stones; there had been no recurrence of that kind of vision, but Bee had seen the horned thing in the yard on Hallowe'en night and that was freaky enough. Now it was the fifth, Bonfire Night, and that seemed appropriate, somehow.

Since their last encounter, Stella had been avoiding Tam Stare, glimpsed occasionally in the village and once in the middle of Yeovil, where she had gone to the dentist. Stella had ducked into a shop doorway and made sure he passed her by. But she was not sure if it was Tam whom she distrusted most, or herself.

Now, she perched on a nearby gravestone and waited. The sky deepened and Venus sparked out between the branches of the yews, a lamp alongside the church tower. The moon was gibbous.

"You'll see it in the east," her grandfather's voice said. Obediently Stella waited, watching, and hoping that the relevant portion of sky would not be obscured by the trees. And then, quite suddenly in an eyeblink, the comet was there: just a smudge of light, like a thumbprint across the sky. Stella put her mittened hand to her mouth.

"Oh my God!"

"Told you."

"That's amazing." She wanted to run back to the house and tell everyone, drag them out into the yard to look. *Honestly, Stella Fallow, you are such a big kid.* But it was amazing. Bee had said of the horned thing that it had been like a transgression, somehow, seeing something that you are not meant to see, and she felt like that herself now, conscious of the honour. She waited, however, in silent vigil with her grandfather's spirit, until the sky was fully dark and the comet stood out against the field of stars.

"There you are," Abraham said. "It's not going to get any brighter than that. Not tonight, anyway. It'll be here for several weeks and it will get a lot brighter before it goes away again."

"Caro's Apple Day is on Saturday," Stella told him. "The astronomy society's coming – I told you that. Dave Reed and some of the others. Everyone will be able to see it once it's dark, if the weather holds." But she knew, deep within, that the frosty bright days would continue for a while, now that the smudge in the sky was there. Comet weather. Stella had faith, and meanwhile they were going to the village bonfire that night. Exceptional. A comet, plus fire, plus explosions. What could be better? *Remember, remember.* She walked home in the comet's light, her boots ringing on the hard cold road, as the first firework exploded in the sky into a shower of stars.

She had dreamed about the white fox, in the trap, but this was not like that dream. In fact, it was not a dream at all. Stella found herself sitting upright in bed, panting as though she had been running a race. She felt clear and chilly, wide awake, and light. Just as she had done on the night when the vision had come, in the stables, she knew that something was outside, and waiting. But it did not feel like that shadowy, heavy presence. This was different and she knew that there was no reason to wake Bee.

She got quickly out of bed and pulled on a sweater and jeans, and downstairs, her boots. Then she slipped out of the back door, closing it gently behind her, and went out into the starry night. It was too late for fireworks now, though the village display had been a good one, down in someone's field. Cold, though, but Bonfire Night should be chilly so you could get the maximum benefit from the fire and baked potatoes. And now there was a further frost. It lay thickly on the roofs of the sheds and the old stable, and fogged the windscreen of the Landrover. When Stella went out into the garden, the lavender was weighed down with it; each floret hanging heavy towards the whiteness of the grass. The half moon was on the shoulder of the hill and the comet – Stella turned, fearing irrationally that it would no longer be there, but it was still flying high in the east, as if in mockery of the sun. She made her way through the garden and then the orchard, the cold latch clicking in her hand. There was no sign of Dark but the orchard felt brooding, as though something lurked within it. Stella thought about the horned thing and shivered. She went swiftly through and into the field, where the piebalds were dozing by the lee of the bothy.

She had expected to see Alys. She realised this only later, looking back and reviewing the evening. They had, all of them, even Dark, gone down to the pub after the bonfire to celebrate the appearance of the comet. It was, Dark said, a fire in the skies and should thus be marked. They had all agreed. Stella must have knocked back the better part of a bottle of Shiraz, celebrating the fifth of November and the accompanying smudge on the pane of the night, almost like marking a birth. But now there was no trace of the wine in her; she was as transparent as glass, the stars seeing through her as she walked across the field. Behind her, the hedge was a ridge of black around the field's rim: the pasture climbed a gentle slope, culminating in a flat plateau and descending to a stream, banked by blackthorn brake, which ran into the Horne and which marked the field boundary between Mooncote and Amberley.

When Stella reached the slight summit, she was not surprised to see a figure walking towards her. The whole walk had the quality of a dream, a hallucinatory sense in which nothing startled and all was meant, although Stella had not liked the atmosphere of the orchard tonight. But orchards were chancy places, and unruly. Now, the figure was no more than an outline of light, a silhouette surrounded by a bright haze, and she expected her mother to walk out of it. But it was not Alys, nor was it the horned figure.

She was reminded of the Behenian stars. She stood, rooted to the frosty earth, with a lump in her throat like a heart, and watched it go by. As it drew closer, she glimpsed its face within the fiery corona of hair, whiteflame starfire streaming down its back, and its eyes were narrow silver. It was smiling, but only a little. It reminded Stella of the white tigers she had seen in Bristol Zoo as a child; there was the same sense of danger, banked but yet not caged. The clothes were, very strangely, reminiscent of Ned Dark's: a doublet and ruff, but then they changed to a pale robe, and then back again. It strode across the hillside and down towards the orchard. Footsteps made of fire gleamed in its wake, before dying and leaving frost melt, bare earth. But, Stella thought, she really should stop thinking of it as 'it.' She knew who the figure was: the comet, and from the look of his face he was clearly male. With horrified amusement, as the glowing shape drew closer to the house, she wondered how much havoc it would cause in the all-female ranks of the Behenian stars.

Serena

"I seem to have become," Ward Garner said, with gloom, "a kind of agony uncle."

"I *am* sorry. Really. I didn't mean to use you as a shoulder to cry on."

The actor sighed. "It's all right. I suppose it's my time of life."

"You're not much past forty."

"Forty is *quite* enough."

They were sitting in the Judge, just around the corner from Eleanor's studio. Serena presumed that it had been named after the Judge's house, which Eleanor and her silent Ethiopian now inhabited. It was an archetypal London pub: dimly lit, with a red lacquered ceiling darkened by generations of smoke and the floor was black wood. It was three o'clock in the afternoon and Serena had run away.

"So what has been happening?"

"I saw Ben. Last night. It was an accident."

"Car crash accident, or inadvertency?"

"It was on the Embankment. Near the Sphinx and the houseboats. He was just walking along." *Head down, shoulders hunched, even though it had been late afternoon, like this, and a sunlit day.*

"Did you speak to him?"

"Yes. He wasn't looking – he nearly ran into me, so I couldn't avoid it. He was –" She paused. *He didn't look well. Pale as paper under the brown curls, and even his hair seemed faded.*

"He was really embarrassed. He muttered something, then he just shouldered on."

"Have you actually had a conversation about all this?"

"No. I tried. When I got back from Somerset I called him, but he said he was busy. He's just putting his head in the sand and hoping I'll go away."

"Men do that. We're basically cowards."

"Well, it isn't good enough! At least you had the bottle to tell me yourself you were going to America."

"I do try to do the decent thing. What about whatsername?"

"Miss Stare? I've not set eyes on her since I saw her in Covent

Garden." Nor wanted to. A pause, then "Have you heard from Miranda?"

"Thankfully, no. I expect, if she is not with her director, she is working her way through Los Angeles' plentiful supply of movers and shakers. Oh gawd, here we go."

A small group of tourists, older people and one young woman, had come into the pub and, spotting Ward, had started whispering. "In a minute, she'll come over."

She did, giggling. "Excuse me. I'm terribly sorry, but I really loved you in *Lionheart Rising*, you make such a great villain, I was wondering...?"

"Yes, yes, delighted," Ward said, perfunctorily. He signed the beermat she held out and posed for a selfie, staring meltingly into her phone. When she had gone he rolled his eyes, but it was an occupational hazard and Serena knew him well enough to realise that he did not really mind. She played up to it anyway.

"You ought to go out in disguise. You are an actor, after all."

"I've often considered a false nose."

"You could grow a beard."

"I had a beard in *Rule of Law* and everyone recognises it. Unless I grow an enormous hipster style beard of the kind that birds nest in – 'it is just as I feared', and all that."

"Two owls and a hen, four larks and a wren? I don't think that would suit you."

"No, neither do I. However, in spite of its disadvantages, it is a job which pays the mortgage. Talking of which, I spoke to my agent earlier in the week and it seems I shall be returning to the stage in the New Year. At the National. *A Midsummer Night's Dream*."

"You're a bit young for Prospero, aren't you? Or are you going to be Caliban? Oh, sorry, wrong play. I can never remember.... How about Bottom?"

"That is quite enough from you, young lady. It's a modern production and I shall be playing Oberon. At least it isn't *The Tempest*, actually. I'd think twice about that because every time I heard the name 'Miranda' I might give an inadvertent twitch."

"Who's Titania?"

"I don't know yet. *Not* Miss Dean."

"I shall come to your first night. If I can get tickets. Do you have anything else lined up?"

"I will put you on the actual guest list. And yes, I do: we will be shooting something called *Melmoth the Wanderer* on location in North Wales later in the year. So I shall be back in Blighty for most of next year which is all well and good." He gave her a considering look which she could not quite interpret. "I've had enough of LA for the time being and I do like a ripe old Gothic. It's the cinematic equivalent of one of those French cheeses that's capable of emptying entire trains."

"If it's going to be a historical Gothic, you might *have* to grow an enormous beard," Serena said.

"I'm certainly going to insist on a false nose."

Later, back at her own studio, Serena cast a critical eye over the clothes that she was planning to use for the little show at Caro's Apple Day. She had picked out dresses that were inspired by the natural world: Nell's unwitting comment about the Behenian stars had stuck. Seafoam and moss agate, bright leaves and trails of anemones, stranded with rosaries of semi-precious stones. The herbs would be given to the models when they arrived, to stay fresh: Caro had promised her the run of the garden. The girls were all local, friends of Laura's. If they weren't all tall and willowy, that didn't matter, Serena thought. She'd put together a range of sizes and lengths.

She went to the window and looked up, into a thin green sky. She was conscious of a sense of anticipation. The comet was coming soon.

STELLA

From the house, Stella watched her sisters bagging apples in the garden. Foreshortened, their figures looked oddly similar. Sam was elsewhere; he'd morphed, fairly seamlessly, into a kind of handyman figure: not, God forbid, a forelock tugging subservience, but a kind of extra brother. Like Dark, Stella thought. They could all do with extra brothers. In Stella's head, Sam had become a sort of counterweight to Tam Stare, as though the universe was sending them pairs. Sam and Tam, like flowerpot men.

Wincing, Stella went down the stairs and out into the yard. She found Sam himself cleaning tools in a shed, whistling faintly.

"I was going to take that stuff to the recycling. The co-op takes metal, they told me. Do you want anything in town?"

"We're nearly out of milk."

"I'll swing by the shop."

Together, they loaded the detritus which had accumulated in the shed: old radios, PC cables, a defunct television. Things that you mark for disposal but which somehow never go away unless a determined effort is made. Stella was not sure what the co-operative did with them, but the important thing was that they were put to good use and did not come back again. She slammed the Landrover door shut and took off down the drive, grinding through mud and cow slurry. It felt rugged, driving the Landrover; Stella liked it. It was higher than a normal car, too. You could see over the bare hedges, down the long slopes of fields made vivid by sudden sunlight. A shaft of watery light caught the tower at the summit of the Tor and turned it to gold. A fairy-tale tower; what it needed now was a princess.

But Stella needed to concentrate on the winding lane ahead of her. There was a person in the road; as the Landrover barrelled towards them, they stepped back into the hedge. It was, Stella saw, Dana Stare. *Shit! Pretend you haven't seen her! She might want a lift!* And indeed, it felt for a moment that smoky tentacles of intent were reaching out from Dana, whose white smiling face she glimpsed for a second as she sped by. *Wanting me to pick her up. Well, I won't.* Feeling childishly relieved at having got away, Stella glanced into the rear view mirror and saw

135

something long and dark slinking into the hawthorn. Either Dana had walked away very quickly indeed, or – Stella gave her head a little shake. She wouldn't put it past Dana to keep polecats, or weasels. Something a bit sleek and vicious, anyway. The tower at the top of the Tor was no longer bright. Stella pulled into the normality of Tesco's car park with some gratitude.

That evening, after a sharp shower of rain, Stella walked to the churchyard to see Abraham. The drain had overflowed, sending a rivulet of water down the lane and transforming it into a little stream. Her grandfather was sparkling about the point of his tomb.

"I thought we'd have too much cloud," Stella said, by way of greeting.

"You're in luck. It's blown through. It'll come in the east."

Stella felt again that prickle of Christmas-night anticipation. "Too early yet, though?"

"A little. But Venus is up." Stella looked over to the indigo ridge of the low western hills and saw a single bright star, hanging beneath the moon. She laughed. "They've all come out in their finery, to greet him."

"They have."

"Abraham, do you know a family called Stare?"

"There was a man of that name near Priddy. A cowman, if I remember rightly. Not a nice man. Not much to say, and violent. His wife always looked afraid."

"Charming."

"He must be long dead now, though – this was years ago when I was a boy. During the war. Why?"

"There's a brother and sister called Stare hanging around the Amberleys. I don't like them."

"Caro has – resources. I wouldn't worry too much."

Stella leaned back against a gravestone. "You're probably right." The evening was deepening.

"Look over your shoulder," Abraham said.

She did as he told her. "Oh!" There was again that smudge on the eastern sky, that cosmic thumbprint. It looked unreal.

I'll come when the comet comes.

"It'll be here for a while, as I told you the other day," her grandfather said.

"For Apple Day."

The wet chill was growing, too, creeping into Stella's bones even through the borrowed Barbour. She said goodbye to her grandfather and went down the church path, between the gravestones, suddenly remembering that this was the lych path, the corpse path by which coffins were carried. And as she thought that, she saw a light in the church itself, through the porch.

The church wasn't even supposed to be open. Normally, due to its age and famous decoration, it was kept locked. A warden, maybe, someone seeing to the flowers? Or the vicar? Stella stepped cautiously forwards. The light was bobbing about, like a will o' the wisp. She didn't like the prospect of going into the church, but her curiosity was impelling her forwards. She should have brought a golf club. Or a fucking shotgun. Surely that ancient horned thing couldn't manifest on consecrated ground? You never bloody knew, Stella thought.

Once inside the porch, she hesitated. The light was still there, moving about, but she couldn't hear anything. The door creaked as she pushed it. The light, a pale yellow ball, was dancing above the altar and as Stella stepped into the church, it changed. The ice plain rolled out before her, the black sky seeded with stars. Her foot slipped on a patch of snow.

"Stella!"

She turned. Alys crouched in a leafless tangle of alder, which stood in a bank of ice. A frozen river ran beside it, its spiralling coils silent and still.

"Mum?" Stella quavered. But it wasn't, not quite. Alys' red locks were bound with wool and silver, hung with bone. Woad-blue bands decorated her wrists. She wore layer of skins. Her face, peering out of the bare branches, was a white curve like a skull.

"Mum? What are you doing there? Where are we?"

Alys grimaced. "I got stuck, Stella!"

"For fuck's sake!"

"You'll have to get me out. I can't – I had to change to get here, you see."

"How?" Stella had been speaking of rescue, not the mechanics of the trap, but she could feel the land pulling at her, trying to suck her in – "Stella, go! Now!" She could see the alarm in Alys' half-familiar face. "It'll take you, too!"

Stella tried to step back, but the land tugged at her, she could feel cold webs about her. Alys did not seem able to move from the tree. Then Stella was surrounded by a cascade of blue sparks. The little lights pulled her away, out of the silent freeze of the land, and into the peace of Hornmoon church. Ornamental texts flowed about the walls and a single night light flickered on the stand for prayer candles as her grandfather faded, over and out.

I'll come when the comet comes.

And so, it seemed, she had.

SERENA

Serena went to bed early. She dreaded waking in the small hours, re-running thoughts of her life with Ben like an old black and white movie, jerky and flickering. But she did not like the idea of taking sleeping pills: they sent her too far under, drowning deep, so that she swam to wakefulness through the consistency of an old London fog. She set the pill box firmly aside and relied on hot milk instead, like an invalid child.

Far into the night, however, she did wake up, startled to find that she'd slept. Something had woken her. The nightlight, beside her bed, flickered, casting long shadows across the familiar comfort of the room. Serena, muzzy, investigated it section by section: nothing was different. She got out of bed, picked up a wrap and went onto the landing. Bella's door stood ajar. Serena, fearing horrors, peeped inside and saw her daughter's still, huddled form. Serena held her breath for a second and Bella sighed and stirred. Nothing to see there. Relieved, Serena padded down the stairs into the hall, feeling as though she was out of place. The front door was covered at night by a heavy satin curtain, partly for effect and partly to keep out draughts, but the shell-shaped fanlight above it suddenly blazed with light as the motion sensor came on. Someone was out there. Probably a prowling cat, Serena told herself firmly. Get a grip. She pulled the curtain aside and looked through the spyhole.

Ben was standing on the step. He stood facing away from her, head bowed, but she would have known his figure anywhere. Hands trembling, she unbolted the door and dragged it open, expecting to find him gone, but he was still there.

"Ben?" she whispered. "Oh God…"

He turned. His face was white in the harsh illumination of the motion sensor and in it his mouth formed a black 'o.' He was speaking, but she could not hear what he said. His eyes looked like river water. She faltered his name, but he did not move, did not reach out a hand or take a step forward. It occurred to her that he did not even know she was there, that he had appeared as a fetch, a shadow on the face of the city, and could not see her at all. Then he was going, moving fast and sailing up like a blown leaf above the knobbly branches of the plane trees, gone against the night. The motion sensor light clicked off, decisively, and Serena sank down into a cold huddle on the step, alone.

Stella did not say: you imagined it. Or, you really ought to move on. Or any of those things. Instead, her voice a little echoing on the other end of the phone in the hall in Mooncote, she said, "I think there's a train at quarter to ten. Sam can run me to the station. I can be in London by noon."

STELLA

Resting her head against the glass, Stella watched the green world whip by with mixed feelings. Back in the Smoke. She might as well be a milkmaid with straw in her hair for all the awkwardness she was feeling – not for the situation, or Serena, but for her relationship with London. It occurred to her that this had been the One. Mr Big. Not a man, at all, or a girl, but a city, ever since she'd started going up to town in her early teens, hanging out in Camden and the clubs, much too young. Didn't seem to have done her a lot of harm, though, and Alys had sanctioned it, in a vague sort of way. The memory of her mother, deerskin dressed, in the alder tree was still with her, like a haunt. She didn't know quite what she was going to tell Serena, but would face that once the Ben thing was out of the way.

She had shared the vision with Bee and Luna and Sam.

"We should go to the church," Bee said. "You go up to town and sort out Serena. Bring her back here if you have to."

"Divide and conquer," Sam said. "As long as someone stays here, your mum said." Luna had, uncharacteristically, reached out and touched her sister's hand.

"Don't worry. We'll find Mum, if she's there to be found. I've seen her once already. We'll find her."

Didcot Parkway, Reading. The Dickensian backs of houses, the distant column of a mosque. Then the train was grinding into Paddington. Stella felt her heart lift. It had been a good thing to go back home and she would return there soon, but it was great to be back in the wicked city. *Young woman, sadder but wiser, returns to the purity of the rural world and is healed by the power of nature* was not going to be Stella's story. Not quite. Clubs and pubs and the swarming streets could not be abandoned for long.

She caught a bus, not the Tube; she did not feel ready to venture into the maw of the underground just yet. She wanted to see. The bus, up top, allowed her to reconnect, first with the babel of streets around the station and then the pale quietness of west London's Georgian facades. Serena lived in one of these lighthouse houses. It was starting to rain when Stella got off the bus; she slipped through the

141

monochrome streets quickly, until she reached her sister's front door.

Serena looked a bit wan and freaked out, but not quite a wreck. Her hair was still damp, curling a little at the ends.

"Showering!" said Stella. "That's good."

Serena pulled a face. "At least I no longer stink. Do you want some tea?"

"Tea is always good."

She waited until they were seated at the scrubbed oak table, in Serena's blue and white kitchen with its view up into the garden, before she began to broach obvious subjects.

"How do you actually know he's dead?"

"I just – really felt it."

"But no one's actually rung you up and told you he's dropped off his perch? I googled him on the train. There's nothing in the news. Okay, he's not exactly a household name but he's not no one, either. If he'd been found dead, it would have hit the papers. Look at poor what'shername Geldof. That was all over the tabloids for days."

"*If* he'd been found."

"And he's not – then what, being eaten by cats?"

Serena actually laughed, though it sounded more like choking. "I don't think Bast and Bertie would have started on him just yet." Those being Ben's cats, Stella recalled.

"A mate of mine had a friend in the police in Bristol – he said cats always eat you. Dogs never do."

"Nice."

"You have rung him up, I suppose? Ben, I mean."

"Yes. Twice. But if he's not dead, I don't want to come across as a bunny boiler."

Stella had to admit that she had a point.

"At the moment, and please understand that in no way am I blaming you, because there is so much weird shit going on at the moment that I would not be surprised if Ben suddenly had the ability to project himself out of his body and astrally visit you… *at* the moment, we don't actually know if he's dead or not. And there's no evidence that he is. So I think we, or probably better I, should go and find out."

Serena, fingers wrapped around her mug, was silent for a minute. Then she said, "Okay. Yes. But I don't think it would be a good idea for me to go."

"I don't think it would be a good idea for you to go, either. *I'll* go." Stella took a final bite of her cracker and stood up. "In fact, I'll go now."

This time, because of speed, she did take the Tube, heading across town from Notting Hill Gate, up on the Northern Line to Camden. Coming out of Camden tube station was a blast from the past: it hadn't changed much, but then, Stella reminded herself, it wasn't all that long since she'd been there. It just felt like a long time. She was tempted to nip into the World's End for a quick restorative white wine, but that could wait. She was on a mission. She avoided a puddle of dried vomit and hurried on.

Ben lived some distance south of the market, above a shop that was now, inevitably, selling cheap leather goods and trying hard to differentiate itself from its competitors by a sequence of peculiar, attenuated mannequins in the window, all with shocks of neon hair and gaping open mouths. They looked like cartoons, Stella thought. She pressed the bell on the door which led to Ben's flat, not really expecting any significant response, but there was an immediate clatter of feet on the stairs. Then the door was flung open and Ben appeared in the gap, in a designer sweatshirt and a pair of jeans that Stella immediately recognised as expensive. He smelled expensive, as well, and he'd had a haircut, which suited him. Not dead, then. In fact, large as life and twice as natural.

He was also apparently delighted to see her.

"You're here! Great!"

Then his face fell.

"Sorry," Stella said, cheerfully, not sorry at all. "I'm not who you were expecting, am I?"

"It's not that I'm not – er, well, not really. You're not wearing a brown and orange uniform, for a start."

"Aha," said Stella. "That well known pastime of 'waiting in for the courier'?"

"They're supposed to be delivering some flyers. The tracking said 'morning'."

Stella was genuinely sympathetic. It was now close to three. "What bollocks!"

"It's like bloody dominoes. I've got to go down to Chalk Farm and see someone before *he* has to go out – look, I mean…" He stopped.

"What you mean is, would I stay in while you pop out? Yes, sure. I was only passing. I'm not in a rush."

She was caught halfway between amusement and outrage, and trying to keep it from her face. So, you dump a girl's sister, then when the latter turns up at your house you immediately enlist her to house-sit for your courier? Fuck *off!* Thought Stella, but – *mission, sister, would be a cunning ruse to get her into the place where she could snoop about...* "Not a problem," Stella breezed.

Ben shot her a grateful smile as she made her way past him up the narrow, creaking stairs.

"Thanks, Stel. It's good we can – you know." Stella, not entirely willing to let him off the hook even for strategy reasons, gave him a bright enquiring smile. "Thing is, Serena and I – we'd run out of road and we both knew it. We both had other people. Sometimes it just stops working. But it doesn't mean that we have to let all connection drop." His brow was furrowed with sincerity, the bastard.

"Sure, I know how it is," Stella said, thinking: *does Serena know this?* Stella was willing to bet that she didn't. "She told you about this other bloke, then?"

For the first time, Ben looked a little bemused. Stella had the unnerving impression that a mask had closed over his face. "Yes, she – she must have done, mustn't she?" Then his face smoothed over. "Of course." He gestured towards the sofa. "Make yourself at home. I won't be long. But they're bound to come when I'm out – I really appreciate this. There's tea in the kitchen. I think there's some wine in the fridge. Help yourself. I've fed the cats."

"Thanks!" Stella said. "Might see you a bit later, then."

She waited until the door shut behind him, then ran to the window. There went Ben, perfectly alive and as normal as he'd ever seemed. But he wasn't. The not-quite-remembering dumping Serena episode had rattled her: he hadn't even looked like himself for a moment. She watched him out of sight and turned back to the flat. No changes here – it was lined with books and vinyl, retro rock posters, carefully and professionally framed. Bohemian, but too tidy really to be a musician's flat. And it was big, too. Either family money or the band was doing well enough to pay actual money; she supposed it was possible. They weren't Coldplay or Mumford and Sons, but they did have a name. Maybe Richard Amberley had coughed up for his son and heir. Lucky

Ben, if so. Stella herself had never been able to afford a London flat. The occasional room in a house share, yes: out on the fringes. Hounslow had been particularly grim, Catford not so bad. Now, when she came to town, she stayed with Serena and took care to give her something for it, which Serena tried to refuse. But Stella wouldn't budge: it wasn't anywhere near the cost of real rent, but at least she could hold her head up.

Thoughtfully she went into the galley kitchen, where Ben's Siameses sat on a windowsill apiece, looking out. Stella liked cats and tried to make friends, but both proved immune to fuss. She sighed. Wine, you say? She opened the fridge and found a half bottle of Pinot, some of which she decanted into a glass. Might as well enjoy herself while she was in residence, although she'd stop at one, just in case Dana turned up: Stella was willing to bet that she had the keys to the flat and she didn't like the idea of losing her edge in front of the other young woman. *Keep your wits about you, my girl.* But Dana was back in Somerset, or had been yesterday: yet she seemed to be in all manner of places at once, and Stella could not quite shake the memory of that long dark thing slinking into the hedge. Thoughtfully, holding her glass of wine by the bowl, Stella went upstairs.

Nothing like nosing about in other people's bathroom cabinets. Ben's had a minimum of masculine product and a large quantity of very girly, very expensive cosmetics and hair stuff. Bingo, thought Stella, unless Ben had decided to explore his female side. It was neatly arranged in the cabinet itself, not down on the floor in a sponge bag; it looked as though it belonged. She didn't want to poke about too extensively, because Dana struck her as the sort who might lay little traps. She closed the cabinet door with care and went back out onto the landing. She found herself balking slightly at the prospect of investigating the bedroom, but her sister's relationship was at stake, Stella told herself. Besides, the door was partly open. She looked through, noting a fairly ordinary décor, no visible sex aids, thank God, and a couple of rather spiffy frocks hanging up on the wardrobe door.

And the thing hanging from the sash window. Which was a – *what?* Stella frowned. A highly unattractive piece of found art? A bird's nest? She stepped into the bedroom for a closer look. It was a fist-sized tangle of stuff – twigs, thorns, small bones. It reminded her of a really big owl pellet and it stank of sour milk. It was tied up with red thread and dangled temptingly from the sash – all she would have to do would be to reach out and take hold and – *oh no you don't,* Stella said out loud. Then the doorbell shrilled, making her jump. What if it had conjured Dana up? – because she was sure she knew the architect of the thing. She ran down to the kitchen window, which overlooked the narrow street, and saw a brown and orange van and a man with a clipboard.

Ben's prediction had been right. Stella opened the door, scrawled a signature with the electronic pen, and hauled a surprisingly large box that felt from its shifting weight as though it contained papers, back up the stairs. Her task complete, Stella swigged the rest of the wine, washed and replaced the glass and went back down to the front door, where she hesitated. No, don't leave a note. Somehow she did not think Ben would be telling Dana about her visit and she wasn't sure that she wanted Dana to know.

Besides, she felt that something else might well be relaying that information. After some thought, she went back up to the kitchen and rummaged about in the cupboards – surprisingly well stocked for a newly single bloke, like the fridge, but Ben always had been a bit of a foodie and perhaps she was being sexist. She found a half-empty packet of table salt and took it up to the bathroom, where she decanted a quantity of the salt into a toothbrush glass, then filled it with water. Watching the little swirling grains of salt dissolve, Stella kept one ear out for the betraying signs of the front door opening. She felt jumpy and twitchy, rabbit-wild, but she was damned if she was just going to slip away without doing *something.* When the water was cloudy white, she went into the bedroom and flicked it over the thing hanging up in the window, whispering all the prayers she could remember and a Buddhist mantra she'd once learned from a yoga teacher for good measure. Just in case; you never knew. Then she plucked a tissue from the neat box beside the bed, ducked it into the glass and ran the wet paper along the sill and up the sides of the window, as far as she could reach.

Just thought I'd do a spot of cleaning, while I was waiting.

She stared hard at the mass of twigs, half-hoping it would shrivel. It did not, but a moment later, following a draft she could not feel, it twisted once on its string and then unravelled back again to rest. It startled Stella, but she felt that, somehow, this might do. For now. Downstairs, something shrieked and Stella nearly jumped out of her skin before remembering the cats. Heart hammering, she ran lightly down the stairs and out, not looking back.

By the time she reached the Tube it was almost dark, a murky blue twilight descending onto the city. She didn't feel quite ready to go back to her sister's just yet; a reconnection with London beckoned now she was here. She caught the Tube down to Bank and walked along the river to London Bridge, enjoying the cold Thames-side air and the lights of the city. The enormous splinter of the Shard loomed over the south bank, dominating the skyline. She looked back once, over her shoulder, but the smudge of the comet was not visible against the brightness of the lights; you might stand a better chance of seeing it from Hampstead or somewhere high. The river slapped against its confining wall and Stella thought of Alys, alder-chained. She felt torn between peculiar responsibilities, but Luna and Bee had shouldered some of the burden. They were going down to the church this evening, to see what might be seen. Stella wondered how they'd get on. In the meantime, she needed to cheer Serena up. Get her out of the house – Bella would be fine for a couple of hours – take her to a gastropub. Get her drunk and get her to have a good cry – time honoured, although it wasn't really controlled Serena's way of doing things.

When she got back to the house, Serena took so long to answer the door that Stella began to wonder if she had gone out. Or – *God, come on, Serena.*

"Sorry," her sister said, when she finally appeared. "I was upstairs." Her anxious face sharpened. "Did you –?"

"He's fine," Stella said, coming into the hall and depositing the bottles she had purchased en route. "Not dead, not catfood. I saw him, we talked a bit, and I'll tell you everything over dinner."

"Thank God." Serena pointed to the ceiling. "Come and look at this."

Stella thought she was referring to a piece of work, but Serena led her all the way up the stairs to the loft conversion, used as a spare room, and the French windows that led onto the roof terrace. From here, one could see out across Portobello, but Serena pointed east, downriver.

"It's our comet!" A smudge was visible, in the direction of Canary Wharf.

BEE

Bee was enjoying Luna's presence in the house. Of them all, Luna had been the one about whom she worried most: Serena was successful, Stella was flighty but, like a swallow, always came homing back again. Yet Bee had always feared that Luna, fuelled by some inner discontent, would go away and never come back. But here she was, with Sam and a baby on the way, and showing no signs of going anywhere. Having a child changes you, Serena had said, you become more fearful and, perhaps, less angry with the world, more protective. Certainly Luna showed fewer signs of her earlier anger now: she wasn't exactly inhabiting a Madonna-like calm, but she was more cheerful, less restless. She had always been practical and now that quality was coming to the fore.

She was being practical now, as they sat around the kitchen table with a map. Stella was still in London, but no one felt they could wait. The accounts of Alys, first on Dartmoor and then in the church, had alarmed Bee. Usually cautious, she felt they should act, now the comet was here. So they were studying the map. Dark thought they should go via the watercourse, that there would be a way in.

"Streams have memories. And wells. They're ancient enough for those memories to linger, even if they've changed."

"What about the lych path?" Sam asked. Bee saw his eyes meet those of the ghost, an understanding pass between them.

"It's too risky," Dark said, and Sam nodded. Bee did not know what they meant, but Luna said.

"What about Grandpa?"

Bee hoped to speak to her grandfather, that Abraham might be able to advise. Sam wanted to come, but Luna persuaded him to stay behind and hold the fort. "Women's work, Sam. Your gran would tell you the same." After a moment, he nodded.

"All right. Is Dark going with you?"

"Hard to tell," Luna said.

They pulled on wellingtons and waterproofs, with thick sweaters underneath. "After all," Luna said, "It's not where we are, but where we might be going, isn't it?"

148

The stream which ran past the church was the same one that flanked the orchard, rushy and shallow. Feeling a little foolish, they stepped into it; Bee half expected the world to change, but it did not. A yellow smear in the west showed the passage of the sinking sun. Apple branches grew low over the water; they had to duck and weave, and the stream breathed out coldness. Bee thought she glimpsed a white cuff through the last of the leaves – Dark, walking alongside. But he did not answer when she spoke his name.

Within a few minutes they were beyond the boundaries of the property and following the road.

"What," Luna said, "will we say if anyone asks us what we're doing?"

"We shall say that we are looking for toads. Helping them cross the road. Do you remember doing that, when we were kids?"

"Let's hope no one sees us."

They had to leave the stream to negotiate a low bridge, and found themselves along the edge of a field. Long grass brushed their knees. It was by now almost dark; Bee had brought a torch, but did not want to attract attention. However, she could see the church tower looming shadowy through the twilight. The stream ran through a small iron gate and down the side of the graveyard; they opened it carefully and were soon among the ancient, lichened graves.

"Nothing seems different," Luna whispered.

"No." She was unsure whether she was disappointed or not. What had she been expecting? The world to turn sideways, alchemical transformation? She stepped soggily out of the stream and onto the grass. A bedraggled wreath of chrysanthemums lay at her feet.

Luna whispered, "*Look.*"

The air was damp and cool, but the stream was curdling, congealing into ice, and a moment later was hard enough to skate upon. Nothing else changed.

Together, bypassing the church, they went in search of Abraham's grave. The pyramid stood silently in the icy grass, but no blue light flickered around it.

"Granddad?"

"Abraham?"

The whispered words hissed in the cold air.

"He's not there." Dark was standing by the tomb, visible in an eye blink. Bee felt warmed by relief.

"Do you know where he is, Dark?" Luna asked.

"No."

"Can I ask – sorry, this is probably really rude. But when you're not – here, where are you?"

"Sometimes I'm in the past. My own day. But not quite as I was. And sometimes – somewhere else. We can't talk about that."

"Can't or won't?" Luna's voice was sharp. Bee knew that tone: heading fast towards confrontation. But Dark did not seem to mind.

"Cannot. There are gardens before death. I am allowed to speak of those gardens – my past, the hinterlands. But not about what lies beyond." He smiled. "Ultima Thule. The land beyond ocean."

Bee knew this; they'd had similar conversations. "It's why, Luna, when people go to séances, they can't come up with anything really interesting or useful."

Luna thought about this for a moment, then nodded. "I get that. They can tell you where your missing earring went to, but not why we have to suffer, or what the afterlife's like."

Dark gave her an approving glance. "You are quick. There's a tie on my tongue. Placed there by angels, you might say. A scold's bridle."

"And these 'hinterlands'. What are they?"

"Like other worlds," Bee said. "Smaller worlds. Parallel universes."

"Like the one Mum's in."

"Maybe." She walked around the tomb and peered over the wall. The stream had now completely frozen in its course, curdled with ice. Hard enough to walk upon? Perhaps. "In any case," Bee said aloud, "all you'd get would be a wet foot." And they had boots on.

They set off down the stream, having tentatively tested it first. But their boots rang iron-hard; it was like walking along a road. They followed it along the wall of the churchyard and as they walked, the thorn trees which also followed the stream's path began to glitter and ring with frost. Above the churchyard the tower of the church, solid and squat, shone in the moonlight. Bee could see stars now, and they were not stars she knew. She swallowed hard and glanced at Dark, but he was walking fast, head down, and he wore some kind of hood, now, which masked his hawk's face. Did ghosts feel the cold? She had always assumed that they did not, but maybe that was wrong. It seemed wrong, too, to ask. When they reached the end of the churchyard wall,

Bee looked back but the church was gone. She was not surprised but she reached out in the quiet darkness and took her sister's hand, and Dark's. She met no resistance. Luna's mittened fingers clung to hers. Dark's hand was warm and living. No one spoke. They walked on, following the ice.

SERENA

They had watched the comet and drunk too much wine, but Serena still thought that this had been a good idea, even when she woke in the middle of the night with a mouth that felt as though it had been stuffed with sawdust. She groped on the bedside table for a glass of water and swigged it back. Water tasted so good in the midnight dark that she wondered why people didn't drink it all the time. But somehow it was flat and unexciting in the middle of the afternoon, filtered through the bladders of thousands of Londoners, even if one used a jug. She didn't buy bottled water, being worried about plastic. Sighing, her mouth refreshed, she lay back into the plump embrace of the duvet and thought about the evening's conversation.

Ben had a woman there, Stella said. She had not wanted to tell Serena, flinched from it, but Stella could not easily lie to her sister. She had been a bit proud of her devious behaviour and Serena was grateful: it had put Stella in a difficult position, after all. And there was a tiny glimmer of hope, too. Ben had seemed 'off,' Stella said. Something wasn't right. He'd told Stella that Serena had another man but this was news to Serena: you couldn't count Ward and a drink in a pub, and the oddness had started before Ward had come back, like a comet, into her planetary orbit. She was big on loyalty and it would have really stung, except – *there's something wrong*, Stella had said. She was keeping things back and Serena knew this, and she knew that Stella knew that she knew… It was like spies. Stella would tell her eventually but what it meant was that Stella was up to something and it had not yet come to fruition. She had always had a tendency to secretiveness, not due to an innately conniving nature so much as a reluctance to worry people about things before they were fully sorted. Serena had faith in her sister; whatever Stella was up to, it would be for her sister's benefit.

The trouble was, Stella sometimes thought she knew best, but didn't.

Thoughts went around and around, a carousel screwing itself into the floor of the fairground field. Serena had long had an issue with insomnia: it was an old friend and normally she would have dealt with it by getting up, making tea, sketching, sewing, surfing the internet. Now, she felt nailed to the bed, sluggish and reluctant to move.

The trouble with you, she thought blearily, *is that you're still pissed.*

This was almost a cheering thought. She hadn't spent so much of her twenties partying without knowing how to deal with that and it was a simple enough fix: drink more water. She half-sat and reached again for the glass. But the glass was not there. Her fingers met something brittle and twisting, prickling like a spider's legs. It moved. Serena gave a yelp and jerked her hand back, fumbling for the light pull above the bed. Don't turn on the bedside lamp, it's on the other side, that thing is there, can't be that drunk if you can – she found the carved bead of the light pull and yanked it. The bedroom flooded with glow. Something fell off the bedside table and scuttled, oh God, oh fuck, under the damn bed.

"Stella!" Serena yelled. "Stella, get in here! Help!" Then she thought: *you idiot. You've just summoned your sister into danger.* Maybe Stella hadn't heard? But there was the sound of running feet, skidding on the parquet floor, and Stella, clad in old yoga pants and a t-shirt that read 'Trollop', was bursting wild-eyed into the room.

"There's something under the BED."

"Jesus!"

Stella took a flying leap and landed amid the billowing folds of the duvet.

"What is it?"

"I don't know! It was like a massive spider!"

"Holy, holy, holy crap," Stella said. She rolled over and peered over the edge of the bed.

"Don't *look!*"

"We've got to know! If it attaches itself to my face like that thing in *Alien,* you'll just have to prise it off."

"I'm not doing that!"

"You'll bloody have to."

Serena grabbed Stella by the ankles and her sister swung down to take a quick look under the bed. She felt Stella stiffen, then her sister said, very quietly,

"Aha."

"What does *that* mean?"

"Right. There was something this afternoon, something that happened at Ben's, that I didn't tell you about."

"I knew it!"

"Have you got a lighter?"

"Yes. What are you going to do?"

"Give me the lighter," Stella said. She snatched it from her bewildered sister's hand and wriggled onto the floor and under the bed.

"Stella! Be careful! What are you doing?"

"I'm sick of this shit!" Stella shouted, muffled by the bed. There was a click and then the smell of burning.

"Don't set the house on fire!"

"Wait there. Don't look," Stella commanded. In a flurry she was on her feet and out of the door.

"Where are you going?"

"Going to get something!"

Silence, then footsteps coming back up the stairs. Stella had returned, carrying an umbrella.

"What —"

"Normally," her sister remarked, "In these situations, I find that I prefer a golf club." She threw herself flat on the parquet boards and hoicked about beneath the bed with the handle of the umbrella. She pulled out a smouldering bundle of twigs, which she beat energetically into ashes, leaving a stain on the pale wood.

"What the hell was that," Serena said.

"Right." Stella sat back on her heels, tapping the umbrella against the floor. "You know that thing I didn't tell you about?"

Some time later, they sat around the kitchen table, drinking mugs of tea. Serena had considered opening another bottle of wine but they decided that clearer heads might be called for.

"After all," Stella said, "We don't know if there might be something on its heels."

"And you found this thing hanging in Ben's bedroom window?" Serena said. She was conscious of a hollow sense of dismay. "Are you sure it's the same thing?"

"I don't know, I didn't get a good enough look. I salted that one at your — at Ben's. Fire and running water for this." They had scooped up the ashes and dumped them in a bathroom sink, leaving the tap on. Its distant trickle could be heard moving through the pipes. "It's some sort of bad charm. I'm sure it's Dana."

"But you don't actually know?"

"No," Stella admitted. "Maybe I've misjudged her." But from the look on her face, she did not think so, and neither did Serena.

"We've got to do something about Ben," she went on. "I don't think he's in his right mind. I think that girl's done something to him."

"I need to be cool about it," Serena muttered.

"Why? Because you don't want to be the mad stalker ex, I get that. But if Dana Stare has done something to Ben, we need to know. We need to rescue him. And we need to find a way of doing that without involving you directly."

"Ward's come back from the States." She didn't know why she had suddenly said this, but it was too late.

Stella stared at her. "Bee said. And?"

"And what? We're still friends."

"Hmm," said Stella. "This could be really useful."

"How?"

"Think about it. Ben dumps you, even if he's now bloody gaslighting you in absentia by telling people it was mutual."

"I'm not sure that's gaslighting. I think it's just plain old lying."

"Well, whatever. Anyway. Ben dumps you, and you? Do you go all *Fatal Attraction* and boil his bunny? No, you do not. You sail serenely on, Serena Swan, and with great grace take up with a man whom half of England, if not the world, would like to shag and who is, moreover, Ben's cousin. What is that going to do to Ben when he finds out?"

"But we're not. Shagging, that is."

"La la la, didn't hear that, doesn't matter. What matters is what people think. Do you think Ward would mind if people thought you were an item?"

Serena considered this.

"He might, actually. I don't know that he's actually that keen to rekindle things, although… Well, he has been calling me quite a bit, in fact. He's on the rebound from Miranda."

"Again? That's not a rebound, it's a yoyo."

"But he probably wouldn't mind that much if people thought we were sleeping together." Serena was aware she was blushing. "He always quite liked showing me off, I think. Even if I do look a bit like a horse."

"You do *not* – well, never mind that now. This is very useful. We need a plan."

"But, look – I don't want Ben to think I'm serious about someone else. I really like Ward, but... Loyalty means a lot to me, Stella. I don't like playing around. It feels wrong."

"As long as you're honest with people, though?"

Serena forced a smile. "I know there's this thing, that Fallow women are supposed not to get attached. But I do, you see. I know it's different for you."

Stella pointed to her own bosom, on which the word 'Trollop' was proudly displayed. "To be honest, Serena, I'm not sure it's in me to stick to one person. Male or female. I was with Mel for what, nearly two years, and if anyone could have made it work, she could have, but we were a bit young. It's just how it is, how I am, and I'm not going to apologise for it. But everyone's different. I haven't noticed Bee or Luna exactly slutting about, you know."

"Bee's going out with a ghost, though."

"Yes. That is a bit different. But Mum never stuck to one bloke. Told me once that she just couldn't do it."

"I did wonder, when she disappeared –" Serena stopped.

"What, that she'd run off with Mr Right Now?"

"Actually, that she might have been strangled by Mr Wrong and ended up in a shallow grave. God knows it happens."

"Yes, it does," Stella said. She spread her hands on the kitchen table and looked down at them. "But it doesn't look like that's what happened here."

LUNA

Luna walked on, following the path of ice, with the life inside her. She was very conscious of a need to be careful, take extra caution, hole up in hibernation until the baby was safe. But combined with that was a kind of recklessness, too. For you never could be safe, could you? Whatever you did, whatever precautions you might take. Something could come and break you, snap you out of your body and the world and into somewhere new. She had always believed that there was somewhere beyond the material plane – how could you not, walking as she did beside a ghost? – and now she had additional evidence. How might it affect a baby inside you, breathing this different air, seeing those unknown stars? She remembered reading a story about a Welsh folktale, the belief that a dog with silver eyes could see the wind. Would her child be silver eyed, far-sighted? In this icy, monochrome country, with only the thorn brakes as shelter from the cold, anything seemed possible.

She stole a look at Dark and Bee. They walked side by side, heads down. Bee's hand clasped her own, firmly. She was glad they were there. The brakes were blackthorn: she could see its long iron spines sharp against the frost. If the tip of one of those thorns broke off under your skin, it would fester, but sloes were a purgative and Luna wondered if that was happening now: that the presence of the thorn trees somehow was a token of the time, of all the petty constraints and resentments against her family starting to be sloughed gently away to leave a clean clear space for the newcomer.

Luna stopped. Bee turned to her, a question in her face.

"She'll be my child's grandmother," Luna said aloud.

"She's already a grandmother," Bee said. Both of these remarks were wholly obvious and yet to Luna they carried the ring of a ritual exchange. She looked around her. There, on the rise of a small round hill, was a ring of frost-crowned stones and around that stood a crescent of thorn. As Luna watched, her mother's crouching figure shimmered into view. Her hair was blood-red against the white and the black, and her bound wrists extended in front of her, snared and tied into the blackthorn by a mass of twigs.

157

"Mum!" Luna cried. But Bee's hand was like an iron band gripping hers, and on the other side she saw Dark's shadowy fingers grasping Bee's other hand.

"Don't let go!" Bee hissed. And Luna did not. They stumbled up the slope towards Alys, who turned her head and stared at them blankly.

"Mum, can you see us?" Bee called and after a moment, Alys nodded. Her mouth worked.

"Told you...when the comet comes." Now Luna could see the sparkly smudge in this sky, too. They arrived at the blackthorn. Luna reached out and grabbed her mother's hand, but the mass of twigs writhed nettlestinging beneath the edge of her woollen mitten, setting her hand on fire. Her instinct was to jerk it back but somehow she found that she was holding her mother's fingers more tightly.

"Pull!" she shouted to Bee, as though it was a tug of war. "Pull!" Her eyes watered with pain. The touch of the twigs was like acid and there was a heart stopping lurch as she thought of her baby within. But Bee hauled on her other hand and Alys stood and stepped from the brake. Something moved out of the shadow of the kingstone, quick and long and dark, pouring down the hill. There were two of them and then more and then the stone itself shuddered and rose and its head turned and looked at them. Its gaze was a weight. Luna's knees buckled but she held on and pulled – and the air was filled with a sweet distant clanging at the church bells sounded. Overhead, the stars shivered as if heat had swept invisibly over them and then Orion, the winter hunter, was striding up the eastern sky with the comet burning at his shoulder. Luna's tingling hand was empty. The church tower reared above them, ringing in the hour.

STELLA

Stella and Serena were heading west. The dual carriageway was surprisingly and thankfully clear, all the way to the Podimore roundabout and the turn-off to Shepton Mallet. Stella had put her foot down, occasioning instances of her sister clutching the edge of the seat and squeaking; Serena was a more cautious driver and it was her car.

"At least," Stella said, as they shot past Stonehenge, "You don't get sick."

"Luna used to."

"*Bee* used to. But they grew out of it. I never did. Or seasick. Or airsick."

"It is a matter of your inner ear."

"I didn't mean it was a virtue," Stella said, overtaking an Audi which had not been competently driven ever since Andover. "Ha! Take that, asshole. This has a bit of poke, doesn't it?"

"Yes. I wasn't sure about a hybrid but it's surprisingly nippy."

The car conversation lasted until the Shaftesbury turn. They were staying away from the subject of Ben. Between them, they had come up with a number of plans, but chosen none and then all of those plans had been blasted out of the water when Serena had phoned Caro Amberley and discovered that Ben was now definitely coming to the Apple Day.

"Is he playing?" Stella had mouthed, when it had become clear that this was the topic of conversation. Serena nodded. "And the band. In the evening."

It made sense, Stella thought sourly, that if you had a musician in the family, to make use of him. And they had known this was on the cards. Pity about the timing, though. "Does Caro *know* that you've split up from Ben?" she'd asked, when the call had ended.

"Yes, I think so, by now."

And Stella thought, but did not say, "I wonder if he'll be bringing Dana?"

Now they were heading west, into the sun, with a carload of dresses draped over the back seat in their protective plastic bags: Stella had not yet found a suitable environmentally sound alternative. The clocks had gone back by now and darkness was not far away. The sunset was fierce, a blazing gold, and Stella had to keep sitting up in the driver's seat to get the benefit of the windscreen shade. The whole countryside, the rolling downs of Wiltshire and the more compact landscape over the Somerset border, was suffused with light. It made Stella feel insubstantial. She loved light, the sun – Ibiza should have been the ideal place for her, really, and yet, and yet.

"Which do you prefer?" she said aloud, filling up the silence. "Light or dark?"

"I don't know, really," Serena said. "You know I like mornings. I'm a lark. Bee prefers it when the nights start drawing in. No idea about Luna. Mum liked the light."

"Yes, she loved India. Surprised she didn't go and live there, to be honest."

"She loved Ibiza, too," Stella said, nostalgic. "It's partly why I went – following in her footsteps. She loved Eivissa – she used to tell me stories about it when I was a kid. She said it was like a city made of light and when I got out there this bloke took me on a boat out into the harbour and it was exactly like that."

"It's not a city, though." Serena shaded her eyes, looking ahead. "But I know what you mean. I thought it was lovely, that time I came out, remember? And Mum always told all of us different stories."

Stella laughed. "Different fathers, different stories."

"She used to tell me stories about princesses. I thought the Behenian stars were princesses. I thought everyone had magical princesses in their house."

Stella, who had heard this story before, smiled. "I know you got into trouble in school over it."

"She and grandfather did say, don't tell a soul. I think I was too little to really get that. I was nearly packed off to the school shrink."

"'Too much imagination'."

"If only they knew."

"Do you think our characters were set, by the time we left school? I was thinking about this the other day. Getting into trouble in school, I mean, like you and your imagination. You daydreamed and cried. I was cheeky. Luna sulked and brooded and still holds grudges years later whereas I apparently took seventeen kinds of shit from Miss Pursage which I can't even remember. Bee – Bee never got into trouble, which is indicative in itself. And we're still all sort of doing that."

"I didn't always cry! I wasn't that much of a drip."

"No, but you mainly did, even if you hadn't actually done the deed."

"You might be right." Serena muttered. She stared out of the window. Then she said, after a pause, "I don't like to think of Mum – trapped."

"I know they saw her. I know they couldn't bring her back. Bee wouldn't say any more on the phone because Nell came in. We'll have to wait until we get there, which isn't going to be very long now."

"You know," Serena remarked, "Someone is going to have to say something to Nell before too long. What's the worst that can happen? She thinks we're all bonkers and goes to stay in a hotel."

"She's really nice," Stella said. "I don't want her put in any danger, that's the thing."

"I know. But – and this is only my personal opinion, mind – I think she's in more danger if she's kept in ignorance."

The familiar signs whizzed by. "Podimore!" Stella said. "Thank fuck. North, out of the sun." She swung the Toyota around the roundabout, putting the glare to her left, but it would not last for much longer, she thought. For some reason, she wanted to get in before dark. They followed the snake of the road towards Shepton, then off, along, down, across and then with a sense of mixed anticipation and relief, Stella saw the tower of Hornmoon church and the weathercock catching the light, a bird of gold.

"Good! Nearly home."

"I want a cup of tea," her sister said.

"I want a glass of wine."

She pulled into the drive and turned off the engine. Serena's car ran quietly, but the silence took her by surprise. Everything seemed in order: the tidy flower beds, the apples in their sacks, waiting to go to the cider farm or the small house press. Down in the paddock, Sam's piebalds grazed peaceably.

"We'll be able to see it clearly from here," Serena said. "The comet, I mean. No light pollution."

"When the comet comes," Stella echoed. "Well. It's here now and I saw it first from the churchyard, so there. Come on. Let's get all these frocks in the house before it gets too dark to see."

Luna and Sam came into the kitchen as they were sitting around the table, dissecting the journey. By tacit consent, Bee was waiting until they were all there before discussing recent events. Nell was over at the Amberley's. Luna had changed, was Stella's immediate thought. She looked older – pregnancy, presumably, and one wrist was bandaged.

"Oh no! What did you do – did you have a fall?"

"No." Luna looked her straight in the face. "It was Mum. We found Mum. But something attacked me and then the church bell rang and I couldn't –" Luna's amber eyes filled with tears "- I couldn't hold her."

"It wasn't her fault," Bee said quietly. "We would have pulled her out, I know we would, except something was holding onto her. You should see Luna's wrist. She was very brave. It looks like someone chucked acid over it."

"She'll bear the scars for a long time," Sam said.

"Jesus! When you say, something was holding onto Mum, what sort of 'something'?"

"It didn't look like anything, really. Just a bundle of twigs."

At this, both Stella and Serena sat up.

"Really? Just twigs, or other stuff, too?"

"Like what?"

"Wool, or moss?"

"I don't know," Luna said, slowly. "It was too dark to see. It was – that other place. The cold place. Like a winter kingdom."

"There were things there," Bee went on. "Animals – like polecats, and a standing stone that stood up and moved. I think it might have been the thing you and I saw, Stella."

"I saw a thing like a polecat when I was down here last," Stella said. "Sliding into the hedge. Where Dana Stare had been standing."

"What was Dana Stare doing in a hedge?"

"Like what was she doing at Amberley when Serena had just seen her in Covent Garden, you mean? We worked out the timing. She couldn't be in two places at once. Could she?"

"Apparently she was," Serena said. "Stella found something at Ben's place."

"You went to see Ben?"

"Yes, and he said he and Serena split up by mutual consent and everything was all hunky dory."

"Bastard!"

"Yes, but Luna, this is the thing. I'm the last person to give an arsehole a pass but I think he genuinely believed it. I think he's been got at."

"By Dana?" This from Sam.

"Yes."

"I have been asking around about the Stares," Sam said.

"And?"

"Not much. I told you someone said they weren't popular."

"What a surprise."

"But there are people who are travellers who know them. And they're not connected. You know, the travelling communities of this country – you might not like them, and there's a lot of bullshit around them – and from them – but they are communities and they're not very big ones, either. Even the New Age lot have got to know a lot of other groups over the years. There are real divisions in the culture. But people do talk. Yet there isn't much talk about the Stares. I'm going to speak to my gran but she doesn't do phones."

"Don't blame her," Stella said. "We could drive up and see her, maybe?"

"There's other ways of speaking to people," Sam said, after a moment.

Stella looked at him narrowly. "You don't mean pigeon post, do you?"

He laughed. "I don't mean the written word at all."

"We've got to try again," Serena said. "Maybe we could all go. Back to the churchyard, I mean. Take weapons."

For gentle Serena to suggest this was, Stella thought, a measure of her alarm.

"Like what? Kitchen knives? We've got a shotgun somewhere. In the attic, I think. Granddad had one. Do you suppose," Bee said, "that if you shot one of those polecat things, it would turn back into one of the Stares? Like those stories of witches who change into hares and get shot in the leg when nicking some farmer's lettuces like Peter Rabbit, and then there's an old lady rolling about on the ground clutching her knee?"

"I've always been against the fur trade but I wouldn't mind a fur hat, actually."

Serena gave a horrified laugh. "You can't turn Dana Stare into a hat!"

"Hey, just watch me."

BEE

Later that night, Bee again woke with a start. She'd been dreaming but the tail end of her dream whisked away, dissolving in the dawn. Beside her in the bed, the impression of Dark remained, but he himself was gone. She had grown used to loving a ghost: sometimes physical, as real and alive as one of her sisters, with at least the illusion of heartbeat and breath, sometimes as insubstantial as a moth. But there was no time to lie in bed and remember. Bee got up, padding across to the window and throwing the curtains open, eager to see what sort of day had started and hoping she would not see anything untoward in the yard.

It was still early, and the mist of last night had not yet faded. It hung around the lower branches of the apple trees, and wreathed the muted glow of the beech hedge along the drive. The hills were lost in shadow but there was a thin scarlet line along the eastern horizon, heralding the oncoming sun.

Perhaps, Bee thought, it might yet turn out to be a fine day. Wrapping herself in her thick dressing gown, she went downstairs to a chaos of cats, all demanding food. She doled out breakfasts, shutting the oldest cat with his special diet in the pantry while the rest yelled, milling about her feet. The kitchen, still warmed by the Aga, was a cradle of light against the morning dark and the breath of cold air when she opened the door. Bee made tea and sat down with a list.

Apple Day. Lots of things on the list: food, equipment, times, things to do. Under the list, she found another one: Serena's list, meticulously noting clothes and the order in which they needed to be packed and brought out of the car. Serena must have left it in the kitchen overnight. Her handwriting was small and loopy, easy to read.

Organisation, thought Bee. She liked organisation. It saved time, effort, stress. Not always achievable, though, particularly with an event that you'd never run before. She wondered what the curve ball would be, then wondered again, aloud to Serena, who had come into the kitchen wrapped in an ancient fluffy pink dressing gown. Her aureole of blonde hair stuck upwards, wetly, and she brought with her a waft of something expensive for the shower.

"It could be anything," Serena said. She sat down at the kitchen table and accepted a mug of tea. "Some kid falling down a well."

"God, I hope not! This is Apple Day, not an episode of *Lassie*."

"Look at some of the stuff we've got going on. More like an episode of *Supernatural*."

Bee had not seen this particular TV show but she knew what her sister meant.

"I've been looking forward to it but now I'm getting to the stage where I'll be glad when it's over."

Serena grimaced. "Know what you mean. I'm like this with shows. But then, halfway through, and you suddenly realise you're enjoying it. Usually. Do you have a schedule?"

Bee did and she handed it over.

"So," Serena said, studying it. "The first music's at three and I'm on before that."

"Yes. The music will go on again after dusk, obviously, the Classical stuff, but not too late because people will be bringing kids and wanting to get them to bed. Or have dinner. Or go to the pub. Your catwalk is at two, as we agreed, when there's still a lot of light."

"I hope it doesn't rain."

"It won't rain. It's too cold." Bee wrenched open the door to let in a breath of frost.

"Oh, it is cold! I'd better get dressed. Bella's dad's taking her to Paddington. She's due into the station around eleven. Who are my models, do you know?"

"Some of them are friends of Laura's or Katie Mount's. The young ones. But a couple of Caro's friends agreed as well and one of them is in her seventies."

"Good. Shows everyone you don't need to be sixteen and three stone." Serena got up.

"Is Bella going to take part?"

"Yes. She likes modelling."

"She's a very pretty girl, Serena. Do you think she might do it professionally one day?"

"Nope. Well, she might change her mind. But at the moment she wants to be an engineer. Or maybe a deep sea diver. She's obsessed with David Attenborough. Always watching things about the ocean." Serena glanced at the clock. "I'd better get dressed."

Bee could already hear the shower running. Serena disappeared to be replaced by Stella, and soon after that, Luna. By half past eight, everyone was up, dressed and ready to engage. Sam strung fairy lights through the branches of the apple trees and, with considerable enthusiasm, found and cleaned Abraham's ancient shotgun, which had indeed been in the attic.

"We don't have a license."

"It's just for the tree."

"I thought that was for Wassail? You're early."

Bee had suggested a kind of pre-Wassail, a little ceremony to greet the harvest, and the shotgun would be fired into the branches of a tree to drive evil spirits away, just as with the proper Wassail in January.

"Be careful with that," Stella said. "I don't think Mum ever fired it. She levelled it at the Hunt once, though."

Sam gave her a wary glance. "We know it can be fired, yeah?"

"Not as such."

"Okay. Well, I'll give it a go."

An hour later, there was a thunderous report from the orchard and a lot of male laughter. Bee, removing a loaf from the breadmaker, recognised Dark's voice and smiled to herself. Shortly after this, Caro's muddy 4x4 pulled into the yard and various Amberleys spilled out. Bee had been worried about this, but Ben was not among them. She pulled Caro aside and asked the direct question.

"Look," Caro said, uncomfortably. "I'm aware Ben and Serena have split up and I'm really sorry and sad about it, but I don't feel I can interfere –"

"I completely get that. They're both adults." *Allegedly,* Bee did not add.

"– he is coming down, and he is going to perform, but he's not due to get here till later. I know Serena's show is at two, so..."

"She knows he's coming."

Caro appeared relieved. "This is so awkward. But when I asked him originally, I didn't know about – all of this. Well, obviously, since I gather this is quite recent."

"I just hope there isn't a row. Bella's here, you know. I'm going to be really tactless now and ask what you think about Dana Stare."

Caro opened her mouth and shut it again. "It's not tactless. I'll be honest. I don't warm to her. Laura doesn't like her, says she can't be trusted. That's my gut instinct, too. I suppose I can see what Ben sees in her."

"She's very decorative."

"She's been very sweet. When I'm around."

"And when you're not?"

Their eyes met.

"What about her brother?" Bee asked next.

"Helpful. A bit too eager to please, but you know, he might just be trying to help his sister out."

"You don't think that, though."

"No, I don't. Laura said to me that suddenly they always seem to be there, you know? And they do. I can't quite get my head around how they do that."

Especially when one of them, at least, is in other places at the same time. "No," Bee said slowly. "Neither can I."

Midmorning. Pans of chilli and soup and vegetarian curry filled the Aga. The kettle was on a permanent boil, adding a fortune, no doubt, to the electricity bill.

"This kitchen," Stella said, "smells fantastic. Why don't we just open a café?"

Bee felt red in the face and unpleasantly damp. "No way. Are you going to be here for a bit? Could you keep an eye on this for me while I get a breath of fresh air and see how it's going in the orchard?"

"I'll do it," said Luna.

Released, Bee wandered out into the yard, the flags still glistening with the last of the frost. The mist had lifted now and the sky was clear and cold and pale. At the far end of the orchard, where there was a wide, treeless strip of grass at the back of the marquee, various men including Sam were swearing over the erection of a little stage. If they peeled back the wall, the audience would be able to sit in the marquee and listen to the music. Talk about the gender division of labour, Bee thought, then saw that Stella had joined the crew and was bouncing about giving instructions regarding sound equipment. Leaving them to it, Bee wandered down between the trees, admiring the fairy lights and inhaling the deep, damp scents of earth and rot. Later, come January, she would come out here one night and Wassail the orchard properly, with Dark, giving thanks in the cold and the quiet. There was a terrible crash from the stage and a shout from Stella,

"Just make sure it extends round the back! Otherwise we're going to need a longer cable."

Bee winced. Three hours to go before one o'clock and she was starting to feel the first twinges, half anxiety and half anticipation. The curve ball. What would that be? She imagined rows between Serena and Ben, the sudden appearance of a Behenian star, a broken ankle. Too much to worry about and not enough time to pack it all into: so stop. She paused in front of a tree and contemplated it. There was a hollow three quarters of the way up the trunk, an oval with a thick rind around it, like a disease. But it wasn't a disease, just part of the ageing tree. This one was close to a hundred years old and sometimes, in spring, Bee and Dark heard chuckling and muttering coming from inside the hole, as the infant owls shifted position in the nest. But now the hole was silent and, as Bee watched, the black oval began to contract. For a moment, Bee was reminded, rather uncomfortably, of vaginas dilating and contracting. Then the hole shut with a snap and the tree itself began to dwindle, thinning down to a tender tip with a single leaf, shrinking until it was knee-height. What the hell? – thought Bee. She glanced quickly around the orchard. It looked quite different now. Some of the trees were no more than saplings, but some were gnarled and ancient, unfamiliar to Bee, who could have drawn the usual trees' shapes from memory. She walked here at least once a day, after all. This was the orchard – when? A hundred years or so ago. She could not see the house from here but there was barley on the hill, summer-bright, and as Bee watched it changed to winter ploughing, then hazed with green. All around her the trees were shifting, growing, dying. The old tree in front of her was now entirely gone. If she scrabbled in the grass, perhaps she would find a pip, tiny and black as a robin's eye. Bee blinked and the old tree was standing in front of her once more, unchanged.

"Well," said Bee, aloud. "That was odd."

STELLA

Stella had a great deal of experience in telling men that they were doing it wrong. Pissed off with Ben though she might be, she wished he were here – that his band were here, because they at least knew how to set up a sound system.

"Look," she said. "Don't put that amp there. I'm not trying to show anyone up, right? But I've done this a lot."

To be fair, they were listening, although Stella was afraid they were just being polite. So she grabbed a handful of cables and set it up herself. Quicker by far. And they'd have to do it over again in the gap between the band and the orchestra. Stella wasn't much of a cook and she didn't want to interfere with Serena's show, because Serena was very picky about what she did and didn't want, but this she knew and she could help, along with lugging equipment about.

Ten minutes later, she stood back and surveyed the stage, which by now was actually looking like a stage on which one might host an event. Thank God for that. Stella had that mid-term feeling of things coming together. She looked down the orchard but Bee must have gone back into the house.

At midday, she made a large and uncomplicated cheese sandwich and ate it in her grandfather's study, out of the way and perched on his revolving chair like a child. Bee had tidied up a lot – the piles of papers and notes that Stella remembered from Abraham's day were no longer there – and Nell had gone through a lot of the historical books for her research, but otherwise the study had been left intact. The tall bookcases were still filled with scientific journals and books on astronomy, military history, and the myths and legends that Stella had pored over as a child. None of them had gone to Sunday school, but Abraham had made sure that all of them were familiar with the denizens of Olympus, the gods of the Nile, the skylords of the North. She smiled with nostalgia, remembering. She could still see the thick orange spine of Larousse's *Encyclopedia of Mythology,* in its familiar place. Another anchor, tethering her wandering ship to its mooring. *Get today out of the way,* Stella thought, *and then think about what's next.* Hibernation, maybe.

She tidied up the remains of the sandwich and went out of the study. As she did so, someone's long skirt whisked around the corner of the bedroom in which the moonhorse stood. Stella quickly followed, depositing the plate on top of a bookcase, and peeped around the bedroom door.

Three of the Behenian stars stood in a cluster around the rocking horse. One wore a dress the colour of sunshine, her hair wreathed in buttercups. A necklace of dark green agate was about her throat and she had yellow eyes like a cat. Her companion, leaning in close and whispering, was dressed in white velvet with a crown of diamonds and carried a posy of hellebores, and the third was Spica, wearing green and emeralds. Stella thought the others were Procyon and Algol, respectively: she found it hard to keep track, which gem, which flower, which star. The Behenian girls seemed amused: even Algol's pale inhuman eyes were sparkling. She looked right through the doorframe and gestured to Stella. *Come in.* Stella, feeling suddenly as though she'd been summoned into the headmistresses' office, went awkwardly inside.

She had never been quite so close to the Behenians before. She had seen them all her life, discussed them with her sisters, but it was as though they inhabited another, parallel realm, gliding alongside the family, barely interacting. They had a habit of vanishing when looked at directly, just as some stars burn brighter when seen sidelong. Now, standing right next to them, Stella could see for the first time how unhuman they really were. They were wearing their bodies as Serena might put a dress on a model, a pin-tuck here, a straightened seam there. Their eyes were emptily blank as though they did not use them for sight, decoration only. They were, nonetheless, very beautiful, with the bones sharp beneath their flawless skin and the silk-flow of their hair.

"Hi," said Stella, feeling like a complete idiot. They all looked at her, with that unnerving gaze, then resumed talking among themselves. At least, she supposed they were talking. It sounded more like the noise water makes, bubbling over stones, or the distant hush and rush of the sea. The sounds did not match the movements of their smiling mouths, either. They were pretending to speak, she thought. Then a voice said, inside her mind,

"You are his granddaughter. Which one are you?"

"I'm Stella," Stella said. The words felt difficult, forced out past the nervousness that constricted her throat.

"We find," said Algol, "it difficult to tell. We hope this doesn't offend."

"We all look alike?"

The star inclined her head. Diamonds tinkled like tiny chandeliers, sparking fire. "At times. We hope this does not offend," she repeated. This time, her lips moved in time with the words.

"It's fine, that's cool," Stella stammered.

"You are having a celebration?" Procyon was looking out of the window where a marquee was in the final stages of erection.

"Yes. Apple Day. We made it up, sort of."

"Harvest end?"

"Yes. You know about that sort of thing, then?"

"We watch," the star said, "as we circle the sky."

Stella nodded, dumbly. How do you make small talk, with a star?

"The comet is coming," Algol said.

"I know. We've seen it. Look, my mother –"

"No," the star said patiently. "I mean he is coming *here.*"

Stella stared at her. "What?"

"He is on his way."

"How can that – why is he coming here?" But she remembered the figure she had seen, his white cold face.

"He needs something which he cannot have," said Algol.

"Or everything will die," said Procyon.

"He does not mean to," said Spica.

"But he must be stopped. He must be taken onto a path."

Stella felt as though something very heavy had been dropped onto her chest.

"But how can we stop a *comet*? And my mum –"

"We will do it together," Spica said.

A blink, and they were gone, just as Stella was starting to feel a little more comfortable in their presence. Cool prefects, not headmistresses at all. Excited and alarmed, she ran down the stairs to tell her sisters.

SERENA

This, then, was Bee's curve ball, thought Serena. Unless, of course, something else happens. She had faith in the Behenian stars, though. If they thought something could be done, then it could be done, and they surely knew more about this strange realm of living stars and walking comets than anyone human. The stars would let them know when the time was right, although the thought of the comet both elated and frightened her. She did not imagine a huge, flaming ball crashing into the planet, no apocalyptic Doomsday scenarios, no Hollywood blockbusters. The comet would be something else – someone? Had Alys known this? Firmly, Serena tried to stuff all this to the back of her mind and concentrate on her show, now a mere forty-five minutes away, but it appeared that the back of her mind was already stuffed with worries about Ben.

Bella, newly retrieved from the station, had already asked the direct question.

"Is Ben coming?"

"Yes. But later on."

"And is he bringing that girl?" Bella scowled. Her mother gave an inward sigh. No chance of keeping anything from Bella, too sharp by half.

"Who told you about that?" she said, trying to sound vague.

"Someone at school. Sorry, Mum. Janie Bower. She said her sister saw them at a gig in the Elephant and Castle and they were all over each other." Bella pulled a face.

Serena felt as though a slender blade had been rammed into her heart.

"I don't like him any more," Bella said.

"Sometimes this sort of thing just happens."

"But why?"

"I don't really know. It just does. I will be polite to Ben, when he shows up, Bella. It's called the moral high ground."

"I think you should kick him in the shins."

Perhaps, Serena thought as she hung dresses on the folding rack, perhaps Bella was right.

Time was Serena's friend, though. She had to get on with it; they had a show to do. Nell was helping her and Serena didn't know if Bee had discussed the situation already, but suspected she had. Nell – practical, sympathetic, calm – would be a good person to talk to, but not right now. Serena stepped out of the marquee and found a line of women, ranging from Bella to the seventy year old friend of Caro's.

"I've organised them!" Bella said.

"Great! So, all of you ready for your close up?" There was giggling. Serena explained how it worked. "We'll be modelling in rotation. First one on – who wants to be first?" No one did, so Serena took charge. "Would you go first?" she said to the older woman, Margaret, tall and rangy in hippy-patched jeans. She reminded Serena of her mother, perhaps a decade older.

"Sure." Margaret's eyes widened. "Never done it before, though."

"You'll be fine. Just walk with a bit of confidence, bit of sass."

"Like this?" Margaret strode up and down.

"Yeah, that's great! So, up and down the catwalk, back behind the curtain, and I'll hand you your next outfit. Don't worry if you tear something, drop everything on the floor or give it to Nell, I'll sort it out. You'll have three outfits each. We're only doing a little show."

There was no time for a rehearsal. Serena forced herself to relax. If something went wrong, it would be funny and everyone would laugh and be in good spirits. It would not be a disaster. Do not be a perfectionist. This is not Paris or Milan: it is boards on bales of hay. Deep breaths! She went into the marquee and found that it all looked perfectly calm. Chairs were out, borrowed from the village hall. The catwalk itself, covered with sheets, ended in two small pillars with a vase of cascading roses on each. Serena stood for a moment, remembering to breathe, and then the first few people started drifting in.

By the time the marquee was full, with people both seated and standing at the back, Bee hopped onto the catwalk and gave a brief speech.

"Hello, everyone, and thank you so much for coming. It's a chilly day but it's a lovely one, isn't it? I've got to give you some safety information –" she followed this with a few comments about parking and where to go if a fire broke out "– and then just to say that it's not a gig, or a fete, or a party, but it's a bit like all of those. It's Apple Day!

And here's Ward Garner, who's going to open it for us."

Serena noted that a lot of the faces in the crowd did not belong to the village, and so appeared impressed (Mooncote itself having long been used to Ward and his celebrity friends, and smug about how little notice they took of him). Ward was brief and funny and made Serena feel a bit better about the whole thing. She climbed onto the catwalk and took the microphone from him gratefully.

"It's not Paris, is it? But it's better than that. It's Somerset! We can do better than Paris, can't we?"

There was a shout from the back about the Wurzels and Serena knew then that it was going to be all right, just a bit of a laugh, just as she kept telling herself. Margaret sashayed out, resplendent in green velvet and a coronet of leaves, accompanied by ribald whoops from a group of her female friends. Serena slipped backstage to find a teenager wrestling with some straps.

"I can't get it on!" she wailed.

"That's because it's back to front. Don't worry." And Serena forgot about comets and love, about everything except getting her models into their clothes and out there and back.

LUNA

Bee and Luna had been hard at work over lunchtime, preparing bowls of soup and crusty bread and cake. They'd be serving at four, but for now, there was another little lull and Luna thought she might as well watch the fashion show. She lurked at the back of the tent and watched as Serena's models, mainly trying not to laugh, traversed the catwalk. They looked lovely, in Serena's trademark floaty-hippy clothes, and one of the teenagers was wearing gumboots: egg yolk coloured Hunters. An older woman standing next to Luna gave her a significant look and said, "She can get away with that frock. Don't think I could."

Luna laughed. "Neither could I. I'd look like a fat baby chick."

"Now *she's* really lovely," the woman said. "But I suppose fashion designers do know a lot of professional models."

Luna took one look at the tall woman in green stepping onto the catwalk and felt a plummeting sensation, as though she'd entered a falling lift. For it was not a model, but Spica, splendid in her emeralds. There was a small, awed hush as she strode down the walkway and some sporadic clapping.

"Oh my God," said Luna, involuntarily. She turned to her neighbour, planning on some kind of damage limitation, but suddenly Dark was at her shoulder. Her neighbour had turned, too, her lips parted, but she did not move and looking around the marquee, Luna was both relieved and alarmed to note that no one else was moving either, save for Spica. The Behenian star was past them now, holding out a trailing hand, then gone.

SERENA

In all the stories Serena had read as a child, when this sort of out-of-time thing happened, no one got left behind. Everyone got to go to Narnia, if they were important. But it was curiously interesting to be the one who was left, Serena thought. She could see none of her sisters, or Nell, but her cousin had nipped back into the house to find a safety pin. She walked slowly around the perimeter of the marquee. Emily was halfway down the catwalk, her gold and silver mesh skirt drifting behind her, but frozen. The audience, too, were quite still: snatched out of time in the middle of lifting teacups to their mouths or chatting to their friends or glancing at their mobile phones. Serena looked over a man's shoulder at his iphone and saw that it was 1.21, unchanging. She went outside and looked up at the sun, caught in an amber moment of emergence from behind a cloud. The air was quite still. Nothing moved. How long would this last, Serena wondered. Going back inside the marquee, she returned to the curtained-off backstage area and checked on her models. Would they get stiff? Or would time, when it started again, simply move on from this stolen moment? She tweaked Georgia's lacy dress, straightening a little, but the fabric fell back into its original incorrect folds. Serena stepped back and saw Dana Stare.

"Hello," Dana said. She gave a tight little smile. "Well, this is all a bit weird, isn't it?"

"What are you doing here?" Serena whispered.

"Don't you mean: why can I move about and talk when everyone else can't? The rules don't apply to me, love."

"Nor to me," Serena said, coldly, although she did not feel that she understood what Dana was talking about. It hit home, though. Dana's pale face flushed into two crimson spots, high on her cheekbones so that she looked like a china doll.

"I suppose you think you're special. You and your sisters. It's not just you, is it? It's a lot of us."

"Maybe you'd like to explain it to me, then." She would not ask *Where's Ben.*

Dana's chin lifted.

"Oh, I don't think so." She walked a little further into the room and picked up a scarf, fragile with embroidered rosebuds. "Pretty. Not my thing, though. Your stuff's nice, I suppose, but it wouldn't suit me."

"There's something for everyone," Serena said, trying to keep her voice even. And if they could actually have some sort of conversation, it might keep Dana here, away from whatever else she was plotting. But perhaps that was the point, to keep Serena herself moth-pinned to the board of time. Where was Dana's brother? "Dana, what do you want?"

Dana snickered. "What do I want that I haven't got already? Like your man? I want lots of things, Miss Fallow. Lots and lots. I didn't just come here to gloat, you know. I came to ask you something."

STELLA

Outside the marquee, Stella found that Algol had paused at the gate which led into the orchard. The star had appeared at her shoulder, when Stella was bending over the sound equipment, and beckoned, so Stella had gone. Now, the star glanced back and opened the gate. Normally, this led onto the lawn that ran along the driveway. But now Stella saw that the drive, and the house itself, were no longer there. Instead, stretched endless fields, bright with frost and moonlit under the darkening sky. Ahead, was the high wall of a moor. And the gate itself had changed: it was the lych gate, now, but there was no sign of the church or the graveyard. A skull had been set high in its eaves and on either side it was crowded by a blackthorn hedge, the spines sharp as talons.

Ahead, down the bright path, a little group progressed, carrying a coffin high on their shoulders. They wore top hats with black streamers and Stella could hear the whisper of bells, like a Morris side.

The gate creaked as they went through. Stella thought it might be a warning and she listened carefully for the voices of the blackthorn hedge, but the thorns were silent. Once through the gate, the air grew colder and purer: no tang of diesel or even the natural smells of the countryside here. Stella glanced back and the gate was no more than an outline against the roll of the land.

It was like walking in dreams, or those times when you'd been thinking about something and realised that you were actually driving, that all the time you'd been reacting automatically to the sights and sounds of the road. Stella was starting to lose track of time and she didn't like that. She pulled out her phone but, not entirely to her surprise, the screen was blank and dead.

Ahead strode the glimmering star. Every so often she turned her head and the diamonds twined into her hair flashed and sparked, as if picking up light from the land. Stella was keeping a sharp eye out for any movement – Alys? – but the land seemed empty, motionless and still. There was no breeze. The sky was a deep, clear green, like that moment after sunset, but as she looked back to the west, a single bright star had become visible, hanging in the heavens like a great lamp.

Elsewhere, it would have been Venus, the Evening Star, but here? Stella was not sure.

She thought that she had only been looking at the star for a moment, so it was with dismay that she stood alone on the track.

"Fuck!" She turned and ran down the path, up and over a slight rise, but no-one was there. Stella balled her fists. "How could you be so fucking stupid?"

She forced herself to think. The choice was actually simple: go on or go back. Don't leave the path, like Red Riding Hood. Who knew what wolves roamed the land?

But as she hesitated, on the pivot point, Stella realised that she was not to be given a choice after all. Around her the landscape was fragmenting. Shards of green grass and black earth swirled upwards, tornado-spiralling. Stella put her arm over her face but the shards whisked painlessly through her flesh. Panicked, she wondered if she herself was starting to disintegrate. They sparkled like Algol's diamonds and above her, the sky grew black.

SERENA

"What did you want to ask me?" Serena said to Dana Stare.

"I have a question, about your grandfather, actually." For a moment, Dana sounded almost friendly. She flicked a strand of hair from her face and leaned against the trestle table. "Was it him who summoned the stars?"

"He was an astronomer," Serena said.

"I know that," Dana was impatient. "You know what I'm talking about."

"I've no idea. They've been around ever since we were children. I don't know where they come from." This was only partly true; Serena was sure that they had something to do with the gemstone box. And the Behenian stars had been attached to the house for generations, coming and going as they mysteriously pleased. She wasn't going to tell Dana that. Dana was looking at her narrowly. Serena kept her eyes wide and, she hoped, guileless.

"Didn't you think it was a bit odd?" Dana asked.

"I suppose so. We weren't supposed to mention them to anyone else."

"But you Fallow girls don't do what you're told, do you?" Dana smiled. "I like that. So it's cool. Did you mention the stars to Ben?"

"Why don't you ask him yourself?"

Dana laughed. "He might think I was a bit of a nutter, mightn't he?"

Serena said nothing. Then she said, "Why do you want to know?"

"Oh, come on. An old house haunted by a bunch of beautiful star girls?"

"So how did you know what they were?" Serena countered.

Dana looked like a sly child. "I know all sorts of things about people. Your sister's boyfriend, for example."

"Oh? Which one would that be, then?"

"Good question, because none of them are quite what they seem, are they?" Dana came across and for a moment Serena thought that the girl was going to touch her. Dana raised a hand, as if she was intending to stroke Serena's face. Close to, her skin was flawless, with no sign of

180

make-up. Serena forced herself to stand her ground. But Dana's hand fell to her side. Her nostrils flared, briefly, and Serena realised with revulsion that the girl was smelling her.

"And are you what you seem, Dana?" she said.

For a moment, something flickered in Dana's eyes. *That's got you on the run,* Serena thought. Then Dana laughed. "Hold that thought, eh? Time's on the move again."

And Serena looked up as an excited model flung herself through the curtains.

"Leave you to it," Dana said. "The show must go on, eh?"

STELLA

Stella stumbled through a snowstorm made of emerald glass. She wasn't even sure what she was walking on, but the whirling shards were herding her, driving her forwards. She hoped she was still on the path but how to tell? Little by little, however, she became aware that the shards were starting to settle. Soon, they had sunk to waist height and she could see both above them and through them. She was walking on bare earth, studded with tough grass the texture of wire. It was soaked and so, therefore, were her Converse trainers. Stella tutted, hoping they would survive the adventure. They were her favourite pair. Around her, the landscape was flat, all the way to the horizon. She could see the gleam of water in between low banks and tussocks of reeds. A marsh, with occasional stands of stunted alder and willow.

"Why are you here?" a willow said to Stella, in a small, whispering voice.

"I don't know! I was caught up in – something. Like a storm. Where is this place?"

"The marsh."

Well, that was helpful, thought Stella.

"Well, I want to get out of it." The prospect of missing her footing and ending up in an actual bog, being sucked down, the Great Grimpen mire, Baskerville territory again... "Which direction should I go in?"

"Follow my sisters," the willow said. "See, the line along the dyke? Follow them and you will come to the shore. Perhaps a boat may be waiting."

Stella did not find that reassuring. Old stories of boats that carry the dead were floating in the back of her mind. Telling herself to get a grip, she nodded.

"Thank you, willow tree." And again she started walking.

It was cold but not freezing; the water that ran in long ditches and pools between the earthen banks was not skimmed with cat ice. *It will be all right*, Stella said to herself. *It will.* She found the dyke and, clambering slightly, made her way up onto it. From here, she could see a line of changing white: the surf. So, the shore was not all that far away, and all Stella had to do was follow the dyke with its willow guardians.

She made her way towards the shoreline. A wind began to blow across the marsh, thin and insidious. Stella shivered and pulled her hoodie more tightly at the neck. She paused, turning to look back over the dark and silver land – someone stood there, watching her. Stella yelped and stumbled but no one was there. She looked around wildly but the marsh was empty. She forced a breath of cold air into her lungs: *in, out, in out. Keep walking.* But the back of her neck prickled as she did so.

At first she was worried that the shore didn't seem to be getting any nearer, but then she saw that this was deceptive. She could hear the rush and hiss of the sea now. And something else – a voice.

"Help me!"

Oh God, thought Stella. *What now?* It was coming from one of the pools – no, that was wrong. There was a boggy area between the pools, and now she could see a figure, struggling. There was a splash. Stella, not without serious misgivings – *a trap? Who the hell knew who or what was out here* – ran along the dyke.

"Hang on!" she called.

Whoever they might be, they were going down fast. Stella grasped the spear-like branch of an alder.

"Can I take this?" It snapped off in her hand, which she was inclined to view as a 'yes.' It wasn't very thick and it might not be strong enough. It might snap. She held it out, braced against the tree.

"Grab that. Can you get your legs free?"

"I think so!" The person was covered in mud; she was unable to tell if it was a man or a woman.

"Try and swim. Don't wade."

A hand grasped the end of the alder pole and the weight nearly pulled Stella in. She gave a small shriek and wrapped her arms around the tree. Slowly, by degrees, the person hauled themselves to the edge of the bog and rolled out into the reeds. Reaching out as far as she could, Stella took the slime-covered hand and pulled the person up the dyke. They stood up, shakily.

"Cheers," the person said and there was something about that voice, something familiar.

"Oh shit," said Stella, aloud.

It was Tam Stare.

BEE

How could you get lost on your own property?

Bee had gone down to the end of the orchard to put some tea leaves from the big urn onto the compost heap. Serena's show was in full swing. The orchestra were just beginning to set up and the sound floated through the trees, rattled by the rising breeze. The wind had swung around, stirring Bee's hair. She reached the compost heap, heaved aside the piece of old carpet which rested on top of one of the sections and hurled the tea leaves into the gently decomposing mass of old cabbage stalks and last summer's runner bean stems. Then she pulled the carpet back over the mess and turned back.

And that had been that, for some time. She remembered coming up to the halfway point of the orchard, the old owl tree, and noting that it had a number of handy twigs on which slices of toast could be hung: they'd do this for the actual Wassailing in January, putting the bread up for the tree spirits as was traditional. But she couldn't remember a great deal after that, and it was now later – much later. The blue, racing sky above the orchard had darkened into sunset storm and the wind was now huge, roaring through the orchard. Bee sometimes felt that the house was a ship, meeting the Atlantic gales head on, and she felt that now and thought of Dark. Come to think of it, where *was* Dark? He was rarely far away when she walked the orchard. The orchestra had been playing for some time, but she had only just realised this. Mercury – they had started with Mercury and then they had gone on to Jupiter. And now – they were still playing but Bee did not recognise the tune and, returning slowly to her own senses, she wasn't even sure if it was the same orchestra, because surely George Hazelgrove wasn't supposed to be on until later and it should be a band now? It sounded different, and very far away. She turned to look back down the marching ranks of trees and found that, instead, she was nose-up against a gate.

Bee stepped back. Well, that had never happened before. The gate was wooden and silvery with age; patches of lichen were scrawled across it in ochre and light grey-green. It had a round iron ring for a latch and it was set in an old brick wall. After a moment's hesitation, Bee raised a hand, took hold of the ring and lifted the latch. It moved easily. The gate opened and she was through.

It was a garden, but not one that Bee had ever seen before. A geometrical arrangement of box hedges – a maze garden, Elizabethan? – ran down a wide green lane to a meadow, and beyond that was a dark stand of trees, and beyond that, water. She could see the gleam and glint of it in the sun, for there was sunlight now, and warmth on her face, and the scent of the box and chamomile and thyme.

"Okay," said Bee aloud. She glanced back. The gate was still there, standing solid. Let's hope that continued. She did not like the idea of adventuring without a way home – but perhaps when she opened the gate again it would lead somewhere else? Bee put that thought firmly aside and walked down between the box hedges. Apart from the oddness of the situation, it felt to her like a normal garden. Her namesakes hummed amongst the spikes of lavender. It occurred to her that this was also a very well-stocked herb garden: there were plants that she did not even recognise, though many that she did. She leaned down and crushed a leaf of mint between her fingers, releasing its wild, fresh smell. It was stronger than the mints she grew in her own garden and there were other, different, things, too. She could not pinpoint it – and then multiple flashes of yellow, white and scarlet shot over the box hedges and came to rest in the big heads of a thistle. Goldfinches, lots of them, and the different thing was birdsong. She could hear a great many birds, chattering and squabbling in the trees and in the high hedges of pleated beech that marked the garden on both sides. Even at Mooncote in the heart of the English countryside, there were not as many birds to be heard. Or as many butterflies to be seen. Bee watched a dance of them, scraps of sky among the spires of lavender. Those were Large Blues – once extinct in the South West, although she'd read in the summer that they had been brought back through conservation efforts and were doing well. Surely not as well as this and she did not remember seeing them in a garden before: they were found on hills, she had thought. But the blue butterflies swirled up towards the light, undeniably present, the sun catching their dappled wings.

Thoughtfully, Bee walked on, noticing other details. No traffic noise. No contrails, blurring lines across the blueness of the sky. The trees at the bottom of the garden were unfamiliar. All she could smell were the scents of the garden, rich as incense. And something else, an indefinable feeling of difference, displacement, *wrongness*? As you would expect, Bee said to herself, if this was in fact the past. The meadow was full of flowers, spikes of orchis as well as buttercups and daisies. As she came closer to the tall stand of trees which separated the meadow from the water, Bee looked up at their elegant draperies and realised that they were elms. The discovery made her gasp. She had never seen an elm like this, outside books. The trees had succumbed to Dutch Elm Disease before Bee was even born, though their names still lingered throughout the district: Elm Lane, Elmbridge Road. But here they stood, healthy and hale. Bee placed a wondering hand on their rough, striated bark, slightly sun warm. Then she wove her way through the grove, through another meadow and down to the edge of the water, coming out onto a pebbled shore. It was an inlet. Nowhere near Mooncote itself, though the red earth of the farther shore looked as though it might be Devon. On the other side of the water, a headland struck out into the silver expanse, covered in trees. And on the water, riding at anchor, there was a ship.

"Oh, wow!" said Bee, aloud. She found herself giving a huge, involuntary grin. A proper ship, a real ship, with a figurehead and furled sails and a great square stern. As it swung around on the tide, she could see the prancing deer outlined on the wood. The scarlet and white of the St George's cross snapped from the top of her mast and someone stood waving on the deck. Bee, abandoning caution, waved back.

Of course it was Dark. Who else would it be? She'd always wanted to see his day and age, had asked endless questions about it. What did London smell like? What did you eat? Did you ever meet a witch? Dark had done his best to answer but some things he simply could not remember. And like everyone, he had favourite anecdotes, which Bee was happy to listen to.

It's only when a person dies that you remember all the things you should have asked them. But that wasn't going to happen here and so Bee asked him anyway, wrote it secretly down. The mysteries of the past should not be lost and now, it seemed, she was about to experience them for herself.

STELLA

Tam Stare couldn't stop laughing. He doubled over, dripping water and mud. Stella regarded him coldly.

"Have you finished?"

"Sorry," Tam gasped. "Can't tell you what's so funny."

But Stella thought she knew. Regardless of his state of filth, she grabbed a fist of his clothes – shirt? T-shirt? Who could tell? – and thrust him into the grove of alder. There was a faint whisper of protest from the tree. "Here's a suggestion. You came here after me – to bring me back? Make sure I didn't get back, maybe? And then you fucked it up and now I've rescued you." She let him go and stepped back. "I wouldn't have bothered if I'd known who it was."

Tam spluttered. "That's why it's so fucking hilarious. Partly, anyway." He sneezed. "Jesus. This mud. I'm freezing."

"You look a real sight."

"I'm not looking forward to when it dries."

"There's always the sea."

"Yeah, the sea. You don't know this place very well, do you, love?"

"Having never set foot here before, obviously not. And don't call me love."

Rather to her surprise, Tam considered this, then said, "All right."

There was a moment's silence. Tam said, "I didn't come after you, actually. I didn't know you were here. It's not all about you, or your sisters, you know."

"So what are you doing here, then?"

Tam gave a sudden shiver, wrapping his arms around himself. There was always the chance, Stella thought with a lift of the spirits, that he might get pneumonia. "I came looking for something else."

"And did you find it?"

Tam smiled. "Wouldn't be telling you that, now, would I?"

"Well," Stella said. "You've got a choice. I'm going to keep walking. You either follow me or you don't."

She did not like the thought of turning her back on him. He was not to be trusted, or believed. But she did not think she could drive him away. Even in his sodden state, he was stronger than she was and any

187

struggle might end both of them up in the marsh. She'd have to try and lose him. She had no intention of teaming up.

"I'm going the same way as you," said Tam. "To the sea."

SERENA

Once the clock had resumed ticking, Serena had no option but to get on with the show. She flung clothes at Emily and Janie, focusing on getting them dressed and out, just as she did in the big catwalks. Dana Stare had melted into the crowd: Serena caught a glimpse of her pointed pale face and then she was gone. Serena looked around for Bee or Luna, but she still could not see them – presumably they were sorting out the food. Stella? She could not see Stella either, and Nell, having only technically been gone for a few minutes, had not returned from the house. Serena didn't like the thought of Dana roaming about the property but she couldn't abandon the catwalk, either. Now just wanting it to be over, Serena got on with the job and it was with a substantial sense of relief that she ran out with her models and took a final bow. As she did so, she saw Ward standing at the front of the audience, holding a cup of tea and looking, in a tweed jacket, as though he was playing the part of an Englishman in a period movie.

As soon as the models had jumped down and joined their families, Serena went out to find him.

"Are you all right?" Ward said, frowning.

"No."

"Serena, what's wrong?" He put a gentle, supportive hand on her arm. Now playing the part of Sensitive Romantic Lead. But actually Serena was grateful. Sod feminism for a moment – she gripped his hand – but she wasn't going to swoon in his arms.

"Ward....could you hold the fort here for a minute? Keep an eye on the clothes."

"Don't let anyone run off with anything? Keep their sticky bun-infested mitts off the taffeta?"

"Thank you!" She kissed him on the cheek and ran through marquee, orchard, garden to the house. Luna looked up as Serena ran through the kitchen.

"Serena, I need to tell you something, about your show –"

But Serena cried, 'Back in a minute, just going to the loo." She spared a moment to be relieved that Luna was there: she felt like a sheepdog, rounding up sisters. The house seemed empty and, after the

189

crowded orchard, somehow civilised. Serena ran into Abraham's study and fumbled the drawers of the desk where the gemstone box was kept. She wrenched it open, knowing that the box was gone.

But the box was still there, untouched.

Clutching it to her, Serena sank down into her grandfather's chair. It was a moment before she thought to tip the stones out onto the green leather surface. They were all there: diamond and jasper, emerald and magnet and chrysolite. She turned them in her fingers, watching them spark in a shaft of the sinking sun. That reminded her that they were still less than halfway through the event. Serena put the stones back in their box and carried it into her room, where she stashed it in a cupboard under a lot of old quilts. And where was Dana now?

She went quickly through the upstairs of the house, opening doors. The place felt fine, but that didn't mean a lot: what if she was wrong? In one room, she found Nell, changing a sweater.

"Oh, Serena! Were you looking for me? I'm sorry I've been so long. I was just putting on something a bit warmer. That wind's surprisingly cold."

"No, no, just looking for the cat. For Tut. Something spooked her," Serena lied. "It makes her throw up."

"Oh, poor puss. She's not in here. Hey, your show was great! I see one of your models came down from London."

It had been Nell who had spotted Spica in the London flat, Serena remembered.

"Yes, so good of her, she had to dash back up to town, though. Her career's really taking off."

"What's her name? I'll look out for her."

"Er, Nadia Radislav," said Serena. "She's, um, Romanian. She might be changing her name, though. Career thing."

"I thought she looked Eastern European. Those *cheekbones*."

"Anyway, so glad you liked it, thanks for your help," said Serena, feeling terrible, and shut the door.

Downstairs, she found Luna was still in the kitchen.

"Serena, have you seen Bee?" Luna looked worried.

"No. Is she out in the orchard?"

"No. Caro's doing the food table. I haven't seen Bee for ages."

"Is Stella still doing sound checks?"

Now that the catwalk was over, it must be getting close to band time, Serena realised.

"I don't know."

"Do you know if Ben's turned up?"

"I haven't seen him or his band." Luna gave a scowl. "No loss either, if you ask me."

"Hold the fort," Serena said. "I'll go and look." Leaning closer, she hissed, "One of the stars turned up. On the catwalk in the marquee. Spica."

"I know, I saw her. That's what I was trying to tell you. She's not still there?"

"No. She vanished. Things went a bit pear-shaped for a bit."

"Nothing happened in the house as far as I can tell," said Luna. "I feel a bit weird, actually. Like something's *going* to happen." She gestured at her belly.

"Maybe it's just this."

Serena patted her shoulder. "Me too. Feeling weird, I mean. As though something's in the wind. Hang in there."

Luna nodded unhappily. "I'll do my best."

Outside again, Serena found that the wind had in fact changed. Rather than that chilly northern whistle, it had swung around to the west and it was stepping up, a big salt-laden Atlantic breeze, chasing the sheep-clouds before its herdsman's breath. It made the whole world feel different and Serena, who loved these westerlies, paused for a moment and took its sea-draught into her lungs. Better! She could hear the unmistakable sounds of musicians tuning up. Chill out, Serena told herself. They loved the show, no one noticed a bloody alien in the middle of it, and now we're going to have some music. And maybe an equinoctial gale into the bargain. But the sky was blue, except for the scudding clouds.

To the background cacophony, Serena ran back into the orchard and conducted a quick search. She glimpsed Seelie and Ben's other band mates but she couldn't see Ben himself. Thank God for that. The bloke on the sound stage said he hadn't seen Stella for half an hour, perhaps more. Serena did a quick circuit but could not find Bee, either. She went back into the marquee where Ward was loyally guarding the clothes.

"We need to take these into the house," she said, picking up an armful.

"Want me to wait here?"

"No, you can help. Everyone's outside."

"Where did you go? Is everything all right?"

"I was looking for the cat," Serena said. *Get your story straight.* "Something spooked her."

Ward raised an eyebrow. He knew her better than her cousin, she realised, or perhaps was more cynical. "Oh really?"

"Well. All right. That's what I told Nell. Actually I was looking for that woman, Dana Stare. Ben's new girlfriend," she added, in case he didn't remember. But it seemed that he did; his eyes widened.

"Is *she* here?"

"Yes. I spoke to her."

Ward frowned. "When was that?"

When a star froze time.

"Not long ago. She snuck back here. Sort of confronted me."

"Shit."

"Then she fucked off and I thought she might have gone prowling round the house to see what she could find – she's that type."

"Look," Ward said. He picked up a rosebud scarf and ran his thumb along its hem, with a curious precision. "You know I said a while ago, when we were talking about Miranda, that I may have been a bit of a tit."

"I do recall that, yes."

"Well, I think my cousin Ben is being a bit of a dick. A lot of a dick, actually. I haven't met this girl he's seeing – at least, I don't think I have but Caro can't stand her, Laura can't stand her –"

"I can't stand her."

"No, obviously. But I'd be surprised if you could. Although you're not really the jealous sort, are you? Or have you changed?"

"I'm not jealous but I do prize loyalty. Well, I'm not jealous when I'm not provoked."

"Mmmm," Ward said.

"Ben didn't tell me we'd split up. I didn't know! He ghosted me – is that what they say these days? On Tinder?"

"I've no idea. I can barely manage a mobile phone even with my opposable thumbs."

And besides, Serena thought, *you wouldn't have to use Tinder, because women have always thrown themselves at you. Or Grindr.* Which of course had been part of the problem originally. She said, "When someone pisses off and doesn't tell you but tells everyone you've become a bunny boiler because you keep texting them and trying to find out where they are?"

"Has Ben actually done that? Told everyone you're a bunny boiler, I mean."

"I don't know."

"He's a shit if he has."

"Ward, the thing is – we think, Stella and I think, that Dana Stare has done something to Ben."

"*Done* something to him? Like what? Poisoned his coffee? Brainwashed him? From what I understand from Caro, she's a Goth, not a member of the KGB."

"I know it sounds a bit mad."

"Okay," Ward said. He put the scarf down and with one hand flicked back a floppy lock of hair. "I think it's time to let you know that I am aware, let's say, that there is stuff that happens around your family which is not, let's also say, totally normal."

"Oh?" Serena's heart gave a big, painful jolt. "What do you mean?"

He was looking at her closely. "Supernatural stuff. Not ghosts – well, all right. Ghosts as well. Not just ghosts. Christ, I always used to think I was articulate."

Serena opened her mouth and closed it again.

"Um," she said.

Ward laughed. "Come to that, I always used to think *you* were articulate."

"I don't know what to say. I don't want you to think I'm a lunatic."

"I don't think you're a lunatic," Ward said, rather gently.

"I feel like Lois Lane. Or Buffy. Maybe Buffy, because Lois isn't pretending to be someone normal, is she? That's Superman."

"Yes, that's Superman. You forget, Serena, that I knew your grandfather, when I was a mere slip of a lad. So did Richard, and so did Caro. We've known your family for a long time – too long to not notice that there is this, 'stuff', that happens around it."

"Oh."

"And," Ward said, "I think you should know that it's not just *your* family."

STELLA

Did he, Stella wondered, ever stop talking? He was trying to get to her, she thought. It wasn't quite needling, Tam Stare wasn't actually rude to her, but it was just on that knife-edge between what might have been curiosity and what was probably an attempt to wear her down.

"So what do you think, Stella?" About all this, about life, about the universe. About music: whether, for instance, Major Sorto was preferable to anything produced by Reo Nada, a subject on which Stella did in fact have an opinion. But then he ran out of musical knowledge and went on to global warming. On and on.

Eventually, Stella said, "Look. Would you mind just shutting up?"

"All right," said Tam, affably enough, and did so, for about three minutes. Then he said, "You can see a long way out to sea, can't you? What do you reckon's out there, then?"

"I haven't a clue." She paused for a moment on the ridge and looked. The shore seemed a long way off again, but she was sure that they hadn't been walking in circles. The landscape was too open for that, with the markers of thorn and brake. Far out to sea, it was even lighter: a thin green sky between the cloud race, the sort of late evening sky in which the new moon's curve might have hung. But somehow she did not think that they would see the moon here yet. And she could hear the sea, its distant boom. Tam seemed filled with an odd, febrile excitement. He bounced slightly on his heels, clad in a pair of worn-down Nike. If the circumstances had been different, Stella might have thought he was on coke, but even if he'd taken some before entering this land, it would have worn off by now and he showed no signs of sniffing. Twitchy, though, and maybe she should be reading that as *shifty*. Probably hiding something, probably hiding lots, but what was it in this particular instance?

"I don't like the look of that sky," Stella said. The mass of cloud was building up over the sea and she could smell the fresh, metallic odour of rain on the wind. The breeze, rising, stirred her hair and then the first heavy drop of water struck her hand. A sizzling flash of bright blue-white lit up the thorn trees and Tam's pale, startled face.

"Shit."

"I think we'd better find some shelter," Stella shouted above the sudden thunder. The low thorn trees wouldn't provide much. As the

194

rain began to pelt down, they stumbled along the ridge. Within minutes, Stella's hair was plastered to her face. The parka would keep out the worst of it, but not for ever. As they ran, Tam grabbed her hand. Stella didn't feel up to a struggle. His fingers were icily strong in hers, and he was pulling her along. Then they came up over the final ridge and there at last was the shore. The breakers were thundering onto the shingle, dragging the stones into the ink of the sea with a crackling rush.

"There's a hut!" Stella shouted. It stood perched, rather lopsidedly, on a spur of sandy soil running above the shingle. They raced for it, skirting the edge of the stones, and wrenched at the door. It opened easily and Stella and Tam fell inside.

"Thank God for that." The hut was very small, furnished only with two benches and a table. You might be able to lie down, but only just, and it would help a lot if you drew your knees up. But you would have to upend the benches or put them outside. Let's see how long we have to hole up in here, Stella thought. She sat soggily down on one of the benches instead.

"Brrr."

"You're not wrong," Tam said, through chattering teeth. He must have been chilled to the bone, given his earlier dunking in the marsh. He sank down opposite her and rammed his cold hands into his pockets. "Wonder how long it's going to last."

Stella shrugged. "Who knows?"

"There's nothing to eat in here."

"I could murder a cup of tea."

For a moment Tam looked wistful and almost sympathetic. "Tea! Yeah, that would be great."

"Except we haven't got any tea. Or any milk, or any water. Or a fire. At least we're out of the rain."

Tam grinned. "Bit like being in the army. On manoeuvres."

Stella gave him a curious glance. "Been in the army, have we?"

"What, me take the King's shilling? You must be fucking joking."

"I think that might be the navy," Stella said.

"I never wanted to run away to sea, either. Landlubber, me. Although I quite fancy being a pirate."

"Yes, I can see that might appeal." She thought wistfully of Dark, whose assistance she could really do with right now.

"Anyway, the army, definitely a big fat no. I don't like being told what to do."

"Neither do I, actually."

"You're pretty fit, though, if I may say so."

Stella regarded him narrowly, but decided to take that remark at face value.

"Yeah, I suppose so. I used to swim. I run a lot."

"Marathons?"

"I've done a couple. I did the London marathon a year or so ago. Came, like, several hundredth."

"Well, it's more than I've ever done. Run for the pub if closing time seemed a bit close. Buses."

But he did not look unfit. He was whip-thin, and Stella could see real muscles under his top now that it was so wet. No, stop that, this would not lead to good things. Maybe he was angling for a compliment. She grunted instead and a short silence fell.

It was, in any case, difficult to be heard. The roof of the hut must be corrugated iron or similar, for the rain drummed and banged on it, deafening and relentless. Behind that was the roar of the sea. Stella shivered, suddenly glad that the hut had no windows. This was a night to be in and now that she thought about it, how was it that they could see? She said so to Tam.

"Eh?"

"I *said,* where is the light coming from?"

He looked genuinely surprised. "I dunno. I thought there was a bulb but now you mention it, there isn't."

"I somehow doubt any electricity company has got this far."

"Yeah, but – sometimes in these places, you come across weird shit. Anomalies."

"Right," Stella said. She wasn't totally sure that she knew what he was talking about but she didn't want to let on.

"Sometimes it's like time's all muddled up. Technology where it shouldn't be, that sort of thing. It's like the Matrix."

"A projection?"

"Yeah, a bit."

"So when did you start – exploring – these other places?"

He shook his head. "It's always been there. Family thing, you know?"

"Sort of."

"Listen," Tam said. "The rain's stopping."

196

BEE

Bee watched the coast slide by. They were leaving the headland behind them now, and the open sea lay ahead. It was, so Dark had informed her, the English Channel. She had been installed on a bench on the starboard side of the boat and it had been strongly implied, if not actually stated, that she was to keep out of the way. Bee, practical as ever, did not take offence at this. But despite the exhilaration of adventure, and the comforting presence of Dark, she could not help worrying. What was happening back at the house? Had anyone else been snapped into another realm? What about Apple Day? She wondered if this was a kind of fairyland experience – would she return to the same moment that she had left, or later, or what? How did this work? She didn't fancy finding that it was a hundred years later and she, all unthinking, might spring out across the strand to crumble into dust. Bee told herself firmly that Dark would never let this happen. He came and went as he pleased, after all, or appeared to.

But then, Dark was already dead.

She brushed a strand of hair from her face, spattered with salt spray. Even the sea smelled fresher, here. Across the boat, she could still see land: red cliffs, very Devonian, and the low hills beyond, more heavily wooded than in her own time but still patchworked with fields. From the way that the sun sat in the sky, they were heading east. She looked up as Dark came to stand beside her, then he plumped down on the bench.

"Captain's going to be on deck in a minute." He said this with a touch of deference, unusual for the usually confident Dark.

"Where are we? That looks like Slapton." She stood, a bit wobbly, and shaded her eyes, trying to see the tower of the chantry.

"Yes, that is indeed. You're well informed."

"We spent a holiday down here when we were kids. Look, you can see the lagoon." Surprisingly unchanged – but then, in geological terms this was hardly a blink of an eye – the long pale bar of the beach rolled by.

"Dartmouth soon."

"Oh, I love Dartmouth. There are some really good pubs."

Dark laughed. "That's not quite what I'd expected you to say, madam."

"I love the Cherub."

He looked at her in surprise. "It's not still there, surely? It was old in my day."

"Built from ship's timbers, so they say. And has a ghostly cat."

"I remember the cat," said Dark. "It wasn't a ghost, though. Not then."

"It's supposed to have a lot of ghosts."

"It can have another one, then. When we return."

Being dead evidently didn't stop you from planning road trips, Bee reflected.

"In my time – this time – a respectable lady like you wouldn't have any business setting foot in a pub like the Cherub."

"Good thing I was born four hundred years later, then. I'd have been able to stay at an inn, though?"

"Yes. But things were different. Are different." He shook his head. "I become muddled, even still."

"So what's a respectable lady like me doing on an English warship?" She paused. "She is a warship, isn't she?"

"She is a warship. Halfway between carrick and galleon. Called the *Pelican*, first, but renamed in honour of Sir Christopher, his arms. A patron is important, you see."

Bee nodded. "Your fellow sailors. Can they see me?" There were men swarming all over the vessel, but Bee had attracted no attention. Something of a relief.

"They cannot. You are a spirit to them."

"My turn, eh?"

He smiled. "Your turn. But the Captain is a different matter. He has what they call the sight."

Bee had not known much about Francis Drake, apart from the story about playing bowls on Plymouth Ho. And he was said to have owned a drum that could be beaten in times of national peril: Drake might return again to save the nation, a bit like King Arthur. Bee had seen its replica in Drake's old home of Buckland Abbey. After meeting Dark, however, she had done a lot of reading. Whereas a boy, perhaps, might have been thrilled to find himself on what was essentially a privateer, Bee could not approve. Drake was a slaver, when all was said and done, and a pirate. She knew it was a different age. Now piracy was seen as romantic, a little comical due to Johnny Depp and those movies, and Bee had laughed along but it wasn't funny, really: it was about murder and theft, and snatching people from their homes into horror lifelong.

She had spoken to Dark about it. All men took others as slaves, he had said, it was commonplace. He did not like the idea himself, thinking that all should be free. But he had not sailed with Drake then, only later, against the Spanish and then to the Americas. Bee thought that he had probably died somewhere near Puerto Rico. But now Dark was here and so was she.

"So where are we going?" she asked.

"Ah," he said. "We have a mission, the Captain says. But I don't know where and what." He stood, quickly. "He's here."

Bee also stood. Drake was on the deck, looking a little like his portraits in a jerkin, if that was the right word, and shirt. Serena would know the proper names for them... She recognised the neat beard and brown hair, but his eyes, when they came to rest upon her, were compelling: almost black and slightly prominent. She called to mind something Dark had once told her, that the Spanish believed Drake to be a witch. She found herself standing a little straighter.

"Madam," Drake said. He gave a small bow.

"Captain Drake." She hoped that was the right thing to say.

"Welcome on board."

"Captain, why am I here?"

The smile broadened, a little vulpine. "You have powerful friends, my lady."

"I do? I am a countrywoman. I don't know many high-ups."

"The star spirits."

"Ah. I see what you mean."

"We are in England's dreaming," Drake said, "untied from time."

"Yes. You – forgive me – you were killed off the coast of Panama, I believe?"

"Yes. No honourable death. A form of the flux. I don't remember much, nor where they put me, save that it would have been into the waves. But now I stand before you, quite restored, and things are as they ever were for me, though I no longer fight. Not the Spanish foe, anyway," he added, with a reflective look. Then, with another bow, he was gone down the deck. Dark stared after him.

"I'd best get on."

"Sure. Don't let me hold you up, Ned."

She sat back down on the bench and watched the coast slide by. There indeed was Dartmouth, the entrance to the river ringed by a myriad small boats. Then the bay and more red cliffs, the slopes of what would one day become Torquay. The *Hind* veered off at this point, out into more open water with the distant blue shimmer of the Isle of Portland in the distance. A breeze lifted Bee's hair: she put her finger in her mouth and held it up to the wind. The coldness told her that it was blowing from the east. The sun was starting to sink, now. She looked back to the hills and saw it reddening. But ahead, over the Isle, the sky was indigo-black. Dark reappeared, with a piece of bread which he gave to her.

"Captain says there's a storm coming," he said.

SERENA

Serena gaped at Ward as though she'd never seen him before. He stared back, mouth tightened in apology, brown spaniel eyes contrite. "*Your* family? What sort of stuff?"

"Not the same stuff. I can't believe I'm having this conversation. *Our* stuff is to do with the women. It's a secret and it's never actually been confirmed to me, but I think I know what it is. Quite honestly, sometimes I wonder if this isn't everyone."

"Everyone?"

"Round here, in England, the world. If every family hasn't got weird magical shit going on under the surface."

"I don't think they do, Ward."

"No, I don't really think they do, either. God, the *boringness* of a lot of the people you meet – all they can think about is their dinner and the football and when they're next going to get laid. Anyway, maybe we shouldn't talk about it. I myself have no magical properties. Apart from my ridiculous levels of charisma, obviously."

"Obviously. I don't think I do either. But, Ward, look, I can't say the same for the house."

Their eyes met.

"That spectacular woman in green, at the end of your catwalk show. I didn't see her around the place beforehand. And trust me, I'd have noticed. She'd give Charlize Theron a run for her money on screen. If I was an agent I'd be down on my knees waving a contract at her. I overheard some woman saying she must be a supermodel and you knew her through your job, but she's not, is she?"

"No, she's not."

"Serena – what *is* she, then?"

"I think she is a sort of star spirit."

Ward's eyebrows had, by now, nearly reached his slightly, if elegantly, receding hairline.

"A star spirit."

"A star spirit."

"And what *is* a 'star spirit?' when it is at home?"

Serena sighed. "Let's start getting this gear back to the house. I'll show you. Sort of."

Soon after this, they were standing in Abraham's study. The box of gemstones had been retrieved from the linen cupboard and the stones were now once more scattered over the green leather top of the desk. Serena handed Ward a chart.

"This is a list of the Behenian stars and their correspondences. Each of them has a stone, and a plant, and a flower. Some of them are male and some of them are female but they all look like women. Don't ask me how that works."

"So how many of these have you actually met?"

"We tried to make a list and it was difficult because we used to see them sometimes when we were little girls, and it's hard to remember. But we think we've met most of them."

"And the one on the catwalk was –"

"Spica."

"I've met another one."

"You have?"

"Yes, when I first started going out with you and we came down for Christmas – that year it rained all the time. Do you remember?"

"Yes, of course."

"I went to the loo in the middle of the night and there was a woman standing on the landing looking down the stairs. She was in a massive dress of blue velvet and she had sapphires in her hair. I could smell something and later, actually when we came down in the summer and we were in the garden, I realised that it was thyme."

"That would have been Capella. Why didn't you tell me?"

"I thought she was a ghost."

"And so –"

"I had it drummed into me as a kid, by my gran, that if you saw something weird – *especially* in someone else's house – you kept your mouth shut about it."

"That does make a lot of sense."

"Gran was very sensible," Ward said. "Despite dressing like Edith Sitwell."

STELLA

Stella felt a little of the tension go out of her shoulders when it became apparent that the storm was actually dying down. She wasn't afraid of the weather itself – though it was always wise to be wary – but she didn't like the idea of having to share this cramped, enclosed space with Tam Stare any longer than she had to. The prospect of needing, at some point, to go to sleep had been worrying her. She wouldn't put it past him to try something on while she lay there inert. So when the last patter of drops sounded on the iron roof and there was only the crash of the waves, Stella bounced up.

"Right! Let's get on with it."

She had been expecting dissent but, rather to her surprise, Tam seemed relieved.

"Yeah, I don't want to spend more time in this shithole than we have to."

Perhaps he, too, had feared the thought of sleep. This was a little heartening to Stella. She pushed open the door and found a still evening, the smell of salt and rain hanging heavy in the air. But apart from the spray cast up by the waves, it was dry. The big clouds were racing away out to sea and the sky was once more green.

"Which way?" Stella wondered aloud.

"Hey," Tam said. "I can see a light."

He was right. It flickered once, dim and wan, and it was moving.

"Someone with a torch?" Tam said.

"What's that stuff that used to lead travellers astray in the marshes, though? Some kind of gas?"

"Will o'the wisp."

"What if it's that?"

"Well, as long as we don't actually follow it, maybe." Tam blew on his hands. Stella had warmed up a bit in the hut but he still seemed withdrawn and shivery. Despite her earlier contemplation of pneumonia, she hoped he wasn't coming down with something. She shouldn't feel responsible for him, and yet, she was beginning to. This irritated Stella and she bit back a snap which he did not really deserve.

"Okay. You're right. It looks like it's heading away from us, anyway.

Look, it's going along the shoreline." The wavering light was growing fainter. "So we can follow it without following it, if you see what I mean. At least we know we've got shelter, if we need it. We can always head back to the hut."

"All right."

They set off along the shore at a brisk pace. Stella's hair was still wet and she shoved it back into the hood of her parka, but she had to keep the hood down, otherwise she couldn't see very well. It narrowed her view, like a horse's blinkers, and Stella wanted as much vision as possible. The light dipped, up and down, following the contours of the low rise beyond the shore. Not high enough to be called a cliff, it was a long snaky dune of sand and coarse grass. The relative flatness of the land meant that the light could be kept in view. Tam and Stella pursued it, trying to keep a distance. At least Tam had finally shut up. As they came up over the dune, Stella saw that they had reached a river. It ran, low and bubbling, through a cut in the dunes to the sea. It had carved channels in a space of sand between the shingle banks and soon merged with the tide. Upstream, a waving blond mass was, after a moment, recognisable as reed beds.

On the opposite bank stood a building, on a spur similar to the one on which the hut had stood, and the light was heading for it. But the building, too, was lit. Within its dark, pointed bulk was the flicker of a candle flame in a window, blue behind stained glass.

"It's a church," Tam said, uneasily. He stopped walking.

"A chapel, surely? It's not big enough for a church." Stella could see that at one gable end, there was a small arch with a bell.

"Whatever."

"Well, I'm going to take a look. Coming?"

"Yes. I'll come." But he did not sound enthusiastic. Maybe he is a vampire, thought Stella. Perhaps he would burst into flames on entering holy ground? Hey, fingers crossed. She was wary of whoever might be carrying that light. It was no longer visible but she had heard the old creak of a door opening: the person, or thing, had gone inside. Stella did not like to think about what it might be, if not a person. She swallowed the fluttering lump in her throat as they came closer to the chapel. A flagstone path led along the spur of land and as they reached the door, the bell began to toll, strangely high and sweet above the sound of the sea. Tam and Stella looked at each other.

"Someone's ringing that," Stella said.

"Or it's just the wind."

"No, it's too regular." The bell tolled nine times and then fell silent. Wasn't there something about a toll of nine? Stella couldn't remember. Nine for a death?

"You still want to risk it?"

Tam shrugged. "We're here now."

She reached out and gave the door a push. It was old, bleached oak, very pale. The salty air couldn't be doing it much good. Her footsteps rang on the stone within. It seemed much bigger inside, a Tardis-chapel, but only for a moment. Stella blinked. There was no sign of the light, or its bearer. The chapel had a ceiling like King's College: she couldn't remember what the style was called, but it was light and arching, reminding her of trees. Columns marched down the aisle to an altar and she could see the candle now, placed high on the ledge of a window. Then she looked again. It wasn't a candle. It was flickering blue-green like a driftwood fire, unattached to any lamp or wax. Marshfire, needfire… words whispered in Stella's head.

And all of it – the columns and arches, the dimly lit walls, were encrusted in seashells.

"It's like a folly," Stella whispered.

"A what?"

"One of those Victorian things. There's one on the Exe estuary – a little house, filled with shells."

Tam looked at her, uninterested. Then his gaze sharpened and he looked past her.

"What's that?"

Stella turned and saw that there was a column standing at the side of the church, also encrusted with shells.

"It's a pillar or something," she said.

"No, it isn't. It fucking *moved.*"

Stella felt a cold prickling blush rush up the back of her neck. She mouthed, repeating, *"Fuck."*

"I'm not going near it," said Tam and this decided Stella, even if it was a bad idea.

"I will, then." Cautiously, she approached the column. As she did so, the marshfire light in the window flickered into further life and she saw that the column was indeed not a pillar, but a figure in a long gown, standing with its back to the chapel. The skirts of the gown seemed to grow up from the floor, or perhaps had grown into it (stalactite, stalagmite, thought Stella, trying to recall the little mnemonic about which was which), and they were heavy with scallops, mussels, tiny whorls of whelks, and skeins of weed. Then the figure twitched, sending Stella stumbling backwards. *Alive alive o.* But it did not turn to face her and somehow this gave Stella courage. She sidled down a pew and back down the side of the church towards the figure. As she did so, the profile turned and looked at her directly. Stella swallowed.

The figure was a woman. She reminded Stella of a ship's prow, with the pale curve of her breasts outlined by the low cut of the gown (at this point, a Joyce Grenfell song beloved of her grandfather came irreverently to Stella's mind: 'stately as a galleon'). Her hair, white as plaster, was piled up and decked with pearls, and her sorrowful face was pale and symmetrical, reminiscent of a Classical statue. Her lips moved but no sound came forth. Her eyes were dark and whiteless. Stella was, by this time, much less afraid and feeling rather smug: she did not get a strong sense of threat from this woman, and she had dared where Tam had not. She said, "Who are you?"

The woman's lips moved again. There was a whisper, nothing more than a breath.

"I'm sorry," Stella said. "I can't hear you." She leaned closer.

"Watch it," Tam said from behind her. But Stella knew the woman wouldn't hurt her.

"Tell me," she said. She was close enough now to smell the woman. There was an odour, very faint, of the sea: fresh and wild and salt, no shellfish or rot. The woman spoke again and this time Stella could hear.

"I am a captured star."

SERENA

All the guests had gone home. The orchestra had played, to great acclaim. No expert in classical music, Serena had recognised at least one piece, because Abraham had played it a lot. She thought it had been Mercury, The Winged Messenger. Earlier, Ben's band had also played, minus their lead singer. The rest of Coldwar 'did not know where he was', they had told Serena apologetically. He was supposed to meet them at Paddington but he hadn't shown up and wasn't answering his phone, so after some debate they had got on the train without him and Seelie had taken over the vocals.

"I'm, you know, really sorry? About all this?" Seelie had shuffled her feet like a child caught out.

"It's not *your* fault."

"Yeah, but it makes things awkward and –" here Seelie looked Serena anxiously and directly in the face "- we don't like her. None of us. We think she's creepy."

"Thank you!"

Despite the disruption, Coldwar had down well, and if the audience had been disappointed not to see Ben Amberley, no one had said anything. What a freaking anticlimax, Serena thought: she had too much to worry about without yet more crap to do with her errant boyfriend and she resented, retrospectively, the energy she'd put into fretting over him. Apple Day had left an empty marquee, a trace of laughter, a few paper plates scattered across the lawn which Luna and Sam had retrieved in case the rising wind took them and flung them across the fields, and quite a lot of money, destined for the church roof restoration fund, which Caro and Serena now sat counting around the kitchen table. Neither Stella nor Bee had been seen for some hours and Serena sat with this knowledge nestling in a thick lump of worry beneath her breastbone.

"They're grown women," Luna said. She seemed less concerned than her sister. "And they will be with the stars."

"Are we sure about that?"

Luna's face crinkled. "I think so. I hope so. I think we just have to trust everyone, Serena."

"This isn't like you," Serena had to say.

"I know. I suppose I've always been a bit – a bit everyone-else-is-always-wrong, haven't I? Maybe I need to take a look at myself."

"Maybe we all do."

"Did you change, when you had Bella?"

"*Massively*. I changed massively, Lune. Everything was different. A whole load of shit that had always been important suddenly wasn't. And it wasn't just me any more. I wasn't the most important person in my life any longer and I never have been since then and hopefully I never will be again, because if I am, it will mean that something has happened to Bells. It doesn't mean that stuff like Ben doesn't matter or doesn't hurt. It's really –" She paused.

"Fucked you over?"

"Yes, it has a bit and there's all this stuff happening around Dana Stare and her brother. I don't know what it means."

"Do you think the stars left us behind because we're mothers? Or soon-to-be mothers, in my case."

"I don't know. I don't know whether that would even be a consideration. They're so unhuman."

"If they wanted someone to hold the fort, you'd think it might be Bee: she's like the linchpin here at the house, isn't she? But it does suggest," Luna said, "that they might have some sort of plan."

"The queen is in her counting house," said Caro Amberley, coming in through the back door.

"Sorry? Oh, counting out her money. Yes. The church's money, anyway."

"I need to say a big thank you to Bee, and to all of you. It went really well, didn't it? I think that ought to do a bit for the Celebrate Somerset campaign and the church roof, anyway."

Caro did not seem to have noticed either Stella or Bee's absence and Serena did not know why this was, for Caro was an observant woman, never complacent. Either the stars had done something to her memory, or she had decided to go along with things, perhaps. But then Caro said,

"Has Bee gone to bed? She must be shattered."

"I think she has, yes, Stella's in the bath," Serena lied. "And yes it did, the day I mean, but I'm glad it's over. Now I can enjoy it." *I hope.* She bundled up all the notes and stuffed them in an envelope. "Here you go."

"Thanks so much. I really appreciate all this." Caro glanced at the clock. "I ought to be getting back. The animals should be fine, someone will have fed them, but…"

"It's been a long day," Serena said. "Do you need a ride home?"

"I'll call Ward. He said he'd pick me up."

"Cool," said Serena, but she was conscious of a little niggle of disappointment. She had wondered if Ward might have liked to come over and keep her company, if there was to be a vigil for her missing sisters. Then she felt guilty, because of Ben – but Ben wasn't here, was he? And Ben had made it abundantly clear that things were over and you shouldn't rebound from one man to another like this. Like what? Serena chided herself.

Caro made her phone call and Luna wandered off into the house and soon Ward swung into the yard in the Amberley's Range Rover and whisked his cousin away into the dark with barely a nod to Serena. Feeling flat and fed up, she went back into the kitchen and opened a bottle of Pinot Grigio. First drink of the day; she hadn't dared touch the cider. She sat, sipping, and checking her phone. Nothing. But in a surprisingly short time, there was the sound of wheels on gravel again and the kitchen door opening.

"Are you going to drink that all by yourself?" Ward Garner said.

LUNA

Luna wandered down to the horses. Apple Day was over and it had gone well. She was pleased, but there had been too many people: she was peopled out. Sam didn't count as *people* and her relatives sometimes did and sometimes didn't. This evening, they definitely did and Luna preferred to seek the quiet company of the piebalds instead of sitting in the kitchen and dissecting the day's events. Besides, she wanted time to think about what was happening: about her mother, about Bee and Stella, about the baby. The child seemed to be absorbing her normal levels of anxiety, dissatisfaction and stress, like a black star sucking in light, except that the light was the darkness and the child itself felt bright inside her, alchemical and transmuting. Luna was, at some level stifled by hormones or something else, worried about this, too: surely it could not be good for a growing baby to be subjected to all this weirdness and angst. Yet she still felt an unaccustomed calm. Guided by instinct and torchlight, she walked down to where the piebalds grazed at the end of the paddock. The grass smelled fresh and wet, the air held a warm whiff of horses. They looked up as she approached, then down again. She was one of their humans and they were used to her. Luna placed her hand on a black and white neck and the horse ignored her, continuing to pluck at the grass. As always, she marvelled at them: at their mild dark eyes, the feathers at their heels, their waterfall tails. Sam had told her that this kind of horse dated to the First World War, when the travelling communities had bred coloured horses so that their beasts would not be taken for the cavalry: the army apparently preferring single shade mounts. She did not know if this was true or a traveller's tale, but it didn't really matter. She switched the torch off, not wanting to dazzle the horses, and the soft cold blackness closed in. She could see lights down the road at the start of the village proper, and the stars were out: it took a moment or two for her to place them, wrapped as they were by the flying clouds. The wind was bitter against her cheek but Luna didn't mind: months in the van had toughened her against the cold and she was bundled up.

Months in the van had also sharpened her eyesight. At first she had found it hard, stumbling about in the dark, and Sam had insisted that she carry a torch with her, or at least matches or a lighter. But Luna had persevered, with notions of getting to know the night, hoping that her sight would catch up. And it actually had: she had glimpsed one of Mooncote's cats, Sable, pure black except for a vicar's white smudge under his chin, slinking through the orchard one night when all the house lights had been off.

"How," Stella had asked in astonishment, "did you know he was there?"

"I saw him."

"You're kidding me. You saw a black cat on a moonless night, with no lights?"

Luna had fought down an urge to make an irritated snap.

"Yes," she had said.

"Wow." Stella had believed her, since the cat was indubitably there, winding around their ankles. Luna felt a moment of triumph: she felt strong, able to see what the common run of humans could not, returning to the ways of the ancestors – all that stuff. It was a bit pretentious, she thought now, but still bloody useful.

So this was how she saw the shadow under the hedge.

The hedge itself was thorn, like the ones further up the field on the way to the churchyard: blackthorn and haw. Luna and Stella had come down here a little while ago, to pick smoky blue sloes and scarlet haw berries (good for the heart, said Sam, if you made them into a tincture). It had been nice, a half hour of sisterly contact doing something productive as they watched the mist roll slowly up off the Moon brook. The resulting sloe gin would be steeped and drunk at Christmas. Their grandfather had made it, so had Alys, and both Luna and her sister felt in need of some continuity. But now the blackthorn, stripped of its fruit, seemed to have retreated into itself. It still bore a scattering of dull golden leaves but the tangle of branches were iron-spined and Luna took care not to get too close.

The shadow was slinking under the hedge. Luna could see it from the corner of her eye. It was long and sinuous, thickly furred. She tried not to move. Was it an animal, or something pretending to be one? Then the piebald shifted uneasily, stepping back, and Luna lost her balance in the wet grass. She did not fall but she had to grab at the horse's mane and that was when the thing slid out from beneath the hedge and confronted her. She saw black eyes in a narrow black head.

It hissed, displaying sharp teeth. It was a mink.

"Fuck off!" Luna hissed back. The mink ran forwards. It was big, though perhaps its fur made it look larger Luna kicked at it and it snapped at her boot, but then the piebald was in between her and the mink, angling its body to push Luna out of the way. She had to move, not wanting to be accidentally knocked flat. The piebald stamped, aiming at the mink, and the mare joined it, whickering in warning. Once, high on the side of a fell, Luna had watched a wild pony go for an adder: the same stamping movement. The snake had been killed; the mink evidently feared the same fate, because it hissed again and slipped back into the shelter of the blackthorns. In silent accord, the piebalds turned and marched up the slope of the field with Luna walking between them, her guardians, as quickly as she could.

SERENA

"What was that?"

"What?"

"That noise."

"I don't know," Ward said. "I didn't hear anything."

Serena sat up in bed.

"Shh. I'm listening."

There was a grumbling sound from the pipes.

"This house still has dodgy plumbing, I see."

"I know. Bee did have it overhauled a couple of years ago, as well, but I suppose all old houses have cranky pipes."

"That wasn't what you heard, though?"

"No."

They had consumed the wine. Then they had gone to bed, not because either Serena or Ward was drunk (not on half a bottle each of Tesco's Pinot Grigio) but mainly because Ward had come back and Serena had an oh-sod-it moment.

"However," Ward had said. "I am conscious of some vestigial responsibility." He looked momentarily appalled, as if at some personal lapse. "What about Bella?"

"Well, I'd prefer it if she didn't know," Serena said. "And I certainly don't want her to catch us in bed, obviously."

"Quite. There is a touch of the Aldwych Farce about the whole prospect. People running from room to room in their knickers."

"Her room is at the end of the corridor and she seems, thank God, to be entering that teenage stage of sleeping a lot and having to be hauled out of her pit in the morning. The battles I have trying to get her off to school! And she's not actually trying to be difficult, she just can't wake up. I was the same. Alys used to say my spirit animal was a dormouse."

"And if," Ward asked delicately, "this develops? Not that I am making any assumptions, you understand."

He was making a whacking big one, Serena thought, but at least he had announced a sort of intention and she felt her spirits lift. Not just lift, but soar. This surprised her, a lot. She had got into the way of regarding old boyfriends, if still around, as sort-of family members. Brothers, perhaps, or cousins; Ward himself had alluded to the avuncular and when she'd met him that day in the pub, she'd been too much of a sodden mess to think about engaging. And she had known Ward all her life, as well: their relationship had been more of old family friends than young-girl-dazzled-by-handsome-actor. She suspected that Ward might have been rather more raw over Miranda than he was letting on, too, and rebounds, as she had reminded herself earlier, are never a good idea. But maybe there really was unfinished business. "Anyway," she had said, "Bella likes you."

"She barely knows me."

"She liked you in *Endless*. She said you were quite cool for an old person."

"So flattering. I should be grateful that I still have a younger audience, I suppose."

But by this time Serena was feeling a little reckless. She took Ward by the hand and led him, with no further protests, upstairs to bed, where things had progressed in a way that was still familiar, and yet not. Ward was older, she was older. Maybe not by that much, given the span of a lifetime, but enough to make a difference. It appeared that they'd both learned a thing or two. At an inopportune moment, she recalled that an unfortunate carnal encounter with a waitress had got Ward into the tabloids, some years before, and the young woman had not only told more about the encounter than anyone surely really wanted to hear, but given Ward ten out of ten. Serena obviously did not bring this up, but she had to admit that the waitress had a point.

She had been initially worried about the changes that pregnancy had wrought, but oh-sod-it to those, too, and Ward didn't seem to notice. If he was too polite to comment, then that was a good thing. And then they had gone to sleep, companionably, and that was also familiar, and nice. Until Serena had been startled awake by the noise.

She could not say what it was. She had been dreaming and something had happened, someone knocking at a door and the door had led to the sea – and then she was awake and knew that the sound had been real. But it had not been a knock.

Ward was listening, as well.

"You know," he said, "I think I *can* hear something."

"What can you hear?"

214

"It's like a sort of rhythmic tapping. A pendulum? No, more like a clock ticking."

Serena was about to say, *it is a clock, you idiot, it's the alarm,* but then she glanced at the little bedside clock, which was an old fashioned one of the kind that you imagine in nurseries. It had stopped, at half past four.

"Right," Serena said. She swung her legs over the side of the bed and stood up.

"Where are you going?"

"I'm just going to have a peek out of the window."

She went quickly across the room and tugged the curtain aside. The wind was still high but then the black clouds parted and she saw the thin horn of the moon. It was very slim, a rind of light, and it was on its back. The sash gave a sudden rattle. It was unlucky to see the new moon through glass, Serena thought, and that was her last proper thought for some time. The sash shot up, though she had not touched it, letting in a blast of cold air. The moon pierced her: she felt it go in under her breastbone like a curved knife. She gasped and folded. From the bed, she heard a startled exclamation from Ward but the words made no sense. She stumbled forwards, falling against the sash window, and through the gap.

When she landed, outside on the flagstones of the yard, it was on all four feet.

STELLA

Stella was, for the moment, stumped. She sat back on her heels and looked at the edges of the star spirit's gown. For the life of her, she couldn't see where skirt ended and flagstone began. The spirit herself had lapsed into something that was like sleep, or perhaps unconsciousness. Her eyes were closed, making her look like a marble statue, and occasionally her mouth opened, but she did not speak. Part of the problem, Stella thought, was that she could not really see. The chapel was dim and the spirit had been caught in the shadows. Tam was exploring, somewhere at the back; she could hear movement, and curses. As long as she knew roughly where he was, she wasn't too worried, but she didn't want to turn her back on him, either.

Stella straightened up and went over to the windowsill. If she stood up on a pew, she would be at eye level with the little light. If she could somehow get it over to the star, she might be able to see better... Closer to it, she could not see whether it was attached to anything, but now, with a better view, it reminded her of something. Of Abraham.

"Are you – alive?"

The blue-green light bobbed. Stella blinked, momentarily dazzled, and saw that there was a fine mesh between herself and the window. The light flickered behind this. Was it metal? It was gossamer fine. She reached out and hesitated. *Oh come on, Stella. It's not likely to be electrocuted, is it?* She touched the mesh but it was like touching spiderweb. It clung to her fingers for a minute and she snatched her hand back, trying to wipe it on her jacket, but the mesh melted away. The light danced.

Stella held out her hand. After a moment, as if making up its mind, or could not believe that it was free, the light shot forwards and hovered over her palm. This close, she could see that it was made up of a vortex, strands of light like DNA, a waterweed presence.

"All right," Stella said. "Okay."

Tam's voice came from the back regions.

"Who are you talking to?"

"Myself," she called. "I'm the only one who understands me round here."

She got down from the pew and carried the light, if that was the right word for something that you weren't actually holding, over to the trapped star. Bending down, the light went with her, flooding the floor with a watery radiance. Stella knelt with care. Now that she could see properly, she noted that there was still no visible join between floor and hem, but this gave her another idea. Might it be possible to get the star out of her dress?

"Excuse me," Stella said. "I'm going to prod you a bit. Sorry if it's inappropriate." The star did not respond. Stella tried to run a finger between the star's bodice and her flesh, but the fabric – if it was fabric – felt more like concrete and the star's skin was cold and hard as stone. Stella was starting to wonder if she actually was some sort of statue, after all, when the light soared up. The star's mouth opened. The light zoomed into it. The star's lips closed with a snap.

"Oh!" Stella gasped.

The star's eyes opened and for a moment they were as opaque and black as before. Then they flooded with marshfire light, blue and green and a lightning flicker of gold. The star's face flushed a delicate blue. She raised her head and there was a tearing, rending sound as she took a tottering step forward and her skirts came free of the floor.

"What's going on?" Tam Stare came down the aisle in a rush.

"She's waking up properly. She's *walking*."

The star reached around and took hold of the train of her gown. She pulled and it tore, coming loose in a rattle of shells. The heavy fabric fell to the flagstones. Beneath, she wore a silk shift. Then the bodice, dropped in one piece like the breastplate of a suit of armour. But the star wavered. She clutched the wooden edge of a pew for support.

"She's having difficulty standing up," Stella snapped. "She's too weak. Give us a hand." She took the star by an arm, no longer so cold and heavy, although it felt unnervingly like the arm of a corpse. How long had she been ensnared? Stella thought about sitting on a long haul flight, how stiff your legs became. How much worse if you'd been standing for – what? Aeons? A hundred years? Poor star, even if they weren't human and might not have the same biological constraints.

"What's your name?" she asked. But she couldn't hear the star's reply. The star pointed to the door.

"She wants to go out," said Stella.

"I'm not completely thick, you know."

"I'm just trying to be clear. Take her other arm."

Tam draped the star's arm over his shoulders and they half walked, half dragged her to the doorway. She was remarkably heavy, Stella thought, for someone who looked quite slight now that she was out of her enveloping draperies.

"Hold her up," she said to Tam. "I'll open the door."

They bore the star through and into the porch. There was a spatter of rain on their faces, blown in on a strong sea wind, and the star seemed to revive a little. She looked up. Stella turned back to the door to close it and there was a sudden violent shove in her back. She was propelled through the door and sprawled on the flagstones. A burst of pain shot through her knee as the door was slammed behind her and bolted. Tam Stare, outside with the freed star, had locked her in.

SERENA

Running was like flying. Serena had never felt so light; she had never run so far. She did not remember why she had run in the first place, only that something had been coming after her, something bad. It was hard to think in words, rather than blocks of shade/scent/shape, and it was too much effort, she was too busy. She dodged and ducked around tree trunks and bushes, dived beneath bramble and briar, leaped a stream with feather-lightness. Ward was a distant memory: huge and alien, as were her sisters and Sam. She shivered at the thought of humans: they could not be trusted, they would kill. She did not know what she was, only that she revelled in her skittering swiftness, pulled along by the vast crescent of the moon and the sparkling stars. Her heart beat like a manic drum; she could feel it thumping as though it would break through the wall of her chest and fly upwards and it rang to the rhythm of her feet. She barely touched the grass, instinct driving her into a weaving zigzag. *Don't run straight.* And the thing behind her, her pursuer, kept on. She did not look back but she could feel it and smell its rank stench, completely different to the fluffy-familiar musky smell of herself and the small fry, who scattered out of her way as she passed and they sensed it coming, too, diving into burrows and into the thick tangles of briar. Serena zigzagged down a slope, past two enormous things who looked up at her mildly as she passed, through a hedge and into another field. She was running along the stream now and she could smell its deep wetness, the mud and weed and the sharp smell of the small people who lived in the bank. Behind her, there was a hiss. It was gaining on her. She could feel its shadow streaming out behind it in the light of the moon and hear it whisking through the damp grass. Something loomed up ahead of her and Serena sprang, scrambling up. There was a snap at her heels, the graze of teeth. But she was over, falling and rolling, hitting stone so hard that it knocked the wind out of her.

"Serena!" a voice said, surprised. And all at once Serena was a woman again, breathless and, to her horror, naked. She was lying against the side of her grandfather's tomb. Something thin and black ran along the top of the churchyard wall and was gone.

"Grandpa?"

"Believe me when I say," the blue light that was Abraham said, "that I didn't know you could do that."

"At least no one saw me." Serena was sitting in the kitchen of Mooncote, wrapped in a voluminous dressing gown that had surely belonged to a man and a larger one than any recent male relatives. It was slightly itchy and smelled of mothballs.

"You'd never have lived that down," Ward agreed. "Arrested. Starkers in the churchyard at midnight. The Daily Mail would have had a field day."

"It was bloody cold without fur, I'll have you know." She sipped the tea he'd just given her, plus a large shot of whisky. The two did not really go together, but Serena was past caring. She was still shaky, from exertion, shock and the relief of seeing Ward pounding down the churchyard path, more or less dressed and waving the dressing gown.

"I found it in the airing cupboard," he said.

"How did you know I might need it?"

He gave her a brooding stare, familiar to audiences. "Stuff," he said.

"Stuff?"

"Stuff."

"Right."

"I must say, just for the sake of clarity, this particular thing has never actually happened to me before. As you know, I have had a number of ladyfriends, including your good self. And a wife. And indeed a couple of gentleman acquaintants. However, no one I've slept with has ever fallen out of the bedroom window and turned into a bloody hare before."

"Well, it's the first time I've ever done it, so there." She stuck out her tongue.

"How old are you, five?"

"Well, I *haven't.*"

"The shock," Ward said, to the kitchen wall, "was substantial. I'll tell you what, I feel every minute of my age. Bad enough that you suddenly took a header onto the cobbles – by the time I'd got to the window I'd got as far as the inquest, the verdict of misadventure, the tabloid headlines... Quite apart from the heart attack when you simply weren't there and there was a large bunny sitting on the step, looking baffled."

"How did you know it was me?"

"Again with the 'stuff'."

She gave him a narrow look, but let it go.

"Did you see what was after me?"

"Yes. A mink. Long and black and slinky."

"Aha!"

"You know who it was?"

"I think it was Dana Stare."

"Animal girls," said Ward. "Don't ask me why but I'm not remotely surprised."

"You're taking this really well. I suppose that's because of 'stuff', too."

"Quite so."

Serena bundled herself more heavily in the thick folds of the dressing gown. She could not seem to stop shivering, in spite of the whisky.

"God, I hope this isn't going to become a regular occurrence." She groped for his hand and Ward took her chilly fingers in what was actually quite a painful grip.

"You might not do it in London. Not exactly hare country."

"It was – exhilarating. But really, really vulnerable."

"I wish I could do more to help." The supercilious, self-consciously thespian mask slipped for a moment. Ward said, "That was fucking terrifying. I thought you might end up in something's jaws – I met a fox in the road, quite apart from Minky Girl. Or get run over. Suppose you'd been flattened by one of those ridiculously enormous tractors everyone drives around here? It's worse than having pets."

"They don't drive them in the middle of the night, do they? Unless they're harvesting, sometimes, and we're way past that now."

"Well, I don't know!"

"Have you learned nothing from a childhood in the countryside?"

"I think I tried to pretend it wasn't happening. I regard Hampstead as overly rural. Hell, *Hackney's* too agricultural for me these days."

"Oh Ward!" But she was smiling now, despite her chattering teeth.

"What? It's got a farm in it, hasn't it? Anyway, at least you are more or less all right and unflattened."

"That farm's for children. It's got baby goats and guinea pigs. I really am awfully sorry about this whole hare thing."

"It's not your fault," Ward said, adding rather fiercely, "*None* of this is your fault. I think I need to beard my cousin in her den and have a serious chat." He knocked back his own scotch. "But in the morning. It's half past three. Is it all right if I stay the rest of the night here?"

"I think you'd better," said Serena. "And tie my toe to the bedpost. Or stick me in a hutch."

BEE

Bee had to grip the railing now, because the ship was plunging up and down. The coast was lost in a blur of rain. They had passed some familiar landmarks, skirting the Isle of Portland and then coming closer to the cliffs: Bee could see the arch of Durdle Door, not greatly unchanged, before the squall hit. She was hoping not to be sent below. It might be more comfortable (the railing had given her splinters and she was soaked) but Bee preferred to see what was going on. If Drake – now standing, legs braced, in the prow – sent her beneath deck, she would have to comply, but she was still invisible to the rest of the crew. As long as she didn't fall in... She clutched harder at the rail as the *Hind* bucked. Above, the sky was inky black and a flicker of lightning briefly lit up a white rim ahead. After a moment's thought, Bee realised it was the distant Isle of Wight.

Dark appeared at her shoulder.

"Captain's pleased."

"He is? Does he like storms?"

"It's a good sign, he says. He's been expecting it. You all right? Do you want to go below deck?"

"I'd rather stay here if you don't mind."

"Be careful," was all that Dark said. But Bee was too excited. Everyone always thought of her as being rooted in place, grown out of Mooncote and remaining there. When she was a child, however, they had come down to this coast often, and she had kept up those visits in adult life. Dartmouth and the beautiful Exe estuary. The Cornish cliffs and bays, Lulworth Cove and Swanage. And once long ago a friend of Abraham's, a member of one of the Cowes yacht clubs, had taken all the girls and Alys around the Isle of Wight, skimming through the Solent and around the Needles on a high bright September day just before the start of the school term. Bee had loved it and at the start of the placid Beaulieu river, Stella had fallen in and they'd had to throw her a lifebelt. It was, the sisters (but not their mother) agreed, the perfect end to a perfect day. They had driven back to the friend's house, Stella dripping triumphantly on the back seat.

And now the island was in sight, a bulk of shadow against the eastern sky. Bee flinched as a great wave broke over the bow of the *Hind*. Perhaps it would be more sensible to go below… but Bee was rather tired of being sensible. She gripped the rail more tightly and risked a look over it at the churning water. The boat was driving into the wind. There was an immense crack of thunder overhead, then a flash. The sails, angled to catch the wind, roared. The *Hind* was tacking against the easterly. Bee did not know how the ship was withstanding it: boats always seemed so frail, somehow, against the wash of the sea. Abraham's sailor friend had told them that the area around the Needles was dangerous. But modern yachts and ferries were all fibreglass and steel; this boat was made of wood. Bee suddenly felt very vulnerable but the sea pulled at her; she had to take another look. In the deep glassy wave, between froth and spume, a split-second face looked up at her. It was wild and snarling, not quite human. An arm reached up out of the water, claw tipped, instantly gone. Bee stepped back from the rail in shock and slipped on the wet wood. She slid down the deck and fetched up against the bench.

"Are you all right?" Dark was there, face creased with concern. He hauled her up.

"Yes – God, I saw something. Someone. A face."

Dark smiled. "A mermaid?"

"It didn't look very maidenly."

"There's all sorts down there."

Bee was about to say that perhaps it might be better if she did go below, after all, when there was a shout from the rigging. Drake called something to the crew but Bee did not hear what it was: his words were whipped away by the wind. But the *Hind* was starting to turn. She could see a long line of headland, rocks, a tiny flicker of light through the storm. The ship seemed alarmingly close to the coast and she thought, *what if I die here?* Would she find herself back in Mooncote, alive, it all a dream? Or would she be dead there, too?

SERENA

Ward stayed long enough to share a belated breakfast before taking the Landrover back to Amberley. Changing into an animal without warning made you very tired, Serena had discovered, and also ravenously hungry. Worse than having a baby. She polished off a plate of scrambled eggs, then piece after piece of toast. Nell was not yet down but sounds of the bath being run echoed from upstairs. Luna came downstairs, raised an eyebrow at Ward, said, "Hi. Still here? Is there any tea?" and, having poured a cup, took it outside. She would talk to Luna later, Serena thought. And Ward had said he would talk to his cousin. She mentioned this now.

"What are you going to say to Caro?"

"I don't know. I've never had this sort of conversation before. There ought to be a Miss Manners set of etiquette guidelines on it. It's going to start 'You'll think I'm a lunatic but'. I will try and be as circumspect as possible."

"Are you going to mention Dana Stare?"

"Yes. Actually, now you mention it, that's a good way in, I think. However, if you see an ambulance speeding past in an hour or so's time, that might be me, in the straightjacket that my relatives have ordered for me. One can always be wrong about things." He downed the rest of his tea. "Right, onwards. Serena, my love, I will be back later on, hopefully with practical advice. Until then, I'm wondering if it's wise for you to leave the house."

"I'm going to talk to Luna," Serena said. "And I'm not the only problem. What about Bee and Stella? And – look, you'd better know. We found something out about Mum, as well."

"Do you mean, she's –"

"No, we don't think she's dead but it's all a bit peculiar."

He took her hand and gave it a squeeze. "No shit, Sherlock."

When he had gone, Serena made another cup of tea and took it upstairs to her grandfather's study. After his death, they had left it to Alys to sort out Abraham's papers, considering this to be the best option. But Serena did not know if her mother had actually done so. Perhaps her mother had not had time? She knew that Alys had got rid of Abraham's clothes and shoes, taking most of them to Oxfam and burning the oldest and most moth eaten jumpers on a large and cathartic bonfire. Her grandparent had been well-dressed on the whole, in an upper class tweedy English way, but had proved male and intractable on the subject of a handful of gardening sweaters and some disreputable hats. But his books and notes... She knew that some, at least, were there.

Calling good morning to the still-bathing Nell, Serena opened the door of her grandfather's study and closed it behind her, shutting herself away from the rest of the house. With no way of knowing where Stella and Bee had gone, or when they would return, and confined to Mooncote, she had to find some way of occupying herself and this might as well be it. Her grandfather's books still stood on the shelves, carefully and methodically alphabetised. His notes were a different matter. Many had been corralled into ring binders and seemed roughly related to topics, although Serena did not necessarily understand what those topics were. There were a great many equations. Stella had once said to her sister,

"You can follow a dress pattern, but you can't do sums. What's that about? Aren't they sort of in the same ballpark?"

"I don't know," Serena had replied. "I can't get my head around music, either."

"Oh, that's easy."

"It's easy *for you.*"

"True. If I sewed anything it would have three sleeves. Even if it was a skirt."

Astrophysics has three sleeves, Serena thought as she leafed through her grandfather's papers. In his case, she supposed it really was rocket science. But it was not all maths and physics. She found a handful of poems, about stars. *Capella walks in sapphire thyme/Spica in emerald green/Algol's diamonds cease to chime/Nephele the never seen.*

Serena stared at the little rhyme. The Behenian stars, but she did not know Nephele. Which one might she be? She rummaged in the shelves until she found an astronomical dictionary, but could find no mention of Nephele. She went back to her grandfather's chair, via the window. Outside, it had started to rain and wet yellow leaves from the ornamental maple on the lawn had blown onto the flagstones and stuck, forming constellations of their own. No sign of Ward yet, but that was okay. Serena needed breathing space. It was at the bottom of a shoebox that she struck, relatively, gold. Along with all the diagrams her grandfather had drawn some of the Behenian stars: she recognised Sirius and Vega, Regulus and Aldebaran. Here were the Pleiades, drawn in nimble outlines with their crystals and fronds of fennel, whispering among themselves. To this, Abraham had added a note in capitals: THE MISSING? Serena frowned. There were seven stars, he had told her, but nine were named including the parents of the Seven Sisters and she remembered that many more were invisible but still part of the cluster. Did the comment in capitals relate to that? 'Sailing starts when they rise', Abraham had noted and this rang a faint bell, too, that the sailors of ancient Greece would not set out to sea in the months when the sisters could not be seen.

There was nothing more at the bottom of the box so Serena turned her attention to the bookshelves and studied them with more care. Astronomy, military history, books about Somerset... and at the bottom of the last bookcase, a series of smaller books bound in black fabric. Serena pulled them out onto the floor and opened one at random. They were handwritten. They were her grandfather's diaries.

LUNA

Luna woke with a start and sat up. Beside her, Sam lay sprawled in sleep. His mouth was open; he breathed as though he had been running, not quite snoring. Luna reached out and put her hand, slowly, on his shoulder. She was glad, as always, that he was there. Without him, and now the baby — had it woken her? — she felt she might become too spindrifty, blown away on the world's wind. But love and birth would anchor her now. She knew she should not let this define her, make her feel real, and yet it did. Being daughter and sister and friend were good things and yet not quite enough: she needed her own family. As this thought entered her head, however, she heard her mother's voice.

"Luna?"

"Mum?"

It was at the door. For a moment, she thought: *don't go. You don't know what's there. It's a trap.* Something damp pushed into the palm of her hand and Luna jumped, stifling a shriek. But it was only Moth.

"Luna, are you there?" Alys' voice was a whisper, urgent.

"Coming." She went to the door and opened it. There was no one there.

"Mum," Luna said in disappointment.

"Can you see me?"

She looked around, a little wildly. "No, I can't. Where are you?"

"Close. I need a door. Can you make me a door, Luna?"

"I don't know how."

"Yes, you do. Ask your horses."

The final words were no more than a breath. Luna said, "Mum?"

It echoed down the passage. She went back into the bedroom. Sam was still asleep. Serena's door was firmly closed and Bee and Stella were who knew where. *This is something I must do,* Luna thought. As quietly and quickly as she could, she stripped off her leggings and t-shirt, bundling up into her usual layers. As she did so, Moth came to stand by her, staring hopefully up.

"No, you stay here," Luna whispered. But Moth trotted out to wait for her on the landing. It was clear that he was coming too. Downstairs, Luna put on her big boots and laced them up tightly. Then she opened the back door and stepped out.

It was now fully dark, but not frosty. The air was cool and damp and there was a ground mist breathing up from the fields, hanging in veils above the shorn stubble. Luna headed through the gate that led into the field. The piebalds were once more at the bottom and Luna marched straight down the middle, avoiding the hedge. She did not want to risk another encounter with the mink. Moth ran beside, the lurcher's long grey muzzle pointing down and skimming the grass. But as they approached the horses, their heads went up. Luna chirped at them. They turned and began to amble away.

"Hey, I need to talk to you!" Luna said, aloud. The piebalds kicked up their feathery heels and cantered off. She paused for a minute, frustrated. Usually the problem was getting rid of them: they would lean, sidle, nuzzle your pockets for treats, see what you had in whatever bag you were carrying: they were as bad as the cadging dog, and bigger. She did not like the idea that she had spooked them. Summoning determination, she trudged in their wake.

At the far side of the field and the top of the slope, she caught up with them. Pregnancy – or having got out of condition, she thought sourly – had made her short of breath and she had now walked down the field and up again.

"You're leading me a merry dance," she said to the horses, who had paused. But then she saw why. They had stopped at the gate which led into the lane and she could see down into the village.

There was a light in the church, casting the stained glass window into glowing jigsaw colours, though there was no sound from within. Sirius was rising over the tower, as though the weathercock had caught her in his beak. Abraham's tomb was in shadow and no light played around its sharp summit, but through the lych gate at the far end of the churchyard Luna could see a faint silvery track.

The lych path, along which coffins had been carried. Luna's hand went to her stomach, concealed beneath several sweatshirts and her big woolly sweater. She felt snared by time, caught between her mother and her child.

"What do you want me to do?" she said to the baby. Nothing. But then she thought *Mum would never do me harm.* Even if Alys had been in fear for her life, Luna knew that she would give that life for her daughters. In spite of all the head butting, the disagreements, Luna's teenage issues with her mother's vague assumption of her own privileges, at the bottom of all that was trust and love.

"You don't understand, Mum. The world is suffering. The environment, global warming – this government is making sure that it suffers and if we don't speak up…"

"You can't save the world, Luna."

Passion had met bemusement and so Luna had, effectively, run away, to do something about it. It had turned out to be more complicated than that, of course. But she knew that, if she'd run into real trouble, out there in the world, Alys would have been the first to drop everything and come to her aid. And so would her sisters, Luna realised. So surely she should do the same?

"Thank you," she said to the piebalds. Then she opened the gate and stepped out into the lane, Moth at her heels. By the time she reached the lych gate, the track was still glimmering along the lane. A ground mist wreathed around the yew trees and when Stella looked up at the weathercock, Sirius had been swallowed by the clouds. There was the breath of rain in the air and the churchyard felt leaden and ordinary. She looked across to the pyramidal tomb, but all was quiet and at last even the light in the church went off. There was the click of a latch as the verger, or whoever had been within, came out into the porch and closed the door behind them. Luna dodged quickly back behind the beech hedge and held her breath but the person did not come through the lych gate. After a few minutes, Luna ventured a glance and found that the churchyard was empty: they must have gone out through the back gate instead.

So. She looked at the glimmering path. She knew where it would lead, into the cold country, and that scared the shit out of her, but she felt, deep in her gut, that this was something that she had to do. Sam and Serena would be worried, she knew. She had left a note, explaining as best she could, but she hoped she would be back by morning, that Sam would not waken and find her gone. Yet if it was a question of on, on until starlight, she would just have to continue.

"Are you up for it, Moth?" she said to the dog. He looked at her and wagged his spindly tail.

"All right," said Luna. "Let's go."

STELLA

Stella did not waste time hammering on the door of the chapel. Of the people outside, one was in no fit state to intervene and the other had locked her in there in the first place. She did her best to open the door, but there were no bolts on the inside and Tam had firmly locked it. She did a quick circuit of the place, but the back regions, which Tam had been so diligently investigating, held neither door nor window. In fact, they didn't hold anything at all, only dust. She tried scraping her foot along the floor to see if it was all flags, or if there was any sign of the trapdoor, but she could barely see now. There was a faint light from the window in the main part of the chapel but no other source of illumination now that the little spark had gone. She went back along the side of the chapel. The shells still lay scattered on the stone floor and her foot crunched on one of them.

That left the window. Crap, thought Stella. She dragged the pew, with some difficulty, closer to the sill and hauled herself up. She thought she could just about squeeze through the window if she could open it, yet she hesitated, trying to remember what lay on the other side. There was obviously a drop, of about eight feet, but was there more than that? She couldn't recall how wide the strip of land between the chapel wall and the edge of the headland had been. It wasn't very high, not an actual cliff, but she didn't fancy bouncing off it, anyway.

Well. At least she ought to be able to take a look. Assuming Tam Stare wasn't standing on the other bloody side of it, but if he had been intent on whacking her over the head, she thought that he would have done so by now. Locking her in suggested that he was trying to keep her out of the way, not dispatch her.

And anyway, this wasn't the first time she'd had to do this. Years ago, in Liverpool, she had gone back with a man to his flat in the upper part of a Victorian house. She had not, in fact, spent the night in his bed, because they had both got a bit past that point, but on the sofa. In the morning, however, she had woken up to find that he had gone out and locked her in. Her phone had run out of charge and her charger was back at her friend's place. There was no sign of a landline. Stella knew that this was stupid behaviour and it would really have been better not to do this sort of thing at all, but there you were, it had happened and now she had to get herself out of it. And anyway, what kind of arsehole locks a stranger in their gaff? The kitchen window had proved amenable – if he was a serial rapist, he wasn't a very good planner – and Stella, acrobatic despite a thumping hangover, had gone out headfirst and managed not to fall the twenty feet into the back garden. Mainly by luck, she had dropped onto the roof of next door's shed instead, climbed over a couple of fences, and marched away down the road until she found a bus stop.

Same sort of thing here, except lack of bus.

By leaning perilously forward, she was able to wrench the window open. Stage one. She stood back, balancing on the edge of the pew to catch her breath before the final assault, and as she did so, something moved in the back of the chapel. Stella froze.

It was a scraping sound, like someone dragging a body. *Fucking hell*, thought Stella. Where had it come from? She'd just been in the back of the chapel and it had seemed and felt empty. She wasn't going to stick around and find out what this was. She reached out, grabbed the sill, and pulled her head through. A quick glance out at the racing sky and there at last was the moon riding low over the waves, although it seemed both smaller and brighter than it should. Stella took a big breath, uncomfortably conscious of her legs still sticking into the chapel, ready to be grabbed by whatever the fuck that was, and that thought impelled her onward. She scraped through the opening and, trying to cover her head and roll, dropped onto the wet turf.

It had occurred to her before that perhaps some martial arts training might be a good idea but she'd never got around to it, and this was the result. She hit the ground awkwardly, which knocked the breath out of her, but she didn't think anything was broken. An impressive display of bruises would no doubt appear upon the morrow. She rolled onto her hands and knees, with the prospect of the thing in the chapel following her out of the window or Tam Stare waiting to shove her over the edge of the low cliffs, and hauled herself to her feet. Then she set off down the headland. She did not dare look back and, besides, it was beginning to seriously rain.

BEE

The *Hind* was plunging. Bee had made up her own mind and gone below deck, more because she didn't want Dark fretting about her in the middle of a crisis. After going backwards down the ladder, she threaded her way through a maze of barrels and crates, and into a long room filled with pallets and hammocks. A single lamp swung to and fro. Bee found a pallet and sat down on it. This ship must have seen numerous storms, it had sailed the world's seas and survived, they knew what they were doing. And besides, they were dead: you could not die twice. Or could you? She did not know how worried about Dark she should be and it was unsettling. Bee herself was strangely untired and anyway, too wired up to sleep. She sat on the pallet with her back to the wooden hull and tried to listen to the wind. But she was not there for very long.

The wind was rising. She could hear it howling against the caulked boards, seeking ingress, and the sea battered the sides of the *Hind*. In a way it would be easier to sit here in the dark: the wildly swinging lamp made her feel queasy in a way that the roaring waves did not. She was glad when there were bootsteps on the stair and Dark appeared in the doorway, bracing himself against the lintel.

"Captain needs you on deck!"

"Needs me?" Bee scrambled to her feet, trying not to go flying. "I should think a landlubber like me would be about as much use as a chocolate teapot up there."

Dark smiled, though she wasn't sure if he understood the metaphor. "Says he's ready for you now."

What did *that* mean? More than a little unsure, Bee followed him out into the passage and scrambled up the steps.

On deck, it was a watery version of Hell. Huge thunderheads gathered above the horizon. Bee covered her hand with her mouth as the Hind began to list, slowly, slowly and a wave broke over the bow. Dark seized her and slung a rope around her waist.

"I don't want to tether you like a dog but if you did go in…"

"Fine!" Once he had secured the end to a stanchion, he took her by the hand and they slithered up the deck to the prow. Drake was by the wheel, shouting instructions, but he turned when they approached and she saw his eyes glitter.

"Mistress Fallow. I need some advice!"

"Good luck with that!"

She could see that he didn't understand. He said, taking her completely by surprise, "Ned here tells me that your sister fell into these waters when you were children."

"What?" She gathered her wits. "Yes, Stella. My sister."

"But she did not drown?"

"No, she was fine," Bee shouted above the gale. "Why on Earth do you want to know this?"

"We are close by to that place. Tell me about that day."

Bee, hanging onto the railing and braced against her rope, gave him a potted version of events.

"And when you say: she fell overboard, did you snatch her up at once from the sea's jaws?"

"Well, no, not quite," Bee yelled. "The current took her and it carried her quite a way from the boat. The captain had to turn it about and go and get her. She wasn't in for very long. We could see her – she was in a white top and shorts. He threw her a lifebelt when we came close enough and reeled her in."

Drake nodded. "Very good. I have my answer, Mistress Fallow. Thank you."

"Glad it was useful," Bee said faintly.

"Set her at anchor," Drake cried. There was a slippery crash as the anchor was cast overboard. "The small boat, Ned."

"What?" Bee said as he went past. "You're not setting out into *that*?"

But Dark was already disappearing along the deck.

Bee turned back to Drake and she saw that the helmsman had stepped away from the wheel. Drake placed his hands on the wheel and he spun it, whipping it around like a child's top. But the *Hind* did not move and the whirling wheel mesmerised Bee, catching her attention so that she felt suddenly sticky and weighed down. She felt her wet skirts begin to grow lighter, her hair spring back from its recent drenching. The wheel seemed to be sucking the storm into itself; she saw an arch of seafoam curving through the air towards her face and she flung up a hand, but when it pattered down around her feet she looked down and saw that it was the petals of meadowsweet. A humming bumble bee, weighted with its freight of pollen, soared past her and the sun was hot and welcome on her skin.

"Captain, what's happening?" Drake still stood in shadow but then it fled away, leaving the *Hind* quite calm in a pool of light.

"Your magic and mine, mistress. Quite the thing, isn't it?" He looked around, smiling a wolf's smile. She would find it easy to be afraid of Drake, she thought.

"How long will this last?" Bee asked. Now that they were out of the storm, she felt paradoxically shaky. She leaned against the warm wood of the railing.

"A good question. It should hold for a time. Now, shall we go for a smaller voyage?"

LUNA

Luna trod the lych path with Moth padding at her side. She was glad he'd come along, wondering if she would have had the guts to go alone. She was not sure that she would. It led across the road from the lych gate, shimmering as it reached the high hedge that stood opposite the churchyard. This was some way from the Mooncote fields: these belonged to a neighbouring farmer, and Luna hoped that she would not be found trespassing, for there had been difficulties over the field boundary in Alys' day. The hedge was high and forbidding but as Luna walked towards it, the branches of beech shivered and parted, crawling back to let the travellers through. Luna did not like to wait, but hastened through the gap and Moth leaped behind her. The lych path led down the sloping field, which was bare now of everything except stubble; Luna thought that it had borne sweetcorn for feed that year and would have been harvested some weeks ago. The remaining stalks of corn, sticking out of the earth like the ribs of an animal, also did not care to carry the lych path, it seemed, for they shrunk away to let Luna stride through.

She was expecting the cold country. But no ice formed on the rain puddles between the cornstalks, and the breeze on her face was damp rather than chill. Moth's tail was up: he was having a dog adventure. Nothing moved in the lee of the hedges. Yet as Luna marched on, she saw that the land was changing, after all. The distant ridge of hills was becoming blurred and she did not think it was rain. The clouds had crept back as though they, too, feared the glimmering road and Orion the Hunter strode over the land with the blue star at his heels.

"Look," Luna said to Moth, to hearten herself. "He's got his dog with him, too."

The lych path was growing brighter. It began to sparkle like frost and all the air was abruptly sucked out of Luna's lungs. She gasped and in the fractional moment between one breath and the next, she was somewhere else.

She instinctively reached down for Moth but the dog had come with her. She touched the rough hair on his neck and the reassuring hardness of his leather collar. She stood in a grove of beech, bare of leaves, on the side of a hill. Beech mast crunched under her feet. Orion still bestrode the curve of the hill but Luna knew where she was, now: on the chalk. The lych path still shone over the earth, littered with white stone, but this land was familiar. She remembered something Sam had said about not needing the written word to speak to his grandmother – was this what he had meant? Over the last couple of months, ever since she had become pregnant, the world around her had seemed to become a great deal more fluid, allowing Luna – and her sisters, and perhaps other people, too – to slip in and out of its interstices. Flitting through the gaps like bats in a leaky barn, not a bad image of the world, maybe. Rather as she and Sam tried to keep under the radar, slip through the cracks of modern capitalist Britain. Better make the most of it while it lasts, just in case it doesn't.

"Come on, Moth," Luna said. "Let's go and see Sam's gran."

She headed off down the hill. It was of course possible that Ver March had moved: unlike her grandson, she had a car with which to tow the little trailer. But somehow Luna did not think this was likely. She had faith in Sam's gran. She hoped Sam himself wouldn't be too pissed off that she'd set off to see Ver without him, but that hadn't been her original intention, had it? And still home before morning. Hopefully. She did not, however, realise that she had been holding her breath until she glimpsed the little white trailer through the alders and saw the candle burning in its window. The lych path, running straight, bordered the caravan at a distance of some five feet. Wondering whether it would allow her to get off, Luna went quickly down the hill and when she reached the van, took a careful step to the left. Moth followed. The lych path ran on and Luna gave a tentative knock on the door, worrying about waking Ver up.

She need not have been worried. The door was flung open and there was Sam's grandmother.

"Luna! It's you. I was expecting someone, you know. I stuck the kettle on. But I thought it might be Sam. Or one of his cousins."

"I hope this is okay," Luna said.

"Come on in. And the doggy."

When Luna got inside, she realised why the candle had been subconsciously bothering her. The black paper that had covered the windows was gone.

"Sorted my sight out," Ver March said. "Took a while, but we got there in the end."

"I think you'd better know," Luna told her, "That I didn't come by road."

The old woman gave her a beady look.

"I know."

"Oh. Right."

"It's not my preferred way of travelling, though I do use the old ways from time to time, because there are some odd things on those lych paths that you might not necessarily want to meet." She said this casually, as someone might comment on traffic levels on the A303. "But I'll give 'em that, they're very quick, all told. How long did it take you to get here?"

"I don't really know. Orion moved a bit but I'm not sure…"

"Quicker than a car, anyway."

"Yes. Much."

"And you left Sam behind?"

"Yes. You see, I'm looking for my mum." The two statements did not really fit together but Ver seemed to understand, for she nodded.

"And I don't think I've got time for a cup of tea, though it's very kind of you."

"No. If that's the case, you'll need to get on before morning. The path will fade when the sun rises. It's a bit chilly out there, isn't it? I'd better find my coat."

STELLA

Fucking rain. It didn't matter where you went in Britain, whether real Britain or alternative Britain or what, it still rained all the bloody time. Stella was following the shore, well away from the chapel. As far as she knew, nothing was following her but she wasn't counting on it. She had managed to find footprints, a few, and they looked like modern ones. Tam had been wearing Nike but she couldn't identify trainer prints exactly. She was not, she told herself, bloody Sherlock Holmes. They had seemed to point eastwards so that was where Stella was going, but even given the amount of time that escaping from the chapel had taken, she had not caught up with Tam or the star. What the hell had he done with her, in that case? He must have taken her another way, but how? The star had seemed in no condition to stand up, let alone be dragged along by a presumably human man of slight build. Stella could testify as to the star's weight. Maybe it was like super-dense matter, not flesh at all. Maybe star spirits could increase their weight, like cats on the bed... The path led through dense reeds. Their tawny tassels would have been taller than Stella, but were bowed down with rain. Stella herself had gone from feeling cold, to too hot, perhaps as a result of exertion. She came out onto a muddy shore and there, again, was a footprint. This time, it was bare.

She tried to remember if the star had been shod but the voluminous skirts had hidden the star's feet. Stella spat out a sudden mouthful of rain, tucked her hair back into the too-big hood, and carried on.

But not, it seemed, for much longer.

The river was wide and it shone in the flickering light of the moon through the stormclouds. Stella came slowly out onto the muddy shore. There was no way she'd be able to cross that without a boat. There might be a path which followed the river but it looked, as far as she could tell in the rainy dark, to head into a patch of woodland. *Don't go into the forest alone, little girl.* But the only other way was back, towards whatever might have got out of the chapel by now. Stella swore under her breath. She walked up the beach, trying to skirt the sea grass and keep out of the worst of the mud, but the river was widening as it reached the sea. Stella climbed a small bluff and tried to get her bearings. Then, down on the seashore, she saw a light.

A familiar light, too. A seagreen marshfire flicker.

Result! So where was Stare? Hopefully he would have fallen in somewhere and drowned. But just in case… Stella searched around her and found a gnarly spine of driftwood. She banged it on a stone to see if it broke. It did not. "You will do," Stella said to it. She seemed to be getting the hang of this carrying-weapons business. Then she ran down the bluff, keeping an eye out on either side.

It wasn't until she was further along the bluff that Stella saw him. Stare, in his dark clothes, blended in against the black background of the sea better than the star herself. She stood, feet braced on the wet sand, with the marshfire light flickering about her face and hair. She looked alien and electric and – if this was some kind of standoff – Stella did not fancy Tam's chances. He had his back to her. If she could sneak up on him and whack him over the head… but as she sidled closer, Tam raised his hand and she saw it glow white.

What the hell? If he could do that, Stella asked herself, then why hadn't he provided its not inconsiderable light earlier on when they needed it? She hesitated, half expecting some kind of magical battle: lightning bolts thrown, light sabre manifestations in frost and seagreen. But this did not happen. She felt a breath of deep cold whistle past her ear and the temperature dropped enough to make her give a sudden shudder. She thought: but stars come from the depth of space, the killing cold, so – then Tam Stare spoke a name.

Stella didn't know how she knew it to be a name, but it wasn't one humans were meant to hear, let alone speak. It made the sea ring. She clapped her hands to her ears to shut it out but the echoes went on and on and she saw the star crumple and fall to the ground. Stella picked up the driftwood, which she had dropped, and raced forwards. She swung the heavy branch at the back of Tam's head but it did not connect. Instead, it was as though Stella had received the blow. She was knocked off her feet and off the bluff, down into the water.

BEE

Now that Drake had taken them out of the storm, Bee was able to see more of the coast. It was like looking through a rainy windowpane, water-streaked but still transparent. She could see the white cliffs of the Isle of Wight to the south, shining in the sunlight, and behind them crouched the grey bulk of Hurst Castle. The little boat skimmed the waves like the swallow inked on Ned Dark's arm. Drake himself stared straight ahead, intent as a hunting cat. Bee did not like to ask where they were going and she was missing the comforting size of the *Hind*, now riding at anchor far down the Solent. In this little boat, even with Dark and Drake alongside her, she could not help thinking of that sharp-toothed face and sharper arm reaching up out of the wildness of the water towards her. If it had reached her, Bee had no doubt that it would have dragged her down and not to make coral of her bones. More probably to suck out the marrow. She'd never be inclined to trail her hand in the water again.

She was not sure whether the storm had dissipated or whether it had turned inland. The coast, apart from Hurst and the island itself, lay in shadow. Dark rowed on, towing the sun behind.

STELLA

Stella went down through green water. The breath had once more been knocked from her lungs although she had managed to take a deep breath just before she hit the waves. There was one thought in her mind: *fuck you, Tam Stare*. She couldn't get her Converse off and they were dragging her under but she struck upwards anyway, strong swimmer's memory kicking in and taking over. The current was too strong, however. She broke the surface and breathed, but saw that the shore was already a long way off. Bollocks. But there was land further out, a kind of bar at the estuary's mouth and it was then that Stella knew where she was. This was the second time she'd fallen into this river. It was the mouth of the Beaulieu and she was being swept out to the patch of salt marsh called Gull Island.

Being marooned on Gull Island was a pain but not as bad as the alternative, which was drowning and she might well do that instead because she could feel herself being pulled under. Stella fought back, but it was night-black below and very cold: it would be the cold that would kill. Then something grasped her ankle. Stella, fuelled by a spurt of adrenaline, kicked out hard but she was rolled over and up. She could see sunlight above the surface of the water – how did that work? It had been pitch black a minute ago. She broke the surface, choked and spluttered, but she was breathing. Something was holding her up. Stella looked down in panic and saw two hands clasped around her waist. The fingers were slender and delicate, human except for the long black claws. It let her go and Stella, splashing, rolled over and saw a white face with enormous black eyes, a skein of brown hair. It grinned at her. Its teeth were points.

What the hell are you? – but she had seen it before. Memory came flooding back like a riptide. Falling over the side of the boat down into the glassy reach of the river and something, someone, had caught her before she had reached the clinging, tangling weeds. It had played with her, laughing underwater, as Stella struggled, and there had been something friendly and cruel about it but it had not let her drown. And it was not letting her drown now. Stella struck out in a breaststroke, heading for Gull Island, but she did not reach it. There was a shout, the

242

clop of oars, and Stella was seized and pulled bodily from the water. She collapsed face down and undignified in the bottom of a rowing boat and rolled over to find herself in her horrified sister's lap.

"Bee!" Stella sat up. Ahead, the grey-green grass of Gull Island waved in the wind and the island was a huge run of shadow across the Solent. At the rivermouth, something brown and sleek broke the water for a second and arrow-waked away.

"Oh, there's an otter!" said Bee, excited. Dark swung the rowing boat around.

"Take us onto the river tide," the captain said.

SERENA

Serena couldn't help wondering how Ward's investigations at Amberley were going, but there were things to be done in the meantime. She was hoovering the ground floor when Nell came in.

"Can I do anything?" Her brow was furrowed. "I'd ask Bee but I can't find her."

"Bee had to run Stella up to Bristol," Serena lied. "One of her contact lenses dropped out." Appalling how easily deception was starting to come to her.

"Oh no! What a nuisance. Isn't there anyone more local?"

"There are opticians in Street but they have some special coating, apparently –" where was she getting this stuff from? "– so Bristol it had to be."

"I hope she gets it sorted," Nell said. "Anyway, *can* I help, in fact?"

"You could vacuum upstairs, if you like. But wait till Luna gets up, she's still in bed."

"I'll do some dusting until she emerges," Nell said. "Then I'll hoover."

Once Nell had disappeared, lugging the Henry, Serena bagged up all the rubbish that had accumulated in the kitchen and sorted it into the recycling boxes. Then she ran the dishwasher a second time and put a laundry basket's worth of clothes in the washing machine. With gadgets whirring around her, and the black and green boxes stacked in the yard, she had a satisfying moment of virtue and good housewifery. At least something wasn't in total chaos. As she surveyed her small queendom, her daughter said through the kitchen door,

"Mum? If I'm careful, can I go up to the attic?"

"Yes, if you want to. Why do you want to?"

"Just to see what's up there. I'm reading this book and this girl goes into an attic and she finds a load of stuff."

"Just watch your footing. Don't fall down the stairs."

"I won't, Mum." Only a mild eyeroll.

"And don't make too much noise! Luna and Sam are still asleep and she'll be tired if she's having a baby, remember."

At this, Bella became quite serious and said, "No, I won't. I'll be really quiet, like a mouse."

She vanished upwards. Maybe teenagehood wouldn't be quite as bad as Serena feared. At least Bella was still reading books, unlike a lot of her school friends. *How middle class you sound,* Serena told herself. *Especially given the amount of time you spend on Instagram.* Talking of which… She checked her phone but there were no messages from Bee or Stella. As she was staring at the screen, however, a text pinged into view.

On my way back.

Ward. When had he sent it? But in the way of important messages, the sender was at the door by the time the text had arrived, looking screen-villainous in black jeans and a polo neck.

"Good morning. Did you get my text?"

"Just this moment."

"Typical. Good thing it wasn't life or death." He sat down at the kitchen table and ran his hands through his hair. "Jesus. Well, *that* was like getting blood out of a stone."

"Oh dear."

"I spoke to Caro. I finally managed to prise her away from Richard and Laura, both of whom kept bursting in with endless questions to do with horses. Why are horses so complicated? No wonder someone invented the internal combustion engine."

"So what did she say?"

"I tried to be subtle. You know me. I can do subtle. I'm not totally clod-hopping when it comes to obliqueness and subtext. I went to RADA, after all. I tried a number of opening gambits, from Shakespeare's more things in heaven and Earth, to whether anyone had seen any ghosts recently, and my cousin proved remarkably obtuse, I must say. So eventually I said "So has anyone in this family ever physically changed into an animal?" and she dropped a cup."

"So *had* they?" Serena was fascinated.

"Well, she wouldn't tell me. She said, was I joking, so I said no, I was deadly serious, and she said what on Earth had ever given me that idea: we weren't living in Harry Potter and it was impossible. Is it really, I said, fixing her with my basilisk gaze, because I could swear blind that someone known to me just did it."

"Oh my God."

"And I'm presuming that she noticed my absence last night, even if she was too polite to mention it. Anyway, she started trembling.

Literally. She got down on her knees and kept picking up the bits of cup and moving them about like a bloody jigsaw until I told her to stop and then she cut her hand."

"Oh, poor Caro!"

"So there was a bit of a hiatus while we found sticking plaster and so forth, then someone else came in with a horse question, and just as I was about to offer to run her into A&E just to get some fucking peace and quiet, she pulled herself together and said I mustn't ever say anything about this, ever. I told her I was not in the habit of propping up the bar of the Ivy telling my mates about shapeshifters in Somerset. Then she calmed down a bit, apologised, and said that it wasn't her secret, but it was something to do with Rich's family – so, *my* family, in fact – and that Richard's mother had entrusted her with a piece of information which she couldn't reveal because, apparently, it is not for men to know. This last was said in capital letters, if you know what I mean."

"Interesting!"

"It is a women's thing. I didn't really know where to take it from that point because Caro obviously wasn't going to tell me anything else and I could hardly beat it out of her. It was kind of a conversation ender. I asked her if Richard knew anything about it and she said that she didn't think he did. This beggars belief according to me, but really, Serena, Richard's a nice chap but he's never been in the top ten when it comes to powers of observation. I once went with him on someone's stag night to Barcelona and we walked past the Segrada Familia on the way to some bar. I mentioned 'that amazing building' and he said, 'What amazing building?'"

"He really notices horses, though. He's brilliant when it comes to something being wrong with the way they walk, Mum once told me."

"Yes, maybe it's like tunnel vision or something. But anyway, that's that. Caro started washing up rather fiercely and she looked as if she was in danger of becoming really upset, so I thanked her for a difficult conversation and slunk away."

"I hope it doesn't cause problems for Bee."

"The thing is, she might tell Bee what's up. She might tell *you,* if you went over and fessed up."

"Would she really want a daughter in law who turns into a hare, though?"

Ward gave her a searching look. "Are you ever going to be her daughter in law, though?"

"I don't know."

"Do you want to be?"

"I don't know. Any more."

"This is the point where I'm supposed to press you to my manly bosom, confess my undying devotion to you and tell you it's going to be all right, isn't it? But I'm not sure that's true. Going to be all right, that is."

"It's not that —"

"Not what?" But Serena was silent.

"Look, I've been around the block. I'm not dim enough to think that just because we had a valedictory fuck, we're back on."

"Would you like to be 'back on'?" Serena asked in a rather small voice.

"Actually, you know what, yes, I think I would. But, depending how you feel about my idiot cousin — would you?"

Serena opened her mouth to reply, although she was not sure what was going to emerge from it, when Bella burst in through the door.

"Mum! Mum, I've found something in the attic."

LUNA

Luna, Moth and Ver March made their way along the silver ley of the lych path. They were not talking. Ver had told Luna to keep her lips sealed.

"Words can drop out when you don't mean them to and who knows where they might end up?"

"All right," Luna said, though she was burning with questions. They followed the track up the slope opposite where the caravan was parked, then down again, then up until they came onto a high ridge of land. Before them, the plain was dark. The lych path was faltering into a scattering of silvery dew on the short turf and a yard or so ahead, it was gone. Luna looked out across the distance. She knew where they were now, but there was no sign of the illuminated grid of Swindon or the line of the M4. But when she looked to the east, she could see the comet, burning bright. From the look of the land, it was wooded all below the ridge.

Ver took her by the sleeve and plucked. They stepped away from end of the lych path and Ver led her into a thorn brake. The earth had worn away beneath the trees and the chalk bones of the world were visible below.

"I hope this is far enough," Ver said. She coughed. "I tell you what, my girl – I'm not used to all this exercise, these days. I ought to sign up to one of those gyms."

"I'm sorry," Luna said, feeling guilty. She had brought a problem to Ver's door, after all.

"It's not your fault, my love. It's just how things are. Your knees get knackered and that's no one's fault. Anyway, we've followed the path as far as it goes and this is where we'll find your mum."

"This is near Wayland's Smithy," Luna said.

"That's right. We're in White Horse Country now. I'll need a drop of your blood."

Luna hesitated, but only for a moment. "Okay." She pulled off her mitten and the fingerless glove underneath it.

"Hold your finger out." Luna did so. She felt a pinprick of pain and then there was a welling bead on the end of her index finger. She knew it was red but in the moonlight it seemed black. Ver snapped off a spine of blackthorn and from her pocket she took a twist of thread.

"It's red wool, if you ever want to do this again." She mopped up the wetness from Luna's finger and tied the bloody thread to the thorn, leaving an end so that the thorn dangled from it. "But you've got to spin it yourself, old school. Can't just go into a knitting shop. There you go."

"What do I do with it? Is it like a pendulum?"

"More or less." Ver pressed the end of the thread into Luna's hand. "See what it does."

Luna held the thorn up to the moon and it began to twist and spin. She held her breath until it settled, the sharp point of the thorn indicating due east.

"Are you coming with me?" she asked Ver March, but the old woman said, "No. This bit you have to do on your own. I'm sure your doggy will go with you, though. But I will wait for you. I'll have a sit down."

Luna nodded and with Moth began walking east. The moon rode low in the sky and she could feel the comet's presence now, a disruption at the edge of the world. It made her twitchy and nervous, like a horse that senses a threat. She held the thorn out in front of her and though the ground was rough and Luna's steps were uneven, the thorn did not falter but remained rigid and horizontal. A dark mass rose ahead: the beech trees in which the Smithy was situated. Luna swallowed hard and walked into the grove.

She could see the outlines of the stones. They rose in a series of shelves and points. The largest stones, vaguely triangular in shape and reminding her of her grandfather's tomb, were taller than Luna herself. As with all standing stones, especially at night, she felt that they were somehow alive and that she was trespassing on their peace.

"I'm sorry," she whispered. Beside her, the lurcher whined. But the stones were still watching.

STELLA

By now, Stella thought she had more or less got her bearings although it was possible that the landscape had changed, and she wasn't overly familiar with the mouth of the Beaulieu river: it was years since they'd been down here, after all. She navigated as best she could, issuing Dark with instructions. Drake sat in the prow, with an expression best described as 'inscrutable,' Stella thought. She wondered who he was taking orders from: Elizabeth the Queen? His Elizabeth, that is, not the current incumbent. Or perhaps in this curious hinterland to life he obeyed his own orders.

The world was shining now, sunlight turning the calm sea to a mirrored shimmer. There was no sign of the storm. The *Hind* rode at anchor just beyond Gull Island. The pale reeds that fringed the saltmarsh were still. They rounded a bend and there was the muddy bluff from which Stella had fallen. She pointed.

"There! It's over there."

"I can't see anyone on the shore," Dark said.

"Neither can I."

"Take her in gently," Drake told him. "Follow the reedbeds."

Stella started as something shot out of the reeds, but it was only a curlew. She saw the long beak and speckled body. As if flew down the river it gave its plaintive cry.

"There!" Bee said suddenly. Here, the oak groves came down almost to the river and a figure was standing on a mossy rock.

"It's her," Stella said. "The star."

"No sign of Tam Stare, though."

"What's she doing?" Stella asked. The star's hands were outstretched. Against the dark green of the oaks, she was surprisingly hidden, given the pallor of her blue skin.

"Be careful," Drake said. "It could be a snare."

Dark began to row towards the oaks. Stella waved to the star, trying to attract her attention, not sure if it was the right thing to do. But the star was looking directly at them. As the boat approached, she stepped onto the dappled surface of the water and began to walk.

"Just like Jesus," Stella remarked, impressed.

It was plain that the star was coming towards the boat. She held her shift out of the way of the river and her feet, moving with careful deliberation as though she walked a tightrope, were bare. For a moment, Stella thought that she was walking on rocks, half submerged, but as Dark rowed them quickly in, she saw that there was nothing beneath the limpid surface, only the banners of waterweed, deep down.

"Get her on board," said Drake. He rose from his seat in the prow to make room. Just as the star reached the boat, Tam Stare erupted from the oak grove. He was wild eyed and at first Stella thought he'd changed his clothes. He had lost his leather jacket and the white t-shirt was red. But then she realised it was mottled and spotted with blood. Maybe that piece of driftwood had actually connected? Serve him right if it had.

"You cunts!" Stare shouted.

"Charming!" Stella exclaimed. He reached out and took a deep breath. The air seemed to hum. A cold draught brushed the side of Stella's face: when she put her hand to her cheek, it came back glittering with frost. Bee's brown curls were silver-dusted. The water between the shore and the boat crackled and glazed. The star took a step and faltered.

"Mistress Fallow," Drake said, "Your assistance is required." He helped a visibly startled Bee to her feet.

"What do I do?" Bee cried.

"Close your eyes. See what comes into the eye of your mind."

"Shall I tell you?"

"Yes, do so."

"Well – I see our garden. Not like it is now – whenever – in autumn, but in summer. It was really hot this year. We had a lot of bees – I can see them humming in the lavender. And Mars has been bright all summer, too – Dark and I used to lie awake and watched it cross the heavens like a dragon's eye. Really hot weather," she repeated, and Stella felt the chill on her face begin to recede. The star lifted her foot with a crack as the ice splintered.

Tam Stare gave a wordless shout and spoke a word that sounded obscene, but Stella did not think it was a curse. It was a spell and a flurry of snow whirled around her – but whatever was happening in Bee's head was changing things, and Stella could see it now, the snow changing to white rose petals and drifting down onto the water. The oaks flushed a darker green with the heavy leaf of midsummer, not solstice but beyond, lammas-tide when the tides of the land grow slower and the days begin to darken and things begin to ripen and die.

"Come on, madam," Stella heard Drake say, softly beneath his breath. "Come up –" as though Bee were a mare to be coaxed.

There was a soundless flash. Stella had to jerk backwards, nearly falling out of the boat. Neither Bee nor Dark were there any more. Two comma-swarms of bees hummed up from the boat, loud with warning anger. Stella watched, open mouthed, as they merged. The new swarm gathered itself up, bunched like a coiling whip and shot out across the river. The star did not flinch or blink as it sailed past, but Tam shouted in sudden fear. His arms went up to protect his face, but the bees covered him. To the watching Stella they looked like black oil poured out of the sky. Tam flailed and she heard him cry out in pain and fury. He threw himself from the bank, hitting the river with a tremendous splash, and sank. The bees, buzzing with frustration, zoomed over the surface like starlings in murmuration, moving as one being. Tam did not reappear. Surely, Stella thought, he couldn't have actually drowned in such a short space of time?

The star had not stopped walking and was now at the boat. Drake's hand also went up, he spoke a word, the star tumbled into the rowing boat and a great wave of river water and ice, green with weed, surged towards the shore and up. Stella saw a form in the water, rolling like a log. The swarm soared up into the oaks, then turned and came back across the water.

Drake gave an exclamation. "Where is he?"

Bee and Dark were back in the boat, looking a little ruffled and insubstantial about the edges. Stella looked over the side, searching. The wave drew back and subsided, causing the reeds to shiver and whisper. Beneath the surface, she caught sight of the sinuous form of a pike, gliding gold-dappled beneath the boat. With a contemptuous flick of its tail, it was gone out into the channel of the river.

But there was no sign of Tam Stare.

"Absolutely bloody typical," Stella said, aboard the *Hind*. "Literally."

"What is it?" They were in Drake's own cabin; a generous offer, Bee thought. Through the porthole, she could see towers of cumulus against the blue sky, rising against the island. Fair sailing and sunlit.

"She means, her blood is here," the star said. She sat on the edge of a bunk with a blanket over her legs, looking somewhat mermaid-like. "I can smell it."

"Oh!"

"My fucking period's started. And I haven't got anything. Or any clean underwear. How did women manage, then? Now?"

"I'm not sure. Maybe they used a wad of linen or something? I think women did go to sea but this seems to be all-male."

"Isn't that where 'son of a gun' comes from? They gave birth on deck, under the guns."

"Hardcore."

The star stared at them uncomprehendingly.

"Do you," Stella asked, "actually eat? I hope it's not an inappropriate question. I'm just curious."

"We eat. But not food."

"Energy, perhaps," Bee suggested.

Stella thought that the star gave a very faint smile. Close to, in this enclosed space, she could see that lights pulsed beneath the star's skin: invisible in strong daylight, but clear to the eye in this shadowy cabin. Now that the star was stronger the inhuman beauty that she shared with her sisters was more evident. Stella felt wan and sticky, and her womb delivered the occasional prodding stab. She wondered if Dark knew any Elizabethan remedies for period pains. Bee was rummaging in a chest.

"Use this."

"What is it?"

"I don't know. It's just wadded material."

"Jesus, what if it's a spare codpiece or something?"

Bee gave a splutter, then laughed so hard at this that she had to sit down. The star watched them curiously.

"Sorry, Cap'n, but I repurposed your crotch padding. At least there's plenty of salt water to soak it in."

"Stella!"

"You've got to laugh. I'm sure he's au fait with the filthy ways of unclean women. I imagine the Elizabethans were pretty rank."

"I'm not sure if that's true, actually. Anyway, it might do until we get home."

Stella went into the head with the material and came out some time later. "It could be worse," she said. "Though I might have to sling these jeans. Where are we, by the way?"

Bee had been looking out of the porthole. "I think we're heading down the river. The sun's to the left and I can see the saltmarshes. I must say, this has been fascinating."

"All very well for you. You've been by the side of your dashing boyfriend and his dodgy magical captain while I've struggled through a swamp, been locked in a creepy chapel by a star-capturing maniac and nearly drowned, and now I'm menstruating."

"I'm sorry you've had a rough time. But if Dark gives me the opportunity to do this again, I certainly will. It's like being Dr Who."

"I know what you mean. I hope I see otter girl again," said Stella. Someone knocked on the door.

"Dark? Is that you?"

"Captain says you can come up on deck if you want. Sun's going down."

It was hovering over the horizon by the time that Stella and Bee joined Dark by the rail. The inlet mouth of the river was rose and silver and pale blue, limpid in the light. A little boat accompanied the warship on her way down the river.

"Where are we going, Dark?" Bee asked.

"To Agamemnon."

"Where?"

"The shipyard."

"Oh, I know – Buckler's Hard. I didn't think that was there, then, though. Now. Whenever."

"It was not yet built in my day. Later. But it is here now."

"So this time is when, exactly?" Stella frowned.

"My day, and others. Like layers."

"Sort of like an onion?"

"Not really. Patchwork laid upon patchwork."

"And it's only the past, is it?"

"Not only."

Bee's eyes widened. "Do you ever visit the future, then?"

"I have not but I have seen things that don't – belong."

There was a shout from above and the rattle of the anchor going over the side.

"She's weighing in for the night," Dark said. "Captain says we're to go ashore."

"Where are we going to stay?"

Dark grinned. "You did say you fancied the Cherub, Mistress Fallow. I think there's an inn here, too."

The sun was fading behind the oak groves when the rowing boat set out. Stella looked upriver, to where the water was on fire from the light. A beautiful, quiet place, but she thought she would prefer to look at saltmarshes from a distance from now on. She shifted uncomfortably on the wooden seat of the rowing boat as Dark took a course between smaller boats and the huge hulk of a half-built ship. Ahead, she could see the two brick rows of the village striding up the hill. There were lamps in the windows and it looked welcoming, small and human.

Dark helped them onto the dock, one by one.

"There's an inn, you said?"

"Yes, and a chapel for mariners."

"Not so worried about that," said Stella, with a grunt. "I've gone off chapels."

The inn was a large, solid building on the end of the right hand row of cottages. Stella could see a sign, still in the breezeless air, but not the name: it was by now too dark. She thought it was Georgian; it had that square redbrick appearance. At least her filthy appearance – covered in half-washed off mud, salt, and now blood – hopefully wouldn't raise too many eyebrows in a dim place with presumably limited washing facilities. Did they have gas lamps yet? She was a little worried about the star, clad in her shift and a blanket, though at least the star was clean. What if people thought they were whores? Did women go into inns in those days if they weren't looking for trouble? Dark pushed open a creaking oak door and they stepped through.

Into a very up to date and brightly lit bar advertising Prosecco 2Nite, with an impressive range of gins and a clientele who had clearly recently come off boats. But not like the one they'd sailed in on. Stella, in one horrified glance, took in their clothes, assessing Toast, Boden, and the White Company. A waitress strode in with a seafood platter and stopped dead when she saw Stella.

And everyone was staring at them.

SERENA

"Can Uncle Ward come with us?" Serena asked her daughter. Bella gave him a narrow look and drew Serena to one side.

"I don't know, Mum," she hissed. "I'm not sure he ought to know about this."

"Oh, not you, too. I'm not quite deaf yet, you know, even if I am entering my dotage."

Serena felt it was time for a vote of confidence all round. She looked her daughter straight in the eye.

"I'm going to talk to you as if you were another grown up, Bella. You can trust Ward. He knows everything I know about this house. Well, probably. We haven't gone through all of it yet. But most things. I don't know if that answers any questions you might have."

"Sort of."

"What have you found?"

"I'll have to show you. I can tell you but I don't know if it'll make any sense." Bella took Serena's hand and, followed by Ward, they went up the stairs and then to the little door at the end of the passage that led to the attic steps. The steps gave their familiar, dismal creak as they went aloft.

Upstairs, the attics ran along the length of the house and the door opened out into an echoing, dusty space walled by the old painted panels that Serena remembered. It contained all the things that attics usually have: a spare ladder, boxes of old tools that Serena thought must have been Abraham's, a crate with children's annuals in it, vaguely remembered. She was tempted to sit down and open one.

"It's not as filthy as the attic at Uncle Harold's," Ward remarked. "Nor do you have his impressive stash of old copies of the *Radio Times*. I found one dating from the Boer War."

"You so did not!"

"Well, whenever television was invented. Nineteen twenty something, if I remember correctly from a long ago tour of the bowels of Broadcasting House."

"I bet the *Radio Times* is more recent than that. We went through this attic and cleared out a whole lot of stuff when Grandfather died.

Swedish death cleaning, it's called. Or maybe that's what you do yourself when you think you might be getting on a bit. What have you found, Bells?"

Bella marched to the end of the attic, where there stood a tea chest.

"This," she said dramatically, flinging a hand at the chest.

"Oh, it's the dressing up box." Serena turned to Ward. "We kept a lot of Mum's hippy gear – you remember she was a model, Ward? She's got a folder containing some cuttings, and in them she's even wearing some of the stuff that we used to dress up in. It's great that you've found it, Bella. I used to play with this all the time when I was growing up."

"No, but Mum, I know that, but I found this." She dived into the box and pulled something out. She held it up.

"It's a dress," Ward said. "Sorry, that was a real Captain Obvious moment there."

"Oh my God!" said Serena.

"You see!" Bella was triumphant.

"It's very pretty." Ward took a closer look. "And rather old, I would say."

"Right," Serena said. "Ward, there is a ghost in the garden. She is a young girl, probably Elizabethan, and I used to see her all the time when I was a kid. Some of us see all the ghosts and some of us just see some of them. Not all the time."

"I get that."

"Anyway. This girl was one of *my* ghosts and I saw her again recently. She seemed a bit more – interactive, if you know what I mean. She smiled at me and she's never done that before."

"Hopefully displaying my lightning intellect, I'd surmise that this might be what she was wearing when you saw her?"

"Yes, that's it. Exactly. This is her dress." Gingerly, Serena took hold of its hem and held it up. The rose silk, pale pinky-grey, was a little thin in places, but otherwise the dress could have been one of her own creations: sewn with seed pearls and caramel gold, fronds of ferns and tiny five-petalled wild roses.

"It must have cost a fortune back in the day," said Ward.

"Yes. It's not as elaborate as some of them, though. I always imagine – well, actually, I don't have to imagine. I *know* how much work went into some of those dresses. This wouldn't have taken quite as long as the ones in some Elizabethan portraits, but it would still have cost a pretty penny. The main thing, however, is that this was not in the dressing up box when I last looked in it."

"Where was it, then?"

"That's the thing. I've never seen this dress in the flesh, as it were, before. Ever."

"Shit! Sorry, Bella."

"No, it's what I said. I didn't actually know that, Mum, about the dressing up box and it not being there. I was just looking."

"So why is it here now?"

"I've no idea."

"So if the ghost pops up again, and she's in her scanties…"

Bella giggled. "Maybe she'll have Wonderwoman underwear."

"Maybe she'll have a thermal vest. I bet it's a bit parky, hanging around outside all the time in the ether without a coat."

"Stop it!" Serena felt genuinely shocked but was not quite sure why.

"Sorry, Mum."

"Sorry."

"Mum, could I try it on? It would fit, really."

"I don't see why not. It's very delicate but I know you'll be careful."

"Turn your back!" Bella commanded Ward, who complied. She pulled off her sweatshirt and wriggled out of her jeans.

"If I undo these buttons –" Serena did so, marvelling at the fragile silk, which rustled like a rosy wave through her fingers. "Then I can just drop it over your head."

She gathered up the skirts.

"Mum?"

"Yes, Bella?"

"Mum!" Bella's voice was very small.

"What's the matter – oh." Serena looked up. The ghost of the girl was standing a few feet away. The dresses were identical but the girl's face was horrified.

"Can I turn round now?" Ward said.

"I think you'd better. Be prepared for a shock, though."

"Good God," he said. He and the ghost gaped at one another.

"I can see the wall. Through that dress."

The ghost held out her hand, indicating the garment. Then she shook her head.

"I don't think she wants me to wear it," Bella said.

"Dearest Bella, it is not for you," said the ghost, in a small, sweet voice.

"No? Then we won't." Serena put the dress back on the box. "I'm sorry," she said to the ghost. "We didn't know."

"Have we upset you?" Ward asked. But the ghost gave him a lightning smile. She held out her hand. A little bird – a linnet, Serena thought – fluttered out of thin air and perched on her fingers. She whispered to it and vanished.

"I'm going to take that as a 'no'," Ward said. "Jesus Christ."

Bella, realising that she was standing in front of a man in her knickers, gave a small shriek and pulled on her sweatshirt. But Ward was still staring at the place where the ghost had been. Serena picked up the dress.

"I assume this has shown up for a reason, but I don't know what that reason is. I don't think this should stay in the box. I'm going to take it downstairs and put it with the clothes from the show."

And it occurred to her, as she laid the beautiful rose dress carefully in a plastic clothes bag, that perhaps this was what Dana Stare had been searching for, and not the box at all.

LUNA

Luna paused at the mouth of the barrow. She found that, in spite of her multiple layers, she was starting to shiver. Beside her, Moth whined and cringed against her leg. But she knew she had to find out what was inside the barrow, that events had pushed and shoved her into this place and time, that she had no choice. She took a deep breath and said to the dog,

"Well then, Moth-mate. Here we go," – and she walked down the short avenue to the black mouth of the barrow.

Inside, it was even worse than she had thought. There was no light at all. She liked dark places, she told herself. She felt safe in them. She'd had no problems spending all that time in West Kennet… But this was not the same. It felt wrong. When Luna, frantic, glanced back, she could not see even the indigo hollow of the sky. She focused on the hardness of the ground beneath her feet and kept a tight grip on Moth's collar. Reaching out, she found the wall, smooth stone. She wrapped the red thread around the thorn and put it in a pocket; it was no use to her in this lightless place. Trying to breathe, she shuffled forwards.

There was something in the darkness ahead. She could hear it moving. Luna closed her eyes for a moment and prayed to the goddess. She imagined her as an antlered woman, dressed in deer skin. Her face looked like Ver March's. The goddess held out her hand in Luna's mind's eye and Luna scrunched up her courage, that ragged, tattered thing and kept going.

The passage twisted and turned. She could not remember how large Wayland's Smithy was supposed to be. From far within, deep in the earth, she could hear a faint, regular thumping sound. It was like a heartbeat; Luna found herself breathing in time to it. Hadn't she heard something similar, in West Kennet? Ahead, something was scraping against the stone.

The passage wall came to an abrupt stop. Luna groped thin air and stumbled. Moth gave a sharp, warning bark. Hands grabbed Luna by the shoulders and shoved her backwards. She gave a yell and struck out, connecting with nothing. There was a flare at her side and she put her hand in her pocket to meet the prick of the thorn.

"Fuck!" She pulled out the thorn and thread: the thorn had become a needle of light, stitching through the blackness. Luna looked into her mother's horrified face.

"Shit! Did I hurt you?" Alys said.

Luna was so relieved that her knees gave way under her. She sank to the floor, clutching at Moth. "Mum! Oh!"

"You made it," Alys said. "I am so proud of you, Luna. You came to get me. And your dog, too! How far have you come?"

"A long way. Sam – my boyfriend – his grandmother helped me."

"Which way? Did you take a lych path or the Second Road? The dead road or the star path? Or something else?"

"I don't know what all of those are. I think this was a lych path. Ver March – Sam's gran – came with me."

Alys' voice was sharp. "Luna, where is she now?"

"She's outside. She said she'd wait for me."

"We've got to go. We can't leave her out there on her own. You don't know what can come down these roads."

"Can you come, though? You were trapped, stuck –"

"I was but I got free. I was way out on the lych path but you pulled me out and I had to run. I took a path back into White Horse Country. You won't know what I'm talking about. There's a lot to explain about this place." She grasped Luna's wrist and hauled her up. In the flaring light from the thorn, Luna saw that her mother's hair was shorn, cropped close to her head and silver-blonde, although there was a faint henna'd aureole around it. Red ochre had dried across her brow and her cheeks and she had those old tattoos. But she was more the mother Luna had remembered: early sixties, still with few lines. From a distance, at the time of her disappearance, she could have passed for thirty, disconcerting a number of male admirers.

"Come on," Alys said.

They ran back down the winding passage, Moth at their heels, and out into the night. The stars blazed overhead and Luna saw that the lych path now carried on, down the hill and into the valley. She could hear a church bell tolling, somewhere below.

"Where's Sam's gran?" Alys asked.

"In that thorn brake, over where those puddles are."

But Ver March was nowhere to be seen.

Luna and her mother searched the hillside, together. Having found

Alys, Luna was reluctant to let her out of her sight, but it seemed Alys felt the same.

"We're not splitting up. It's too risky."

"I don't know what's here."

Alys stood still for a moment, head cocked to the sound of the tolling bell. "Eight... nine. Keep away from the path, Luna."

"Why?" Luna asked but Alys, grabbing her hand, was already striding back towards the beeches. They searched the side of the hill but there was no sign of Sam's gran. Luna felt a pang of despair: she'd found Alys only to lose Ver.

"Luna, come here!" Alys' voice was urgent. She drew her daughter behind the trunk of one of the beeches. "Don't make a sound and don't argue."

Luna did as she was told. Independent as she was, there was a relief in having someone else make decisions. Even if she did seem to have reverted to her teenage relationship with her mother. Together, they watched as a group of black-clad men came over the brow of the hill, following the lych path. The church bell once more began to toll, a set of single strokes. The man wore frock coats and top hats from which shadowy streamers fluttered out. They were carrying a coffin.

"Do you know who it is?" Luna murmured into her mother's ear.

"Let's hope it's not Sam's gran. They're not bearing a body to rest, Luna. They're looking for someone to put in that coffin. Now shhhh."

SERENA

"What do you mean – you're in a pub?" Serena had been so relieved to hear Bee's voice on the other end of the phone that she felt quite faint. She sank into the kitchen chair. On the other side of the table Ward mouthed *"Who is it?"*

"It's my sisters. Bee and Stella. Now please shut up. I need to concentrate." She ran a hand over her head as if trying to hold it in place. "Where have you *been*? We've been really worried."

Bee said, quite calmly, "We're in a pub called the Master Builder. It's in the New Forest, near Beaulieu. Dark was with us and so is – someone else." She lowered her voice. "I don't want to say too much over the phone because this is also a hotel and the receptionist has very kindly let me use the phone for free, but she might come back at any minute. She's showing a guest to their room. We don't have any money and we're going to need a lift."

Stella glanced at the clock. It was six in the evening.

"I'll come and get you, of course. We'll come." She glanced at Ward, who nodded. "But how did you get there?"

"*Really* long story. We told the hotel we'd been in a boating accident. God knows whether they believed us although it is sort of true."

"Are you all right? You said Dark 'was' with you."

"We're more or less okay. Dark was with us when we came in but he disappeared. Look, the receptionist's coming down the stairs. I'll have to go."

"One quick thing," Stella said. "Luna's gone missing."

"Oh God! Serena, she could be anywhere, literally. Is Sam there?"

"Yes, and he's worried. I'll tell him to stay here in case she comes back and Ward and I will drive down. Expect us in a couple of hours. Set up a tab. Get some dinner and I'll pay for it."

"I'm going to hand you over to reception," Bee said. "We'll sort it out later."

Serena read out card details, while Ward's eyebrows rose higher and higher. When she finally put the phone down he said, "So what's happening?"

"Fancy a drive to Hampshire?"

She came clean to Bella.

"Can I come?"

"No, darling, because there won't be room in the car for all of us."

Bella frowned but she was not a sulky child. Serena said, "You can do what you like. Surf the net. Read books. Make chips – well, maybe not make chips because that involves a deep fat fryer and I don't think…"

"Can I make a cake?"

"Yes. Do you know how to use the oven?"

"I can work it out."

"Please don't set the house on fire. But Nell and Sam will be here."

Sam took her explanation surprisingly well and agreed to remain behind in case Luna showed up. Nell, however, was nowhere to be found.

"She must have gone for a walk," Serena said, firmly rejecting a host of other catastrophic possibilities. "She does do that sometimes."

"I'll keep an eye out," Sam said. "For all sorts of things." He clammed up then, for Ward had come back into the kitchen.

"He knows," said Serena. Ward's mouth twitched.

"Fly, fly, all is discovered."

"It's a bit of a relief, though, mate, to be honest."

"Apparently there are family secrets in mine, too."

Sam gave him a curious look. "Really? What sort?"

"I'm not quite sure."

Serena ran up to Stella's room and fetched, on Bee's instructions, jeans, a sweatshirt, knickers, a sponge and a packet of sanitary towels, which she loaded into a carrier bag and stuffed onto the backseat of the Landrover. Then they set off, Serena at the wheel, bumping down the drive and onto the lane which led past the churchyard, and then at length out onto the A37, once the old Roman road of the Fosse Way. As they sped along, Ward said,

"You mentioned something on the phone about it being dark?"

"Okay. It's Bee's boyfriend."

"I didn't know she had one. Caro told me a couple of years ago that she'd been worried about her, that she'd tried to set Bee up with some chap but Bee didn't seem interested in men. Or anyone."

"That's because she's been seeing someone. Except that, how can I put this, there's a bit of an issue…"

And that conversation lasted until well onto the A303 and the turn-off for Salisbury.

There wasn't a sat nav in the Landrover so Ward navigated by phone, and did so well enough that, two hours after they had left and despite some confusion around Beaulieu, they were pulling into the car park of the Master Builder.

"This looks like it might be rather nice in daylight," Serena said.

"If things ever calm down, we should come back and have lunch."

They found Serena's sisters sitting at the back of the main bar, nursing drinks and the wreckage of a fish and chip supper. They were not alone.

"Thank God," Stella said. "Did you bring the bag?"

Serena held it out.

"Thank you so much. I'm going into the Ladies and I may be some time. Send a search party."

Ward was staring at the third member of the party. She did not have an empty plate in front of her.

"And who is she?"

"I'll explain in the car," Bee said.

"She's rather – blue."

"I know. That's why we're sitting in the back of the pub although actually most people don't seem to be able to see her. Thank God. One lad gave her a bit of a funny look, though, so I don't want to risk it. We'd sit outside in the beer garden but it's too chilly."

"Does she speak English?"

The woman – surely one of the Behenian stars, Serena thought – was staring straight ahead.

"Yes, but it seems she doesn't really like to."

"Fair enough. What's up with Stella?" Ward asked.

"Women's mysteries," said Bee. "I hope she's not going to be too long. I want to get back. Any news of Luna?"

"Not yet. Also we couldn't find Nell in the house but I'm hoping she's just gone for a walk or something, I did send her a text but I don't know if she's seen it."

"Any sign of Dana Stare?"

"I'll tell you in the car."

At this point Stella returned, wearing clean clothes and looking a lot more confident in herself.

"Better! Are we going?"

"Yes. I'll sort out your bill."

"We haven't been sitting here quaffing endless rhubarb gins, by the way. We had a half of Old Peculiar each and stopped there in case you wanted to share the driving. But *she's* a cheap date."

The star rose, fluidly, and drifted out in their wake. She accepted a seat in the back of the Landrover without comment and Serena pulled out into the 40 mph zone that enclosed the heart of the forest.

"It's not really a forest, though, is it? More like a heath."

"Dark said one of the Henries – King Henry – cut a lot of it down for shipbuilding."

"Wasn't it actually planted for shipbuilding?"

"I think so."

"This is an old land," the star said suddenly, causing Ward to drop his phone on the floor. Due to the rather cramped conditions of the Landrover, she had spoken almost into his ear.

"Jesus! Sorry."

The star did not speak again. When they pulled into the driveway of Mooncote, it was not far from midnight: roadworks had held them up. Serena and Ward had swapped the driving.

"Are you staying here tonight?" Serena asked him in an undertone as she stepped out of the Landrover.

"If you'd like me to."

"Yes, I would."

Stella was hauling the bag of dirty clothes out of the boot.

"Might as well put this straight into the washing machine. Or on the bonfire. Pity we've had Guy Fawkes."

"Are you coming in?" Bee said to the star. But the star was fading. Serena could see the hedge through her silk-clad frame. She gave her faint smile and was gone.

"Without even a word of thanks," Stella said. "You're welcome."

"I don't think we can hold them to our standards," Bee said.

"No, I get that. But it's been a hell of a couple of days."

"Never mind," Serena told her. "Hopefully you'll get some rest tonight."

But the kitchen lights were still blazing and when they walked through the door, it was clear that rest wasn't going to be an option.

LUNA

The lamp was swinging, casting wild shadows through the beech wood. Alys and Luna, crouching behind a bramble thicket, kept silent and still: mice before the hunting cat. The lamp bearer did not call out, nor did his footsteps make any sound on the layer of mast that covered the floor of the wood. Luna had glimpsed his face as he strode by and it had been a white, gaunt oval, lit by eyes like copper coins. They glittered and glinted, not a man's eyes, but something else, something wearing human clothes. There was an insect stiffness to his limbs; he strode with jerky, puppet motions, but very fast.

Alys breathed into Luna's ear, "If he takes hold of you, don't try to fight him. You'll die."

Luna gave a very small nod and kept her hand clenched around Moth's collar. The dog was very still and he trembled: she had never seen Moth afraid. She kept thinking of old Ver March in the hands of this man and the thought made her cold with horror. She did not know how she was going to face Sam and tell him that somehow she had led his grandmother into the hands of a monster, left her alone in the woods while things walked the lych path intent on hunting women. *But Ver knew more about this world than you*, her rational voice said. *She must have known what dangers it contained – she said so. She made you stand away from the path.*

She kept very still. It must be like this for badgers, with the cull running and the men and dogs and guns and no way out. Luna hated hunting and killing, one reason she'd become a vegetarian, and the prospect of being seized and stuffed in a coffin was certainly reinforcing that decision. Into her ear, Alys hissed,

"Luna? Who is this with you? I don't mean the dog."

At first Luna didn't understand. She looked around, trying to keep her movements as small as possible. But then she got it.

"I'm going to have a baby, Mum."

"Oh, crap!" As maternal reactions went, this was not what Luna had hoped for.

"He'll smell it. Luna, I'll have to draw him off. Take this." Something long and hard and round, like a small pencil, was thrust into

Luna's hand. "Don't lose it. Run down the hillside as fast as you can."

"But, Mum –"

"Go!" Alys stood up. The hunter saw her at once. He made a sound like a crow, a harsh bark. Echoes came from across the beechwood. The hunter began to bound over the ground, the streamers from his hat ringed him with shadows. Luna wasn't going to leave her mother. She stepped in front of Alys, shrieking abuse. Moth barked, sharp and high. The hunter was upon her, she saw his hand, long black claws shining as if oiled and when he opened his mouth his teeth were sharp needles and his breath was charnel-sweet. Luna flung her arm in front of her face as the dog raced forwards, growling. She could hear Alys shouting behind her but then the hunter was plucked up into the air and there was a blinding flash of whiteness. The beechwood lit up. Luna felt a strange cool heat on her face and when the dazzle faded and she could make it out, she saw a white horse, as perfect as a heraldic figure, stamping the ground in front of her. On its back, perched high and ridiculously like a bundle of rags, sat Ver March.

Later, they walked the road together. Not the lych path, this time, but the Second Road, the star road. The white mare trotted along it, with Ver still on her back, Luna and Alys on either side, holding the horse's long mane and Moth running heraldic beside. Bridesmaids flanking a bride, thought Luna, who didn't normally have much time for weddings.

"When you went off," Ver said, from on high, "I thought: I don't like this. I got a feeling, you see. Something, I said to myself, is coming down the pike. Remember I told you there was some funny stuff on the lych paths?"

"Yes. You said there were some odd things on it and Sam mentioned it, too. He was speaking to Dark. A friend of my sister's. He said it was 'too risky'."

"Well, now you know why. So I thought I'd better go and enlist help, so to speak."

"She's a beautiful horse," said Alys.

"Well, of course. And where do you think she comes from?"

"I don't know."

"Think where we are."

"Oh!" Luna said. "Of course. The Vale of the White Horse." She'd seen it many times, this one and its kindred. Cut into the chalk slopes of the Wiltshire downs.

But the one near Wayland's Smithy was the oldest, the most mysterious: some people said it was prehistoric. To Luna, who had often seen its curving lines over across the face of the hill, it looked more like a dragon, or even a cat. But the mare, shining with her own faint light like the dappled moonhorse which rocked all by itself in the bedroom at home, was definitely a horse.

"Is that what you meant by White Horse Country?" she said to Alys.

"Yes, sort of. But I didn't mean Wiltshire. This is somewhere else. Like and yet not like."

"I owe her a favour now," said Ver from high on the mare's back. "And that's a bit of a problem but I'll sort it." She reached down and tapped Alys on the shoulder.

"Which way did you come up, then?"

"I've been on the run. I started out on the Switch from Dartmoor, and from there I went up to Northumberland, and from there to Cumbria and then back down here."

"You didn't get all the way up, then?"

"No. I didn't finish the Switch. In fact, I barely started it. I didn't know what I was doing. Completely fucking clueless. I knew where the thing I was looking for was to be found, I found it, and I thought that would be it. Like Hell it was."

Ver gave a snort of laughter. "Easy to say in hindsight, though: *I should have done this, that and the other.* Not so simple at the time when you don't know what you're walking into. I'd say you've done all right."

"What was it you were looking for, Mum?" Luna asked. She fingered the thing in her pocket. It felt like stone, but too light: bone, perhaps?

"I'm not going to talk about it until we're in a safer place," Alys said.

"Best not to draw attention," Ver agreed. "There's all manner of snares and traps along the lych paths and this one's not so perfect either, believe me."

Luna looked down. The white chalk beneath her feet was broken by ridges of earth, where tiny white flowers grew, but for a moment, the chalk was transparent as glass and the flowers were stars. An unimaginable darkness lay beneath. She blinked and was once more traversing the quiet Wiltshire ridgeway.

"There are points along the way, Luna, where you can step onto these old tracks," Alys said. "Wistman's Wood is one of those, so is the land around Wayland's Smithy."

"Stone circles?" Luna asked, thinking of Avebury and the great henge to the south of here.

"Oddly enough, only sometimes. Some of those monuments were built to close a door, not to open one. But there's so much I don't know," Alys sounded frustrated.

"Lovey, you've come to it a bit late," Ver said. "There's a lot even I don't know, coming from that background so to speak, and probably I never will."

"Well," Alys said. "I've had some adventures, that's for sure. But I won't mind being within four walls for a bit."

"While we're on the subject," Ver said, "I won't be coming all the way with you. The mare will go back under her own steam."

"Don't you want to see Sam?" Luna asked, disappointed.

"I do, but – don't take this the wrong way – I can't spend all night at this time of year looking after other people. I've got stuff to do. Don't think I didn't want to help you out – that was essential. But I'll make sure you're safe for the rest of the journey and once you're back, Sam will know what to do once Alys tells him what she knows. Well, he should, anyway, more or less, even given that he's a man. It's always hard to know if they've got the right end of the stick, even the best of them."

The mare came to an ambling halt. Ver slid down with an ungainly thump.

"Thank you, my lovely." She patted the mare's neck and the horse stood patiently. "Right, this is my stop, as it were. You'll know where to get off, won't you?"

"Yes, I think so," said Alys. "Nice to meet you, Mrs Fallow. I'm sure we'll see one another again. Goodbye, doggy." She bent to pat the lurcher's head and Moth wagged his tail.

She shook their hands and stepped from the chalk path. Luna had a glimpse of her fading figure, with the alder grove visible through it, and when she turned back to the path, the mare was no longer there.

"Come on," Alys said. "Let's get home."

BEE

Stella had fallen asleep at the kitchen table. Hardly surprising, thought Bee. It was long past anyone's bedtime, although she wasn't sure about Ward. He didn't precisely appear bright eyed and bushy tailed but he, too, had had a long day. She stood up.

"Right. Stella needs to go to bed. So do you, Luna. So do you." She favoured her mother with a stern eye. She had not yet recovered from the shock of walking into the kitchen and finding Alys sitting at the kitchen table as though she'd never been away. Now she knew why cats were really pissed off when you'd come back from a trip. Bee had rehearsed Alys' homecoming so many times, imagining her relief, her love, the embraces and are-you-all-rights and the where-have-you-beens and now that this had actually happened, she just wanted to turn her back on the bloody woman and ignore her for a day and a half.

"I don't feel particularly knackered, actually," Alys said, irritating Bee further.

"You might not." Ward knuckled his eyes. "I suspect it's an accurate description of the rest of us, however."

"My sleep patterns are all over the place," Alys said. "I suppose it's a bit like mega jetlag."

"I just feel really drained," said Luna. She sat holding tightly to Sam's hand. Bee did not yet know how he had reacted to his girlfriend's rescue attempt, though they had been brought up to speed on recent events.

"...then Sam's gran left us and we just walked on, up hill and down dale like Pigling Bland until we came to a landmark I recognised."

"What was that, Mum?" Serena asked. "For future reference."

"I could see the Hornmoon church steeple with its golden weathercock. In bright sunlight from the road, even though it was night. So we stepped off and there we were in the churchyard, and we just walked home as though we'd been down the pub for the evening. There was Sam, waiting, and clever Bella had made this rather wonderful cake and gone to bed, and so had Nell."

"Well," Ward remarked. "All this is most curious, I must say. I've passed into a state beyond astonishment and now I'm going to follow

Bella's example and go to bed as well." He looked at Serena. "And I'm past shame, too. Are you coming?"

"What?" said Alys. "Are you two – What happened to Ben?"

"Good question," said Serena. She took Ward's hand. "He buggered off with Dana Stare. We told you about her brother. I haven't got to Dana yet and I think she can wait till morning, the cow."

"Well, it's nice to see you back in this house," Alys said graciously to Ward.

"Thank you. You, too, to put it mildly."

"Mum, I don't care if you're tired or not. The rest of us are going to bed." Once she had put aside her unreasonable annoyance, Bee was delighted to see Alys back safe and sound, but she'd had enough of her mother being mysterious about what she'd been doing. For Alys had by no means told them everything. And there was another, unfamiliar emotion lurking in the wings, too, which Bee was too tired to examine right now: doubt. When Alys had disappeared, Bee had been left with no option, or so she believed, other than to become Mooncote's mistress. That had brought some interesting things in its wake, like Dark, who had not joined them in the kitchen but melted away into the orchard, as was his custom. She couldn't yet face the thought that Dark might not return, now that Alys had, but there was this lesser worry, too. Bee was by no means sure that she wanted to hand the reins of the house back to her mother and she had a very harsh word with herself about selfishness: after all, they had wanted nothing more, or so they thought, than for Alys Fallow to come back.

Well, now she had.

"We're going to bed, too," Luna said. She patted Bee on the shoulder as she passed. "Goodnight, Mum."

Alys looked up and smiled. "Good night, my darling."

"Well," said Bee, rather more sharply than she intended, "We could all sit here like the Waltons but I, too, am going to turn in."

"Yes. I'll see you in the morning."

"Do not go wandering off."

Alys grinned like a small child, caught out. "No, miss. I wasn't going to, actually. I was going to let everyone have a fair crack at the bathroom and then come up myself. I really could do with a proper wash."

Bee kissed her cheek. "Can't say fairer than that."

Later, teeth cleaned and face scrubbed, she lay in the coolness of her bed watching the moon as it sailed through the clouds. She thought back over the long, strange day, her summer powers. If they were hers. Bee remembered lying here with Dark, watching Mars on its journey through the sky, chasing Sirius who chased the Hunter who chased the bull who chased the seven sisters like one of those Russian doll nursery rhymes, embedded. The old woman who swallowed the fly, indeed. She closed her eyes, shutting out the moon and the scudding clouds, and she did not think that she slept, but she must have done so for when she next opened them, surely only a moment later, Dark's familiar presence was beside her. Bee gave him a big hug.

"I'm so pleased you're here! Why didn't you stay when we got back? Mum's come home! Luna brought her."

"I know." Dark said into her ear, very quietly, "Mistress Fallow — are you sure that this woman really is your mother?"

STELLA

Thank God for ibuprofen. And the entire modern age. Stella, showered and in a t-shirt and pyjama bottoms, stood by the window, looking out over the dark garden. She barely remembered going to bed, having apparently fallen asleep at the kitchen table and been sent upstairs by her sister. She had woken, fully clothed and uncomfortable but no longer so exhausted, and had decided that the day needed to be taken in hand. It was around seven, so Stella had occupied the bathroom before anyone else was up and was now about to get dressed. But she wanted a moment of quiet before heading down to the kitchen. She wanted to think.

Her mother was back. Stella now felt even worse about that argument with Bee. She had known perfectly well the extent to which Bee had liaised with the police, with the organisation that had been the Susy Lamplugh trust, the informal enquiries. And know she knew that even if her sister had taken personal charge of a police investigation, they still wouldn't have found Alys. Having experienced one of those patchwork layers of time and place for herself, the thought of her mother – resourceful but hardly young – having to face who knows what otherworldly shit made Stella feel physically ill. She told herself that Alys had survived, however, and they had succeeded – *Luna*, bless her, had succeeded – in bringing her home. It was time to get on with things and the family was still entangled: she somehow did not think Tam Stare was dead, Dana almost certainly wasn't, and the Behenian stars were still in mysterious orbit around Mooncote. Stella remembered those comments about 'the cold man'. Who was the cold man? Had the trees meant Tam? That was some sort of winter magic, surely. Or the comet? And who was the star they had rescued?

Slowly, Stella dressed in a sweatshirt, jeans and one of Bee's woolly jumpers. It must have reached her sister's knees: it was long enough on Stella. But it was warm and comforting and she felt like being bundled up. Ibiza's summery warmth was a distant memory; Mooncote was not terribly well heated.

She went downstairs, trying to be quiet, but there was a line of light beneath the kitchen door. When Stella pushed it open, she found her mother sitting at the table.

"Oh, Stella. You're up early. Want some tea?"

Alys wore a velvet blue kaftan as a dressing gown and sheepskin slippers; her normal winter attire for bedtime. Apart from her shaved head, which lent her a rather ascetic appearance, she looked exactly as she had at the time she had left. She was reading a letter.

"Rather nice to get a letter, isn't it? In this technology-obsessed day and age. Bee's done her best to weed out all the junk mail. I must say, I didn't realise I'd been gone for quite so long."

"Well, you had," Stella said. She folded her arms. Alys sighed.

"Have I really pissed you off?"

"Pissed off doesn't really begin to cover it, Mum. Terrified, grief-stricken, baffled…"

"I promise you, Stella, I didn't mean to be gone for so long. A week, not more. And it started out well enough, although as I said to Sam's gran, I now see that I didn't know what the hell I was getting into, not really. Then I got trapped."

"Look," Stella said. She accepted a mug of tea and sat down. "The trouble is, this doesn't start with you going off like that, right? Or even with your disappearing. This starts way before that. I can't speak for anyone else in this family, but I didn't know, prior to this week, that it was possible to travel through time, that another world – or parts of worlds – exists alongside our own in some kind of Celtic twilight style thing and that you can pop in and out of them as you please, or that there's so much weird shit going on. I mean, I knew there was *some* weird shit. Like the ghosts and the stars. But not all this. So how did *you* know?"

Alys sighed again. "I know. It's a lot to take in. I grew up here, with Abraham and your grandmother, and stuff happened then. But it happened from time to time – a ghost on the landing, something slipping out of sight in the garden. That was it. I thought it was normal. My mother was proud of it. I can see her now – she was very tall and willowy, very elegant, a great gardener, and she loved to go and dead head the roses and potter about and I would watch her. She told me stories about the ghosts as she was gardening. It was a fairy-tale childhood and I suppose I wanted to give you girls all that as well, not that I could have stopped it. Abraham wouldn't have moved house. I suppose I could have done and I did travel a lot, but I always came back. Anyway, one day, when I was nineteen, I was home for the summer. It was really hot – 1976, everyone remembers it. None of you were born then, obviously, and I hadn't even met –" here she paused and Stella almost heard the whisper of a name on her lips "– Bee's father at that point. I was out on the lawn, the sun was setting, and the heat of the sun had brought up all these old patterns in the dry grass of the lawn. Parch marks, they're called. They show things like old watercourses and where buildings once stood, and I was looking at this square on the grass where the soil had been a different colour. Suddenly there was a building there, a little hut-like thing, and I was in the middle of a maze. I wasn't in my own time at all. It was like a dream. The sun was high and there was this powerful scent of box from the hedges of the maze. I went into the hut. And there were two girls there, winding silk onto spools."

"Did you recognise them?"

"One was a pretty girl in a rose coloured dress and the other one was in mourning black, with violet ribbons in her black hair and a little pointed face. They both stared at me. There was a tiny bird in a cage and it fluttered up in fright when it saw me. I was going to say something but the girl in mourning opened her mouth and a shower of golden sparks came out. They whirled around my head – they were stinging, like tiny wasps, or needles – and I threw my arm up to protect my face and when I lowered it, there I was on the lawn again. So after that, I started looking into the history of the house. And into other things. I got to know a man in – well, never mind where, later on, after Bee was born, and he told me about the Gipsy Switch and how his family said that you could use it to travel, to other places. Not normal places. So I started to look into it."

"Did you ever see the two girls again?"

"I used to see the one in the rose coloured dress quite a bit and I think Serena has seen her, too. She certainly used to when she was a little girl."

At this point, Serena herself came into the kitchen. She was dressed. "Oh, you're up. Ward's still asleep. Bella's still asleep." She joined them at the table and rubbed her eyes. "I wish I was still asleep."

"You could have stayed in bed," said Stella.

"I woke up, and started overthinking and I got sick of it. I didn't want to wake Ward up. I thought I might take the dogs for a walk."

"I won't come with you," Stella said. "I've done quite enough walking for this week."

"I'll come, if that's okay," Alys said.

"I should think *you've* done quite enough walking as well."

"Yes. I suppose it's left me restless. I could do with some fresh air."

"Actually," Serena said, "I don't think you ought to come, Mum. I don't think it's very safe right now. I'm not going to take the dogs past the orchard."

Alys' eyes flashed warning blue. Then she subsided. "You might be right."

"In that case, I will come." Stella drained her tea. "I'll keep an eye on you and Mum can sit here."

They reached the edge of the orchard, silent after the bustle of Apple Day and now denuded of marquee and stage by Caro Amberley's helpers. Stella released a breath that she had not realised she had been holding. The orchard seemed to enfold them both, though Bee had told her that it was through the orchard that she had time-travelled.

"Don't you try that nonsense with me," Stella said, aloud.

"Sorry?"

"I didn't mean you. I was talking to the trees. There's been quite enough of that sort of thing."

Serena gave a grim nod. She threw the spaniels' ball for them, over and over. It never grew old. Hardy and Nelson fought and snarled and gurgled at one another, play fighting across the newly shorn grass. It would, Bee had said, be the last cut of the year. Stella looked back at the house repeatedly, just in case it had decided to disappear, but it still stood, solid with the kitchen light pooling in a welcoming glow across the courtyard. As Stella watched, a bedroom light went on. Luna and Sam were getting up. *That's better*, she thought to the house. *You stay right there.*

The dogs' ball hit her foot. She picked it up and threw, watching them race about. Serena was in sight, not moving too far away. After a few minutes, she said, "Stella?"

"Yep?"

"Have you noticed something?"

"Oh God, what now?"

"It's not getting any lighter."

Stella looked at the sky. Serena was right: the grey halflight of dawn, into which they had taken the dogs, was still present.

"It's quite cloudy. I don't think we'll see the sun come up."

"But it should be up by now, Stella. We're on more or less the same latitude as London and I have to be up really early because of Bella and school and so on and I can see the sky from my place. It should be quite light by now. It's nearly eight."

She was right, Stella realised. She shot a wild look back at the house but more lights were on by now. Nell's window still lay dark. In the next room, she could see her niece at the glass. Bella waved.

Above, the stars were suddenly very bright; not the faint morning stars, soon banished by day, but those of deep night. The blue lamp of Sirius burned over the apple trees and the Hunter strode overheard, with Aldebaran crimson beyond. The Pleiades sparkled over the Bull's shoulder and in the east the comet was blazing.

"I think we should go back indoors," Serena said.

"I think so, too."

Serena corralled the spaniels and they hastened across the lawn. Everyone except Sam and Bella was now in the kitchen. Bee was up, cooking breakfast in a comedy apron. There was no sign of Dark. Her mother was, Stella noted with relief, still where they had left her.

"Dogs all walked? Who wants bacon? I don't mean you, Stella and Luna. Although we've got veggie sausages. I'm going to do scrambled eggs."

"I don't want to freak everyone out," Stella said, "But what happened to sunrise?"

Ward went into the hallway and came back in short order. "Your impressive clock has stopped."

"So has my watch," said Bee.

Serena ran for the staircase.

"Bella? Can you come down here, please, sweetheart? Quickly!"

"Where's Sam?"

"He went out to the van with the dog," Luna said. "I'll get him."

But as she opened the door, Sam came in, all in a rush as if blown.

"Something's not right. It's too dark. And it's getting really cold."

Serena, returning, said, "Bella's coming down. But Nell won't answer her door and it's locked from the inside."

"You're going to have to tell her something now," Ward said.

"How? Slide a note under it? I suppose we could send her a text if we can get a signal."

Stella was watching the windows of the kitchen. With the Aga

278

quietly roaring away and the hob switched on, the kitchen was a warm haven. But fingers of frost were starting to climb up the glass, each one a tiny diamond point, and it was growing colder. All three dogs, Moth and the spaniels, were up and staring at the back door.

"This bacon's not frying," Bee said. She switched off the hob with a click but Stella did not think it would make much difference. Frost was creeping beneath the back door, turning the flagstones to faint silver.

From behind, Dark said, "We are under attack."

"What do we do?" Ward was glancing around him, as if seeking weapons.

"Wait. I don't know what will happen now."

Stella marched to the back door.

"Don't open it!"

"I'm not going to open it, Mum. I just want to have a look out."

The whole courtyard was covered in frost. Icicles crept down from the guttering and Stella could hear them chime.

"Where are the stars when you need them?"

Stella turned away from the back door but as she did so, there was a thunderous knock. The dogs roared.

"Fuck!"

"That's not the postman," said Ward.

"I'm certainly not opening it to find out!"

The knock came again. It sounded as though someone was trying to kick in the door.

"Is that going to hold?" Bee snapped.

"Push the table against it!"

"Don't invite them over the threshold!"

"I think that's vampires, darling. Help me with the table."

Bella, very pale, and Serena started to shove the big table across the flags but the knock came again and the door flew open.

Dana Stare stood on the step, in her leather jacket and a long lace skirt. Her face was paper-white and her eyes blazed.

"You've got something of mine, and I want it back!"

Ward said, "Miss Stare, I presume? I'm sure if anyone's got your property, they'll be happy to return it."

"Oh," Alys said. She pushed back her chair and stood up. "It's you."

"Give it back, you thieving cunt."

"Language, language, so important," Alys murmured. "It's not yours – it's mine. Can't steal your own belongings, can you?"

"No," Serena said. "but you can steal other women's men, just because, can't you? Enspell them just because you can?"

"It didn't take much spellcraft," Dana said. "He was gagging for it anyway." She spat on the kitchen floor and the spittle sizzled and hissed, evaporating into a cloud of small winged flies that spiralled upwards.

"Conjuring tricks," said Alys with scorn. But the cloud comma'd out and settled around Serena's head. She gasped. Stella made a move forward, to pull her sister back, but something was happening. Serena was surrounded by light, a mist, a glow. It was as though she'd walked into thick fog, lit by headlights. Ward Garner said, "Oh, *shit*."

The mist faded but Serena wasn't there any more. Instead, a white hare sat poised on the kitchen floor. Dana snarled. The hare darted forwards. It shot between Dana's feet and out into the cold dark. Dana said something, a long liquid word. Black mist surrounded her and then she, too, was gone. Stella glimpsed the mink, shooting arrow-swift, after the hare.

STELLA

Stella ran for the door but her mother got there first. Alys slammed the back door shut, scraping frost from the floor.

"What are you doing?"

"We can't help her! We can't go after her, we can't run that fast."

"What about the lych path?"

"Luna, we don't know where they've gone."

Stella pulled open the door into the hall. "I heard something."

There was an arctic breath of air blowing through the hall. Stella raced into the dining room. The French doors that led to the garden were wide open. Ice was already fringing the long curtains.

"Get this fucking door shut!" Stella shouted. But the door was ripped out of her hand and she stumbled forwards. Someone caught her by the arm. She caught a glimpse of the garden, black and silver in the shimmering light. Ned Dark pulled her back.

"Careful."

"What is it?" Bee had been right behind her.

"It's Tam Stare, I know it is. Look!" A figure was running through the trees, flickering like a magic lantern.

"The orchard is my domain," Dark said. He stepped through the French windows. "Leave him to me."

"No chance." Bee and Stella were already in the garden. Stella turned and pulled the French windows shut from outside, then she ran.

SERENA

She remembered this, the flying dance. Instinct had propelled her through the door but she was more herself, this time, as if growing accustomed to this business of changing shape. She fled, darting, down the lawn and through the hedge and over the grass and leaped a wall, landing in the lane. The roadway was silent, free of even the infrequent cars. Serena bolted down the lane, heedless of the cold, heading for the churchyard.

Of anyone outside Mooncote itself, Abraham would know what to do. And she might change back. Draw Dana away. Then fight?

The mink was not far behind. As before, Serena could hear it, hissing as it ran. Dana wanted her to know that she was following. And Serena did not think that Dana would be quick with the kill, no quick snap and oblivion, or a catapult into ghost-form. Dana struck her as the type who would play with her food. But it was not far from the church. She could see the lych gate and, running from it, the faint, pulling lure of what must be Alys and Luna's lych path. No, mustn't, won't.

Serena scrambled up over the churchyard wall, paws scrabbling in the ivy, and fell into the churchyard itself. She could see Abraham's tomb, looming large and pointed. Above, the weathercock swung and gave a scream. She was still hare, not woman.

Serena ducked behind the tomb and hid. She felt, rather than heard, the mink pour over the wall. Into one long ear, she heard her grandfather say,

"Sweetheart? You've got to go back."

BEE

Dark had become a swarm of bees, flying up into the shadows of the orchard, but a moment later the swarm descended and he stood there in human form once more, out of breath.

"It's too cold."

"He's gone through the hedge gate," Stella said. She stood, bouncing up and down on the balls of her feet.

"There's nothing there, except the meadow."

"I'm not going to let the bastard give me the slip again." Stella drew a breath and set off. She was a fast runner; Bee not so. More heavily built but on her feet for a lot of the day, she was not unfit, but she could not keep up with her marathon-running sister. By the time she reached the gate in the hedge, Stella was halfway down the field.

But she could see Tam Stare. He was standing at the end of the meadow, arms outstretched in mocking welcome.

"Come and get me then, you slippery bitch. Come on, little Tarka – come to Uncle Tam!"

"Fuck you!" Bee heard Stella shout. But she slowed to a halt, allowing Bee to catch up, panting.

"I can't just go for him. He's stronger than I am. I haven't got a weapon."

"We took him before. I took him." But the sunlit magic which she had conjured up on the southern shore was too weak now without Drake's back-up. She could feel it inside her mind, like a breath of summer, but it could not combat this iron cold.

"He comes, he comes!" Tam Stare shouted. His head went back, his arms up, in a gesture of exultation. "He is here!"

The hedge parted, the thorn bushes shrivelling back. Through the thorns came the figure whom Stella had met on the stairs, whom Bee had glimpsed in the yard on Hallowe'en night. It was huge, eight feet or more, towering over the slight figure of Stare. It wore a heavy cloak of skins, fringed with ice, and its face was now human but wrong, the colour of fir at night, a deep black-green. Its obsidian eyes had moonlight in their depths and it moved swiftly, on back-jointed legs. The stubby horns above its forehead, half concealed by a hood, began to grow as they watched, shedding strips of skin, until the great antlered rack spread outwards. Stella could not see fully inside the depths of the swinging cloak but she thought it might have an erection.

"What is it?" Bee whispered.

"Nothing I want to meet!"

"He is here," Tam said, in a voice filled with delight.

LUNA

"Come with me," Alys said, to Sam and Luna. To Ward, she added, "Stay here and look after Bella."

"I'll do my best!"

"Where's my mum?" Bella was in tears.

"Don't go out of the house." Luna watched as Alys bent down to look her granddaughter in the face. "Don't worry. She will come back. She will be all right. I promise you."

Bella gave a shaky nod.

Alys tugged an old Barbour off the rack and struggled into it. She pulled on a pair of hiking boots. She was still wearing the blue velvet kaftan.

"I know I look ridiculous. I don't care."

Luna was putting on her own boots.

"No one's going to see you, Mum."

"I'm sure the neighbours gave up long ago."

"Wait –" said Ward, but Alys had already opened the back door.

"There's nothing out there now. That girl won't stop till she finds Serena, except she isn't going to find her, because my daughter's too clever. So don't worry, Bella."

Then she was gone. Luna, hastening after with Moth, saw her marching out of the courtyard and down the drive. She did look ridiculous, but somehow dangerous as well. How had she managed that?

"Do you know where's she's going?" Luna said to Sam.

"She's going to the lych path. Look, you can see it."

The path, by now familiar to Luna, ran over the fields. She could see it beyond the hedge that separated garden and meadows and orchard. When she looked across to Hornmoon church, the weathercock gave a flash of fire, as if caught in the light of the sun. But it was still pitch black, with the stars motionless overhead. There were shapes in the meadow. At first Luna thought they were trees, because they were so still, but then she realised that they were people. Bee and Stella and Dark. And someone else.

SERENA

Serena crept around the tombstones. The blue spark of Abraham danced before her, showing her the way. She could hear the mink, sniffing around on the other side of the churchyard: Dana had not yet picked up her scent, but it wouldn't be long. Abraham led her under the fronded branches of a yew, berries black-wax in the lack of light, and she felt its poisonous needles brush her face before she was out, heading around the side of the church to the smaller back gate.

"Go!" Abraham whispered. "I'll distract her," and the firefly spark flitted away. Serena, as if shot out of the greyhound traps, was off. Under the gate and down the field, running for her life. She tore through the hedge, leaving white fluff behind, and back along the road. There was an animal squeal of rage from the churchyard. Serena ran and ran, everything going into the power of her legs and her flight, until the gates of Mooncote once more came into view. She was nearly home.

STELLA

It was so cold. Stella's teeth chattered and her legs felt leaden. She tried to push Bee away, tried to run, could not do a damn thing. The being that was coming up the hill fast towards them had hands like clubs, it was too big, she would claw and kick and bite if she had to but not even adrenaline was enough to carry her out of the cold's locked embrace. She was suddenly and unpleasantly aware of the surge of blood between her legs, one of those floodings which sometimes overcame one, soaking the sanitary pad. Beside her, Bee was still and Dark was transfixed, staring.

"We're fucked," Stella whispered.

"Look what I've brought you!" Tam Stare sang and whatever accent he'd been assuming fell away; Stella did not think he was even human any more, if he had ever been. His eyes were blue fire. The being was here, a few feet away, and it opened its mouth and she smelled smoke and blood, its peatfire breath, heard the clack of bones from beneath its cloak, tried not to look into the wells of its eyes – and then there were pattering hooves on the frost ground, ringing out like Christmas.

Stella turned her head. A doe stood close by on the meadow. She would have been almost invisible if she had stood against the meadow, but she was whitefire, silhouetted on the frost of the field like a heraldic figure. The being saw her. It flung up the cloak, which fell to the floor in a bundle of leaves, and dropped onto all fours, a green stag. Stella looked into its wild golden eye and felt scorched. The doe gave a cry and bounded up, then she was off, across the field with a roe deer's springing leaps, and over the hedge. The stag went after. They watched as the two animals raced away to the west.

"Well," Stella spat at Tam Stare. "So what are you going to do now?"

"It's getting warmer," Bee said.

SERENA

Up the drive and over the lawn. Leaping the flowerbeds and into the yard but the kitchen door was fast shut and Serena gave a hare's scream. She ran right around the house, heading widdershins, past the dustbins and the feed for the horses and the potting shed, with the mink pelting behind her. What if she ran into Moth? Would the lurcher know who she was, and what? They were programmed to chase rabbits... She no longer knew what to do but with some idea of going back down the drive, she completed a full circuit of the house and collapsed, naked and gasping, against the brick wall.

Dana Stare walked up to her. She did not even seem out of breath. "Better put some clothes on, love, or you'll catch your death. Oh wait. You're going to catch that anyway. I'd like to have sunk my teeth into you but I've got a better plan now." And Serena saw the dull blue glint of the blade in her hand, its ivory handle.

"It's slate, just in case you're wondering. Sharp, though. Better be careful, hadn't I? Wouldn't want to cut my fingers."

Serena scrambled to her feet. She looked around but there was nothing to defend herself with. Dana saw this and her smile vanished, She became intent, a hunting look. She feinted with the slate knife and Serena darted back, bare feet stinging on the gravel. If she became a hare once more – but Serena felt deep into herself and there was no hare there, nothing but fright and fury. She thought for a bright bloody second that it might just be worth it, just jump the bitch and see what damage she could do... She dodged back and Dana came forwards with her eyes shark-dead and her mouth almost lipless with concentration.

Above Serena's head, the window rattled as the sash went up.

"Your sister Linnet says – you always wanted it and now it's yours. Good luck!" It was Bella's voice and Serena, startled, saw something in the light from the bedroom window, floating down like a huge pink rose petal, billowing out as its skirts caught the draught in a parachute pattern. Dana looked up and her mouth opened but it was too late. She dropped the knife as the skirts of the old rose coloured dress fell over her head. Then she screamed and as the dress ignited, taking her into a sunset column of flame, she went on screaming.

BEE

The frost sank into the ground once the horned thing had gone and a wet breath touched Bee's cheek, a gathering sense of rain.

"Borrowed your power, eh?" Stella snapped.

Tam Stare gave her a filthy look. "Not all of it." He caught his bottom lip between his teeth and gave a smug, self-regarding nod. "No, not all." He still didn't look human. What on Earth was he, Bee thought? Bare branches were coming out of the ground, bramble twisting. Bee cried out as the sharp thorns, too long for real blackberry, pierced her ankle. She stumbled as she stood but Dark was steadying her.

"This is *her* land. You don't command it, this is not real, this leaf-in-the-morning magic of yours. I know you now. How long have you been out of the hills?"

"As long as I fucking well like." But the brambles had stopped growing and Tam doubled up suddenly, coughing. Dark reached down and brushed the coils away, to melt into shadows.

Tam stepped back and straightened up. He raised his hand. The tips of his fingers glowed silvery. He opened his mouth and spat. A hornet hummed out, enormous, and made for Bee's face. She felt a sudden strangeness in the palm of her hand and looked down. Something black and soft moved between her fingers. Bee gave a cry and dropped it. A blackbird fluttered up. She glimpsed the sharp yellow beak as it snapped. The hornet was gone and so was the bird. From the hedge, she heard its long morning song.

"You can't attack me, miss Bee. It's still too cold." But Stare sounded uncertain.

"You weren't invited," hissed Dark.

"Oh yes, I was. You paid me," he said to Bee. "Good money, too. It's a bond, in the human world."

"I didn't pay you to summon a demon!"

"That was no demon. An old being, true. And prone to the whiff of a cunt in heat like any other male, it seems." Stare spoke a word and even the vestige of light went out. Bee heard Stella give a muffled yelp.

"Take my hand!" She reached out and grasped her sister. From close by Dark's voice, quite calm, said, "This is her land and she commands the snares, the traps. Give me *your* hand, Bee."

Bee put her hand in his. Quite human, warm and flesh and blood.

"His tricks aren't real. He seeks to make you doubt yourself."

Doubt. The word was a fishhook, snagging her thoughts. Bee suffered as much from doubt as anyone: am I doing the right thing, have I done the wrong thing, what if what if what if? But deep down, past the fishhook's snag, Bee knew who she was. Beatrice Fallow, sister to Stella and Luna and Serena, daughter to Alys, granddaughter of Abraham. It was like an obituary. And deeper than that? She belonged to the land, to this place. She felt her feet settle strongly on the cold earth, planting down and rooting in, and as she did so, she caught a sidelong mental glimpse of Tam Stare.

Flimsy. Barely rooted, drifting. Old, yes, though not nearly as old as the thing he had sought to summon and control. Not human, not born of flesh but made out of scraps and patches, coming from an ancient magic, long long ago, which had grown thin and attenuated down the centuries but still sought to bring back the source of its power: that ice age world in which men fought to survive but in which some things flourished. Bee felt his link to his sister, spilling over with hate and warped desire but under that a bottomless, painful thing that might have been love. She suddenly felt terribly, unexpectedly, sorry for him and Dana both, just as the blackness was split by a bolt of lightning pink. Stare shrieked.

"Dia, no!"

Bee felt a wash of heat. Flames flickered through the shadows, blossoming with the colour of roses and far away a woman was screaming. Into her ear Dark said urgently, "Now, mistress! Strike while he is weakened – his sister is gone and his powers are waning."

But she didn't know how to strike. She looked within, seeking what was to be found there. And the first thing that came to Bee was a memory: standing in the orchard at the start of the autumn, waiting for Dark, and talking to the elder tree. As the thought entered her head, Tam Stare cried out and she could see again. He began to shrink, to change, his white face and black clothes reducing and turning on their side and splitting. The distant screams subsided. Within a few minutes, a stand of elder rose out of the field, whip-thin and white withy against the darkness of the hedge. It thrashed once, a frenzy as though a gale blew through it, and then it was still.

"Well, that's an improvement," said Stella.

"We need to get back to the house." Bee turned to Dark. "I don't want to face that horned thing again, Ned."

"Nor I."

"Agreed," said Stella. "But if we ever get to leave the house again, I suggest coming back down here with a fucking chainsaw."

LUNA

Luna stood on the lych path on the churchward side of the lych gate, waiting. She did not like it but she tried to feel strong, holding the space. Sam and Alys had gone ahead, further into the churchyard, to open the gate. It was very dark now, and Luna could no longer see what was happening in the field, or what had become of Serena, or anything. She fretted, events having long since slid out of her control or even her view. She wished Ver March were here, was glad that Moth had come with her. But the sky was moving again. She watched the fire of the comet gradually slide round, as though some vast hand turned the wheel of an astrolabe, sending planets and sun and moon spinning on their approved courses, with the anomalous comet roaring between. When it reached the weathercock, the golden bird creaked on its stand and Luna blinked. For a moment, the whole church tower was in sunlight, with the bare chestnut tree beside its northern wall in full Maytime candlehood. Then night, once more. But the church bells were pealing out and someone was coming up the field.

He was very pale and bright. Luminescence poured out around him and he left a frosty sparkling track. Luna recognised him from her sister's description: he was the comet, its spirit, and he had come at last. She stood, rooted to the spot, watching him pass through the stone wall as if it was not there and stride past her. He wore ribbons of light and his eyes were closed. *He is dreaming*, thought Luna, and she stopped being so afraid. He went down the path and into the church. Luna held her breath. Then her mother appeared in the doorway.

"Luna. Come in out of the cold."

SERENA

While Serena was getting dressed, her sisters gathered below to look at the smear of ash that had been Dana Stare. Bella was sitting on the bed, as Serena hastily put on her jeans and sweater, which had been sitting neatly on the bed after her transfiguration, transported upstairs by some unknown force and in the case of the jeans, uncreased.

"When everyone had gone out, the ghost came. Her name's Linnet. Like grandma's middle name is. And she spoke to us."

"She did," Ward said. "She gave quite a concise, but coherent, explanation. Dana, not her original name, by the way, is her sister – was her sister, they'd had what you might call a dysfunctional relationship, and the ghost has been on the watch ever since in case little sis rocked back up."

"But how long has that been?"

"Rather a long time judging by the Elizabethan nature of that garment."

"But Dana wasn't a ghost. There was nothing ghostly about her. How come she was still alive? She was a human. She had a brother, after all."

"I'm not sure that's true, actually. The ghost implied, but did not actually say, that Dana might have come from somewhere else."

Serena paused mid-jumper. "What sort of 'somewhere else'?"

"She didn't say. But from what Stella just said, one might start looking a bit more closely at stories about changelings."

"Right."

"I mean, normal girls can't change into mink."

"Or hares." She paused. "So what does that make me?"

"I've no idea. Quite cute?"

Bella made a throwing-up noise, then said, "Oh. Or me, either. What am I?" There was a short silence.

"I'm pretty sure I'm not anything really supernatural," Stella said. "I grew up. I remember growing up. Everyone else remembers me growing up. With changelings, they notice. Because they're not right."

"I suggest a conversation with your mum might move to the top of the *to do* list," said Ward.

"Yes. Wherever she is. *Again.*"

Someone knocked on the bedroom door. "Hello?"

"Stella?"

Her sister came in. She said, "As if we hadn't had enough excitement, Cappella is at the door. We are wanted in the church."

LUNA

Luna sat in a pew, holding Sam's hand, with Moth lying at their feet like a stone dog on a tomb. The old oak door creaked as her sisters filed in, with Bella, with Ward. Seven people were now in Hornmoon church, and one ghost. And the stars of the sky.

Luna felt very shy. She had seen them before, but never altogether, and there were a lot of them. She tried to count them but it was like counting the yews in the churchyard, a different number each time. There was Arcturus, jasper in her red-gold hair and a stem of plantain in her hand. A woman with a frond of succory smiled at Luna and Luna recognised the woman whom she had sometimes seen sitting by her cradle, at night when the fretful baby could not sleep. Here was Antares, black-skinned and flashing eyed, with a skein of sardonyx beads across her brow, and Aphecca, also black and topaz-crowned. Algol's diamonds sparked fire from the altar candles and the Pleiades clustered in a corner, whispering to one another. Procyon strolled by with a garland of buttercups. And in the centre of the ring that they were slowly forming, the comet stood, dreaming still.

Stella nudged Luna.

"That one, the one who looks a bit blue – that's the one I rescued."

"Do you know who she is?"

"I do now. I asked Capella and she said she's called Nephele, but she couldn't remember her own name, poor thing. But she's starting to remember things again now. She's been lost. There should be a piece of lapis in the gemstone box. And she carries speedwell."

Algol, resplendent in a gown of black and white, walked forwards and held up her hand for quiet. She gave the Pleiades a rather stern look, Luna thought. The stars all joined hands. Algol spoke a word, a hissing, fizzing word and the comet slowly opened his eyes. He smiled, and replied: it was a language like fire, crackling up into a blaze. Algol gave a bow. She spoke again and the conversation continued for a little while, formal and measured now, somehow like a dance, Luna thought. Then all the stars bowed, paying tribute to their visitor, and he held out his long fiery hands and laughed, delighted.

To the family, Algol said, "The comet is here, our little brother has come. And with the greater cold that he brings from deep space, he will seal the gateways to the Winter Kingdom, the world of ice whose legacy your enemies have tried to steal, by right of their blood, which yet does not belong to it. We need to send him into it, for if he remains in this world too long, he will bring the cold and the world will die. He will go now, but do not follow him: you will die also. We will tell you when it is safe." She turned to Luna. "All except you. We need you, Luna, to open the door for him."

"What?" Luna felt cold with panic. "I don't know how to do that."

"You do, Luna," her mother's voice said, not far away. "I gave you the key. It's yours, now. Once it's passed from the eldest to the youngest, the youngest must bear it."

Luna remembered the thing that her mother had given her, when they were in White Horse Country. She had forgotten, or perhaps the thing itself, hiding in plain sight, had made her forget. She fished into her pocket and pulled it out. The object, small and hard and round, lying in the palm of her hand, was a flute made of bone. It had five little holes, a narrow lip. She held it up to her mouth.

"Do I blow it?"

"Go on, Luna," her mother urged.

So Luna blew into the flute. At first she thought that nothing was happening, that the flute was blocked or that she had blown it the wrong way. But then a high, sweet note sang out, closer to birdsong than to a sound made by an instrument. Luna blew again, but she did not need to. The humming sound rang through the little church, making the air hazy and blurring the figures of the Behenian stars. Everything shimmered, shivering. Luna felt an electric pause, a suspension in the world, and deep inside her the baby stirred. The comet turned and walked back down the aisle, and out through the door. Luna followed, her fingers frozen to the little flute. The oaken door shut behind them with a crash. She looked down and saw Moth. The lurcher stared gravely up at her: *I will not leave you.*

Outside, it was very cold and very still. The gravestones were rimed with frost and Luna thought she must be able to see every star in the sky. Apart from that, it was utter dark: no sign of the orange glow that was distant Bristol, or even the closer illumination from Bridgwater. The comet paused, waiting, and the temperature dropped still further. In her ear, a voice said,

"I think he's waiting for you, Luna."

It was her grandfather's voice. She looked up to see a small blue spark. She and Moth were not alone out here after all and this gave her strength. She raised the flute to her lips and blew again.

The note sang out. The lych path was suddenly very bright but across the hills, the sloping fields, Luna could see other paths, too: some fainter tracks, criss-crossing, and, running towards the Tor along the floor of the valley a great burning road that she thought must be the Michael-Mary line, the ley that is said to bisect southern England from West to East, from Cornwall to Walsingham. A patchwork country, stitched together by these old roads, the tracks and pathways. And along the lych path, stood a gateway: not the in-our-world entrance to the church, but a great dark door.

Luna heard a tune in her head and she began to play. It was a simple tune, only a few notes, very faintly familiar. As she played it, she turned her head and looked up. Orion the Hunter, the Winter King, was striding over the ridge of the hill. When she looked back, a man was standing by the lych gate. He wore skins, black and white furs which covered his body, and at his belt hung a sword. A silver-white dog slunk around his knees and when it looked up its eyes blazed blue. Moth whined in greeting. The hunter smiled at the comet, gestured, "Come."

The comet's attenuated figure gave a bow. He stepped forward as Luna repeated the little tune. The lych gate loomed ahead: winter's king showed the comet through. Beyond, Luna had a glimpse of the dead kingdom: not White Horse Country, but the post-Ice Age wasteland of snow and wind-blasted scrub and icy pools. This, she knew, had been the land to which Tam and Dana had sought entry: was it where they had come from, perhaps? Or had they wanted to open its ways, to bring through the things that lived here into the world?

Far away, there was a flash of spring. A green stag, running.

Better it's closed, Luna thought, and finished the tune with a flourish just as the comet closed the gate. She hoped Moth wouldn't take off after the deer. She had a last glimpse of the comet, moving fast through the cold land, faster and faster, then the gate slammed soundlessly shut and the winter king, too, was gone, back to his rightful striding place in the sky.

The oak door opened behind Luna.

"Are you all right?" Sam's voice was thin with worry.

"Yes! Yes, I'm fine. See, Moth came with me." She ran back down the church path, seeing from the corner of her eye the blue spark of her grandfather's spirit sink down into the pyramid of his tomb, and took Sam's hand. He drew her back into the church where her sisters were anxiously waiting.

Above their heads, the biggest bell of the tower rang once, a singing note that shook the church and the world beyond, as though the little flute had struck an echoing note. The stars bowed again and then they began to fade, one by one, as stars do fade when morning comes. The Pleiades went first, then Arcturus, winking out, then Capella and her sisters. Algol vanished when all but one had gone. The star Nephele, clad now in seagreen silk and a necklace of lapis, stood with her hands folded together. She looked gravely from face to face, passing over Ward and Dark, but lingering on the sisters and Bella and their mother. Then she nodded once and was no longer there. In the eastern window, coloured like all the stars, there was a fire in the sky behind as the sun at last came up.

SERENA

There were footprints all along the muddy lane. Small pattering feet, small claws. And others – not footprints, thought Serena, but hoofprints, cloven. Some of these were very large, others not so big, but they wove in and out of one another in a braided dance that went all the way up the lane and into the drive, to where a pale doe was grazing on the lawn. Her head went up when she smelled the humans and the dog and she immediately pranced away, leaping the low beech hedge and disappearing into the orchard.

"I hope she's not been after your carrots," Ward said to Bee.

"I'm not growing carrots. Anyway, it's November. Do you know nothing about vegetables?

"I sometimes eat them in quality restaurants."

There was nothing more to do, Serena felt, than put the kettle on. Luna went upstairs for a rest, taking faithful Moth with her. Sam and Dark went out, to do man stuff in the yard, Sam said with a grin. Ward sat down at the table again, looking shell-shocked.

"I suppose we ought to do brunch. Or breakfast. I feel like I've been up for hours."

"You possibly have."

"I'm definitely going to the pub tonight," Stella said. "Just so you know."

"Did someone mention the pub?" Nell came into the kitchen, fresh from the shower and wearing a silk robe. Her long fair hair, unbraided, was damp. "Bit early, isn't it?"

Stella stared at her. "It's never too early to go to the pub. Have you just woken up?"

"Oh, no," Nell said. "I've been up for a while." There were dark circles under her eyes. She yawned and smiled. Her eyes met Serena's with the faintest hint of a challenge. "Had some funny dreams, though," Nell Fallow said.

ALYS

Night. The house was quiet, though Alys thought she had heard the moonhorse rocking against the boards. She walked quickly down the landing, making no sound. You learn how to do that, in certain places. Here in the old house, it was hardly a matter of life and death, but she didn't want to wake anyone up. Partly because they'd had a challenging few days and she thought, maternally, they needed sleep whether they were her kids or not, and partly because Alys didn't want to field awkward questions.

Such as "Where are you going at two o'clock in the morning, Mum?"

It had been a good day. She had spent most of it in the kitchen, over endless cups of tea, as family members came and went. She had spoken, in turn, to all her daughters. There had been enough questions.

What are you going to do about Ben, if all this was the fault of that girl? What about Ward?

Are you going back to Ibiza? What are your plans, now?

Are you sure, really, that you want a life with someone few other people can see? Although he is rather good looking, I must say.

When is the baby due, darling? Are you going to stay here? Or will you be back on the road before long?

And enough answers.

I don't know, Mum. Maybe Dana didn't use a whole lot of magic when it came to Ben. Maybe it really does take two to tango. And Ward's going to be in town for the winter.

If you and Bee are okay with it, I might stay put for a bit. I'll pay my way. I've got some gigs in Bristol coming up. London, too. And I was going to do a bit of exploring myself if I'm going to be in the South West for any length of time. Maybe some wild swimming. Might go down to Cornwall and learn to surf.

Dark's part of the house, Mother. If he stays, I'll stay. Is that okay, with you? It's your house, after all – what? Oh, that's a nice thing to say. Thank you. And Dark understands things. He told me about the Stares. He said they were – I'm not to say the name? All right. Maybe that's wise. But they're not the only ones out there. He says they're drawn to magic, like moths to flames, that they steal it just as they steal everything else from the world of men, that the world they come from is very

300

old and they want it back again, but they're not quite strong enough on their own. So I feel as though we're guardians, somehow. That we're here to stop this happening.

I think I'd like a roof over my head for the winter, Mum. Is that all right? Do you mind Sam being here? Maybe until the baby comes. I don't think Sam would want to stay living in a house forever but there are some things I'd like to do. There are some courses in woodland management that he was talking about…

Enough answers that Alys was reassured that her children, all long since grown anyway, had plans. That they did not need her, although they might think they did. A year and more without her, however inadvertent, had proved to them that they could manage on their own and so could the house, under Bee's sterling management. Life had gone on without Alys, maybe not perfectly smooth (but nothing ever was) and would go on without her again.

She had reached the end of the landing and the door of the spare room. She listened for a moment, but there was no movement from Nell within. Their cousin would be flying back to the States at the weekend.

Bee — and all the girls — really have been fantastic, putting up with me for so long. But I promised the folks I'd be back home in time for Thanksgiving.

And did you get all your work done, Nell?

Their eyes, so similar, locking in mutual understanding. Nell's hand straying to her stomach, a protective gesture, very familiar to Alys.

Yeah, I think I got everything done that I came here to do.

Nell had not asked where Alys had been all that time, and Alys had not told her.

She did not think she needed to.

Alys went down the stairs and reached the kitchen without anyone stirring. The spaniels were upstairs, sleeping illegally on someone's bed. The black cat, Sable, gave her an indifferent look.

"Still not speaking to me, eh?"

She sat down by the warm range to put her boots on. Honestly, heading out to battle otherworldy forces in a fucking kaftan… For this trip, she'd dug out thermals and an Arran sweater. Heavy cords. Taking no chances. The kitchen really was cosy: it would be so easy to stay, but Alys had done *easy* for a lot of her life and she knew now that it wasn't always the answer.

This time, however, she would leave a note in plain sight on the damn table. She wrote out about a page, with clear instructions, and weighted it down with a bowl of Bee's still-dormant hyacinth bulbs.

I will, the note ended, *be back for Christmas.*

No one could surely have a problem with coming home at Christmas. People did it all the time.

She fished in the collar of her heavy sweater and took out a locket, spinning on a golden chain. That needed to stay here, too. She should have left it in the gemstone box. One last look. She flicked the catch and once more marvelled at the tiny miniature within: a young man in a ruff, a little bit like Ned Dark but with fair hair, standing in a meadow full of flowers. William Fallow, his likeness. At his side was a young woman, very beautiful, in a dress the colour of the sea. And, though the light was low, Alys could see that her lovely and familiar face had the faintest trace of blue.

She snapped the locket shut and put it on top of the note. Then she took a last quick look around the kitchen and opened the back door. It had started to rain. Alys grinned and stepped out into the wild and the wet.

Some time later, she stood alone with the antlered staff in her hand, looking out over the empty land. Without the thorns in her flesh, she felt as light as a leaf on the wind. She'd let herself be trapped but she wouldn't be doing that again, wouldn't make that mistake a second time. It wouldn't be fair on anyone.

She had a thief to catch, after all.

So don't fuck this up.

The land was dark and in the distance was the silver of the sea. There was salt on the wind, cutting through the cold. Time to start walking. She wondered where the old roads would take her this time, now that the gate to the Winter Kingdom had been shut: White Horse Country again, or the realm of the hollow hills, perhaps. That might not be a bad starting place, if dangerous. The lych path was faintly visible even though the light had nearly gone, glimmering green. Alys looked up and saw unfamiliar stars. Some day, she would know their names.

ABOUT THE AUTHOR

Liz Williams is a science fiction and fantasy writer living in Glastonbury, England, where she is co-director of a witchcraft supply business. She has been published by Bantam Spectra (US) and Tor Macmillan (UK), also Night Shade Press, and appears regularly in *Asimov's* and other magazines. She has been involved with the Milford SF Writers' Workshop for 20 years, and also teaches creative writing at a local college for Further Education.

Her previous novels are:: *The Ghost Sister* (Bantam Spectra), *Empire Of Bones, The Poison Master, Nine Layers Of Sky, Banner Of Souls* (Bantam Spectra – US, Tor Macmillan – UK), *Darkland, Bloodmind* (Tor Macmillan UK), *Snake Agent, The Demon And The City, Precious Dragon, The Shadow Pavilion* (Night Shade Press) *Winterstrike* (Tor Macmillan), *The Iron Khan* (Morrigan Press) and *Worldsoul* (Prime). The Chen series is currently being published by Open Road.

Blackthorn Winter, the sequel to *Comet Weather*, is forthcoming from NewCon Press, and a non-fiction book on the history of British paganism, *Miracles Of Our Own Making*, will be published by Reaktion Books in 2020.

Her first short story collection *The Banquet Of The Lords Of Night* was also published by Night Shade Press, and her second and third, *A Glass Of Shadow* and *The Light Warden*, are published by New Con Press as is her recent novella, *Phosphorus*.

The *Diaries if a Witchcraft Shop* (volumes 1 and 2) are also published by New Con Press.

Her novel *Banner Of Souls* was shortlisted for the Philip K Dick Memorial Award, as were three previous novels, and the Arthur C Clarke Award.

NEW FROM NEWCON PRESS

Rachel Armstrong – Soul Chasers

Scientist and SF writer Rachel Armtrong delivers a tale of Death, but not as we know it. When Winnie's house is swallowed by a giant sinkhole, her body starts to break down, becoming one with the planet, and her components begin an incredible journey around the globe, where she encounters characters from different times, different places. A novice soul chaser is determined to claim her soul before it dissipates forever.

Ian Whates – Dark Angels Rising

The Dark Angels – a notorious band of brigands turned folk heroes who disbanded a decade ago – are all that stands between humanity and disaster. Reunited, Leesa, Jen and their fellow Angels must prevent a resurrected Elder – last of a long dead alien race – from reclaiming the scientific marvels of his people. Supported by a renegade military unit and the criminal zealots Saflik, the Elder is set on establishing itself as God over all humankind.

RB Kelly – Edge of Heaven

Creo Basse, a city built to house the world's dispossessed. In the dark, honeycomb districts of the lower city, Turrow searches for black-market meds for his epileptic sister when he encounters one of the many ways Creo can kill a person. A tinderbox of unrest finally ignites when a deadly plague breaks out, which the authorities claim is a terrorist weapon manufactured by extremist artificial humans hiding in the city, but is the truth darker still?

Nick Wood – Water Must Fall

In 2048, climate change has brought catastrophe and water companies play god with the lives of millions. In Africa, Graham Mason struggles to save his marriage to Lizette, who is torn between loyalty to their relationship and to her people. In California, Arthur Green battles to find ways of saving water and root out corruption, even when his family are threatened by those he seeks to expose. As the planet continues to thirst and slowly perish, will water ever fall?

Lightning Source UK Ltd.
Milton Keynes UK
UKHW011114130120
356862UK00001B/141/P